Kinsey linked her arms around Luke's neck, pulling in closer.

"See what happens when you work with me, Luke? Teamwork is so much more productive, don't you think?"

Luke shrugged, which was harder than it looked with a hot woman wrapped around his waist, her breasts smashed to his chest. The heat between her legs pulsed an erotic rhythm against his abs.

"It's just a game, baby," he said, his voice low, rough.

"It's never just a game."

Pr...
KATE ...

"Meader tugs at the heartstrings."

—*Publishers Weekly*

"Meader's books are absolutely fabulous to read and impossible to put down."

—*The Best Reviews*

"A wonderful author."

—*Harlequin Junkie*

"Nobody does it like Kate Meader—Kinsey and Luke set the pages on fire."

—Lauren Layne, *USA Today* bestselling author

ALSO BY KATE MEADER

"Rekindle the Flame" in *Baby, It's Cold Outside*
(anthology)

FLIRTING
WITH
FIRE

KATE MEADER

POCKET BOOKS
New York London Toronto Sydney New Delhi

Pocket Books
A Division of Simon & Schuster, Inc.
1230 Avenue of the Americas
New York, NY 10020

This book is a work of fiction. Any references to historical events, real people, or real places are used fictitiously. Other names, characters, places, and events are products of the author's imagination, and any resemblance to actual events or places or persons, living or dead, is entirely coincidental.

First Pocket Books paperback edition April 2015

POCKET and colophon are registered trademarks of Simon & Schuster, Inc.

For information about special discounts for bulk purchases, please contact Simon & Schuster Special Sales at 1-866-506-1949 or business@simonandschuster.com.

The Simon & Schuster Speakers Bureau can bring authors to your live event. For more information or to book an event contact the Simon & Schuster Speakers Bureau at 1-866-248-3049 or visit our website at www.simonspeakers.com.

Interior design by Kyle Kabel

Manufactured in the United States of America

10 9 8 7 6 5 4 3

ISBN 978-1-4767-8590-5
ISBN 978-1-4767-8594-3 (ebook)

This book is dedicated to the brave men and women who run into burning buildings instead of out of them. Your hard work and heroism are awe-inspiring. Thanks for everything you do.

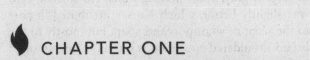

CHAPTER ONE

So this was where jock straps went to die.

Kinsey Taylor's nose twitched at the aromatic combination of sweat, dirty laundry, and an unhealthy abundance of testosterone. Three stinky brothers had inured her senses to the more disgusting habits of the male species, so she remained largely unfazed as she marched through the makeshift gym of Engine Company 6's quarters on Chicago's north side.

Judging by the slack jaws and horrified expressions of the men she passed, her composure wasn't catching.

"Hey, lady, you can't be in here," a Popeye-gunned lug said as he reset dumbbells he'd been curling with ease.

Ignoring him and the supporting grumbles of his workout crew, she continued to her destination—the locker room of Chicago's oldest firehouse—for a showdown with a man she had never met, but who had already pissed her off so much she was ready to set his head on fire. The guy might have a reputation as one of the bravest and most decorated firefighters in the Chicago Fire Department, but she'd like to see how Mr. Luke Almeida would handle that particular conflagration.

She rounded a corner with purpose and crashed

through the swing doors at the end of a corridor flanked by gray, paint-peeling walls. The smell in here was slightly better, which Kinsey attributed in part to the scent of shampoo and soap, but mostly to the broad-shouldered specimen standing before an open locker.

He turned slowly, his eyebrows veeing over a face more weathered than handsome.

"This isn't part of the tour, miss."

Miss.

That word flicked across her sensitive brain like a fingernail over a raw wound. She should have been *Mrs.* David Halford for almost a month by now, and the painful fact that she wasn't apparently still had the capacity to surprise her. Oh joy. Now she had to steel her mind against the word *miss* along with other nuggets like *incompatible* and *nonrefundable deposit.* Her vocabulary of not-words had expanded considerably since her cross-country move from San Francisco to Chicago four months ago.

"I'm here for"—*the head of*—"Luke Almeida," she said to the man before her.

The slight twitch of his mouth acted like a lever for his eyebrows. "Luke. Visitor," he called out in a tone that said Luke hosted a lot of visitors.

Kinsey had a truckload of reasons to dislike Luke Almeida. Any man who instigated a bar brawl involving half his firehouse and a vigorous complement of the Chicago Police Department was already at the top of her shit list. When that same man refused to return three phone calls from the mayor's Media Affairs Office, he was on his way to carving out a special place in her affections for his about-to-be-reamed ass. Now that smirk from Tall, Dark, Whatever confirmed what she had suspected the moment Almeida's file landed on her desk at city hall four days ago: he thought he was all that and a bag of chips.

"You must be lost, sweetheart."

A low rumble spiked every fine hair on the back of her neck to attention. On four-inch heels she pivoted and encountered a plume of steam, which, like a magician's cloud, dissipated to reveal a half-naked man.

Whoa.

The clearing mist had the opposite effect on her rapidly fogging brain. Bye-bye, Tall 'n' Dark; this brute streak of male had that guy beat in the masculinity stakes six ways from Sunday.

Across his broad chest, the slogan of the U.S. Marine Corps, Semper Fidelis, formed a rolling script that joined forces with the tattooed cuffs on his biceps, the letters of which she couldn't quite make out, short of staring.

And she wanted to stare because this just got better.

On lean hips, a towel draped threateningly low, highlighting cut indents on either side of his abs. Was there anything hotter than that V shape? As if the killer bod wasn't enough, he had eyes so fiercely blue she wondered if they were natural. Surely those things had come out of a lab.

Then again, the whole picture was one of a genetically engineered firefighting machine. Or fighting machine, considering his fondness for hitting first and to hell with the consequences.

He rubbed a towel through damp hair, returning life to mink-brown waves that framed strong cheekbones and more jaw than was strictly necessary. The movement showcased the tattoo on his right bicep: *Logan,* combined with the intertwined letters of the CFD. She would bet the two-carat engagement ring she had hurled in her ex-fiancé's face that the ink on his left arm spelled Sean, the name of Luke Almeida's foster father. A renowned fireman who had been awarded every medal in the book, Sean Dempsey made the greatest sacrifice during a high-rise fire eight years ago. Logan, the oldest brother, had also died during the blaze.

A smudgy ocher bruise around Almeida's left eye webbed out to his upper cheek. No need to inquire how he came by that. It was why she was here.

Snapping back to the reality of her mission, Kinsey held his now curious gaze. "What did you say?"

"I think you're a little lost." He enunciated each word as if she was some sort of dimwit who had never seen a man's naked chest before. "Tours of the firehouse are every other Wednesday."

"I'm not here for a tour of the firehouse."

He streaked the towel he'd been using to dry his hair across chiseled pectoral muscles, then a meaty swatch of scar tissue covering his right shoulder.

"Okay," he said, parting his lips to reveal straight, white teeth and a gorgeous smile. So the city dental plan was a winner. "Other types of tours can be arranged. How does tomorrow night sound?"

"Excuse me?"

"Well, I just got off my shift and I have forty-eight hours free ahead of me. Usually I sleep the first twelve, but if you need me sooner, sweetheart, I suppose I can rework my schedule."

Kinsey didn't hold much truck with cocky. Or

with men who called women they had never met "sweetheart." Luke Almeida seemed to be under the mistaken impression that . . . Did he actually think she had crawled into this stink pit to get a date?

"You haven't returned any of my messages. I called three times—"

Tall 'n' Dark snorted. "Shit, Luke, they're chasin' you down now."

"Who's chasing Luke down?"

Another man had entered, wearing board shorts and a ripped CFD shirt, through which his extremely defined muscles played peekaboo. Tall and blond, with a fresh-faced Thor vibe, he looked like he'd stopped off at Engine 6 while on a break from his modeling gig for *GQ*. Truly, she must have missed the entrance to the hot-man laboratory on her way in.

"Luke's takin' a leaf from your book," Tall 'n' Dark said to Baby Thor. "As if we don't already have enough of that with your castoffs showing up every other week looking to clean your hose."

Baby Thor grinned, a little lopsided, a lot sexy. "Can I help it if I've broken half the hearts in Boystown?"

Boystown. Chicago's gay neighborhood, which confirmed that Baby Thor played for the other team. The gorgeous ones always did, though in all honesty, it looked like there was gorgeous to spare. The other two members of the triple threat were still taking up all the space and sucking up all the oxygen.

Greedy.

Almeida stared at her, the cogs of his Neanderthal brain clearly working overtime as he tried to piece together when and where they had met, and exactly how much trouble he was in because the memory refused to take shape.

She decided to help him along.

"So you didn't get my calls?"

He lifted a broad shoulder. "Sure I did, but I've been busy. Puttin' out fires."

More like busy leading a fistfight that had turned him and his firefighter brothers into YouTube sensations and prompted the mayor to action. Now it was Kinsey's job as the mayor's assistant press secretary to create solutions to a media nightmare. Almeida wasn't even supposed to be on duty. He had been placed on presuspension administrative leave, but when he hadn't shown up for a meeting with Media Affairs at city hall, she had called the number she had on file for him and left a message. And another. And another.

"Ignoring phone calls is incredibly rude."

"Yeah, bro," Baby Thor said. "You were brought up better than that." He offered his hand. "I'm Gage. The handsome, sexy, interesting, and well-mannered one."

Kinsey shook, enjoying the firm grip. According to his file, at twenty-four, Gage Simpson was the youngest of the Dempseys, a family of foster siblings who had all followed their late foster father into the service.

"And this is Wyatt." Gage jerked his strong chin at Tall 'n' Dark. "He usually only opens his mouth to criticize."

Wyatt Fox, oldest of the brood at thirty-three, threaded burly arms over his chest and clamped his mouth shut. Kinsey supposed she should be grateful.

There was also another brother, Beck, and a sister, Alexandra, one of only 120 female firefighters in the CFD. None of the foster siblings bore the same last name or were related by blood, but their bond—the Dempsey bond—was strong enough to ensure they were all assigned to the same firehouse. It was unusual, but then so was the family.

"And you already know Luke," Gage went on, amusement sparking his silver-gray eyes. "Though how well you know him is another story. Are we talking fluids exchanged or just phone numbers?"

Almeida eyed her with interest. This moron really thought they might have hooked up in the not-so-distant past, and that she had rushed down here at 7 a.m. on a Monday when he hadn't made good on his sweetly worded promises to call.

At her pointed look, Luke spoke into the pause she had no intention of filling. "She knows me well enough to think she can walk into my firehouse and get results. Pretty ballsy, sweetheart."

"Sometimes you have to take matters into your own hands, and after the other night . . ." She twisted the toe of her pump, as if she was terribly, terribly unsure of herself. Time to kick this up a notch. "I thought we had something special."

Those electric blues widened as he moved into her personal space, and while she wasn't a small woman, she felt curiously diminutive in Firefighter Almeida's mountainous presence. Her former fiancé, David, had barely three inches on her. He hadn't liked when she wore heels that made her taller than him.

Neither had he liked when her five-mile runs came in twenty seconds ahead of his, or she beat him like a dusty rug at racquetball, or god*damn* it, had three orgasms to his one. Though usually she had to help herself along there.

Competitiveness isn't terribly feminine, Kinsey.

No, honey, but it sure as hell beats losing.

Luke pinned her to the spot with that ocean-sparkly gaze. "So the other night when we were—"

"Dancing."

"We had serious moves."

"You certainly thought so. My toes are all bruised, but you made up for it later."

His lips twitched.

"With your scintillating conversation," she continued. "I had no idea firemen knew so much about *The Bachelor*."

"Lots of downtime in between runs." He rubbed his chin. "And then we had that discussion about . . . what was it again?"

She sighed her annoyance at having to remind him of the amazing conversational highs they had reached together. "The Cubs' pitching roster. You were confident Arrieta could hold his form through the late season and I had worries about—"

"The rest of the bullpen." His indolent gaze dropped to her mouth. "Or how deep it could go."

"Yes," she murmured, realizing a tad late that she might have waded in too far here. "You never really put me at ease about that."

"Rest assured, sweetheart. It goes deep. Deep as you need it."

Holy wow. She felt her stomach dip and roll at his provocative words.

About baseball.

"You're a lot prettier than Vargas, Miss . . . ?"

"Taylor."

"Well, Miss Taylor, Commissioner Freeman is

a good friend of mine, and Luis Vargas from CFD Media Affairs is handling this, so it seems we have it under control."

Ha! So Luke Almeida knew exactly who she was—and that he had ridden shotgun with her game sent a rush of unexpected heat through her.

"Under control? Your four minutes of fame is already the subject of a *Trib* editorial, you made the national news on all the major networks, and the city council is calling a special meeting to discuss your situation this week. Sounds like the opposite of under control."

She felt a chill emanating from Wyatt's direction now that the true reason for her early morning visit was out in the open.

Luke narrowed those blue-on-blue eyes at her. "Your message said you were from the mayor's office, Miss . . ."

"Taylor," she gritted out. "And it was messag*es*. Three of them."

"Right. And while the fire department technically reports to the mayor, we have our own way of handling things. Our own commissioner. Our own Media Affairs. I'm not sure why you've been sent here, but it would probably be best all around if you turn on those heels and toddle back to city hall."

Huh, he did everything but tell her she should pop her cute little tush into the kitchen and fix up some biscuits. Get the hoses ready, boys, because any minute now, she'd be expelling enough steam from her ears to burn everyone in the immediate vicinity.

"I'm afraid that won't be possible. You see, I have a problem, Mr. Almeida." She infused her words with the businesslike tone she could usually manage in her sleep, but which wasn't coming quite so easily today.

"Oh, it's mister now? And I thought after the other night we had something special."

Not bad, Almeida, not bad. Struggling to hide the burgeoning smile that she should not be surrendering to, she also tried to ignore the fact that he had moved closer to her on the utterance of the word *special*. She had to tip her head back to meet his gaze directly. No way was she having this conversation with his thick, muscle-corded neck, even if it meant putting a crick in her considerably less muscled one.

"My problem is this." She poked a finger in his chest. A not unpleasant sizzle fizzed through her fingertips. "You're. Still. Here."

"*Here* is where I work."

Irritation had the unfortunate effect of dilating her blood vessels and making her warm all over. Not his nearness. No, not that. "This is where you *used* to work. As of three days ago, you were placed on administrative leave pending a hearing on your bone-headed actions. You're not even supposed to be on CFD property until your case is resolved."

Visibly bristling, Luke cocked his jaw like a weapon. "I happened to be on site when a call came in. I'm hardly going to sit around while my men head to an incident. It was a tough run and we needed all hands on deck."

Reluctantly, she admitted a grudging admiration at that, but it didn't change the facts. He had already cast a pall over the entire CFD when a grainy video of his fisticuffs got a million hits on its first day online. She needed to get through to him, and coming down to his intellectual level was her best option. Men like this only understood threats: to their livelihood, manhood, and food sources.

"I've done my research on you, Mr. Almeida. You have the commissioner in your pocket, the unstinting support of the union, and a rather overweening sense of entitlement owing to your family's contribution to the CFD, but the mayor is tired of his civil servants thinking they are above the rules."

A number of scandals had recently rocked the foundations of city hall. Bribes for permits. Backroom deals. A CPD detective discovered with more vodka than blood in his veins—and a Baggie of coke in his glove box—right after leaving the scene of an accident. Almeida's outburst might not relate specifically to endemic corruption, but it highlighted all that was wrong with Chicago's local government.

"The city has a zero-tolerance policy for violence by its employees," she continued. "You have five more days of leave and then if—and that's a big *if*—you get out of the hearing with your balls still intact, you have work to do scrubbing the reputation of your firehouse clean. And I've been asked by the mayor to take charge of the cleanup."

Thunderous rage stormed over his brow. "You?"

"Me."

"I've already explained my side of the story in an incident report. I assume your meticulous research covered that."

She reached back into her memory, mentally scanning the witness accounts of the bar fight. Mostly bland reports with little variation. A code of silence encompassing CPD and CFD had kept lips sealed tighter than bark on a tree.

"One minute you're serving drinks in your family's bar. Next, Detective McGinnis is laid flat and several members of Engine 6 and the Third District are duking it out like it's an episode of *Real Housewives*. All because he made a pass at your sister." She tilted her head, taking his measure. "I would have thought an experienced bar owner would know how to handle boozy, grabby customers. Why do I feel like there's more to this than the black and white of those reports?"

It was a long shot, but she knew immediately she'd hit pay dirt. His eyes darkened to navy, swallowing all that had-to-be-fake blue, and some shutoff in his brain checked what he was about to say. He flashed an unreadable glance at his brothers.

"Too much alcohol, tempers easily frayed," he murmured. "And it was game seven of the Cup finals. I believe Detective McGinnis is a Rangers fan." He punctuated that with a pressed-on smile. Still gorgeous, despite being a big, fat phony.

"So just a typical night of boys will be boys?"

He looked bored. "I'm not exactly clear on what you want from me, Miss—"

"Taylor," she finished before he could drag out the annoying what's-your-last-name-again thing.

"She wants you to shake hands with McGinnis," Gage chimed in. "Preferably after you've both spearheaded a very public event that benefits the community. Maybe a block party where you grill the dogs and the detective squirts the ketchup. Would I be right, Miss Taylor?"

"No decent idea is off the table," she said to Gage, "and please call me Kinsey."

"We already do a lot for the community," Wyatt murmured.

"Yes, the foster kids support program your father created. I saw that in your file." And definitely something they could use to turn the tide of public opinion. "We have a lot of options here. A team sporting event, a chili cook-off, maybe even a calendar of all you manly men getting your manliness on."

Gage snorted loudly, but not loud enough to drown out Almeida's growl, a sound that signified his manliness would never be at issue. Yeah, she got it.

"I'm sure the Chicago taxpayers, especially the female ones, would love to see a scantily clad muscle factory carrying a big hose in one hand and a kitten in the other. With the proceeds going to charity, of course." She was starting to enjoy herself now, so she winked. "Sweetheart."

Wyatt rubbed his mouth, evidently concealing a smile. Gage grinned broadly. As for Luke? She may as well have suggested he wear a matching bra-and-panties set while he stroked that fluffy lil kitty cat.

"Oh, this should be good," Gage said, and Kinsey no longer bothered hiding her amusement. She'd found her ally at Engine 6.

Determined to have the last word, she leveled Luke Almeida with her most hard-nosed gaze. He opened his mouth to speak, but she raised a hand of, *Stow it*.

"Keep that silver tongue of yours for your hearing, Mr. Almeida. Once you're in the clear, we'll work on making you a star for all the right reasons."

And then she dropped the mic and skedaddled out of that locker room before he could get a volley off.

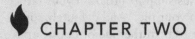

CHAPTER TWO

Luke slammed his locker door shut, only to have it spring back open like a bad-news boomerang. The violence wasn't enough to dislodge the photo tucked into the upper right-hand corner: Sean Dempsey and Logan Keyes, his foster father and brother. Frozen in time, their smiling faces shone back at him, a constant reminder of the bittersweet joy of being both a Dempsey and a member of the Chicago Fire Department.

He grabbed clean clothes from his locker and got dressed, covering muscles that still ached even after the hot, pulsing spray of the shower. This morning's 3 a.m. run to a warehouse fire on Elston could have been tricky, given the hazardous chemicals stored illegally on the north end of the lot, but they had managed to suppress the blaze quickly and seal it off, ready for the boys at hazmat to take over. All in all, a good night's work.

The mouthwatering smell of bacon hit him like a semi before he pushed through the door to the kitchen at Engine 6. No matter the time of day, everyone was usually starving after a fire. The adrenaline pumping through a firefighter's veins was like a drug that needed constant feeding. Food first, then sex. If some eggheads ever did a study on birth dates of children in the CFD, Luke bet there would be a clear relationship between the most taxing incidents and when those kids were conceived. He was always primed for a woman after a fire—and the appearance of Miss Hot in Heels was like introducing oxygen into a nonvented room.

Luke poured a coffee, grabbed a seat beside Wyatt, and spared a glance for what Gage was working at the stove. It looked like eggs, but with his aspirations-to-gourmet-chef brother, that would have been far too simple. Thankfully the kid hadn't made good on his threat to install an espresso machine with a milk frothing attachment. Luke's old pal Mr. Coffee did the trick, and hazelnut-flavored half-and-half was as fancy as it needed to get.

"You should call your union rep," Wyatt said to Luke around his chewing.

"Why? To tell them to get the mayor off my back? Or to tell them I can't handle his attack dog with the big mouth?"

The full, lush, and crazily lickable mouth, if he was being honest. A dangerous habit he rarely indulged in these days, especially with himself.

"Hmph." From Gage, who served up a veggie-studded omelet complete with home-fried potatoes. His youngest brother looked a whole lot more serious than he had fifteen minutes ago when he was playing mental footsie with Kinsey Taylor.

"Something to say, Chef?"

"For your dining pleasure, we have a vegetable frittata, with apple-Gouda turkey sausage and salsa verde." He tilted his head. "And yeah, I do have some colorful commentary with your delicious meal. You should have been more forthcoming in your report."

"And how exactly would that make a difference?"

"If you told them what McGinnis did—"

"It would just add more background color to the constantly evolving story of me and Detective McGinnis, but it wouldn't change a thing about what happened a week ago." Just saying that prick's name aloud raised a heat rash on his skin. "He laid his grubby hands on Alex, he got my fist in his face, and now I'm on leave." Luke smirked. "Or supposed to be, anyway."

He pointed a fork to shut down Gage's next complaint. "Talking about my history with the detective only gives them more fuel. It makes it look like I have a grudge and that I was just looking for an excuse to rearrange his face." So what if he was. He'd rather the CFD brass and those pencil-pushing assholes at city hall didn't know his entire sorry business.

Luke stole a glance at Wyatt to gauge his response to all of this. His oldest brother was as steady as a rock, cool under pressure, and spare with his speech, even if he had been indulging in a few more daredevil stunts than normal on rescue squad these last few runs.

"You're right," Wyatt pronounced, and punctuated it by shoveling a forkful of the fancy omelet in his mouth. Just in case he was tempted to embellish, which he never was.

"See?" Luke said smugly.

Frustration furrowed Gage's brow at yet again being caught on the wrong end of an argument with the elders who always knew best.

"Yeah, because Wy's such an expert in the affairs of the human heart. Look at him." Gage considered Wyatt like he was the saddest thing on God's green earth. "The guy wouldn't know passion if it hit him over the head with the Jaws of Life. I'm sick of throwing my lady posse his way only to have them all report back how dull he is."

"I'm not interested in your froot loops," Wyatt said so seriously that Gage and Luke broke into laughter.

Gage shook his head. "I love you, man, but you are never going to get laid with that attitude."

Per usual, Wyatt looked uncomfortable at Gage's fulsome display of affection. It was the way of the Dempseys to love deeply and hate to show it, except for Gage, who was the well-adjusted one. A frickin' miracle, considering what he'd been through before Sean took him in at the age of ten. They all had tales to forget and sorrows that had molded them, but Gage was the one who had come furthest the fastest.

"We still trying to get Wyatt laid?" A woman's smiling voice rang across the kitchen.

"Aren't we always?" Gage groused.

Luke grinned at his sister, Alex, who had just arrived for the start of her shift. Dark chocolate waves, shot through with fire-engine red streaks, framed a heart-shaped face. Possessed of the killer combo of dry wit and no filter, she also had a temper that made her green eyes flash like winking jewels when tested.

Gage handed her a just-buttered piece of toast, one bite already gone. A preemptive move, because Alex would have plucked it from his hands in about three seconds anyway.

She grinned in acknowledgment of her victory. "Forget about Wy and focus on finding a hot man for yours truly. Don't you know any hetero guys?"

"I've got your hetero right here, baby," leered Lieutenant Tony "Big Mac" McElroy as he strutted into the kitchen.

"We'll pretend the fact you've been happily married for thirteen years is the only reason I'm not jumping all over that very attractive offer, Antonio," Alex said with a good-natured leer of her own. Luke tamped down the protective instinct that boiled up— it was just too early for a fight, and Big Mac actually was happily married. Anyway, Alex could handle herself against all comers.

That's not what he had put in the report, though.

Big Mac's semi-lecherous grin slipped at the sight of Gage's fixins. "Can't you just scramble them like a normal person, Simpson? This isn't the fuckin' Ritz in here."

"You want it or not? I even made bacon for you because you're my favorite lieutenant."

"I'm your only lieutenant," he muttered.

"*Mangia, bambini, mangia.*" Gage placed a piled-high platter with extra bacon down on the table with one hand and, with the other, passed Alex her coffee the way she liked it.

Wyatt's usually razor-straight eyebrows hoisted slightly, drawing Luke's smile. Close in age, Alex and Gage lived in each other's pockets, for which Luke and Wyatt were eternally grateful. Partly because neither of them had the energy to hang with the youngsters at the ripe old ages of thirty-two and thirty-three respectively (dance clubs were usually involved), but mostly because their tight-knit bond meant they would always have each other if something were to happen to their older brothers. Sure, they were all in danger on every run, but Luke and Wyatt did their best to protect their youngest sibs, including Beck, who was currently on vacation in Thailand with his girl, Darcy. It was the most important one of Sean Dempsey's many lessons: defend the people you love to the dying embers.

"Speaking of performing a public service and trying to get my elders laid," Gage directed at Luke. "It's time you jumped back on the pony. How long has it been now?"

Too long. A year and two months, give or take, since he'd ended things with the woman who was supposed to be his future. Kids, rocking chairs, the whole nine. Lisa had crushed his heart, then took her Porsche and ran back over it to eliminate any remaining electrical activity.

"I'm with Wy. Not interested in any woman who wants you for a friend."

"What about Miss Taylor?"

"Who's Miss Taylor?" Alex asked.

"This chick Luke was flirting with."

Luke grunted. "I was not flirting—"

"You should have seen him, Alex," Gage said. "It was all zingers and eye fucking and enough heat to set off the smoke alarms. Our Luke's ready to get his wang back in the game. So proud."

Ker-ist. Luke looked to Wyatt for support.

His older brother shrugged. "It was kind of cute." Back to his eggs.

Cute did not apply to Miss Taylor. That woman

was a heap of trouble, and not just because of the warm, hazel eyes that had shot sparks when he'd gotten her riled. He wondered how their color might change if he stroked her touchable, golden skin, or how big they would bloom if he tangled his fingers in all that honey-silk blondeness that cascaded over her shoulders. She'd had an enticing twitch to her hips as she sashayed her world-class ass out of the locker room, clearly pleased with herself for hijacking the last word. That ass would feel so good crushed against his palm and . . .

He really needed an orgasm that did not come courtesy of his right hand.

But not with Kinsey Taylor. Because then he'd have to listen to her, and Luke was done with know-it-all harpies who got off on bringing a guy to his knees for all the wrong reasons. Next time he set his sights on a woman, she would be soft, pliant, and ready for kids as soon as he put a ring on her finger. Maybe an elementary school teacher or a nice, sweet girl who worked with rescued puppies. Someone easy.

And if she had a world-class ass, all the better.

CHAPTER THREE

The grim, sagging walls of CFD HQ on South Michigan could definitely do with a sprucing-up, which wasn't far off from how Luke felt as he sat, stiff as bamboo, outside the hearing room a week after Daniel McGinnis had walked into Luke's fist. God, he felt like crap. The collar of his button-down was pulling double duty, cutting off all the air to his lungs and making him sweat so much he thought he might die of dehydration.

In a few minutes, he would learn his fate. He'd almost prefer a kick to the curb rather than mandatory counseling for some perceived anger-management problem, because the idea of talking out his problems with whatever four-eyed nut doctor they assigned to him was enough to give him the shakes.

As a kid, he'd endured countless sessions with psychologists and social workers, everyone eager to get to the root of his emotional problems. Like the facts of Luke's life so far hadn't clued them in. Mother a crack whore. Father MIA. Baby sister ripped from his arms and stashed in another group home, miles away from Luke.

Most of the time during his two-year stint in the group home, the arranged visits to see little Jenny had been canceled because some social worker wasn't around to drive him, but more often because Luke had acted up and been placed in a time-out. Splitting up siblings was common in foster care, but his anger at everyone—his drugged-up mom, the parade of do-gooders, the other sniveling kids—wouldn't allow him to see reason and play ball long enough to figure out how to game the system.

Nine-year-olds aren't really known for their problem-solving skills.

Apparently, neither are thirty-two-year-olds.

The promise of reuniting with his family was extinguished when his mom set herself ablaze while hanging with a gang of tweakers at a meth lab, incinerating any hope Luke had of salvaging a good life with Jenny. His sister, an indomitable streak of sunshine, was snapped up by an adoring family in one of those white-bread suburbs on Chicago's North Shore. Safe at last, or so Luke thought, but not even happy-as-a-pig-in-shit suburbia can guarantee that. Of course they had no room for a "behaviorally challenged" kid in their picture-perfect family. If they had—if he'd been less of a pill—maybe he could have saved Jenny from that speeding car barreling down a quiet residential street.

Fortunately, Sean and Mary had room in their house and their hearts for a kid whose primary method of communication was with his fists. Shame rolled through him. Neither of them would be particularly proud of him right now.

"Can't leave you alone for a second, Almeida."

Shit, just kill him now.

Luke didn't bother to look up as the hard bench

groaned and nearly splintered under the new weight. His seating companion's thick, widespread thighs, encased in CFD uniform navy, shifted to diffuse his heavy bulk.

"Said your piece yet?"

"Any minute now." Counting the cracks in the tile wasn't going to prevent the ball-breaking lecture he knew was coming. Unable to avoid it any longer, Luke turned his head to take in Commissioner Laurence Freeman, better known as his godfather, Larry. Big, bald, and black as midnight on a moonless night, this man had been just as instrumental in Luke's upbringing as Sean Dempsey. Luke had cried just once in his thirty-two years—and the man currently invading his personal space was the only person to have witnessed the meltdown.

"You need to cooperate," Larry said. "There's only so much I can help you with."

The steel in the older man's voice pulled Luke up short.

"What gives?" Luke wasn't so stupid as to think he'd emerge scot-free here, but he figured a short suspension and a couple of rounds with the CFD shrink would be enough to move it from the loss to the draw column.

Larry's usually smooth forehead crinkled. "You're the straw, Luke, and they mean to make an example of you. The mayor's under a lot of pressure to clean up city hall, especially from some of his bigger donors like Sam Cochrane. I've promised you'll cooperate with his press secretary. Anything they want. And not just token, blow-it-up-their-asses cooperation. You'll have to mean it."

"Or what? The union's not going to stand for some bullshit media campaign that makes us look pretty."

Larry's expression was pained, which looked mighty strange on him. The guy was the calmest person Luke knew.

"They're threatening to split you up."

Cold dread pooled in Luke's gut because that . . . that was the worst thing that could happen to the Dempseys. He and Wyatt had made a pact when Logan and Sean died: insofar as was humanly possible, they would ensure no harm came to the kids. The oldest Dempseys had pulled strings, called in favors to make sure the five of them stayed together at Engine 6. And, short of persuading their pain-in-the-ass sibs not to join the CFD, which would have gone over like a fart in church, keeping them intact at 6 was the next best thing.

It was also why Luke had placed his own ambitions on hold. Because as soon as he passed that lieutenant exam, he'd be transferred out to another house.

Now that dickhead bureaucrat on the fifth floor of city hall thought a crusade against the CFD—against the Dempseys—was going to help his reelection. Not exactly fair, but as Sean used to say, the only thing fair in life is the hair on a Norwegian albino's ass.

"That's not going to happen," Luke finally ground out.

Larry's face turned as hard as the bench that was numbing their asses. "Get your temper under control, go charm the brass in there, and cooperate with the mayor's girl."

The door to the hearing room swung open with a whoosh, ejecting Detective Daniel McGinnis like a halfhearted upchuck. Larry placed a placating hand on Luke's arm, but so not necessary. Luke's anger had found a new target. As disgusted as he was with Dan, his fury was now focused entirely on Mayor Eli Cooper and his click-clacking lap dog, Kinsey Taylor.

McGinnis strode by in a sharp-looking suit, not a bead of sweat rolling down his forehead. Smooth as a slug's slime. But Luke was pleased to note that his splotchy bruises looked far worse than Luke's. His once close friend had the common sense to keep his mouth shut and his eyes forward as he passed.

"Firefighter Almeida?" a voice called out. "They're ready for you."

And he was ready for them. Time to put on his game face and power through this. He'd keep the good stuff for the PR princess.

Jimmy Choo could kiss her ass.

Kinsey leaned against the wall outside her office and rubbed her sore feet. For the second time in a week, the cranky old elevator in city hall had crapped out and she'd taken it as an opportunity-slash-sign to get some much-needed exercise after a calorie-laden lunch with Jillian Malone, a reporter from the *Chicago Tribune* (Bloody Mary, extra bitters). The endorphin high of scoring 70 percent off the Choos at Nordstrom's semiannual shoe sale a week ago had long faded. These fuckers hurt.

A musical tinkle of laughter perked up her ears. Her assistant, Josie, who Kinsey shared with two more senior members of the Media Affairs team, was a sweet girl who spent all her time on Facebook when she thought Kinsey wasn't paying attention. Now, from the sounds of that throaty giggle, she was flirting with one of the staffers—probably Caleb, who liked to sniff around the admins—instead of working on that press release about the summer learning program assigned to her an hour ago.

But Kinsey couldn't have been more wrong.

At the glass door to the media suite, she stopped cold as the source of Josie's chuckle fest became clear: Luke Almeida. His expansive back, covered in a charcoal suit jacket, filled her vision. A band of white peeked above the collar, a nice contrast to those mink-brown waves that today looked a little damp from the humidity of the asphalt-melting June heat. Casually, he sat on Josie's desk, one strapping leg swinging back and forth.

Strapping. That was the word that came to mind when Kinsey saw Luke Almeida.

Josie was all aflutter, alternating between leaning back in her chair, a view that stretched her blouse taut against her twenty-two-year-old breasts, and leaning forward, dipping so as to place her cleavage directly in Luke's line of vision.

"Ricky is five and he's a terror," she was saying. "Well, I'm sure you know how awful boys are at that age."

"Know from experience, having been one," he murmured.

Josie laughed so hard she risked dislodging a lung. "If he wasn't my nephew, I'd be tempted to disown him, but sometimes he's just so adorbs."

Luke's meaty paw gripped a pewter photo frame, the cat whiskers one that held an ovary-explodingly cute pic of Josie's two nieces and nephew.

"I see you're an animal lover, as well," he said, gesturing to the array of critter photos on her desk.

"I am!" she squealed. "They're just so unconditional in their love, aren't they?"

"They sure are." Said in what Kinsey assumed was his seductive voice, if you liked that kind of thing. Which she most certainly did not.

Lately, Kinsey was feeling a tad raw at how flirtations and relationships had the nerve to proceed without her. Not that her never-ever-after with David should be cause for love the world over to come to a standstill, but she was getting increasingly fed up with being confronted by other people's happiness at every turn.

Her abused feet back in their prison cells, she stepped into the office and cleared her throat like a scene-interrupting cliché. She placed a grande Frappuccino on Josie's desk.

"A little pick-me-up for the afternoon." Not that the girl needed it, as she seemed to be getting picked up all by herself.

"Oh, thanks, Kinsey," Josie said, a guilty blush tinting her cheeks.

Luke barely moved a muscle except to raise his startling blue eyes in Kinsey's direction. They revealed nothing but disdain. Shocker.

"We need to talk, Miss Taylor."

The way he said her name confirmed his less-than-sunny feelings toward her, but he followed it up with something unexpected. Surely this was a figment of her imagination, but in those eyes, she thought she saw a flash of appreciation for her legs, the prolonged visit to her hips, the flare of arousal as his gaze touched her breasts like a kiss. Perhaps she should upgrade Josie to a venti next time for getting Luke primed.

Blinking herself back to Earth, Kinsey looked past him to her assistant. "What does my schedule look like this afternoon, Josie?"

"You're free for the next thirty," Luke cut in as he unfolded to his full height. All six four of it. His suit was a little rumpled from the heat. The blue-and-silver striped tie had been loosened to the point that he may as well not have bothered. The snow-white shirt still bore just-opened-from-its-package creases. Bought special for the hearing, she assumed, which had taken place this morning. Wearing a suit did not come naturally to him. His body fought its bonds, and her brain stuttered with the image of him tearing it from his hard, ripped torso as soon as he got home.

A lot less skin was on display than the last time they met, but what she saw was just as enticing. Smooth, buttery cocoa that looked good enough to taste. His ethnicity was not listed in his file, but she had overheard two of the flightier interns gossiping about his Cuban-Irish roots in the restroom yesterday.

Drooling over it, to be precise.

Uninvited, he walked ahead of her toward her office, devouring the carpet with long, muscular strides. Jodie raised an eyebrow but Kinsey ignored her. This wasn't the time for girly camaraderie.

She followed him in and shut the door, the resounding click loud and final to her ears. Luke stood stiffly at the window, hands in pockets, scoping out the busy Loop streets.

"I expected the view would be better," he said, not turning around.

"The mayor's office up one level has it best." She needed to alleviate the deadweight she suddenly felt in her legs, but she certainly wouldn't be the one to sit first while he took in the view like a king on his perch. The pain of gender relations in the twenty-first century.

"Would you like a seat, Mr. Almeida?"

He turned and leaned against the window, his flinty gaze clashing with a forced smile. "I think it's time we did away with the formalities. After all, we'll be working closely together."

She nodded. "I assume your hearing went well . . ."

"Luke."

Heat pooled in her abdomen with that simple word, said in the huskiest, sexiest tone she had ever heard.

"Luke," she said, annoyed to find she sounded breathless.

"It went as well as can be expected, given the circumstances. I have to speak with the CFD shrink and work up a publicity plan with you. Apparently, you're going to have some say in how soon I can return to active duty."

Shock sloshed over her at this unwelcome news. "Why would I have any input? I just need you to cooperate with me to make Engine 6 look good."

He laughed, short and bitter. "I have a history of not playing nicely with others, Miss Taylor. And there are some people who don't like me or my family and would welcome any excuse to make things difficult for us."

The "Miss Taylor" wasn't lost on her. There was no trust here despite his invitation to get less formal. He assumed she was part of some conspiracy to bring his family down, which was worrisome. Not that there was a conspiracy, but that he thought there was.

Violent *and* paranoid. She'd let the CFD psychiatrist sort that one out.

"My job is to show how important the Chicago Fire Department is to the lifeblood of this great city—"

"Sounds like you're reading from a press release."

Her throat worked over a swallow. It did sound like that. A PR professional learned quickly to speak in guarded statements, though she was beginning to realize that keeping her bodily defenses in place around Luke Almeida might be the true challenge.

Willing her hand to move deliberately, she flipped through a pile of file folders on her desk until she found the one she needed. From it, she extracted a multisheet document. Her ideas for rehabilitating the rep of Engine 6.

"So I thought we could host a community party. Kids could visit the firehouse, climb on the fire engine while supervised of course, hang with real-life heroes."

Luke rounded the desk and leaned beside her, an action that strained the suit fabric over his thighs. *His strapping thighs.* His clean, male scent topped with a hint of—was that smoke?—curled through her blood. God, he smelled incredible.

She blinked and returned to her list.

"We could host a barbecue and set up a bouncy house—"

"A bouncy house?"

She studied him past her lashes. "Yes, you know, a bouncy house. My nieces love bouncy houses."

Why had she mentioned her nieces? So what if Josie had nieces and Luke had spent a few moments poring over that photo and—dammit, she had nothing to prove here.

Competitiveness isn't very feminine, Kinsey.

Oh, shut it, David.

"A bouncy house," he repeated dazedly, as if his entire life had been distilled to this one moment and he couldn't believe his rotten luck.

She pressed her lips against a smile. "I also think your connection to the foster kids would make a great promotional piece. I had lunch with a reporter from the *Trib* today, and she'd love to see the other side of Luke Almeida. The one who gives back to honor his foster father and brother."

He cut her a look, and she felt it to her perfectly manied toes. "The kids stay out of it. I won't have them used as pawns to make me or the CFD or your damn mayor look better."

While it was impossible to predict what would stick in the minds of voters, sad-eyed, underprivileged kids playing softball with firefighters had *win* written all over it.

"It would really be the easiest route—"

"Not happening, Kinsey." He took the list from her with one hand, her pen with the other, and slashed through that bullet point. "Next."

Kinsey wasn't quite ready to give up on that idea, especially as he had used her first name. They were finally getting somewhere, though she couldn't be sure where exactly. Or if it was a place she wanted to visit.

She tried another tack. "The members of CFD, and Engine 6 in particular, are heavily involved in the city's community, from their great service and public education to volunteer work and charity drives. Our campaign needs to focus on those efforts so we can minimize the negatives. Maybe even wipe those negatives out of existence."

Laying the list down on her desk, he stared at her in a way that completely unnerved her. "When the negatives are caught on camera and blasted onto YouTube, sweetheart, there's little chance of scrubbing the record. It's out there forever."

"True—"

"Plus, there's a place in our society for those negatives, as you call them. Usually, men channel their anger into approved routes of violent expression— the military, sports, a charity boxing match between CPD and CFD. When it's unapproved, that's where there's trouble. But, Kinsey, if I had a chance to do it over, I'd still punch the living daylights out of McGinnis and take my lumps."

Butterflies dive-bombed in her belly at all that passion and conviction. After working so long with constantly remorseful politicians, it was . . . refreshing.

He ran one large hand over the edge of her desk, mere inches from where her thigh flexed tight at the skirt of her cream-colored suit. Momentarily mesmerized by those masculine fingers, Kinsey worked to drag herself back to reality.

"Are you telling me that men are compelled by the mere fact of their gender to choose violence as their first resort?"

"Partly. It satisfies our sense of justice, it makes us feel good, and it always improves our odds with women."

He hoisted an eyebrow, drawing her laugh. It had been awhile since she wanted to laugh, and now she was choosing to let loose at Luke Almeida's argument for channeling his inner Ultimate Fighter.

"It won't improve your odds with *all* women."

He considered that for a moment. "No, there'll always be some who pretend they aren't turned on by the idea of a man who can defend himself and keep his woman safe. Usually, it's the same women who wear sexy heels that accentuate their shapely legs or open that top button of their blouse to hint at beautiful, cuppable breasts, then scowl when a guy takes a lingering look."

Cue lingering look. His gaze fell to the V of her blouse (top button *not* undone, but cut low enough to get things simmering) and continued downward, the intensity in his eyes sending her sex into a clench.

Kinsey knew she looked good, and with that scorching appraisal, she felt better. How long had it been since a man had looked at her with such candid interest? David had stopped looking at her, really looking at her, a long time ago.

"Are you one of those women, Miss Taylor? The kind who showcases her gorgeous assets and then hides behind the electric fence of feminism to keep the animals out?"

Animals. That word snapped her out of her reverie. So she would never consider herself a raging feminista, but she didn't need a degree in women's studies to recognize Luke Almeida's type. He was the alpha predator, a guy who turned to violence to solve his problems, a man who looked like a suit or a job or a woman could never contain him. She needed to get her head in the game and focus on the mission.

Operation Clean Up CFD. And Don't Let Luke Almeida Distract You.

The first part would be a cinch. As for the second . . .

"I think we're getting off track here, Mr. Almeida."

"Luke." Warm, sexy, inviting. Oh my.

Her mouth felt as dry as the golden sands of Baker Beach back home, the sensitive area between her thighs not so much. She smoothed clammy hands over her skirt. Drawing her palms down her thighs magnetized his gaze to her heat-saturated body. Every cell was on fire.

Maybe she should call CFD.

"Luke," she said, liking far too much how his name sounded on her lips. "Let's start with the community block party idea and go from there. I'll make sure we have media coverage and enough city bigwigs on hand to give it the validation we need."

"And the foster kids stay out of it?"

For the moment. "We'll have to add something else, then." She paused as if she needed time to think. "Maybe the calendar."

The cold set of his mouth contrasted with the hot flash of annoyance in his eyes. "You were serious about that?"

"As a heart attack. I've done some unscientific research around the office. The Men on Fire calendar idea was very popular, even with the guys."

He snorted.

Emboldened, she carried on.

"It'll take awhile to set up the community event, but I think a photo shoot with the heroes at Engine 6 could be laid up pretty quickly." Hell, she could sell tickets. The minute word about this wildfired around city hall, she just knew she'd be making a bunch of new friends who wanted in on that sexy action.

Straightening, she took a step backward and into the safety of professionalism. Getting back on the terra firma of the job she was pretty damn good at was the best way she knew to center herself. But she had to admit that his appreciation of her as a woman made her feel just as powerful.

"I need to get ready for my next meeting. Thanks so much for stopping by."

"And thanks for hearing me out." The quirk at the corner of his mouth was probably the only ac-knowledgment she'd get that this round had gone to her—the calendar was the kill shot—and that, more important, he didn't mind. Wow, how sexy was that? Meathead Luke Almeida had managed to surprise her.

He lifted his big body off her desk and moved lithely toward the door, then turned when he got there. "Your assistant . . . ?"

"Josie?"

"Josie. Is she seeing anyone?"

Her heart leaped into her throat. "Not as far as I know." Insisting that her quickening pulse was purely a reaction to all the caffeine she'd had today was an assertion she'd take to her grave. And just when her feelings toward him had crossed into warm fuzzies territory.

Score one for Mr. Almeida.

He nodded and made to leave, but she wasn't quite done with him yet.

"When's your birthday, Luke?"

Turning to face her, he speared her with those electric blues, now contracted in suspicion. "July."

Try as she might, she couldn't hide her grin. "Mr. July has a nice ring to it, don't you think?"

On that, she pivoted quickly to maintain her grip on that precious last word and bent over the desk to grab, oh, the stapler that was a few inches out of reach. She could feel his penetrating gaze on her ass as it shifted under her tight skirt. A cheap thrill, perhaps, but the way her sex life was going, she'd take the thrills where she could find them.

Only when she heard the door close behind her did she let go of the breath she hadn't even realized she'd been holding.

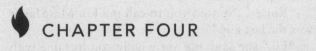

CHAPTER FOUR

"The chef here is amazing, Kinsey. He'll knock your heels off."

She didn't doubt it. Though San Francisco had its own thriving food culture, the culinary options in Chicago beat it hands-down. From deep-dish pizza and pierogi to five-star tasting menus and molecular gastronomy, you could eat out at a stellar restaurant every night of the week for a year and still not have exhausted all your options.

Kinsey tried to imagine how the firm, fit body of her dining companion would handle a daily assault of butter, carbs, and sugar. Probably very well, considering Eli "Hot Stuff" Cooper—as Chicago's female denizens referred to their disruptively handsome mayor—usually ran six miles to work and back instead of taking the car that his predecessors had seen as their due. Every morning, Kinsey checked Facebook and found photos of the mayor high-fiving other joggers on his run along Lake Shore from the tony streets of Lincoln Park. Occasionally, he took the "L" so he could glad-hand commuters while proclaiming the CTA the best transit system in the country. It was far from it, but ridership had skyrocketed as hopeful women vied to rub shoulders (and other body parts) with the most eligible bachelor east of the Mississippi.

"Well, Mr. Mayor—"

"Kinsey, I've told you to call me Eli. Mr. Mayor was the last guy."

"Eli," she said, not yet wholly comfortable with the informality. Having worked for a board supervisor and numerous big shots in San Francisco after earning her communications degree at Berkeley, she found this loosey-goosey style of her new boss disconcerting. Marching into her office without going through her assistant was standard. Texting her before she had made it to work at eight was par for the course. He called whenever he felt like it, including this morning's 5 a.m. wakey-wakey with an idea to win the hearts and minds of Chicago's public librarians. In recent months, they had been raking his ass across the coals over his threat to cut their funding.

"Cupcakes with cat-face icing, Kinsey. Those bookworms love cupcakes and cats."

Why the mayor had lately singled her out for special attention was hard to say. Working under two other members of the Media Affairs team—John Hernandez, aka "Porn Stache John," and Mark Baker, senior to her in position, junior to her in age—usually kept her out of Eli's orbit. Since starting in February, her daily grind revolved around press releases about the city's parking app or the popularity of Divvy, the bike share system. The puff pieces. The feel-good stories. That all changed a few weeks ago when the mayor began soliciting her opinion in the morning meetings. This CFD-CPD bust-up was the first meaty project she'd been given in her four months on the job.

Tonight he had invited her to a late dinner at Smith & Jones, a trendy new addition to Restaurant Row in the west Loop. She had agreed, hoping Eli's motive was just business, because despite the fact that she could cut a steak with that jawline, sleeping with the boss was not an option. Anyway, the man wore far too much product in his hair.

A plate of meat appeared before them. "The sausage bonanza with lamb merguez, pimiento-cheddar chicken sausage, and fennel kielbasa. Compliments of the chef," their hipster-Goth server tossed off with just the right amount of practiced indifference.

Glancing over his shoulder, Eli gave a one-fingered salute in the direction of the kitchen and the white-jacketed chef who stood sentry at the entrance. His thick, inked arms, folded like armor across a barrel chest, gave the impression of a man who had ways of "making" people like his food. With a curt nod, he spun around and headed back into his culinary sanctum.

"Someone you can't work your charm on?" Kinsey teased.

"We got unsolicited sausages, didn't we?" Eli slathered one encased meat tube with stone-ground mustard and took a bite. A little grease spattered on his French blue shirt and the suspender bisecting one of his broad shoulders. Yes, the mayor wore suspenders.

"Chef Brady Smith and I go way back," he said around his chewing. "Served together in Afghanistan." He inched the meat platter toward her.

"No, thanks. I'm a vegetarian."

She might as well have asked *him* to go veg, if the

horror that crossed his brow was any indication, but he quickly recovered and caught the attention of the server.

"You eat cheese, Kinsey?"

"Like it's going out of style."

"Bring her the goat cheese and sweet corn dumplings," he said to their server, "and I'll take the bone-in rib eye, medium rare."

Well, that was unexpectedly thoughtful, if a little high-handed. Not at all like her ex-fiancé, who had never really made peace with her vegetarianism, usually going out of his way to take her to steak houses where the only option was the slim-pickins salad bar. Strange now to think of how she had let pass his sly digs about her life choices. How she'd made excuses for him and allowed him to take the lead in their relationship because his ego was as big as all outdoors.

Then came the ultimate insult. She moved here. *For him.*

A woman in love should not be allowed to make life-altering decisions at the behest of the fiancé who thought his career was more important. She had left behind her family, her friends, and a great job working for the city of San Francisco for a man whose spine was so soft he needed scaffolding to stay upright. Not that her new job wasn't decent—it was—but the bitterness of compromise was a tough pill to swallow.

She had thought they were the golden couple. The handsome cardiac surgeon and the savvy media professional, a match made in the pages of a glossy lifestyle magazine. So maybe she spent more time hosting catered parties for David's colleagues than enjoying the fruits of their high-powered pairing, and maybe the sex had waned to zilch in the last year of their relationship, but moving to Chicago a month after he was appointed chief of cardiac surgery at Northwestern Medicine was supposed to fix it. For all his complaints about her lack of support and self-absorbed focus on her own career, he had sounded so pleased when she said she'd found a job in Chicago.

But within two months of her cross-country move—and less than three weeks before their May wedding—the rat bastard dumped her for a soft, feminine nurse with shoulders broad enough to prop up his fragile ego. Ten years together and—*poof!*—it was over. The replacement understood his needs, David had explained in his reasonable voice. She wasn't always trying to engage in power plays and one-upmanship. She *got* him. A man in his position just wanted to come home to a double Lagavulin, not a ball buster—or worse, an empty house and no dinner on the table because Kinsey was out working an event for *her* job.

Ooh, she wished she'd taken a rusty spoon to his 'nads. See how reasonable his voice sounded then.

Setting her fury aside until later when she could feed it with Cherry Garcia, she looked up to find the mayor's knotted expression fixed on a spot at the end of the densely packed bar. Or more particularly, on an Amazonian brunette with a rumpus of red-streaked curls and an unimpressed expression, which she was using on . . . well, well, well, if it wasn't Gage "Baby Thor" Simpson.

Gage was enthusiastically waving his hands to explain something *really important*. With each increasingly dramatic gesture, the woman's eyebrows hitched higher in skepticism until finally he shook her shoulders impatiently and she laughed. Their easy camaraderie and obvious bond radiated off them, even from paces away. If those two weren't related, Kinsey would sacrifice her meat virginity to the sausage bonanza.

"Do you know Gage Simpson?" she asked Eli, who was still riveted by the exchange at the bar.

"Who?"

"That's Gage Simpson, one of the Dempseys. And if I'm not mistaken, the woman with him is his sister, Alexandra."

"Tell me how it went with Almeida." There was a snappishness to his tone as he tore his gaze away from the Dempseys, or more specifically, from Alexandra. Interesting.

"Nothing to worry about. The wheels of rehabilitation are in motion."

"Sam Cochrane is making a bigger fuss of this than I expected," Eli said, with not a small amount of weariness in his voice. "He's siding with the police."

One of the mayor's biggest campaign donors, Chicago real estate baron, media mogul, and Trump-style billionaire Sam Cochrane owned the *Chicago Tribune*. His paper had gone to town with a scathing editorial on the video and repeated calls for head rolling every day since. Cochrane had also made clear his intentions to neither endorse nor support financially his reelection bid if Eli didn't come down hard on anything that carried the faintest whiff of scandal.

"However it goes, he comes out a winner," Kinsey said, knowing full well how sharks like Cochrane operated. "Calling out the bad behavior of public servants allows him to preach from the mountain while selling more newspapers and tightening the vise on you."

"Didn't take you long to figure out the lay of the land." Eli's smile was wry. "There's a bit more to it, though. Cochrane has history with the Dempseys. Used to co-own that bar of theirs with Sean Dempsey before they fell out. Now his daughter, Darcy, is shacked up with Beck Rivera."

The Dempsey foster brother she had yet to meet. This just got better and better. "And let me guess? He and Firefighter Rivera get along like a house on fire."

"Exactly. Darcy's a sweet kid, though, and Rivera's got a great left hook. Helluva boxer. I won a packet on him at the last Battle of the Badges."

Marvelous, another Dempsey with homicidal tendencies.

"So, Almeida and McGinnis," the mayor prompted. "What do we know?"

"The fight was apparently over Alexandra Dempsey. She's a probationary firefighter with six months' service at Engine 6. Her report said McGinnis had too much to drink and was getting handsy with some of the female patrons, including her, but I have a feeling there's more to it." That significant look Luke had shared with his brothers said there was a mile-deep root of "more to it" underneath that iceberg of silence.

Mr. Mayor—*Eli*—sighed. "*Cherchez le femme.* Where there's trouble, look for a damn woman." His gaze slid to Alexandra at the bar and turned brooding. "And Lord save us from women who think they can do everything a guy can do. The female firefighters are the worst."

Every hair on Kinsey's neck shot to indignant attention. "How enlightened of you, Eli. I'm sure your substantial female voter base would love to hear this."

"Hush, now. It's all well and good to rage about sex equality, Kinsey, but there are just some jobs a woman is not cut out for."

Pulse sputtering, she fought for calm. Not once had she ever felt that her vagina disqualified her to do anything, but there was always some dunderhead who believed the glass ceiling should be lowered instead of smashed.

"Remind me again how you got elected."

He grinned, and his dimple did a quickstep in his dark-shadowed cheek. *That's how.* Sometimes she had no idea if he believed half the crap he spewed or if he was just testing the limits of employee loyalty. Perhaps it was a unique attribute of Chicago men. Luke Almeida had certainly enjoyed pushing her buttons. Bet he was good at pushing all sorts of buttons.

"I promised to be tough on crime, to curb spending, and not stand for bullshit," Eli said, as if her request for information had not been rhetorical. Like all politicians, he loved to list his accomplishments. "Since I've been elected, the White Sox have clinched the World Series again and the Blackhawks have won the Cup two out of three years."

"What about the year they lost?"

"I was out of town during the playoffs. And while I'm good, even I can't lift Billy Goat's curse to help the Cubs." An arrogant smile touched his lips. "I'm happy to say women are my strongest supporters. They like what they see."

Screw the formalities. "God, could you be any more of an ass— Oh, hello!"

Gage Simpson had materialized at their table like a grinning, golden god.

"Miss Taylor, fancy seeing you here. Of course, your connections will get you the best tables. My connections only get me as far as the bar."

"Meet my connection," she said, gesturing to Eli, who thrust out his hand, eager to parlay with another voter even if he was one of those pesky Dempseys. "Mayor Cooper, Gage Simpson, one of our finest with Engine 6."

Gage shook the offered hand. "Mr. Mayor. Pleasure." Kinsey detected the slightest lowering of Gage's vocal register to bedroom level on that last word. An equal opportunity flirt, apparently.

He turned to the woman behind him. "This is my sister, Alex Dempsey. Alex, this is Kinsey Taylor and, of course, you recognize the mayor from his innumerable TV appearances."

Alex's smile was brief and in no way unfriendly, but she seemed more reserved than her brother. On the statuesque, curvy body of a swimmer, she wore red cowboy boots, dark-wash jeans, and a T-shirt emblazoned with "Gandalf Hates the Yankees." Kinsey liked her immediately.

"So how are the entrées?" Gage asked, unashamedly eying the smorgasbord of meat. "I've been dying to try this place but we were limited to the bar menu."

"We haven't gotten very far. The mayor knows the

chef." Kinsey gave an "of course he does" shrug and gestured to the protein platter. "Sausage?"

"I can never say no to sausage," Gage said with a conspiratorial wink. Alex smiled at her brother's joke, but Eli's expression was stony—and lasered in on the striking woman.

"So, Miss Dempsey, or should I say Helen of Troy?" he threw out.

Alex's smile faltered. "Excuse me?"

"Helen of Troy had a face that launched a thousand ships, and she's best remembered for instigating decades of warfare. After what happened last week, perhaps we should refer to you as the face that launched a thousand fists. You *are* the reason we had an unofficial Battle of the Badges in your brother's bar, are you not?"

Kinsey balled her hands under the table, itching to smack her boss, but it wouldn't do to undermine him in public. She'd bring out the slap in her bitch later.

"I can handle myself," Alex said, holding Eli's gaze boldly with a pair of incredible green eyes, "but my brothers were brought up not to show disrespect to women. Or tolerate it in others."

"All the same, I'd have thought a woman with your training would be more used to the rough-house atmosphere of an all-male environment, and wouldn't need your brother to intercede for you." Eli considered Alex with interest. "Sometimes I wonder how appropriate it is."

Alex bristled, as did Kinsey. Even Gage, who had radiated nothing but affability since the moment she met him, looked put out.

Hearts and minds, Mr. Mayor. Hearts and minds.

"How appropriate what is?" Alex asked, and though Kinsey had just met her for the first time this evening, she could tell her voice was pitched a few angry octaves higher than usual. Kinsey suspected it might go higher before her boss was through.

"Female firefighters."

Yep, here we go.

"I know we lowered the physical requirements a few years ago to get more women into the profession," Eli continued, "but I'm not sure it's good for the service. Especially when it causes these types of disruptions and leads to headline-grabbing brawls."

"Mr. Mayor," Kinsey warned.

"Kinsey, I told you to call me Eli." He swiveled his strong jaw back to Alex, who looked like a sewer had opened up beneath her feet and the scent had just struck her nostrils. "The same argument was made for women in combat, and now that it's a reality, I suspect we're going to see some backlash about it. Women are a distraction when lives are at stake."

"Do you feel the same way about gays in the military or in the CFD, Mr. Mayor?" Gage cut in, strain underlining every word. "Are you worried a homosexual might get so distracted by the hot ass of one of his fellow firefighters that he'll forget to pull your little old grandma from that burning building?"

Eli met Gage's gaze head-on. "I've no problem with gays in the military or my fire department. To be honest, it's also a strength issue, and if my ass is on the line, I want the person who can handle the physicality of the job at my side. A woman in that environment complicates the dynamic."

Kinsey could see Alex running down a ten-second

count in her head. After a long beat, she framed a response through gritted teeth.

"Well, it's a good thing the decision isn't up to you, Mr. Mayor, though I'll happily run against you next year if you decide to make 'Patriarchal Woman-Hating Asshole' part of your platform."

Deathly silence fell over the group, the tension so thick the steak knives on the table would have a hard time slicing through it. Though by the glitter in Alex's eyes, the blades might find other ready uses. A stiff moment later, Eli broke the heavy quiet with a smile that would usually have the female voters faint with lust.

"Well said, Miss Dempsey." He turned his attention back to Gage. "Would you like to meet the chef? As Kinsey mentioned, he's a friend of mine."

Gage stared at Eli, perhaps trying to puzzle him out. Did he want to meet the chef badly enough to accept a favor from the man who had just dissed his sister's career and ambitions? Sending a sidelong glance Alex's way, he appeared to wait until she smiled her permission. The sharp pang in Kinsey's chest reminded her all too well of how much she missed her own brothers.

"If it's not too much trouble," Gage said easily.

Unfolding his long body from his seat, Eli stood, displaying his unabashed masculinity in all its glory. The man was a media wet dream. If only he wouldn't use so much hair gel—or spout off every politically incorrect thought in his brain.

"What about you, Alexandra?" he asked. "Are you a chef groupie?"

A flame of heat lit high on her cheekbones, though whether it was because of Eli's familiar use of her first name or his apparent peace overture was impossible to tell.

"I'm no one's groupie, Mr. Mayor," she said in a low voice. Tension of a different sort now filled the space between them.

Flustered, Alex broke their eye contact first, and Eli and Gage strode off toward the kitchen.

"Would you like to take a seat?" Kinsey asked Alex. "It might help you get inside the mind of the dinosaur who just occupied it."

With a husky laugh, she sat and picked up Eli's steak knife, turning it over thoughtfully. Oh yeah, she had gone there during that exchange.

"He didn't say anything I haven't heard a million times already. In my profession, there are plenty of naysayers who hate the idea of a woman daring to think she can do what's traditionally been a man's job."

"Even your brothers?"

Alex quirked a rueful smile. "They know how much it means to me to be treated the same as anyone else, but they can't help feeling protective. It's more their fraternal instinct than anything else"—she let loose the sigh of a billion women before her—"or at least that's how I choose to see it."

"I know what you mean. I have three brothers myself."

Alex raised her chin, and a look that only a tortured sister could understand warmed those amazing green eyes. "So, what has having three brothers taught you about dealing with bullheaded men?"

"Enough to know I can handle both my boss and your brother with one hand tied behind my back."

That pulled a surprised bark of laughter from Alex

that faded as quickly as it erupted. "Luke's a good guy. I know you have a job to do, but maybe you and the mayor should cut him some slack."

"Maybe you should tell me what's going on between your brother and Detective McGinnis."

Alex's previously open expression shuttered to blank, and Kinsey realized there would be no prying any Dempsey family secrets out of her tonight. Knowing what fueled the bad blood between the two men shouldn't be a priority anyway. Her only goal was to rehabilitate the reputation of Engine 6, and by proxy the entire CFD, which had taken a hit with Luke's bad behavior. The underlying reasons for his lack of self-control were unimportant.

Then why was it all she could think about?

If, by some magical stretch of the imagination, Gage hadn't followed his brothers and father into the family business, he would have become a professional chef. He loved to cook and he was excellent at it, so stepping into the kitchen at Smith & Jones was like walking into a fantasy world. Avidly, he drank in the bustle of the crew as they moved in perfect symmetry, their obvious expertise washing over him pleasurably. Add to that the smells, and he was tempted to sneak a peek in the gleaming chrome reflection of the countertops to see whether he was drooling.

Then his mouth went as dry as the unsuccessful angel food cake he had ventured last week, the one that tasted like reconstituted cardboard, because at the head of the line stood the hottest, scariest motherfucker Gage had ever seen. This guy was built like a tank—broad shouldered, broad backed. Just broad. His forearms were as thick as ancient oak branches, their dark skin a comic book tapestry weaving a million stories in vibrantly colored ink. Above the collar of his immaculate chef's jacket, a black ribbon curled around his neck like a wisp of smoke.

Hot diggity.

Gage wanted to lick that neck tattoo, then lave his tongue all the way over this guy's close-shaved skull. Claim every inch of his rough-cast head for his own. Later he would take the time to explore the rest of his body, but for now, he would work with the pleasures of the neck up.

He hadn't even seen the man's face and he was as hard as granite.

"Brady," Gage heard beside him, and he jumped at the mayor's voice, having forgotten he was there.

Brady. Please, baby Jesus, let it be him.

The hulk turned around, and damn if he didn't look like a mob enforcer, the kind who probably presided over an underground fight club after the restaurant shut up shop. On the right side of his face, he rocked a zigzag of scars. Dark eyes, hard and suspicious, stared above a strong Roman nose and a cruel-set mouth. This guy was so not his type. Gage liked men with smooth edges and well-formed features, and who weren't likely to snap him in half.

He had never wanted anyone so much.

There was no smile of acknowledgment at Eli as Brady walked over, just a careful blankness.

"Brady, this is Gage Simpson. He's a big fan. Mr. Simpson, meet Brady Smith, chef/owner of Smith & Jones."

Gage thrust out his hand much too eagerly. He wanted to touch this man. He had to.

Brady considered Gage's hand as if unsure what should be done in this tricky situation. Perhaps he was wondering if he should shake it, slap it, or lick it. Suck Gage's fingers into that hot pocket of a mouth and make him beg for release.

All of it, Gage thought desperately. He could do all of it.

Several seconds passed to the soundtrack of kitchen clanking, cooking sizzle, and Gage's pounding heart. Brady finally clasped Gage's outstretched hand, and his cock stirred in response. Christ on a crutch, what was this guy doing to him?

His body had never gotten the jump on his brain this quickly before. Gage had no problems with who he was and what he liked, and he had no problems acting on his healthy libido. There was always some hot guy—a couple of hot guys—ready to give him what he wanted, wherever and whenever he needed it. But this . . . it was like every hormone had decided today was the blessed day to revert to horny-as-all-get-out adolescence.

And with that came the brain freeze, the best jump-start for which was of course his trusty pal, verbal diarrhea. He'd always been a silence filler.

"I'm here with my sister and when we couldn't get a table, we had an appetizer at the bar. The fried calamari with the bacon-herb aioli? It was genius. Fucking genius." Too late, Gage realized he was still crushing Brady's hand and that this one action was the only thing holding him up. All the blood in his brain had rushed to his crotch. There was an excellent chance that if he let go, Gage would fall down face-first, his dick so hard he'd end up spinning like a top.

Brady Smith remained as silent as the grave Gage wished he could crawl into. But he couldn't. Stop. Talking.

"One day, I'll come back and have the full tasting menu. Your food is a touch expensive for someone on a firefighter's salary and I'd need to save up for a few months, by which time I might be able to get a reservation." Gage laughed at his own razor-sharp wit, the sound hollow and maniacal as it bounced off the polished chrome counters. Shit, where was he going with this? "From what I've had tonight, I know it would be worth it."

Brady stared, cocoa eyes dark as sin, not a single muscle moving on his forbidding face. Not even an eyelash. His expression hadn't changed one iota since he'd walked over from the line, and now Gage was beginning to wonder if the guy had heard any of the word vomit spewing from his mouth.

Finally, Gage extracted his hand, which had started to sweat from the heat of the kitchen. Sure, let's go with that.

"As you can see, Brady just lives to talk about his work," Eli said in a thoroughly amused tone, earning a filthy look from the silent chef.

God, that scowl was hotter than a shirtless Joe Manganiello.

Aaaand . . . crickets.

"Do you like to cook?" the mayor asked Gage, in his new role of interpreter-facilitator. Someone had to pick up the conversational slack, which was about the only thing in the immediate vicinity that was anywhere close to loose. Everything else—Gage's body, Brady's mouth, the air between them—was tight and fraught.

Slowly, Gage nodded. "Love to." It came out of his throat raspy, an undeniable invitation to the brooding cliff face of muscle before him. The things he would love to do to this man. The things he would love to have done to him by this man.

"Well, we'll let you get back to it," Eli said, seemingly satisfied that this introduction had gone swimmingly, "though I need to talk to you about the food for the fund-raiser. How's Monday sound?"

Brady Smith only raised an eyebrow in response, because why waste precious energy on anything so ridiculous as an acknowledgment that the mayor—*the frickin' mayor*—had spoken to him? Eli, clearly used to this manner of communication from Mr. Talkative, appeared unperturbed as he nodded and turned to leave the kitchen. Had Gage missed the Morse code blinks for yes and no?

With one last—possibly blistering, possibly just bored—look, Brady Smith twisted his broad shoulders and gave them his back, but not before Gage heard a gravelly "Call me" from deep in the bear's throat.

Holy shit, was that for him or Mr. Mayor?

If Gage was expecting clarification, clearly he'd be a long time on the hook. Eli was already heading to the dining room, Brady was back to grunting orders at the end of the line, and Gage was left wondering what in the hell just happened here.

CHAPTER FIVE

"Ooh, Almeida, are you ready for your close-up?"

Luke froze in the act of pulling on his bunker pants, counted off the five seconds in his head that kept Firefighter Jacob Scott safe from a pounding, and then continued getting ready.

For his fucking close-up.

"Jacob, you just wish someone thought you had a bod worth snapping," Gage cut in. "But as your flabby muscles won't even get you a date, never mind a photo shoot, you should probably keep your fat mouth zipped."

Jacob, who did like to overindulge in Gage's pasta puttanesca and could probably stand to put forth a touch more effort in the station's gym, slammed his locker door shut with a scowl.

"This whole calendar thing is so gay," he muttered as he slithered out of the locker room.

"Good one, Firefighter Scott," Gage called after him archly. "Jon Stewart–worthy."

Sucking in a ragged breath, Luke debated which T-shirt he should wear, not that it would make a blind bit of difference because he would be shirtless for the shoot.

Shirtless.

"You have to admit this *is* pretty gay," he mumbled to Gage while he pulled a standard-issue navy CFD tee over his head.

"I know. It's gonna be awesome. Reminds me of nights at the Manhole, dancing on the bar, throwing my sweaty shirt at the guys I liked."

Luke groaned. Forehead, meet locker door. "Tell me it's not going to be like that."

Gage clapped a strong hand on his shoulder and grinned triumphantly. "Bro, it's going to be the gayest thing you have ever experienced."

Luke hadn't quite known what to expect, but certainly not the shitball hurtling his way like that scene in *Raiders of the Lost Ark*. Engine 6 and the rest of the units had been taken out of dispatch rotation for the morning, meaning they had four hours where no calls would come in. All so they could ensure an interruption-free shoot for the calendar.

His crew would usually see that as a golden opportunity to run errands or sleep in or just stay the hell away from work, but oh no. The A shift had arrived on time, everyone coming off C had stayed, and the boys on B had strolled in on their day off. All three platoons were in the house, ready to bear witness to how low Luke could go.

No big deal, right? Just his homies raggin' on him for taking his shirt off and shooting *Zoolander* stares at the camera. He'd take crap for it for months, but if it got the mayor off his back and kept the Dempseys together, it would be worth it. Then the impossible happened.

It got worse.

About an hour ago, the vehicle bay started filling with people. An assistant working with the photographer he could understand, even a couple of pencil pushers from city hall to wrap the whole event up in a pretty red bow. But no way in hell had Luke expected the seventy or so people—mostly women—who were now hanging out in a makeshift tailgate party.

He could hear the Doritos crunching from in here.

"I wonder if they'll let me choose the music for my shoot," Gage said distractedly, scanning his iPod playlists.

"Can't believe you volunteered for this." Luke knew why *he* was doing it, but his head almost exploded this morning when Gage told him he'd called Kinsey and asked to take part.

Lost in his own world, Gage fingered through assorted briefs, his expression deathly serious. "Black, gray, or white? I think the white shows my hip flexors better, but the black is a classic."

"I don't give a shit what color shorts you wrap your junk in."

"You sound nervous, Mr. Almeida," he heard behind him.

The sizzle between his shoulder blades almost hurt. Almost felt good.

"He is," Gage said. "I'd watch your shoes, Kinsey, because he's probably going to puke any minute now."

"I need a word with you," Luke spat out as he turned and got a load of the PR princess. She was wearing her standard dick-raising uniform of hip-hugging skirt and gauzy blouse, a little sheer but not sheer enough. Sleeveless, it showcased her tanned, toned arms and nicely curved shoulders. This woman kept herself in shape. He liked that.

But right now, he didn't like her.

Tucking his hand under her elbow, he steered her to the other end of the locker room. The clack of her heels reverberated like jeers in his skull.

"I'm not doing this," Luke said in his best not-fuckin'-around tone.

A citrusy scent wafted off her skin, reminding him that he was still cupping her elbow. Elbows should feel coarse and bony, but not hers. She was so damn silky he never wanted to let go.

He dropped that elbow like it was a burning doorknob.

"You *are* nervous," Kinsey said with something approximating glee in her voice.

"I. Am. Not. Nervous." He just didn't want to be the laughingstock of the whole department. There was a difference. "When did this turn into a billion-ring circus? There's an awful lot of flesh tourists out there."

She delivered a look of boundless patience. "Now, don't be petty. The gray life of the city worker needs a splash of color every now and then."

Petty? This was his reputation, his job, his life they were talking about. "You've got Gage, who actually wants to be your puppet. I mean, look at him. He's the most colorful person I know."

In unison, they turned to Gage, who was bobbing his head to a song on his iPod while rubbing something oily all over his chest. Christ Jesus. He caught their stares and held up his underwear choices. "Kinsey. White, gray, or black?"

"Black, babe. It's classic."

With a smile and a nod, Gage returned to his task of making his chest greasier than a slab of bacon.

"See?" Luke hissed.

Kinsey's lips flattened, and she made a strangled "I'm not laughing at you" sound.

"What can I do to get you out of your shirt today, Luke?" Her voice held a husky, wheeler-dealer tone, the kind of voice for which he was likely to do anything. He imagined that voice whispering in his ear, issuing wicked orders, making him hard as steel.

Come to think of it, he didn't have to imagine. The tug of desire in his groin turned painful as his dick climbed to half-mast.

She smiled sweetly. "The big stars usually make demands like a bowl of M&M's with all the green ones removed, or fresh heirloom roses for their dressing room. I'm not sure the city's budget can stretch to that, but we'll do what we can. What do you need, Luke?"

Now she was making him sound like some preposterous prima donna. Feeling more foolish by the second, he racked his mind for leverage. A checklist of the things he wanted scrolled through his brain, half of them shockingly lurid and all of them involving Kinsey's long, luscious legs wrapped around his hips. Asking for mind-blowing sex in exchange for his cooperation was probably not kosher, though.

What else? *What else?*

"The proceeds of this calendar go to charity, right?"

She nodded.

"I get to pick the charity." The kids at St. Carmen's

could do with a new rec room and, while he was under no illusions that this skin-fest would actually raise much in the way of Benjamins, every little bit would help.

"As long as you don't choose something controversial that could embarrass the city."

"Such as the Committee to Elect Anyone but Eli Cooper?"

A smile lifted the corner of that lush, pink mouth. "I'm fairly certain that wouldn't count as a charity, despite the great service you might think you're performing."

That pulled a laugh from deep in his gut. Cute. Kinsey Taylor had a sense of humor about her boss. "I'd like any proceeds to go to the foster home where I volunteer."

"Oh. That sounds very . . . worthy." It was the first time Luke had seen her flummoxed, but a few seconds later, she squared her shoulders and was all business again. "You ready to do this, Luke?"

He sighed heavily. "Make me a star, sweetheart."

The boom-boom bass out in the truck bay wasn't quite loud enough to drown out the whoops and hollers of the ladies—and a few guys—who had gathered for their splash of color. Thankfully, Luke wasn't the only one who would be making a total assclown of himself. Like Gage, several firefighters from other houses had stepped up to be part of the "Man Titty Extravaganza," as Alex had dubbed it. Gage's enthusiasm, Luke could understand. The kid was a grade-A exhibitionist, and if it improved his chances of getting dick, he'd do it. But why anyone else would willingly strip in front of seventy ravenous women and a bunch of men feigning disinterest was beyond Luke's understanding.

When he looked over to his crew gathered on the far side of the bay, he caught a glimpse of bills being shoved into McElroy's hands, quickly followed by the lieutenant scratching a note on a piece of paper.

Shit on a stick. Big Mac was running a book.

Luke took a leisurely stroll over to the guys. "What's up, ladies?"

Insolent stares greeted him, except for Wyatt, who looked like, well, Wyatt. From the expressions of the rest of them, though, respect for Luke was slowly circling the drain of the hose-drying tower. Even Derek Phelan, the new recruit who usually looked up to Luke in wide-eyed admiration, was now staring at him with a healthy dose of derision.

Captain Matt Ventimiglia, better known as Venti because of his name and the fact that there were twenty ways to piss him off (the list was posted in the kitchen), strode over to join them. Luke breathed a sigh of relief. Surely the presence of the senior officer at Engine 6 would add a much-needed influx of order to these shenanigans.

The Cap passed over a Jackson to Big Mac. "Twenty on Almeida to not make five."

So much for the gravity injection.

"Gambling is illegal on city property," Luke ground out, marveling at the irony of the hothead who was currently on admin leave for punching out a guy becoming the firehouse's hall monitor.

Jacob crossed his arms. "Just a little fun, Almeida. We're taking bets on how quickly you raise wood under all those lights."

The crew practically fell off their folding chairs. Even Wyatt smiled. Traitor.

"You know something, Jacob? That sounds pretty gay." Luke stalked off to the tune of Jacob's sputtering denials and the guys' noisy guffaws.

Not that Luke needed his crew's mockery to clue him in. The sucking sound in his head told him exactly how this morning would go down.

In a crashing ball of flame.

Two hours later, eight guys including Gage had taken turns strutting their stuff. Popular poses included jaunty-angled helmets, hanging off the side of the pumper in a way that might prompt an OSHA audit, and competing to see how low their briefs could go without getting a triple-X rating.

"Almeida, you're next," the photographer's assistant called out, a cute pixie type covered head to toe in black.

Luke felt the stares of the entire crew and city hall workers as he walked toward his harshly lit nightmare in the staging area. The photographer, a pretty, olive-skinned woman with *Jersey Shore* hair, shook his hand.

"Pleased to meet you, Luke. I'm Lili. Is this your first time being professionally photographed?"

"Other than for my dress blues on CFD graduation."

"YouTube doesn't count, huh?" She winked. Everyone was a comedian today. "Okay. Take off your shirt and I'll try to make it as painless as possible."

Deep breaths.

He peeled off his tee from the back, and by the time he found light again, his ears were ringing with cheers. Someone took the shirt from his clammy hands.

"Good," Lili said. "Now pull the suspenders of your bunker pants up and open the snaps to halfway down your crotch."

"Get 'em off, sugar. Nice 'n' slow," a woman's lewd voice called out, earning a chorus of lusty catcalls in response. And women were supposed to be the gentler sex.

He closed his eyes. *You can do this, Almeida.*

When he wrenched his eyelids open, his gaze targeted and locked on Kinsey Taylor like a heat-seeking missile. She stood off to the side, leaning against the front of Bessie, their fire truck, giving it a brand-new shine by her association with it. Annoyance roared through his veins like rocket fuel. It was her fault he was standing here, half naked, at the mercy of this crowd of vultures.

She'd wanted this. Now he was going to give Miss Taylor exactly what she had asked for.

Watching Luke as he traced one incendiary finger below the border of his bunker pants, Kinsey was struck for the first time by the true meaning of Not Safe for Work. And not just because of the location of his fingers. It was all in the eyes.

He was staring at her so voraciously her skin burned under his focus.

Pop.

His six-pack—*groan,* eight-pack—revealed itself inch by inch.

Pop.

A tight band of elastic bisected the lower half of his cut abdomen. Smooth beauty above. Untold pleasures below.

Pop.

She inclined her shoulders forward just a smidge because hell if she was missing—ah, yes. An intriguing bulge pushed against the snowy white fabric of his boxer briefs. Not classic black, but she couldn't imagine him in anything else.

Luckily, she had more than enough imagination to picture him in nothing at all.

The noisy cheers were deafening, but who needed auditory senses when every other one was heightened? Her skin tingled with the need to touch. Her mouth watered with the need to taste. In her nostrils, motor oil and pheromones created an intoxicating concoction of pure, raw sex. But sight was the victor here. There was no beating the image of a half-naked firefighter putting on a sexy show.

The photographer coaxed him out of his shell with soothing instructions, not that he needed much encouragement. The man was born for this. His earlier discomfort apparently forgotten, brazen grins came easy. Each turn revealed more smooth planes and defined muscles of his sculpted body. Playfully, he'd dip his head, then peek past his dark eyelashes with a "come hither" look for the camera.

For her.

As if he didn't have enough going on with the drop-dead bod and rough-hewn jaw, those tattoos were completely badass—*Sean* and a pulsing green shamrock on the left, *Logan* and the CFD's seal on the right, *Semper Fidelis* emblazoned across his chest: Family, Duty, Country. Coupled with his request to donate the calendar's proceeds to his foster kids' charity, the whole package hinted at something more than an inked-up, brawling thug. Yet another layer to the surprising Luke Almeida.

Her lips felt as dry as tinder, and she darted her tongue to wet them. She crossed her legs and squeezed her thighs together, desperate for relief, yet eager to agitate and enjoy this moment for as long as possible.

He was teasing her, driving her insane with lust as payback for having put him in this position. Wasn't revenge supposed to be a dish best served cold? Well, the delicious sight before her just went to prove that the best revenge was a man served hot, hot, hot.

Bring it on, Mr. Almeida.

Out of the corner of her eye she caught the ghost of movement, and she turned to take in a stunning redhead. Rail thin with creamy, freckled skin, she wore a gray pinstripe suit and peep-toe leopard-print pumps. Last season's Louboutins. Super cute.

"Hi," Red said, offering a hand with an easy smile. "I've seen you around city hall, usually on the upward slog when the elevator craps out."

Smiling back, Kinsey took her hand. "I thought you looked familiar. Where do you work again?"

"Legal on the third floor. I'm one of those people everyone loves to hate." She laughed a little too long at her joke. "My, my, quite the display, huh?"

"Something for everyone," Kinsey said with an eyebrow waggle.

They spent a minute or two chatting about the new fro-yo place in the city hall food court and how summers were so much better with cute college-age male interns and their cute college-age asses. It was easy, kind of nice. Maybe she'd found a new friend. It had been tough these last couple of months in a strange city, and her misery over David had kept her locked in a bubble of gloom.

Feeling optimistic, she was about to suggest that they meet for drinks Friday after work when Red spoke first.

"So you're working with Luke to turn him into a good little boy?"

Something about her tone rankled. Kinsey felt her gaze being dragged back to Luke, but he was no longer looking at her. All his heat was now reserved for her new friend.

"Just a word to the wise," Red continued, passing smoothly over the fact that Kinsey hadn't answered her question, which had sounded more like an insult. "Luke's only ever been good at three things: firefighting, sex, and being a Dempsey. His family has always come first and there's no room for anyone else."

Kinsey mentally recoiled as if struck. "And you're telling me this because . . . ?"

"He used to look at me that way."

Kinsey's mouth felt like an ash pit. "I didn't catch your name," she said, compelling her voice to calm when every cell in her fingertips burned to scratch this woman's eyes out.

"Lisa Sullivan," she said, walking away. "Formerly Almeida. Good luck with the Dempseys."

That ash in Kinsey's mouth ignited to flame. An ex-wife? And from the way Luke's gaze had scorched over Lisa, "ex" was a moving target.

Kinsey was so taken aback by what had just transpired that it took a moment to notice that the photographer was calling her over. "I need someone with decent nails for the next shot." Lili looked down at Kinsey's nails boasting a three-day-old manicure. "You in or should I poll the crowd?"

Her eyes met Luke's unbelievably blue gaze and slid to the blood-tinged color that flagged his cheeks. A tsunami of passion waved off him. Because of her. *Lisa.*

Knowing that every single woman in that audience—maybe even the former Mrs. Almeida—would jump at the chance to grope the hunky fireman, Kinsey made an instantaneous decision. There had to be some perks to being the founder of the feast.

Keeping her focus on Luke, she spoke to Lili. "I'm in."

"Miss Taylor," he said, tipping his helmet.

"Mr. Almeida."

Lili glanced up from her viewfinder. "Kinsey, stand behind Luke and place your palm under his arm and over his pec. Then wrap your other arm around his waist."

Kinsey rounded Luke's imposing form and rested her palm between his shoulder blades. *Oh!* Volcanic heat dueled with barely leashed fury at her touch. Both sizzled through her fingertips, buzzing her skin, sparking her body to glittering life. Slowly, she coasted her right hand along the crease where his ink-cuffed arm met his body. Weaved it through under the strap of his suspenders. Explored the thrilling new territory of this man's incredible body.

She palmed his chest and encountered a pebble-hard nipple. He shivered.

"Oh yeah, that's what I'm talkin' 'bout," a female voice rang out, whipping the lady horde into a frenzy of emphatic appreciation.

Kinsey had to tiptoe to whisper into his ear and the urge to brush her lips against his skin almost undid her. Was he sensitive there, in that soft hollow behind his lobe? Where else might her touch produce sensuous shivers?

"We okay?"

After a long beat, he coughed out, "Fine."

Why she had chosen "we" was beyond her. There was no "we" here, just two people forced to work together toward a common goal, but as soon as it passed her lips, she recognized its unerring rightness. David, an expert in healing physical hearts, had taken a scalpel to hers, and Luke was battling demons of his own. Whatever had happened between him and his ex had left him angry. Hurt.

He held his body iron-rigid, every muscle straining to break the skin barrier, including that scar tissue on his shoulder. It appealed to a very womanly instinct deep within her. What daring feats had he performed to earn that badge of courage? Who had lived to see another day because Luke Almeida exuded heroism from every pore?

Slowly, as if she were dealing with a dangerous, caged animal, she encircled his waist with her forearm and splayed her palm over his rock-hard abs. *Gently does it.*

"Screw her," Kinsey whispered, and then she drew a nail across his nipple, absorbing another delicious shiver into her skin. "Sorry, am I cold?" she asked, knowing she wasn't.

"Yeah, you're as cold as ice." Within the span of a heartbeat, the stress in his body vanished and he relaxed in her arms. "Get in close, sweetheart, I'll keep you warm."

Yowza. Unable to resist that offer, she molded her body flush to his. At shoulder level, he was twice as wide across as she, the perfect male specimen. A perfect fit. His strong back felt like the reason she had breasts. Her nipples, already stiffened to bullets, now registered painful, the only relief for which would be a friction-inducing rub. With every fiber of her being, she resisted doing just that.

Ninety-seven erotically charged seconds passed while the photographer took several shots. Off in the corner, where the Engine 6 crew had gathered like a witches' coven, boisterous cheers rose up, punctuated by a shout of, "Pay up, McElroy. Told you he wouldn't last."

Luke's growl rumbled in his chest, an animalistic vibrato that rolled through her body like the precursor to a brain-melting orgasm.

"Okay, that's it," Lili said. "Kinsey, anything else?"

Kinsey extracted her hand—and her overheated breasts—from the hazardous cocoon of Luke's body, but it felt like she lost something in the separation. Crossing her arms over her nipples, she wrapped her palms around herself, desperate to hold on to that life-affirming male heat for a few more precious seconds. Behind his back, a few shallow breaths started the rocky road to composure.

When her mind had defogged somewhat, she glanced at her watch. "We have a few minutes before break, so I think we could get some more shots. For fun." Because, dang, that had been way too serious. She needed to get control of her hormones—and her emotions—pretty damn quick.

She sought out Josie, who was getting her flirt on with one of the barely clad firemen.

"Josie, we're ready."

Her assistant jumped into action and brought a carrier to the front.

With her game face back on, Kinsey turned to Luke, now refastening his bunker pants and hiding all that manly magnificence. So sad, but it was really for the best. It would be too easy to lose herself in his dangerous heat. In those eyes.

"Haven't you had your pound of flesh from me yet, Miss Taylor?" Luke murmured as he finished buttoning up, languor in his motions.

She fisted her hands at her hips and shook her head.

"Not quite, Mr. Almeida." Meeting his smoldering gaze head on, she issued the next order in her brightest voice.

"Josie, release the kittens."

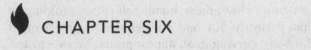

CHAPTER SIX

Luke balled his fists against the cool tile and let the spray crash over his body. He had no idea how long he'd spent in the shower. Long enough for the water to run cold. Long enough for the crew's ribbing to dwindle to chirps and for the ravenous crowd to clear out.

But not long enough to quit his brood over his ex-wife's appearance, apparently. Who the hell did she think she was showing up in his house?

Of course, that was just the beginning of the Lisa torture fest. Not enough to waltz in with her smug airs and expensive perfume, she had to cozy up to Kinsey in that conspiratorial huddle. Two sophisticated, out-of-his-league women getting a kick out of the man meat on display. That's what had truly enraged him. Not just that Lisa had shown her face in the last place she was welcome, but that she might have been corrupting Kinsey. Telling tales out of school about what a terrible husband he had made, how inadequate he had been as a provider, maybe even a dig about his family.

Lisa really hated his family.

His ex and Kinsey gettin' chatty. His past and his . . . nothing. An easy-on-the-eye distraction, the

PR princess was barely his present, never mind his future.

But she had sure felt shockingly present when she'd gotten up close, those bombshell curves molding to him perfectly. She had put her slender arm around his body, curving in an almost protective sweep, and whispered those two beautiful words in his ear.

Screw. Her.

Damn, he didn't need her defense. He wasn't used to it, either. From his family, sure, because that was their default setting. But another woman—a strong woman like Kinsey—stepping up like that confused him with its heady brew of territoriality and care. More likely she was playing some game to make him look like a dumb, horny beast in front of his crew.

And now he was stupid with anger again.

Out in the locker room, he took a moment to absorb the blessed quiet now that the firehouse was back to its usual state of watchful readiness. The lull before the twister. He grabbed at his locker door hard enough to send the picture of Logan and Sean floating to the floor. As he bent to pick it up, a taunt of heels broadcast her arrival.

Miss Kinsey Taylor.

His eyes traveled upward, his crouch giving him an excellent view of her well-toned legs, skirt-hugging thighs, the flare of her hips. Standing, he caught the scent of fragrant citrus that made him dizzy.

Unable to think above the haze of emotion short-circuiting his brain, he deposited the photo in his locker. Then he slammed the door shut, making a lot of noise while he did it.

Kinsey raised an eyebrow. "Use your words, Luke."

Good fuck, she had not just said that. This woman was determined to drive him insane. Between her know-it-all flounce into his house last week and this day from hell, her edging under his skin was city-sanctioned torture of the highest order.

She leaned against Gage's locker. "Want to know what she said to me?"

Speech was impossible, but she must have taken his raging silence as permission to continue because she went on. "She said you were only good at three things. Two of them I already knew about. All those commendations for bravery."

He strained to hear the derision in her tone, but his mock-o-meter was off.

"She said you'll move heaven and hell in defense of your family."

He doubted Lisa had put it in quite those terms. Her resentment of Luke wouldn't allow a kind word. Kinsey's slightly crooked smile acknowledged her re-working of whatever his ex-wife had said about the Dempseys.

"The third thing she mentioned . . ." She looked him up and down, her visual dissection turning him hard. "I can only imagine."

Sex. That's what Lisa had said. Damn straight, that had never been a problem.

"A woman who can make you mute, Mr. Almeida? Or perhaps all the blood that's usually fueling your cerebral cortex is busy elsewhere." The challenge in her tone was unmistakable. She was goading him into losing his head, compelling him to play to type.

"She cheated on me with Detective McGinnis."

Okay, that was *not* what he had planned to say. He

had planned to put his mouth to a more rewarding use, meet her expectation of him as the brute who led with his emotions. But something checked him at the last nanosecond. He wanted her to know that he wasn't a complete animal. That occasionally he had God's honest reasons for his outsize behavior.

Kinsey drew a sharp, audible breath. "When?"

"Over a year ago, she left me for him after they had been . . ." Fucking for months. In the bed they had shared. In the bed he no longer slept in.

Christ, he needed to eighty-six that bed.

A flicker of something in her eyes registered his pain and offered understanding. He resented it despite the fact that he had invited her sympathy by basically handing her his balls on a platter. *Would you like them sautéed or roasted, Miss Taylor?*

"The fight in the bar was about your ex-wife?"

"He used to be a friend of mine. We'd play hoops, get sauced together, dinners at my house." Luke had invited the bastard into his life and he stole it. Stole her. Dan and Lisa hadn't even gone the distance, but broke up not long after Luke's discovery of them one fateful March morning over a year ago. "He got grabby with Alex at the bar but she could have taken care of it. Instead, I did. Because that's what I do."

She laid a warm palm on his arm. Sparks ignited beneath his skin. "I'm sorry—"

He coughed out a caustic laugh. "No, you're not. Because my little outburst just gives you a chance to shine, right? You're having a blast, Miss Taylor."

Her eyes widened in shock. It was bordering on mean, but right now he was the meanest sonofabitch who ever lived.

He stepped in close, a howl of pleasure ripping through him when she placed a hand on his chest to keep him at bay. "I'm just some panting piece of flesh to you. The assignment. A means to my end."

His gaze fell to her lush, full mouth and then she—Christ Jesus—moistened her lips with the briefest flash of her tongue. This woman knew exactly what she was doing to him. Somewhere between his cock thickening in need and grasping a lungful of her intoxicating scent, he made a decision. Unable to cage the beast any longer, he pushed back against her hand and crowded her until she met the next locker over. Gage's with its rainbow sticker. Then he stamped his mouth on hers and let his emotions be his master.

So good to give in.

So good to give in *to her*.

If he had expected her to go meekly, then he clearly needed to think again. When he could think clearly. Dominance was something that came naturally to him. It suited his need to punish—his birth parents, the people who took Jenny and couldn't take care of her, the whole world. Sometimes his head was more demon than human, and heaven help whoever got in his way.

Most women surrendered to him. Lisa had, then complained later he had been too rough because he abraded her skin and left his stubble rough mark on her. *My bedroom brute*, she had called him.

Kinsey was . . . different. Against his lips, she gave in by degrees, then fought her way back up to equal his carnal assault. She kissed like he imagined she did everything. With fervor and passion and a healthy dose of, *Screw you*.

"Luke," she rasped when they both came up for air.

Oh, the way she said his name, like the whisper of a fallen angel. It was a long time since he'd heard it uttered so desperately, so loaded with need. The sound stroked his spine, tightened every cell.

Her hands rose to rake his hair, pulling him closer, marking her nails over his scalp. Tingles started there and rippled through his body, the same prickle he got when he sensed danger. A roof ready to collapse, a door too hot to touch. This woman might be the next thing to pull him down, the bullet around the corner.

He tore his mouth from her sweet lips and held her lust-sparked gaze. Hands splayed on his chest, her dreamy expression gave way to reality, and she pushed him back and away from her pliant body. He blew out a breath, already knowing the spell had been broken and he wouldn't like what was coming.

The fact that nobody would be coming.

"That," she murmured, "probably shouldn't have happened."

She was right. Fooling around with the woman who held his career in her hands was a dumb-as-dirt move. But he had no intention of letting her off the hook just yet.

"Are you going to admit to your animal impulses getting the better of you, or am I to be the villain here?"

She ran her hands over her skirt, smoothing fabric that didn't need smoothing. He had the distinct impression she was stalling.

"I'm not going to pretend that was all you. I take responsibility for pushing your buttons, but it probably shouldn't happen again."

"Probably?"

"Definitely." She swallowed. Loudly. Kinsey Taylor, ball breaker extraordinaire, was nervous—and it was cute as all hell.

"Let me guess. Something about blurring professional lines and you've got a job to do. Etcetera, etcetera."

"Uh-huh." She lowered her dark golden lashes, eyes widening when she found a button on her blouse that had popped open. With visibly shaky fingers, she set it right.

Well, depending on your perspective.

"I should go." She moved a few steps to her left. Then a few more.

As orgasms were no longer on the menu, Luke resigned himself to getting his kicks elsewhere. With heightening satisfaction at Kinsey's obvious discomfort, he let several seconds pass before speaking up.

"It's that way," he said, thumbing the opposite direction.

"Oh, I know. Just wanted to check . . ." Without missing a beat, she popped her head around the wall that led to the shower room. "Just as I thought. Good-sized shower."

Chin pushed high, she strode by him toward the exit on her gravity-defying heels. Just the tiniest wobble. "Nice work today, Mr. Almeida."

"You, too." Smiling at her departing back, his gaze followed her world-class ass as it switched all the way out of his locker room.

Very nice work, Miss Taylor.

In the bunk room at Engine Company 6, an hour after the shoot, Gage paced between the single, neatly made beds, psyching himself up. He took a seat on one of the bunks and pulled out his phone. Stood. Sat down again. Finally, he clicked the number on the restaurant's website and waited.

Ring frickin' ring. Not even a voice mail pickup. Was that normal in the restaurant industry? It was only one in the afternoon, but shouldn't someone be around to take reservations?

Maybe it was the universe telling him that this was the worst idea since Jimmy Dean Pancakes & Sausage on a Stick. If the guy really wanted him to call, would he have been so—what was the word?—ambivalent about it? He was Gage Fucking Simpson. On any night of the week, he could walk into a bar on Halsted and score a blow job within sixty seconds. Thirty. Calling a guy—an ambivalent guy, no less—was not his style.

Still ringing.

Still holding on to the damn phone.

Screw this.

"Smith & Jones."

Not him. "Could I talk to Brady?"

There was mumbling in Spanish, the thud of the phone hitting the floor, what sounded like a rooster, then about two minutes of nada.

Finally, a gruff "Yeah?"

"Is this Brady?" Nothing but strained silence and the echo of Gage's thudding heart. "Hey, you there?"

"Call back after three to make a reservation."

That crusty baritone walloped him like a fifth of Jack to his bloodstream.

"It's Gage," he said, though he suspected Brady knew exactly who he was talking to. "We met the other night when the mayor brought me back into your kitchen." Long, intimidating moments of quiet ticked by while his heart tripped out a ragged beat. "I thought I'd see if you wanted to get together for a drink sometime."

More lengthy beats passed, each one weighted with Gage's increasing sense of stupidity and humiliation. If the man didn't want to talk, then why the hell was he on the damn phone?

Ticktock.

"I work a lot," Brady said.

Brady. Said.

Result!

"Yeah, I know what that's like. Sometimes it feels like all I do is work but I can usually find the time." He swallowed around a lump the size of a hose coupling in this throat. "When it's important."

You don't care. It's no big deal. Just forget—

"You said you cook."

Oh yeah. Gage could feel a smile conquering his face and he just knew his next words would be filled with the sweet joy of that smile. "I said I *love* to cook."

"Come over now." The line went dead.

Huh. Pretty cheeky, that chef. What if Gage was working or had a previous appointment or didn't answer to barked orders followed by rudely ended phone calls? Brady had hung up like people did on TV. Whenever some character on a show did that, Alex and Gage would exchange incredulous headshakes. *That guy just hung up the phone and he didn't even say good-bye. No one does that in real life.*

Except Brady "No Manners" Smith, apparently.

Yet less than forty minutes after Brady had issued

his demand, Gage was knocking on the door to Smith & Jones because it seemed he had a thing for churlish, bossy chefs. Or he just really wanted to get laid.

The door opened outward and Gage stepped back. Brady's arm stretched up, pushing his biceps agreeably—so frickin' agreeably—against the hems of his heather gray tee. USMC was scrawled across the front under the eagle, globe, and anchor insignia, and you know what Gage's first thought was on seeing that: Luke and Wyatt will like him because he was a fellow Marine.

Boy, you are so fucked.

"Hey," he managed to scratch out.

Brady held open the door for Gage to walk in, which he did, inhaling as he went. Something spicy tickled his nostrils and bucked his dick. Welcome to the world of a healthy gay male loose in the city.

Close to two in the afternoon and the restaurant was eerily quiet. Fully set tables, lights down low, the feel of Brady's hot gaze on his back—all mixed into a heady brew that Gage wanted to knock back like a shot of Jäger. The strip of condoms in his wallet burned against his groin. How would this go down? How would Brady go down? Easily, Gage imagined, infusing that single word with bone-deep belief.

He had already walked in a few steps when he realized that Brady hadn't budged from the door. Gage smiled. He was used to being admired. From the moment he had figured himself out, he'd made use of all his assets like the attention-loving whore he was. A psychologist might say it had something to do with his cracked-up childhood, bounced from home to home, always searching for the one family that didn't balk at the crazy-eyed little queer with the mom who spent more time in drug rehab than out.

"Why you here?"

Gage turned to let Brady see his interest. Were they really going to play games?

The look on Brady's face stopped the wiseass comment on the tip of his tongue. Whereas before the impassive chef had looked sexy-stoic, now he looked genuinely puzzled. Disbelief clouded around them like a third person in the room.

Why *was* Gage here?

I want to kiss you with a fierceness I can't even fathom. I want to feel your shaved head on my stomach after you've milked me dry with your incredulous mouth. I want something I haven't had and I can't even name.

He gave a negligent shrug, forcing the lie into his shoulders. "It's not every day a guy gets the chance to play chef with a professional." So Gage was still uncertain whether that terminating bark last week had been for him or the mayor. But Brady knew exactly who Gage was when he had called today.

He had been waiting for Gage to connect.

Closing the gap between them, Brady halted about two feet out. The full length of his right arm was taken up by a tattoo of the Scoville heat scale, which determined pepper heat levels. Pretty hard core. From bell peppers at his wrist to habaneros at the hem of his shirtsleeve, that arm made Gage's mouth water as if he had bitten into one of those throat-burning buggers himself. If his fingers could sneak beneath the sleeve's hem, what would Gage find there? How high did the Scoville heat scale go?

Brady's upper body seemed to bevel forward slightly and there was that hint of spice again, shot through with something else. A slight sweetness that seemed to increase in intensity with each passing second.

The big chef was going to touch him. *Please, for the love of Scoville, do it.*

He didn't.

So Gage took matters into his own hands. Just a whisper of a touch, he rested his finger on Brady's chest over the globe of the USMC insignia. *A world of pleasure awaits you, Chef.* That massive chest expanded on an inhale, so space filling that it seemed to strain for more than just Gage's hand.

"My brothers were in the Marines. Iraq and Afghanistan. What about you?"

As if bitten, Brady stepped back out of Gage's greedy grasp radius, sending his heart into a plummet. Thoughts did the rounds on his face, the most expressive Gage had seen during their brief acquaintance.

"It was a long time ago." Brady crossed his arms over his chest, covering up the tee's logo. Got it. Brady's time in the service was out of bounds. It was also the first time Gage had noticed an accent, the vowels long, lazy, and lilting. Southern, he guessed.

Gage nodded when really a million questions competed to find voice. *What happened to you? Is that why your face is fucked up? Should we do it on a table here or in the kitchen? Any concerns about health codes?*

"I'm makin' enchiladas," Brady said, low and rough. "You like 'em hot?"

"Hotter the better."

"Sure you can handle that much heat? You seem kind of . . . fragile."

Fragile? Gage was six feet two of unapologetic, hard muscle. He could bench-press three hundred pounds, run five miles in under forty-five minutes, save cats from fucking trees, and Mr. My-Body's-an-Etch-a-Sketch thought he might be fragile?

"Peppers are my specialty. If it's spicy, I'm in."

"I use guajillos." Brady pointed about halfway up the scale on his arm. "They burn the skin. Can be real damagin' if you're not used to it. If you're too—"

"I'm not fragile, Brady."

Brady's eyes darkened, and Gage realized that he had used the chef's name face-to-face for the first time. It sounded too familiar, too sweet for Gage's lascivious plans. Gage would never have considered himself the sharpest tool in the shed, but it should have hit him quicker that they were talking about something other than peppers. Was Brady warning him off?

"Maybe not fragile," Brady said, a thoughtful air to his harsh demeanor. "More like . . . golden."

Jesus, that sounded worse than fragile. Gage opened his mouth to protest, but Brady was already bypassing him on his way to the kitchen.

"Let's see what you got, Golden."

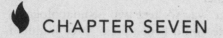

CHAPTER SEVEN

The day after the calendar shoot, Kinsey sat at her desk and tried to analyze what in the world had prompted yesterday's outrageous behavior. As a creature of logic, she was determined to get to the root of it.

She couldn't blame alcohol, though on that note, she should stash a bottle of Grey Goose in her desk for emergencies.

She couldn't blame her time of the month, not that she would ever use *that* as an excuse.

One other possibility came to mind. PR professionals were more than a little familiar with the concept of herd mentality, the idea that crowds can start acting as one and influencing people around them. The bandwagon effect. Being part of that female host at Engine 6—the lascivious catcalls, the rampant estrogen, the sheer objectification—had flipped a switch and conjured up Kinsey's cavewoman side.

That had to be it. Not Luke Almeida's cut body. Not his catty ex-wife. Not even how forlorn he looked when he opened up about his failed marriage. Those were all reasons that might sway a woman with a loosening grip on her self-control, but not Kinsey. She had merely been caught up in the moment, like a dizzy girl at a raunchy bachelorette party in a strip club.

So what if the man was hot enough to melt butter? It would be outrageously inappropriate to get involved with Firefighter Almeida while she had some say in whether he could return to active duty. That's probably why he'd kissed her in the first place.

Wait one second, Taylor. Never mind his motives or the clear ethical conflict, it was just wrong to get involved with him. Period. This was a man who was on far too intimate terms with his id. Apart from the potentially earth-shattering sex, she could see no benefits whatsoever to getting up close and personal with an instinctive beast like Luke Almeida.

Apart from the sex.

Which, judging by that kiss, would be earth shattering.

But she would never know because since David, men—and sex—were off the menu. Only the job mattered. Speaking of which . . .

The pounding of what sounded like a herd of rampaging rhinoceroses shook the foundations of city hall. Kinsey wondered only what had taken so long.

She rearranged her facial muscles, preparing to go neutral in *three* . . .

"Kinsey!" came the mayor's bellow.

Josie, bless her, made a token effort to do the "Let me check if she's free" thing in the outer suite, but Kinsey could have been in a meeting with POTUS and Eli Cooper wouldn't care a whit.

Two . . .

Her door exploded open with a splintering crash as it hit the wall.

One.

Neutral be damned. Kinsey smiled up into the scowling face of her boss.

"Explain." He slammed the door behind him, though if privacy was his aim, chalk that one up to an epic fail. Without a doubt, Josie was already broadcasting news of the mayor's meltdown on the city hall grapevine. The cubicles were alive with the pings of IMs.

"I assume we're talking about the Summer Learning Program," Kinsey said, all innocence. "The speech to the press sounded great on WGN. You really sold it."

With one hand, he raked his dark, wavy, overly produced hair furiously. In his other, he held an iPad, the older model he used as a backup. Oh, that wasn't good.

"*'Yet again, our esteemed mayor is seen to be siding with the delinquents at the Chicago Fire Department,'*" he read from the iPad, or more specifically, this morning's op-ed from the *Tribune*. Sam Cochrane claimed his staff had editorial independence, but all those opinions came out sounding suspiciously like the blowhard himself.

"*'First we have the city employees at Engine 6 brawling with their brothers in arms at CPD and making the mistake of getting caught on film. Now we're paying them to strip on city property and re-enact* Magic Mike *for a chorus of administrative workers. During this spectacle, city hall practically shut down, emergency calls to Engine 6 were put on hold and'*"— he held up a dramatic hand of wait-for-it—"*'everyone got paid.'*"

Fury molded Eli's features to the ferocity of one of the Harold Washington Library gargoyles overlooking State Street. "This is a PR-fucking-disaster. You're supposed to be fixing it, not making them into Chippendales. What in the hell were you thinking?"

Moving a finger to her lips, Kinsey tried for contrite, but that had never looked good on her. Honesty suited her much better. "I'm thinking that maybe I know how to do my job better than you do."

She rounded her desk and removed the iPad from his hand. "Other one cracked?"

"Yep," he ground out.

That was the third tablet the mayor had gone through in her close to four months on the job. Technology was far too fragile for a man with this much passion, or faced with this many blows from the press.

"Believe it or not, I have a strategy here." Her gaze fell to the iPad and a smile tugged at her lips. The editorial couldn't have been more perfect if she had dictated it personally.

Step one in the plan: complete.

A couple of incendiary images from the shoot had somehow made it into Jillian Malone's email box. Kinsey had selected the photos to be leaked to the veteran reporter herself, including a nice one of a sheened Gage Simpson, but the paper had used a scorching shot of Luke unsnapping his bunker pants, his eyes directed at some point over the photog's shoulder. At Kinsey, in fact, about ten seconds before he had set her panties ablaze.

"Explain to me how this helps me get reelected in February," Eli said, sounding slightly appeased, or at the very least hopeful that her claim to be good at what she did carried weight. The guy might be a chauvinistic dolt when it came to female firefighters, but she could hear a grudging respect in his tone.

Her personal phone rang and she spotted the caller ID from three feet away. "Just a second, I need to take this." Those respect levels in the room hitched higher, keeping pace with the mayor's arched eyebrow. Ignoring the boss to take an important call? Power play at its finest. After a minute of pleasantries, she finished with her demand. "Ten o'clock news, Marisa, not the six. Those pictures aren't really fit for dinnertime now, are they?"

She hung up and turned back to the mayor.

"That was the anchor at NBC local," she said, the surge of euphoria in her veins threatening to give her an orgasm on the spot. "The story will air at ten."

Step two: complete.

Skepticism pinched his mouth. "You mean the story about the city's stripper firemen?"

"I mean the story about the brave men of CFD showing off their fine physiques, all so unfortunate, underprivileged foster kids can get new footballs." Her heart skipped a few beats remembering Luke's request for the calendar's proceeds.

"You're controlling the message?" Eli asked, a glitter of approval in his eyes before going dim again. "I think you're forgetting I need Cochrane's money and endorsement. If we make him look stupid, that doesn't exactly help me."

"It's a fine line, but as soon as the charity connection emerges, he'll have no choice but to retract his fangs. We feed Malone tidbits about our rehab plans and then it's up to them how to spin it. *I* think the public will see it as a fun summer distraction. Like the Taste of Chicago."

She hoped. Screwing up the mayor's reelection bid would be catastrophic, and she'd have zero chance of getting off the fluff beat. But her gut told her this was going to work. It had to.

Eli's lips firmed as he thought it over. "Okay, I'm letting you run with this, but the minute I see evidence that it's not having the desired effect—which is to make CFD look like they are all part of the cozy city family—then I'm pulling you off it and it's public shaming all around. Though I can't imagine Almeida was too happy with getting half naked to make his problems go away."

The mayor sounded pleased that Luke's forced cooperation was putting him through the wringer. Weirdly, Kinsey's stomach lurched in defense of the sexy firefighter.

"In my experience," she said archly, "the half-naked solution works for fifty percent of the male species. Dropping trousers, the ultimate problem solver."

"And the other fifty percent?"

"The full monty works for them."

His laugh was warm. "Funny how you women always sound so above it all. It's always the men who can't keep it in their pants, yet I hear it was a firehouse filled with our dickless staff at this hootenanny."

"Oh, that must have made things difficult over here—did your penis people have problems figuring out how to turn on the photocopier up on five? Or was the Starbucks run a touch too much for their testosterone levels to handle?"

That drew a sardonic grin. "The city is not paying its female employees to ogle naked men."

"No, just to do Starbucks runs."

"You have the wrong impression of me, Kinsey."

"Don't think I do. But it's okay, I still like you."

She smiled.

He did not.

"Just to be clear," she said, a touch testy she had to defend her strategy here. "Twenty-three staff, *both male and female*, elected to take vacation time so they could support CFD's charitable efforts during the calendar shoot. This was not done on city time and no one got paid to be there. The rest of the crowd were members of the community we serve."

Eli looked unimpressed. "You're sure this isn't going to blow up in our faces?"

She mentally crossed her fingers behind her back. "Trust me, I've got this." Step three would be the cherry on top, but she'd keep that to herself for the moment.

"Think it's time you met M Squared and share your expertise. Keep the message on target," Eli said. "Set it up."

"Of course." Kinsey schooled her expression to blank. Meeting M Squared, Eli's election campaign manager, made her stomach roil like a bag of scrappy kittens, but damned if she'd show any weakness. Back to the take-charge professional who was *hell yeah* good at her job.

But as she watched the mayor's tight ass journey out of her office, and pondered on how beautifully shaped it was and how it filled out his pinstripe pants so very well, her mind inevitably slid to how it was not nearly as enticing as the one belonging to a certain stripper fireman.

Where Luke Almeida was concerned, it seemed that rational, cool, and collected Kinsey Taylor had left the building.

Luke was heading west on Foster to St. Carmen's Group Home when he almost crashed his truck.

It couldn't be . . .

No way in hell would she have . . .

He blinked. Refocused.

It was . . . and she had.

Above the Metra track, kitty-corner to the Chase bank, a humongous billboard showcased in glorious, gleaming, sharp-edged color a shirtless Luke Almeida.

Going on the assumption that he might have been hallucinating, Luke circled the block praying for a different result. Back on Foster, he parked the car at a hydrant. He had no intention of staying longer than it took for his brain matter to erupt in a volcanic mass down his spine.

Yep, that was him up there. Twenty feet tall, chest shining (how did that happen?), his fingers in a suggestive hover over the snaps of his bunker gear. He wore what someone with a better vocabulary than him might call a smoldering look. At thigh level, a line of text asked the provocative "Did Someone Call the Fire Department?" and then a link to a website capped it off. Thankfully, this shot was before the kittens were introduced. Those kittens had been damn cute, though, especially that little calico one with the big eyes—*shit*. He bit back a snarl, not liking the direction of that train of thought.

She was behind the camera. Several feet behind it, but that's who he had been looking at. Smoldering at. The woman better have her catcher's mitt ready because he was about to pitch hell.

He pulled out his phone and scrolled through his old calls. There it was, with an area code he didn't recognize. Gage had said she was from San Francisco, and while he waited for her to pick up, he imagined her on a pristine California beach, soaking up the rays. Her honey-blond hair would cascade down her bare back, bisected by wispy strings that scarcely held her bikini together (a white one, perhaps, or red . . . Yeah, definitely red). It would take the work of a moment to pull on the tail of the bow and watch as it unraveled to reveal—

"Hello," she said in that husky tone that sent shivers barreling down his spine.

"Hey," he said back, softer on his lips than it sounded in his brain. Hell to the negative. Time to get his head out of his lately famous ass and stomp down with his size-twelve boot. "You've gone too far, Miss Taylor. I was driving down the street and what should I see but me in some ridiculous pose on a billboard. I don't remember giving you permission to do that. The calendar, yes, but billboards?"

His rant was met with a pause, likely because she needed a moment to craft some claptrap to soothe his temper.

"Who *is* this?"

He growled and her throaty laugh shivered in his ear. His cock reacted predictably.

"Mr. Almeida, I told you I was going to make you a star. Together, we're going to raise lots of money for your charity—"

"At the expense of my reputation. People can see that billboard from space." A newly horrific thought slashed through his haze. "How many of them are there?"

"Just a couple." She paused. "No more than ten. Fifteen max."

He slapped the steering wheel with the palm of his hand.

"Did you just hit something?"

"No."

Her silence said she was unconvinced.

"Kinsey . . ."

"Don't worry," she said blithely. "Gage is featured on some of them. We're all about equal opportunity at city hall. Now, I have a firehouse party to plan, Mr. Almeida—that bouncy house won't erect itself." She broke into a laugh. "Or maybe it will! I'll have to look into that." *Click*.

Twenty minutes later, Luke dribbled a basketball past one, two, three of the defense and fired the shot. It hit the backboard, flirted with the rim, and popped off without screwing the basket. Story of his life these days.

Bending over, palms on his knees, he hauled air into his burning lungs. His watery gaze wandered to the cracked tarmac of the court so far west on Foster Avenue to be practically in the burbs. Weeds struggled through the crevices, stretching to the sun, making life where they could find it.

"Pussy," a voice said behind him.

Straightening as he turned, Luke shot arrows of disproval at the fourteen-year-old punk kid with the trash mouth.

"That's Mr. Pussy to you, Anton."

Anton grinned that shy smile that was so at odds with the salty language that came out of his mouth with every other word. He liked being treated as an adult by the mentors, and letting some of his jokey disrespect slide was a calculated move on Luke's part. All the kids at St. Carmen's needed something different. Some wanted to be left alone, some wanted an assurance that there was light at the end of the tunnel. Some wanted love or what passed for it in this messed-up universe. What they all had in common was a need for respect and to not be treated like they were stupid.

"Saw that video of you in the bar," Anton said, a cheeky twist to his mouth.

Shit. Luke had been dreading the moment one of the kids brought it up.

"Yeah, about that . . ." How could he put this without sounding like an after-school special? "You know that was not the best way to handle it. That guy pissed me off, but I should have let it slide."

"Turn the other cheek and shit?"

"Right." Just like Our Lord Jesus.

Anton rolled his tongue around his mouth, which meant he was thinking. Never good.

"But you didn't get into trouble. You still got your job, you still here with us, you showin' off on the TV news."

And that would be *double shit.*

He needed to assert control here and assure the

kids that bad behavior truly had negative consequences. Though the way Kinsey Taylor's mouth and
body had responded to his kiss was about as far from
negative as it could get.

"Hey, guys, listen up."

The teens turned, wearing their usual impudent
stares like armor.

"I know you've probably all seen that video of me
going psycho on another guy. Well, this behavior got
me into a lot of trouble at work. Sure, I still have my
job, but if I don't cooperate with my bosses, I could
lose it. You understand what I'm saying here?"

"So if we want to have jobs, we shouldn't get into
fights," Kevin said through his gum chewing.

"Yes—well, no."

"Nah, man," Denny chimed in, with a hitch of
the low-slung shorts that showed half his underwear.
"If we wanna fight, don't go gettin' caught on the
vee-dee-oh."

The kids busted their guts at that.

Luke crossed his arms and delivered a badass
staredown before continuing. "What I'm saying is
that violence is not the solution when you get mad
at someone." Even if that someone screwed *your*
wife in *your* bed and then showed up at *your* bar
during game seven of the Cup finals to smirk about
it. McGinnis was lucky not to be pissing blood. "And
just because I ended up on a billboard, looking like
a pansy-assed model . . . well, believe me when I say
that it's not a reward."

Except for the hot woman with the hot mouth and
the hotter . . . *down, fella.*

Nothing but squinty-eyed stares greeted that. After

a long, long beat, Mickey placed his hands on his hips. "You're modelin' on a billboard now?"

The rest of them shook their heads in pity.

So it would seem this billboard business was not yet common knowledge.

Kinsey was trying her best not to act like a complete country bumpkin, but the view from the Signature Room on the ninety-fifth floor of the Hancock was nothing short of spectacular. Seated at a south-facing window with the magnitude of nocturnal Chicago spread out before her, she could only stare at the blur of bright lights and tall buildings testifying to the city's beauty and progress. And yet again she was faced with the chilling fear that as stunning as it was, it meant little without the right person to share it with.

She smashed that gem of self-pity with a mental karate chop.

"How long since your relationship ended?"

Kinsey snapped her eyes away from the stellar sights, surprised at her dining companion's question. *Really?* She had been careful to keep her personal business to herself, so how Madison Maitland had come by that gossipy tidbit made her curious. Owner of M Squared, Chicago's largest public relations firm, this woman had managed countless political campaigns and corporate rebrandings. Ethics and finance rules prohibited the mayor from using city employees like Kinsey for his reelection, so Madison's outside firm was brought on board to keep Eli's ass on the mayoral throne.

"I've no doubt you have your finger on the pulse,

Ms. Maitland, but I'm surprised you'd be interested in me enough to check my background."

Madison sipped on her Glenfiddich eighteen-year-old and speared Kinsey from beneath dark lashes. Effortlessly put together with an ebony Anna Wintour–esque bob and a white Marc Jacobs suit, the woman looked no older than thirty-five, though Kinsey knew for a fact her real age was ten years higher. An endorsement for switching to top-shelf whiskey, perhaps.

"That ring of paler skin on your third finger is all the background check I need."

Under the ambient lighting, Kinsey would have thought that slight discoloration would be barely visible, but then that was Madison Maitland's job: notice the unnoticeable.

She gave a resigned sigh. "Just over a month."

"Moved to Chicago to get away?"

"I wish."

"Ah, you moved for him? Even worse. Now you're working for a man who thinks you shouldn't be left alone in the sandbox."

Kinsey took a sip of her dirty Grey Goose martini and let the moment sit. This wouldn't have been the first time a woman issued a camaraderie vibe only to later stab her in the back—and use the knife to get a handhold on her climb to the next rung.

"The mayor's being careful," she said diplomatically. "I work for the city, you work for him. It's important we coordinate our efforts and no doubt I have a lot to learn." A shot of humility, the perfect chaser to diplomacy.

"Well, your firefighter did look good on the ten

o'clock news, not to mention those billboards. I'll admit it was a good move, Kinsey. We just have to be careful it doesn't trivialize the issues."

"I think it provides a healthy distraction from idiots going at it in a bar." Though the reason behind the bad blood between Luke and Detective McGinnis had put a different color on it, for sure. Every time she tried to relegate Mr. Almeida to nothing more than brainless beefcake, a niggling thought warned her against it.

Madison narrowed her eyes. "There's something to be said for the bait and switch, I suppose." Touching the rim of her almost empty glass, she arched a sultry eyebrow at their handsome waiter before he reached the table. He immediately about-faced and made work for his idle hands. "My job is to make sure Eli gets reelected. Your job is to make sure the city of Chicago's reputation as a dirty, corrupt, pay-for-play cesspit is turned around."

Kinsey laughed heartily. Good as she was, that was expecting a bit too much. "Right now, I'd be happy with changing minds about one particular firefighter at one particular firehouse."

"One rock-hard ab at a time?"

"Exactly."

Both women *hmmed* as they savored a few X-rated visuals. The moment ticked over, not unpleasantly.

"This all seems a little"—Madison carved the air, seeking whatever word she was no doubt already prepared to use—"lowbrow for a woman of your talents. I've seen some of the work you did in San Francisco. The recycling campaign, the breast cancer one. I know your specialty is city government, but you're better than hot firemen and kitten pics."

A year ago, Kinsey had crafted a breast cancer screening campaign for San Francisco's health department—Check Your Boobs—that saw a 32 percent increase in self-reported breast exams over six months, along with more women visiting their doctors and getting mammograms. Her recycling campaign may have preached to the choir in the earthy-crunchy, granola-imbibing Bay Area, but she had posted gains there, too.

Again, the shrewd Madison had hit it on the head: stuck in Chicago on the equivalent of the entertainment beat was not the plan. "I won't be doing this forever. I was headed somewhere different and I took a left turn, thinking it might fix things with my fiancé. I compromised because I thought it would create a work-life balance and make me happy." She had hoped kowtowing to David's needs would give her some Zen-like insight into how the game was supposed to work. Please her man, please herself. Or maybe that the job wouldn't matter because she had nabbed the real prize: a guy who checked all the boxes. Career, wealth, prestige.

Being single and alone was still a frightening fate for a woman in a way it was not for a man. A universal truth, and one she hated.

Kinsey took a generous swig of her drink. "I'll admit I'd rather be dealing with more important issues like education, health care, links with the nonprofit sector, than whether a guy with a force-ten temper and a penchant for the fists-first solution can be brought to heel."

The waiter switched out Madison's empty glass for a fresh one. She studiously ignored him. "From time immemorial we've been cleaning up after male messes. When a man does it for a woman, it's called being rescued. When a woman does it for a man, it's housework." She looked out the window, a pensive expression softening her sharp features. "I moved for a man once."

Kinsey started at this abrupt move from the woe-is-a-woman's-lot to the personal.

"My second husband took a job with a prestigious law firm in New York. I had just gotten M Squared off the ground and we tried the every-other-weekend solution for a few months but—"

"Soon it became all your weekends there and none of his here?"

Madison nodded. "My career was never going to be as important as his. I saw how all the other wives at the law firm acted. They were expected to entertain, support, stay back. I've worked at male-centric companies where mentioning previous successes in a job interview looked like bragging. Where success and likability are positively correlated for men and negatively for women. Where women end up compromising because they want to be liked."

"And not just by men."

Madison's smile was grim. "Yes, we do it with other women, too. We play down our strengths in case we're seen as uppity. Like we've failed some marker of womanhood." She leaned in. "Well-behaved women don't make history, though, do they?"

"What about Mother Teresa?"

Madison coughed as if her drink had gone down the wrong way. "Self-sacrificing saint? That's my only option? No, thanks. When my husband asked, I moved to New York, found a job I sort of liked, but he was less interested in me once I had capitulated. He was attracted to me for my strength, and trying to please him made me weak in his eyes. We divorced after six months and I came back here."

Capitulated. That word set off a vibration of resentment in Kinsey's body at the memory of how she had sacrificed for David. Never would she allow a man to rule her emotions like that again. "And you're happy with how things turned out?"

The older woman's lips twitched with disappointment, not at how her life had turned out but that Kinsey had asked the wrong question. Happiness was too abstract for a woman like Madison Maitland. Kinsey was starting to wonder if it was too abstract for her. Perhaps it was impossible for both life and career contentment to coexist for ambitious women.

"I haven't met a man yet who can handle what I bring." Madison hesitated, her eyes misting over with memory. "There was my first husband, but he was too unformed, too young to get it. These days I put food on my table. I'm responsible for my own orgasms." Her gaze drifted to the waiter. Guess someone was getting lucky tonight. "Eli put us together because he thought you couldn't handle this assignment."

"What do you think?"

"There's only one opinion that matters here. At least, publicly. The ego management is a full-time job, but I think between us, we can ensure that opinion is crafted to everyone's best interests."

With a sly smile, Madison picked up the dinner menu. "The food here's not so good, but the views, both inside and out, are amazing. Another round?"

CHAPTER EIGHT

The scene of the crime—the original crime that got her this assignment and put Luke Almeida on her radar—was already hopping by the time Kinsey walked in at close to eight on Friday of the July Fourth weekend. Dempsey's on Damen was your typical Irish bar. High tables, low lighting, Bono wailing about how he still hadn't found what he was looking for. As befitted an establishment owned by firefighters, there were also plenty of nods to the service. Sepia photos of Chicago firehouses and crews. A brass bell that sounded the alarm back in the day.

And then there was the gorgeous streak of heat behind the bar in the form of Gage.

He grinned wide as she approached and hopped onto a stool. Baby Thor was looking particularly fine tonight, wearing a T-shirt announcing: I'm a Firefighter—It's Kind of a Big Deal.

"You are *sooo* lucky," he said. "He's not here."

"Who?"

"Mr. July."

Her smile covered nicely her disappointment that Luke was not in the house. "You think I'm scared of your brother?"

"I think you ought to be." He leaned over the bar

and tapped his phone. "My favorite is the one of Luke where they Photoshopped in the glistening sweat. He was so pissed about that little detail."

Swiping at the screen, Gage zeroed in on what Kinsey had to admit was also her favorite pic. Luke's oh-my-God abs and that sexy V of his hip indents screamed sex, and on a sky-tall billboard, were damn near unmissable by every driver heading into the city this morning on the I-90.

"Can't believe the city sprung for those bill-boards," a female voice chimed in to her right. Alex took up residence on the next stool and nodded at Gage, who passed her a Goose Island summer ale and raised a questioning brow at Kinsey.

"I'll have the same," she said, then turned back to Alex. "The billboards were donated. Once I explained that they were for a good cause, they were more than happy to provide them. I only need them for a month to drive up orders for the calendar."

"You mean people are actually going to buy that shit?" Alex asked.

"People are already buying that shit," Kinsey said with a laugh. "The 311 city services line was inundated with calls today, and the website we're selling it on crashed for thirty minutes this morning." She might have ordered the boys in IT to take it offline for a while to fuel the frenzy. Threats to the hunky firefighter calendar supply chain could only help the effort.

Alex clinked her beer bottle companionably against Kinsey's. "Damn, woman, you are taking names. Between those smut boards and the local news, it's the perfect FU to that ass at the *Trib*. He called Gage a pretty boy!"

They both looked at Gage, who shrugged his shoulders. While most people seemed to enjoy the calendar, there had been a backlash fronted by the *Tribune* about the unorthodox use of taxpayers' money, especially on something so "deviant." Though the tone of the op-eds made it clear that the deviance was not half-naked men per se, but half-naked gay men.

"When Darcy and Beck get back from their vacay in Thailand, I'm going to tell our girl she needs to keep Ogre Dad in check," Alex said. "We're practically related to the dude. You'd think he'd be less of a dick."

Gage shook his head. "That's exactly why he's being a dick, Scooby-Doo. He hates that Beck sullied his darling daughter."

"Sounds more like he's feeling threatened by hot, half-naked firemen," Alex said. "Speaking of . . . Did you tell her?"

Kinsey eyed Gage. "Tell me what?"

A sexy grin bloomed on his handsome face. "I had a call from a modeling agency this morning. They saw the billboard on Western and want me to come in for a test."

"As if you need more help keeping your bed warm," Alex muttered. "Puppy Eyes has it bad over there. Probably wants you to autograph his hard-on."

In unison, the trio swiveled to take in a cute frat boy with sun-kissed hair and a hopeful smile. Gage assessed him with a coolness Kinsey wouldn't have thought was part of his repertoire.

"That's awesome news, right?" She assumed most

guys would be totally on board with an offer to play part-time model, though the thought that Luke might have received a similar request dragged a shot of bile up her throat.

And it was no concern of hers. A few blazing looks and one smoking kiss, and now she was worried that the man's options to connect with women not named Kinsey Taylor had suddenly opened up wide. She had no claim on him—and no desire to make one.

Then why was she here?

Because Gage had suggested she stop by, no other reason. She was single, friendless in a strange city, living in a cookie-cutter corporate suite with her furniture in storage and nothing but Chinese food in her fridge. There were only so many Friday nights she could spend tooling around Whole Foods, trying to cobble a full meal together out of Cabernet and asiago cheese samples.

Turning away from the college hottie, Gage smiled, but it didn't quite reach his eyes. "Yeah, it's all good. I'll never say no to more opportunities to get laid."

"What gives? Are you coming down with something?" Alex's eyes flew wide. "Or going down on someone?" Standing on the foot rail, she leaned over the bar and grabbed her brother violently by the shoulders. "Who is it? Deets. Now, Simpson."

"It's no one. It's not even a thing." As he pulled out of Alex's grasp, he flicked a glance to Kinsey, and an uncanny awareness struck her.

"Oh my God, it's the chef. The mayor's pal." On Eli's return from the kitchen that night at Smith &

Jones, he had boasted about his matchmaking skills. The scary chef and the budding male model seemed like an oddball pairing, but what did she know?

Gage rolled his eyes as if Kinsey had disappointed him greatly.

"Sorry, I didn't know it was a secret."

"It's not," he said quickly, putting her at ease. "Like I said, it's nothing. Not yet. It's just . . ." His smile lit him from inside as secret thoughts, the ones you held on to at the beginning of something special, fueled his grin. "It's nothing. Guy's playing hard to get, anyway."

"I know he served with Eli in Afghanistan. I could get some more details about him," Kinsey said mischievously before turning to Alex. "And if you need to know anything about our fearless leader, by the way, feel free to ask. Boxers or briefs. PJs or nude. Ribbed or flavored. There's a list doing the rounds at city hall."

"Why would I want to know anything about him?" Alex asked, suddenly fascinated by the label of her beer bottle.

Gage and Kinsey shared a knowing glance. In the face of their scorn, Alex colored, but quickly surrendered her pretended ignorance. "Mayor Eli Cooper is an arrogant, chauvinistic jerk who probably calls his own name when he comes."

"*Eliiii* . . ." Gage threw back his head and moaned orgasmically, an impression that sent Alex and Kinsey into peals of laughter.

Alex pointed her bottle at Kinsey. "Your boss is a dick, I live with dicks, and I work with dicks. So, up to my neck in dick, thanks very much."

"Can never have enough dick," Gage said wisely. Kinsey lifted her beer. "I'll drink to that."

Luke jerked awake, scrubbing at imaginary eight-legged visitors crawling over his face. When he was in his own place next door, the cockroach-filled crack house nightmares usually stayed buried deep in his dream conscious. But on his siblings' sofa, where he had dozed off waiting up for Gage and Alex to return home, comfort and safety eluded him. Not even the two glasses of Jack he downed when he came home from his shift at the bar could send him into a deep enough sleep.

Luke loved that damn bar, even though he knew that owning it—or keeping up its legacy—was probably one of the reasons his marriage had failed. There were times he'd needed space, and surrounding himself with a bunch of drunks was the best way to get it. Lisa had hated it there. Just one more manacle to his family.

Sean had opened Dempsey's on Damen with Weston Cooper and Sam Cochrane before Luke was even a twinkle in his meth-addicted mother's eye. A firefighter, a lawyer, and a businessman walked into a bar—and bought it. It sure made for an unlikely partnership, but by all accounts it had been a successful one until Cochrane fell out with Sean, reasons unknown. Then Cooper—or "Coop," as he was known around the Cook County court system—sold off his share a few years later in preparation for a bid to become state's attorney.

Prosecuting lowlifes and mob bosses had put him

in the crosshairs of some pretty nasty elements, one of whom murdered him along with his wife. All for doing his job as a public servant. Now his son, Eli Cooper, Mr. Fucking Mayor, was choosing to ride Luke's ass so hard that he wondered how much more shit he could take—or if Cooper even knew that their fathers had once been partners. Even friends.

Between this calendar crap, his probation, and Kinsey Taylor, Luke was half a spark away from igniting like a powder keg. Probably not the best night to be serving a bunch of sloppy frat boys. Gage and Alex usually worked Friday nights pulling brewskis, but it was the start of the holiday weekend and Luke had said he'd cover while they went clubbing. Let the kids have their fun shakin' their asses at the other kids.

Wyatt said he worried too much, that he needed to let them make their own mistakes. Luke agreed, for the most part, but tonight he had still taken up residence on the sofa in the home he had grown up in so he could play overbearing father figure to his youngest sibs. As soon as they came home safely, he'd go back to his place next door and shoot for a dreamless couple of hours. Not in his bed, though. Not since . . .

A familiar scraping sound told him his trip to Nod would be starting blessedly soon. Someone was having trouble getting the key in the door.

"Gage, give it here, you cabbage," he heard his sister slur. Gage with motor coordination issues. Alex ten sheets to the wind. And Wyatt said he worried too much.

He headed out to the hallway and yanked open the door with Gage still attached. Clumsily, he fell into Luke's arms.

"Bro! Don't say you waited up again. You need to get a life." Straightening, Gage dusted off Luke's shoulders as if he was the one who had picked up his older brother instead of the other way around. "And speaking of getting a life, we brought you a present."

Over Gage's shoulder, Luke found his very drunk, very unsteady sister clutching the arm of—huh—Kinsey Taylor.

"Surprise! K's staying over," Alex said before collapsing in a fit of tequila giggles. She only broke out the chuckles when she'd downed too much Jose C. "God, I would give my left tit for a burrito."

Lurching forward, she abandoned Kinsey to head to the kitchen.

"Let's make popcorn," Gage said, following her.

Luke took a long, hard look at Kinsey, who took a long, hard look back. The expected wear and tear of a night out seemed to have no impact on her, though her eyes were overbright from alcohol.

"Don't worry, Almeida, I'm not staying."

Maybe not, but she made no move to leave. Just stood there looking so good that tearing his eyes away would be a sin of the highest magnitude. The jeans she wore molded to her slender form like snakeskin. Red heels below, a red tee up top with sparkly bits around the V-shaped neckline. The swell of her breasts pulled at the clingy material in a way that made him pleasantly warm.

"I just wanted to make sure they got home safely," she said with the deliberate diction of someone trying not to be drunk. "Now, could you please point me in the direction of the closest cab . . . um, place?"

He pulled her inside and shut the door. "You're not going anywhere. How much did you drink?"

Insolence plucked at the corner of her mouth, a cheeky little smile he would like to kiss off. Repeatedly.

"Not enough to let you have your wicked way with me, Mr. Almeida." She snort-giggled and cupped her mouth as if she'd made a naughty sound—or revealed too much. With both hands flat on his chest, she said in a stage whisper, "*Mr. Almeida.* I like that thing we do, *Mr. Almeida.* It's sexy as hell. You're sexy as hell with all these hard muscles."

She moved her hands over the planes of his chest, assessing, groping. Claiming, to be honest, and his world was a million times better for it. His arms locked naturally around her slender waist and held her in place for his viewing pleasure. Her gold gaze fastened on to him. Those beautiful eyes. Those beautiful, drunken eyes.

"Stop that," she hissed.

"Stop what?"

"That dark, disapproving, smoldering thing. It's illegal in Europe, you know. Genetically modified eyes, that's what you've got." She squinted up at him. "They have to be fake. All that blue, like the Pacific Ocean out at Baker Beach."

Her forehead fell to his chest. "God, I miss it. Fucking David. Stupid fucking David." She punctuated each word about "stupid fucking David" with a bump of her head against his pec. Felt kind of nice to hold her and listen to her unravel. Cool, unflappable Kinsey letting go of that well-crafted image she went to such pains to maintain.

"Who's stupid fucking David?"

"No one," she murmured into his chest, and then something that sounded like "dead to me."

"Her fiancé," Gage said as he pulled out the stockpot he used for from-scratch popcorn. "Her ex-fiancé."

Alex was opening and closing cupboards, and making a lot of noise while she was at it. "Who she hauled ass across the country to be with—"

"Shush," Kinsey said, curving her gaze around his shoulder. Her breasts brushed tantalizingly against his chest. "Don't tell him."

"—and who decided to dump her because apparently she didn't square up to his ideal of womanhood," Alex finished, sounding mighty ticked off on Kinsey's behalf.

Stupid fucking David was right. The chump clearly had eyesight problems, because Luke's ideal of womanhood was here in his arms. Strong, sexy, and take no shit.

Hold up there now. Had Luke not just resolved to pursue only pliant, easy, nurturing women who liked puppies and kids? For the long term anyway.

As for the short term . . .

He tightened his grip, pulled her flush. "What a loser."

"I know, I am!" she said passionately. "I gave up a great job, friends, and my family to move here for a guy, only to get screwed over. Never again. We clear, Mr. July?"

He could feel a smile shaping his lips, but she sounded so serious he kept it on lockdown. "Crystal, Miss Taylor."

She laughed, a heartily unapologetic sound that warmed him from the inside out. He liked a woman who was unafraid to let go like that. He wondered idly if she liked *him*.

Or puppies.

Or kids.

No more hard liquor for you, Almeida.

Every part of her anatomy registered with him on some cellular level. Slim waist, rounded hips, legs a mile past eternity. Breasts made for his mouth to suck deep and long. And don't forget the devilish glint in her eyes, the one that said she could take him on—and would relish the challenge of making him work for it.

God, he wanted her.

He turned to Alex and Gage. "All right, kiddos, can I trust you not to burn down the house I was raised in?"

Alex gave the Dempsey stare-down. "We're trained professionals, Luke. If we *were* to do something that *might* burn down the house, we could handle it."

Not comforting in the slightest.

"I think I need to close my eyes," Kinsey said faintly. "Can you call me a cab?"

No way in hell was he putting her in a taxi in this state, and with the current ratio of Jack to plasma in his bloodstream, driving Kinsey himself was out. She would sleep in his room next door, and Luke would take the sofa.

He pushed a honey-blond strand of hair behind her ear. "You're not going anywhere. I'll take care of you, sweetheart."

The scent of her filled his nostrils, curled into his

chest, and settled there, both strangely arousing and pleasingly familiar. Circling his palm around her waist, he let a few seconds pass to get her used to the idea of how he would possess her space. There was something about a strong, fine woman like Kinsey surrendering to his will that got him harder than mahogany.

Blinking those big golden eyes up at him, she held her plump bottom lip between her teeth and dragged. Slowly.

"Thanks, Luke. You're sweet."

And sweet he would stay until she sobered up. Savage could wait for another day.

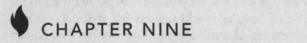

CHAPTER NINE

Waking up in a strange bed was so 2003—or it would have been, if Kinsey had ever been the sort of woman who got trashed, got laid, and got her morning-after exercise with a brisk walk of shame. But that kind of behavior had always been foreign to her. She had met David at an Alpha Delta Phi fraternity party her freshman week at Berkeley, and they had quickly become exclusive and serious. As a third-year med student, he shouldn't have looked at her twice, but her California freshness and nonthreatening communications major had appealed to him. His goal-driven manner had appealed to her.

Now it appeared she was making up for her goody-two-shoes college days with a dive into girl gone wild in Chicago.

Cautiously, because tiny jackhammers were drilling into her skull, she scoped out her surroundings: Luke Almeida's lair. More gender-neutral than she would have expected—not that she had spared it a single thought at all—with eggshell blue walls and quality balsam wood furniture from Ethan Allen or some other high-end home furnishing purveyor. The ex-wife's taste, no doubt. The hunter green bedding clashed with the decor, the most obvious hint that

Luke had made a token effort to put his marriage in the past.

She raised the sheets. Breathed out her relief. Her skinny jeans bagged at the knees, but they were still on her body. Ditto for her top, though it might have lost a swatch of sparkle around the neck, but overall as it should be, covering up the girls.

New snatches of early morning horror flickered with the pulse of those jackhammers in her brain. Last night with Luke, there had been flirting and groping and oh God, whining—all on her side. Quickly, she shot up to a sitting position, and immediately regretted it when her head and stomach joined forces in rebellion. There had been something else. Something shameful. She had—

"It lives."

With her stomach in a pitch and roll of regret, Kinsey creakily turned her head to find Luke at the door. Wearing battered jeans and a muscle-molding CFD tee, he looked so fine her mouth watered. Or perhaps that was nausea.

Covering her eyes with her forearm didn't help. Neither did laying her head back down on the pillow. Gently. The man-on-fire hotness was already imprinted on her retinas.

"I'm sorry I put you out," she mumbled, partially into the pillow.

"You didn't." He placed a coffee cup on the nightstand, the sound like a cymbals crash in her ears. "I added a splash of half-and-half. Can grab sweetener if you need it."

The aroma hit her nostrils, snaking through to activate caffeine-deprived neurons. Leaning up on one elbow, she took a sip, closing her eyes as the liquid gold did its holy work. "Mmm, this is perfect, thanks. What time is it?"

"A little after seven."

She glanced up, suddenly all too aware that she was in Luke Almeida's bed, drinking coffee he had made for her, and suspecting she wasn't quite as put together as she would have liked. And there were the memories. The horrible memories.

Oh. Shit.

"I puked on your shoes last night."

"Never liked that pair anyway."

"I am so, so sorry." But that wasn't all. Fresh horror thumped her skull as her fuzzy memory began to clear. "You held my hair while I threw up. Multiple times."

"I've graduated with honors in hair holding. Used to do it for Alex back in her teens. Gage, too, when his hair was longer." He gifted her a superior yet wicked grin she felt all the way down to her panties. Which thankfully were still on. "How're you feeling?"

"Not so good. I haven't drunk that much since . . ." She hesitated, not wanting to go there.

"Since your ex dumped you after you hauled ass across the country to be with him?"

Ah, that was the confession part she vaguely remembered from the night before. Though, if memory served, it was that snitch Alex who had blabbed the salient details. As for her last bout of drunkenness, on finding out David had decided to up and plan his life without Kinsey, she'd bought a bottle of Skinnygirl Island Coconut vodka and holed up in a hotel room at the Peninsula on Michigan Avenue. Avoiding the minibar was supposed to save both money and the ignominy of housekeeping finding her passed out in a sea of tiny bottles. Instead of, as it happened, in the company of one large bottle.

Several hours and one mother of a hangover later, she had rented her temp apartment so she could get on with her temp job and her temp life. In the months since, she had been living in a misery cocoon, and last night was the first time she'd let loose in forever. To be honest, she missed her family. Alex and Gage had embraced her in their cozy Dempsey circle, and hell if she didn't like it there a bit too much.

"Sounds like I got chatty *and* barfy last night."

He nodded, unexpected understanding in his eyes. "We're all entitled to let our hair down every now and then."

"Go a little crazy?"

"Go a little crazy."

"Did you go a little crazy . . . ?"

"When I found out my wife was cheating on me? Oh yeah. You can still see the fist-shaped dents in the living room walls. Sort of artistic, if you catch it in the right light." He hooked his thumbs in his pockets. "So what happened with your ex?"

She inhaled a bolstering breath. Took a sip of coffee. Inhaled again. "In January, he moved here to become head of cardiac surgery at Northwestern Medicine. A month later, I took a pay cut and a demotion to move here to be with him. In April, he dropped me three weeks before our planned May wedding in Napa."

"Ouch."

She waved the hand not holding her coffee cup.

It shook a little, which she preferred to credit to her delicate physical condition. "He met someone else. A nurse." A nurturer by nature, Kinsey's polar opposite.

"How come you stuck around in Chicago?"

Countering with "Out of spite" would be pathetic despite the germ of truth in there. Really, she had refused to give her ex the satisfaction of watching her slink back home with her tail between her legs, and the stiff-upper-lip attitude kept her family's concern at manageable levels. "I like Chicago. I have feelers out for opportunities back on the West Coast, but until something better pops up, this city suits me."

Luke studied her for a moment as if he didn't really understand that line of reasoning. Sometimes she barely understood it herself. After a taut moment, he gestured to a chair where sweats hung over the arm.

"I grabbed some clothes for you from Alex. There are clean towels in the bathroom. Breakfast's up in ten."

"Oh, okay, thanks." Breakfast might be a problem given her wayward internal organs, but she'd hate to be a bad guest on top of everything else. Hopefully, he wasn't too fond of his current footwear.

After a quick shower, she donned Alex's sweats and CFD hoodie. The clothes swam on her because Kinsey didn't have the dynamite proportions of a female gladiator, but she was grateful to be out of her evening-cum-sleepwear. Mr. Thoughtful had left out a spare toothbrush, so she brushed her teeth, then tore a comb she found in one of the vanity's drawers through her damp hair. With her lukewarm mug, she headed downstairs toward the sound of a radio and the smell of bacon, the one thing she missed about going vegetarian.

Picture hooks—but no pictures—hung on the wall abutting the stairs. Banished memories of Luke's marriage, she assumed, waiting for new ones to take their place. She wasn't sure when exactly their relationship had ended, but the stasis of his house decor implied he was in some sort of holding pattern. She wondered how long it would take to get over her own relationship fail. Or, if a certain streak of walking, breathing temptation might be willing to indulge in a spot of naked sex therapy.

Bad brain. She needed to remember that Luke was a job. An assignment. And he'd made it clear that she was the enemy.

Time to do a little reconnaissance across enemy lines.

Taking advantage of his position with his back to her while he stood at the stove in the fifties-style kitchen, she let her gaze drink him in. Those broad shoulders. Tightly woven back muscles. Slim hips. Her breasts tingled in memory of how wonderful it felt to cradle him in her body's embrace. How hard he was for her that day in the locker room at Engine 6. How good—

"You're not my favorite person right now, Kinsey," he said without turning around.

Le sigh. Luke Almeida, creator—and destroyer—of fantasies. Needing a moment to rally her defenses, she walked over to the coffeemaker and heated up her cup.

"Not enjoying the attention?"

"I let you spread your wings with the calendar, and the way you countered the *Trib* with the local TV news piece was nicely played. But billboards? Now we have badge bunnies lining up outside the firehouse to have their picture taken. Not to mention the increased demand for ring cutting."

Badge bunnies? Alarm pop-popped in her chest. "Ring cutting?"

"We get a couple of women a month coming in to get their wedding rings removed rather than go to the ER. The day before last we had five, yesterday close to fifteen." He glowered. Sexily, of course. "They seem to think it's as good as a divorce. Snip the ring and they're free to roam. And they'd like to roam right into my arms."

When she came up with this idea to make Luke and his crew minor celebrities while raising the profile of CFD and cash for charity, she couldn't have suspected how much female attention it would garner. Of course, Luke was gorgeous with multiple exclamation points, and women would have to be blind not to see that.

He placed a plate of bacon and scrambled eggs on the table—with attitude. "Have some grease. It's good for your hangover."

"I don't eat meat."

"Of course you don't, Cali girl." He folded his arms and blew out a frustrated sigh. "You like to win, don't you?"

"Doesn't everybody?"

"Not as much as you do, but that's okay. I'll let you lead me around by the dick in public if it makes you feel better. As long as we both know that in private, it's different."

Heat bloomed between her thighs. In private was exactly what she would like more of, but his implication that she had some diabolical agenda here rubbed her the wrong way. "Is that what you think I'm doing? Busting your balls for my own amusement?"

"Your career. Your boss. Your amusement." He shrugged those immense shoulders. "I don't care what your reasons are. I only care about mine."

"Which is to keep your job at Engine 6."

"Wrong. To protect my family at Engine 6."

The oddity of that struck her anew. "You said that before. As if the city or the mayor is out to get you."

He opened his mouth to respond, but clammed up as Wyatt strode in, looking as tired and worn as Kinsey felt. Wordlessly, he divided a glance between Luke and Kinsey before pronouncing with brows drawn tight that the situation was below his interest. Mr. Coffee was his aim. Kinsey moved out of his way.

"Did you come home last night after the bar closed?" Luke asked him, concern bracketing his mouth.

"Not one of the juniors, Luke. No need to keep tabs."

"Maybe I wouldn't have to if you told me where you were one of these nights."

Wyatt sniffed, doctored his coffee with cream and three packets of raw sugar, and turned his squinty gaze on Kinsey. "Unless you enjoy constant cosseting, Miss Taylor, I would suggest you get out now before it's too late."

No clue how to respond to that, so she went with a soft "Call me Kinsey."

"A couple of the kids from St. Carmen's are stopping by," Wyatt said as he headed out the back door. "I'll be in the garage working on the Camaro."

For a few extra-charged beats, Luke's troubled stare followed his brother.

"Everything okay?" Kinsey asked.

"No, he's . . ." Luke appeared to course correct, perhaps remembering that he was talking to someone unworthy of his confidence. "Have a cinnamon roll. They're from Ann Sather's. A Chicago institution."

On any other day, she'd be all over that like white on rice, but her stomach roiled at the prospect of an iced pastry on top of all she had subjected it to last night. "Best not. I'll stick with coffee." She took a seat at the kitchen table. When he sat and pulled her plate of eggs and bacon toward him, she felt a satisfactory glow in her chest at the domesticity of it all.

"So you and Wyatt live here and Gage and Alex are next door?"

He nodded. "I used to live here with my ex, but after we split, Wyatt moved in. Beck's with his girl, Darcy, a few blocks over. We all grew up off and on in the house next door and when this place came up for sale, we pitched in to get it."

"Your mother isn't around anymore?"

"No, she passed away a couple of years before Sean and Logan. Breast cancer."

Same as Kinsey's mom. Mentioning it would look like she was trolling for sympathy or trying to curry favor, two things she never did.

He squinted at her. "You ever heard of the Sullivan rule?"

"You mean the one that prohibits family members from serving together in the same military platoon or company?"

"Right, but it also applies to firehouses. Technically, the Dempseys should be split and assigned to different houses in case there's some catastrophe and we all bite the bullet on the same day. It's meant to offer some measure of comfort to those left behind that they'll be limited to one coffin in the ground instead of five."

She winced at his cavalier reference to the danger he faced on a daily basis. "But you're not legally siblings, so it doesn't apply to you."

"And there's no one left behind, just us looking out for each other. Wyatt and I worked our asses off to ensure we all ended up at Engine 6. After Sean and Logan died, we had to be certain the kids would be protected. That *we* would be the ones protecting them. And your boss wants to take what we've created here and rip it apart. He said as much to the commissioner."

"I didn't know about that—"

"No, I don't suppose you did. But you know now. I might not share the same gene pool as Sean or any of my family, but I've got something better and stronger running through my veins. Fire and smoke and ice. Wyatt, Beck, Alex, and Gage are who I care about. I'm not doing your bullshit campaign to save my ass. I'm doing it to save theirs."

The Dempsey dynamic coalesced into clarity. Luke was the rock, the one who waited up to ensure his siblings came home safe from a night on the town, the one whose heart beat faster with every second they were out of sight. His family was the mission.

Her hand crept over to his and curled around his clenched fist. "I don't want to split you up, Luke. I have family, too." Family she craved like a piece of her heart was missing. "I'm just trying to do a job here."

Not unlike when she wrapped her body around him at the calendar shoot, he seemed to relax at her touch. Unexpectedly, he opened his fist. Entwined his fingers with hers. The serrated breathing that lifted his chest with every roughly grasped inhale steadied to an even draw. The effect she had on him surprised her—she wasn't a restful person by nature, so that she was capable of inspiring calm in this passionate man both stunned and electrified her. Something about how they connected just worked.

The moment seemed to expand between them, until suddenly the back door flew open and two bodies crashed in. She jumped at the intrusion. Luke released her hand.

"You ever heard of knocking?" he barked.

The new arrivals, African American boys in their midteens, presented a mix of mildly chastened with challenge to authority.

"Thought Wy was here," one of them said, his curious gaze slipping to Kinsey.

"Eyes forward, soldier," Luke said. He stood and did some complicated fist bump/handshake move with each kid. The tallest one snuck another look at Kinsey, one at Luke, and chuckled.

"Is that yo woman?"

"Have they stopped teaching English in school, Anton? The word is *your*, not *yo*."

Kinsey's heart clattered, though she knew Luke was just using the yo/your example to make an excellent point about grammar, not to actually claim her as his.

"You eat any breakfast this morning?" Luke asked the boys.

"Just the Grape-Nuts shit they serve up on Saturdays," Anton muttered. "And fuckin' apples," he added, as if those green-skinned suckers had offended him deeply.

"Grab a couple of forks and have at the cinnamon rolls. One each, then out to the garage. Wy's expecting you."

The boys moved around the kitchen knowledgeably, grabbing plates and forks before settling in at the table. Standing at the counter, Luke speared them with a paternal gaze, then caught her eye.

"You can get that idea out of your head, Miss Taylor."

The kids looked up as if they had forgotten she was there. "I'm Anton," the tall one said to Kinsey around his chewing. He thumbed to his friend. "That's Kevin."

"And she's leaving." Luke placed a hand of brook-no-argument on the back of her chair. "C'mon, I'll drive you home."

"You don't have to—"

"It wasn't an offer."

Got it. Kinsey went to grab her clothes, blood boiling. Mr. July was Mr. Mercurial today, it seemed; one moment warm and fuzzy, the next cold as a Chicago winter. Kinsey guessed feeling threatened in all manner of ways could do that to you: his family, his job, these kids he mentored. Luke clearly felt like everything was at stake, and that it was up to him to protect everyone around him. But he didn't need to treat her like a soulless PR junkie at every opportunity.

After taking her time grabbing her jeans and shirt, she met up with him at his pickup truck, unsurprised that this man's man would own a Chevy Silverado with a turbo diesel V8. Fewer cylinders might be misinterpreted as sensitivity. In torturous silence, except for her directions, they headed to her home on Erie in the River North neighborhood. Luke drove like he was on a five-alarm-fire run, weaving in and out of traffic, apparently hyperfocused in his goal to offload her from his life. Ten minutes of meat-locker cold blew between them, rivaling the truck's air-conditioning, but inside her body heated with the fire of a thousand planet-destroying suns.

Who the fuck did this guy think he was? She would put this job to bed ASAP—but not in his bed with his hard body spreading her thighs wide and pistoning into her with those trim hips and—*argh!* It was time to wrap up Engine 6 Makeover: Asshole Edition stat, and move on to projects where block-heads were thinner on the ground.

The craptastic Chicago parking situation meant no space was available outside her building, but to her surprise, Luke flipped on the hazards and skipped around to the passenger side. He opened her door as he looked up at the awning for Burnham Corporate Apartments. "Temporary accommodation?"

"Temporary everything," she snapped back, ignoring his outstretched hand as she stepped into the street. In a snit, she marched to the entrance of her building, mentally warning herself to let it slide. To just go inside. To just—*oh damn him!* She turned and pounded back. Poked a finger in that hard chest. Got all up in his grille.

"I took this job, Luke, because it was the best one I could get in the city where the man I planned to spend the rest of my life with had moved. Now the reason for upping sticks and coming here is no longer part of the equation, but that doesn't mean I get to bail on being a professional. You might not like it, but this is what I do. Fix big fucking problems."

"Like me?"

"Like you."

That would have made such a fine scene-ending line, if this infuriating man had the decency to let her have the last word. But then she guessed that the definition of *decency* must be fluid as far as Luke Almeida was concerned. Because while he was shaping up to be one of the most decent men she knew . . .

Exhibit A: his family.

Exhibit B: those foster kids.

Exhibit C: he had held her hair *and* rubbed her neck while she hurled her guts out last night.

. . . there was nothing remotely decent about how his granite body maneuvered her flush to the truck's door. As for the proof of his arousal, thick against her belly?

Not decent, but decently sized.

More than decently sized.

"You're lucky that right now your job objectives coincide with mine, Kinsey." Brute hands caged her on either side. Sweet breath, flavored with sugar and cinnamon, fanned her lips. "But when you stray your honeyed ass onto my turf, in my firehouse, in my bed . . ." He brushed his lips against her ear. "When you come within a five-mile radius of my body, which is so fucking hard for you, baby, you need to leave your job at the door and let me take charge."

Pleasure howled through her, but it was immediately tempered by disappointment. Luke Almeida was no different from David. Yet another nitwit who felt threatened by a strong woman.

And "baby"? Honest to God, the man was not to be believed.

"What if I want to leave my job at the door and still bust your balls, Almeida?"

He rubbed his stubble-rough jaw against hers. Want coiled deep in her belly. Deeper.

"I think I can get down with you on top as long as you're prepared to spend equal time underneath me."

Oh, mama.

"It's hard to strike that balance. Someone always feels like they're losing."

"Then you haven't been doing it right," he said before stamping his perfect mouth on hers and showing her just how right it could be. Their tongues tangled and parried, thrusting forward, drawing back. Shared dominance and surrender, control and submission.

No losers here. Luke Almeida was just one fantastic kisser.

Too soon, he unlocked those fantasy lips from hers. Was that a whimper she heard from her throat? Surely not.

"You stayin' in town for the Fourth?"

She nodded, still dazed by the sensual assault.

"We'll be at North Avenue Beach this afternoon at one, near the volleyball courts. Wear the least amount of clothes possible while keepin' it legal."

Indignation snapped her out of her sex-addled haze, but as she was learning, this infuriating man was ten steps ahead of her.

"I'll be the one in the barely there Speedos."

She laughed. Nice way to defuse, Mr. Almeida. Even so, as the fog cleared from her brain, the need to set something straight kicked in.

"You know that while we're working together, Luke, we have to keep our interactions professional." Or more professional than what they had been doing.

Amusement brightened his eyes. "Just askin' you to hang at the beach, Kinsey. Don't fret now, we'll have chaperones, so you'll have to keep your greedy little hands to yourself."

Right, because *her* hands were the problem. With a devilish grin and a wink, he started to head back to the driver's side of his truck.

Not so fast, Mister. "Aren't you forgetting something?"

"Don't think so."

"How about an apology for being a card-carrying jackass earlier?"

He narrowed those stunning blue eyes. "Thought I just did."

That kiss might have been on the upper end of the Richter scale for moisture creation, panty scorching, and nipple hardening, but as far as apologies went, she was unimpressed.

Her expression made that clear.

Back in her personal space, he drew a thick finger across her jaw, all while staring deep into her eyes. "I'm sorry for being a dick, Kinsey. Feel free to call me out on it anytime."

Then he squeezed her ass, and for the briefest moment the words of one of those foster kids in his care came back to her: *Is that yo woman?*

As her butt cheek was shaped by his rough hand, her hormones chanted, *Hell, yes.*

"Now go sleep off that hangover, Miss Taylor."

CHAPTER TEN

Alex had a theory that farmers' markets had replaced bars for the quality hookup, but as Gage surveyed Green City Market on this fine Saturday morning, he was extremely doubtful. Spread out before him were couples, gay and straight, as far as his hungover eyes could see. This market might be loaded with potential of the homosexual variety, but all of it appeared to be taken—and not looking.

At least if you ran into a so-called committed couple at a bar, the chance of being invited into their fucked-up sex games was high on the list. Between the lighting, the music, and the alcohol, the atmosphere conspired to toggle those "Ooh, I'd never" switches to "We're just a block away, handsome."

Nobody got laid with kale as the backdrop. Or gleaming chrome professional kitchens in the heart of Restaurant Row, apparently.

Fucking Brady Smith.

Three times Gage had gone over to his kitchen so far, with zero to show for it but a recipe for pork carnitas empanadas. The man barely spoke. Barely spared him a glance. Didn't even admire his ass when he thought Gage wasn't looking. Gage was not a happy camper.

Enticing the Grumpster over to Dempsey's bar in

Wicker Park, where Gage might have a chance at loosening him up, was a similarly dead end. *Too busy,* Brady had said. He worked every day from noon to 2 a.m., a fact Gage was mildly embarrassed to have come by during a stakeout of Smith & Jones one night, thinking that maybe Brady was seeing someone. But no, he closed up and walked half a block to the loft building on the corner. The next night, the same. Gage checked and found Brady's name on the buzzer. The guy lived there, and not once had he hinted that they could get away for a little afternoon delight at chez Smith.

Gage had turned into a stalker, and this morning, he was at it again.

One of the servers at Smith & Jones had tipped him off that Brady hit the market on Wednesdays and Saturdays around eight, scoping out fresh produce for the restaurant's specials. An oh-so-casual, accidental meet-up might put some fire under this thing that was going nowhere. Once they had fucked, Gage would get this guy out of his system and move on to easier pickings.

"Bit early for you, isn't it?" he heard behind him.

God, he loved that man's voice. A spot of Google-fu had thrown up that Brady was from Louisiana, and that lazy-as-fuck drawl that occasionally crept into his speech made Gage so damn hard. Tamping down his triumphant grin, he turned to find Brady in his usual stance: arms crossed in defense, face bored with, *Who are you again?*

Gage's hackles rose. What the hell was he doing here, chasing an uninterested guy? While he was hungover, no less!

"I like that Wisconsin cheddar they sell over there," Gage muttered, with a nod to the Michigan cheese monger near the entrance. The Wisconsin cheddar on the Michigan cheese stand. Genius.

Brady's response was so weird that Gage had to rewind his brain for verification.

The guy smiled.

If he'd known Brady was turned on by Gage acting dumber than a pail of bait, he would have played up his blond weeks ago. Quicker than double-struck lightning, the smile disappeared, leaving Gage to wonder if he had imagined it.

"Saw you on the news," Brady said with a derisive sniff. "And on those billboards."

"I know, it's crazy. Kinsey—she works for your pal the mayor—is crafting a PR campaign to rehab the reputation of my house. And you'll never—" He had been about to spill about the modeling agency interest, but he stopped short. Brady didn't look so much stoic as just plain bored.

Okaaay. "So what's on the menu today?" Gage asked instead.

"We'll see," was the cryptic response.

Gage fell into step with Brady and, like a golden retriever, followed him around as he made his purchases. About five minutes in, Gage accepted the position of assistant-without-benefits, carting around two bags filled to bursting with produce. Twenty minutes later, and still nothing verbal from Brady. Christ on a cracker, could this get any more painful?

Finally, after one last gunfighter squint at the stands, the big chef made tracks toward the main entrance.

"Gotta get some Wisconsin cheddar," Brady said gravely. "I hear those Michigan cheese mongers use a special recipe to give it the Wisconsin flavor."

"Jesus, is that you making a joke?"

Brady's mouth contorted again into something approximating a smile, and yet again, as if it pained him to do it, he shut down. Shit, this was so messed up. Rising panic dogged Gage's steps as he followed Brady to Cannon Drive where he had parked his SUV. Wordlessly, he took the bags from Gage, loaded them in the trunk, and shut the door.

"*Icameherelookingforyou,*" Gage said in a single burst, as though he had been gagged for the last half hour.

"Why?"

"Why do you think?"

"Dunno. Judging from your billboards, looks like you could have anyone you want."

"I could, but I want you." *Conceited much, Simpson?* Well, when that's all you have, you may as well play it to the hilt. "Are you not attracted to me?" Gage took a step forward, and Brady edged a shaky step back. "If you're not interested, just say so."

Brady flashed him an answering grimace and Gage was suddenly struck with an unpalatable and wholly unexpected conclusion.

The man was just not that into him.

"Sorry to have wasted your time," Gage bit out, feeling cold and shaky, the disappointment heavier than a bowling ball in his gut.

He turned to leave, but got no farther than a few steps before his body was slammed against the back of the SUV. Brady's callused palm curled around his neck and drew him closer, closer, so close until *fuck, yeah,* his lips found Gage's mouth and seized possession. Brady drove his tongue deep, searching, at the same time as Gage anchored his hands to Brady's hips and pulled him in for some cock-on-cock action. Holy smokes, that felt so right. It had been a long time coming, and like a man who hadn't eaten in days, Gage wanted to experience it all even if it left him with a stomachache.

The man kissed like he had been custom built for it. Those lips were made for Gage's, that tongue couldn't make anyone else feel this good. A moan escaped Gage's throat, answered like a mating call by Brady slanting his mouth to find a more penetrating angle.

Perfect. So frickin' perfect.

But it was over much too soon. Brady pulled away, breathless, and gaped at Gage. Then he edged back farther, out of Gage's immediate reach.

"Can't do this," he rasped.

"Can't do what?" Gage looked around. Sure, it was a bit public, but the liberal-minded set of Lincoln Park could handle it. "I need you to take me back to your place. I need you to fuck me. Now."

"I-I can't. I can't do this."

Gage fisted Brady's shirt, absorbed the thud of the man's heart. "Do not tell me you don't want me because your body says different. It's begging for my touch, for my greedy mouth. I could make you feel so fucking good, Brady. Best you've ever had."

Brady was breathing hard, his broad chest rising and falling. Apparently, he had been struck mute, so Gage continued to coax. Calling on skills he rarely had to use.

"If you're worried about people knowing you're gay . . . I can work with that." He would despise the dishonesty of it, but for a chance with this man, even once, he would put aside what few scruples he possessed. "Brady, I want you. Any way I can have you."

"That's not it. I'm not hiding who I am. I just can't do this." Brady scrubbed his mouth, removing all traces of that kiss. Of Gage. He placed a hand over Gage's fist and unfurled his grip like he was dealing with a grasping child who needed a stern talking-to. "Can't do you."

Shock froze Gage in place and numbed his throat, and hell if Brady didn't take advantage of his compromised state. Two seconds was all it took for him to make like the wind and hightail it out of there in his SUV.

With those squealing tires sounding like a bank robbery getaway, it was easy to believe that someone had just committed a crime.

"Kinsey, over here!"

Alex's strong voice carried over the heads of sun worshippers and families soaking up the midday sun at North Avenue Beach. Perfectly situated on a curl of land, the beach was made even more spectacular by the impressive Chicago skyline watching over it like a steel-and-glass guardian. Passing by a restaurant shaped to look like an ocean liner, Kinsey picked her way across the sand to the volleyball section, where the Dempsey crew had set up camp.

Alex sat in a collapsible chair, as did Wyatt, Gage, and a few other firefighters she recognized from the

Engine 6 crew. Gage made the introductions—Jacob Scott, Derek Phelan, Murphy (*just Murphy*), but Kinsey couldn't help the disappointment chilling her gut that the one person she had been expecting to see was nowhere in sight.

"Glad you could join us," she heard in a deep rumble behind her.

Mental fist bump. She turned and looked her fill.

Gloriously bare chested, and wearing black board shorts that indecently covered his tree-trunk thighs, Luke stood sentry behind her with his arms crossed, aviators gleaming. Like a lifeguard ready to come to her rescue or a Secret Service agent itching to bounce her back to city hall if she made any threatening moves.

"Expected a bit more skin, Almeida." She punctuated that with a pointed glance at the shorts area. The man *had* promised Speedos.

"Think Chicago's seen enough of me, don't you?"

Chicago might have, but Kinsey most definitely had not.

Feeling flirty, she dropped her bag to the sand and peeled off her midthigh-length Tommy Bahama cover-up. The red bikini she wore underneath was a favorite, though David had thought it too revealing. *May as well be wearing napkins, Kinsey.*

"I see you followed my instructions," Luke murmured, his aviators-covered gaze reflecting heat off her skin. *Dayum.* One look was like twenty minutes of foreplay.

"What'd ya bring?" Gage cut in with a nod to the plastic bag at her feet.

"Just some cinnamon rolls from Ann Sather."

"Goddamn it, woman, why didn't you say so?" Alex made a dash for the box. "The perfect hangover food."

Like ravenous wildebeests, the crowd demolished the sweet rolls Kinsey had bought on the way to the beach. "Now we can eat," Gage pronounced, licking a sliver of sugar from his lips.

Cooler lids were unleashed and out came lunch; evidently Gage had spent all morning in the kitchen. On a fold-out table, he lay out the spread of hummus, dips, and raw veggies—cucumber, zucchini, colorful peppers, cherry tomatoes. One of the firefighters whose name she missed during the introductions tended to hot dogs and burgers on a portable Weber. A couple of beautiful salads rounded out the selection, perfect for the vegetarian. Guess she wouldn't need that bag of pretzels she'd brought along after all.

Wyatt stood and gestured to his seat. "Kinsey, sit."

She obeyed, partly because she wanted to and partly because Wyatt was a wee bit intimidating. No man scared her, but she suspected that if she were to encounter the eldest Dempsey on a badly lit street, she might cross to the other side with her finger hovering on that last digit in 911. She wondered what his story was. What all their stories were.

As foster kids, it had to have been rough. No one escapes that kind of upbringing completely unscathed, but all of them came across as well adjusted. Tight. If the bond between them wasn't obvious from the good-natured insults and ribbing, the commemorative tattoos they all sported on their biceps—even Alex—said it as clear as day. Family, duty, Dempsey.

Throughout lunch, Kinsey tried to focus on eating and laughing, but mostly on restraining herself from staring at Luke. He lay stretched out on a beach towel, skin glistening like his billboard counterpart, thick, corded forearms crossed behind his dark head. Her fingers itched with the need to wander over those sunbaked muscles and spend time exploring. Lord, the man was a visual orgasm.

But there were only so many times she could get away with diverting her not-so-surreptitious gaze. After her fourth attempt at covert glances, Luke curved his wicked lips, making it abundantly clear he had caught her admiring stare from behind his obscuring aviators. *Busted*. She blushed and looked away, insisting she was unmoved by that sexy grin. There had been a lot of insisting lately.

Gage stood and stretched. "Think I'll go for a swim."

"Don't forget, little bro," Luke threw out.

"Forget what?"

"Wrap it before you tap it," all the Dempseys, even tight-lipped Wyatt, chorused.

Gage caught Kinsey's eye. "See what I put up with? Frickin' homophobes. You wouldn't say that if I was hetero."

Wyatt snorted.

"Dad said it to us all the time," Luke said, leaning up on one elbow and eyeing his little brother over his sunglasses. "No glove, no love. He shoved so many condoms in my pocket I could've opened a rubber stand."

"Unless his new honey is on the beach, I think he'll be okay," Alex said.

"What's this?" Luke pulled his long, lean body

upright and grabbed Gage in a headlock. "You're delivering the package to one address now?"

"No packages are being delivered," Gage replied patiently, extracting himself from Luke's grasp. His cheeks were flushed and the downturn of his lips emphasized his annoyance. "Later, family unit."

With a loose-limbed swagger, he ambled toward the water while every woman in the vicinity looked on appreciatively. A few guys, as well, including Firefighter Jacob Scott, a blond hulk with a neck thick enough to categorize him as genus bovine.

"I know, right?" Alex said to Kinsey sotto voce, with a significant glance in Jacob's direction. "Guy's so far in the closet he's sucking dick in Narnia."

Kinsey's laugh drew a sharp look from Luke, which she ignored. But there was no ignoring how he sprang to his feet with a catlike grace and headed to the volleyball court about twenty feet off. In some unspoken male ritual, Wyatt, Jacob, and Derek followed him.

About time. Oiled-up men flexing rock-hard muscles while they pounded a ball over a net? Kinsey had been waiting for it all day, though she was clearly not alone in her interest. Amused, she watched as assorted women gravitated to the court and the very fine testosterone showcase on display.

"Put your tongues back in your mouths, *bishes*," Alex muttered. She handed off a beer to Kinsey from a nearby cooler and settled back in her chair. "Hair of the dog."

The guitar strains of the Pixies' "Here Comes Your Man" comingled with the shouts of kids playing Frisbee and splashing in the lake. Sitting in comfortable silence with Alex, Kinsey felt truly at ease for the first time since she had moved to Chicago. So Alex was never going to be her shopping-and-makeup gal pal, but Kinsey enjoyed a real affinity with this woman who got it from all sides in one of the toughest jobs on the planet.

"Wyatt freaks me out," Kinsey said after a few swigs, needing to lay it out there.

Alex laughed. "He's a pussycat, but I can see your point. He used to be chattier when Dad and Logan were around."

"I can't imagine how hard it must have been."

"It was hell, but Logan's death in particular hit Wy and Grace hardest."

"Who's Grace?"

"Logan's wife." Hurt tightened the lines of Alex's mouth. "After the funeral, she moved back to be with her folks in Boston. Too many reminders here. She wanted to forget, and there's no forgetting around us. We refuse to be quiet. We want to talk about them, remember how Dad told these long, seemingly point-less stories that always managed to get back on track just when you thought he'd lost it. Remember how bad a singer Logan was, but he was the first one up singing 'Country Roads' on karaoke night. Keep them close, you know."

She chugged her beer and Kinsey took that as a prompt to do the same. She needed to swallow down the emotion clotting like custard in her throat.

"So," Alex said. "You doin' my brother yet?"

Kinsey narrowly avoided a spit take, only to have the beer go down the wrong way. So much for the heart-to-heart. "Nope," she choked out around her coughing. "He sees me as the enemy." Even his body trapping hers against his car this morning was more adversarial than seductive. Okay, adversarial *and* seductive.

"Besides, right now, he's my job. While I'm in a position to recommend his return to work, I can't be—"

"Giving comfort to the enemy?" Alex looked over at Luke, her brow furrowed. "We've been worried about him. He hasn't been interested in anyone since that bitch fucked him over. Until you."

"How long were they together?"

"Three years, eight months of it married. Their divorce was finalized just over six months ago." She grinned. "Maybe you could both rebound with each other."

"Or off each other," muttered Kinsey. Something they were doing a whole lot of already. Violently clashing and bruising, which turned her on unbearably. "We'd have to get to the point where he sees me as more than the mayor's lackey."

"Oh, we're *waaay* past that. Now he's at the point of 'What's goin' on inside those bikini bottoms, Miss Taylor?'"

That drew Kinsey's reluctant laugh. Time for a subject change. "What about you? Are your bikini bottoms seeing any action?"

"Just my washer-dryer."

"You don't date?"

Sighing, Alex slumped further in her chair. "Want to know how many dates I've been on in the last six months?"

The poor thing. "Hey, that's okay. Since my ex, I haven't exactly been whooping it up on the singles scene myself."

"Twenty-five."

Kinsey gaped. Surely she hadn't heard that right. "Twenty-five dates . . . in six months?"

"Yup, and not one of them a repeat offender. Guys are either intimidated by my all-around awesomeness, or I exude man repellant from every pore. Can't figure out which."

She stood, all va-va-voom curves in a stunning five-ten package. How was this woman not cleaning up on the man circuit? On a smile, she jerked her head toward the volleyball courts.

"C'mon, K, time to make like a tampon commercial. Let's show the boys how it's done."

Kinsey in her power suit was one thing, and in second-skin jeans that molded to her curvy ass, she was quite another. Now Luke was seeing yet a different side: bikini-bombshell Kinsey. Red, just like his California beach girl fantasy, and every part of his anatomy was enjoying the view.

"Kinsey, you're the guest, so you get to choose your partner," Luke said, curious to see how she would play it.

She wanted to win. He could see it written all over her face, which meant teaming up with one of the guys was her best option. Wy and Derek had already bowed out, leaving Jacob Scott, who was actually pretty good at volleyball.

Luke was better.

Kinsey thrust out her hand to Jacob. "Hey, partner."

Luke turned to hide his smile, but not before he caught her challenging one. Not only did she want to win, but she wanted to beat him. Game on.

Ten minutes later, Luke was reassessing the situation. Kinsey was a good player—it was clear she had spent some time on the golden California beaches spiking the ball—but Jacob wasn't giving her room to breathe. The guy was so competitive he was calling for every ball that came into the back court, even if Kinsey was already there. Shoving her out of the way, too, which had Luke grinding his teeth like a trash compactor. Defending her wouldn't win him any favors, and frankly she could take it. But damn if it didn't rile his Irish side, which was usually the calmer part of him. The Cuban half was always up for revolution.

Stranger still, Kinsey seemed deflated, as though letting Jacob wear the pants was the best option for keeping the peace. The set finished with Luke and Alex coming out on top twenty-one points to twelve. He grabbed some water from a cooler and walked over to Kinsey.

"Here. Keep hydrated."

"Thanks," she muttered, taking the bottle from him. Their fingers brushed and electricity fired through him, enough to power the Navy Pier Ferris wheel he could spot off in the distance.

"Why're you lettin' Jacob push you around?"

She wrinkled her nose. "I don't find fighting with my teammates to be all that productive. If he's not going to work with me, I'm not going to waste the energy."

Was that a dig at Luke's unwillingness to surrender his life and image to Kinsey Taylor's molding hands? He tried to lighten the mood. "Thought maybe you were second-guessing your girl power and decided that men are just better at ball sports after all."

She downed half the bottle of water in one long gulp that made her throat bob. He wanted to lick that throat and move on down.

"The sun must have gone to your head, Almeida. You're usually a little sharper with your button pushing."

So, not his most subtle comment. But he didn't like when Kinsey played less than 100 percent. Backing down didn't suit her at all.

"We're switching up. Alex, you're with Jacob." He turned to Kinsey. "If you can't beat me, sweetheart, looks like you'll have to join me." Before she could respond, he walked back to the other side of the net, his back warm not from the sun but from her heated gaze.

"You look like you might be better in the back court," he said to her when she trotted over twenty seconds later. "You're a good mover."

A grin broke wide at his compliment. "I'm not afraid of getting pummeled in the face. I survived three brothers and two nose breaks in my teens. You'd hardly notice, right?"

He took that as an invitation to tip her chin up and examine her fine features. That nose of hers was perfect and so were her golden-umber eyes, filled with uncommon intelligence and determination.

"Looks like you had a good plastic surgeon."

Sexy offense curved those beautiful lips. "I'm all real, Luke. Every single inch."

This was more like the Kinsey he had come to expect. Smart-tart and giving as good as she got.

"You ready to kick some firefighter ass, Cali girl?"

She nodded and took a part-crouched position in the front court. Those beautiful back dimples above her gorgeous ass winked at him. Best. View. Ever.

"Let's do this."

For the next fifteen minutes, they played like winning was more important than breathing. Watching Kinsey punch that ball—once in Jacob's incredulous face—was about the sexiest thing he'd been privileged to witness in all his days. Every now and then, her bikini bottoms would fail in their objective: to cover completely her made-for-his-hands ass. Or perhaps that *was* the wily objective. Give him glimpses of that curve where her thigh met the round of her perfect ass and, in turn, give him a whole new appreciation for the female form.

Together, they were dynamite on the sand. He'd known they would be. The sooner this probationary shit was sorted, the better, because if they were a tenth as good a force between the sheets as they were on the volleyball court, it was going to be unlike anything he had ever experienced.

Soon they were celebrating every won point with a high-five.

Then a hip check.

Then a light mutual pat on each other's asses.

And when she sealed the game-winning point with a powerful spike, his reaction was instinctive. Up high, then down low with his arms under her gorgeous rear.

Kinsey linked her arms around his neck, squeezing

in closer so she could whisper in his ear. "See what happens when you work with me, Luke? Teamwork is so much more productive, don't you think?"

He shrugged, which was harder than it looked with a hot woman wrapped around his waist, her breasts smashed to his chest. The heat between her legs pulsed an erotic rhythm against his abs.

"Just a game, baby," he said, his voice low, rough.

"It's never just a game."

The truth of that lanced through him. For all their snarky quips and joking foreplay, it had never felt like a game. Something unfurled in his chest. Something warm and unexpected that he hadn't felt in a very long time. Never, not ever, had he wanted a woman like this.

But in the span of a thunderous heartbeat, the mood shifted. Her whiskey-colored eyes flicked over his shoulder and widened. Sensing something was off, Luke lowered her to the hot sand.

"Still doing anything to win, Kinsey?"

Luke turned to the source of the voice and found a sandy-haired, stocky guy of average height. He wore a tee that proclaimed his affiliation with Northwestern Medicine and a blonde that proclaimed him very fertile indeed. As big as she was, the woman had to be expecting twins.

"David," Kinsey said, almost choking on the name. "What are you doing here?"

So this was Stupid Fucking David, the chump who had dumped. He threw an arm around his pregnant companion and pulled her close.

"We're meeting Natalie's family further down the beach." David waved a hand casually to some distant spot.

Kinsey's gaze had magnetized to the woman's swollen belly, made even more conspicuous by her revealing bikini.

"I hadn't realized . . . you're . . . you're—"

"—going to be a father," the guy finished smugly.

Aw, shit. Silence reigned while the emotional landscape was reshuffled.

"This . . . this is Luke." She turned to him, her face drained of all color, eyes vacant and unseeing. "Luke, this is David and . . . Natalie."

Yeah, got it. Dave the Douche, who she upended her life and hauled her sweet ass cross-country for. What a cluster. Knowing that Kinsey needed his protection and not caring that she might not want it, Luke placed his palm on the small of her back.

It wasn't enough. He inched his fingers below the lip of her bikini bottoms. Staked his claim.

Kinsey's thoughts were so loud they might cause a tsunami out on the lake. She was doing the math, God love her, and it was adding up to one whopping great negative in the ledger of, *I got screwed*.

Don't ask, baby. Do. Not. Ask.

"When are you due?"

"October 3," Natalie said blithely. Was she really that oblivious to the fact she had stolen another woman's man? That while she was having her fun and cooking up that bun in her oven, Kinsey was planning a life with the sperm donor?

Proud papa had the decency to look sheepish. "We should talk, Kinsey. I feel we haven't reached the necessary closure."

"Not sure that's a good idea, David. Closure for me can only mean grievous bodily harm to you."

"Christ, you hate to lose. You can't stand that you didn't get to end this."

Kinsey positively vibrated under Luke's claiming palm. "You know what I can't stand? Not that you cheated on me, which I long suspected, or that you knocked up a nurse in a supply closet or wherever this happened"—she waved a shaky hand at Natalie, who was *finally* red-faced with embarrassment—"but that you didn't have the common decency to call and let me know that we were over before I fucking moved here!"

"Our relationship was on the skids for a while. I tried to tell you—"

"Just not hard enough. Maybe you were getting your miniature dick sucked by Blondie here and it slipped your mind." She stepped forward, but Luke tightened his hold, restraining her from doing something she might later regret.

"That mouth of yours, Kinsey," the Douche said with a condescending shake of his head. "Always have to be one of the guys. Hanging around with foul-mouthed politicians has made you less of a woman."

"And spending time with me made you less of a man."

"That's okay, honey. I don't mind admitting you're a better man than I'll ever be."

Ah, hell, no. Something imploded in Luke's brain, pinwheels of fury propelling him forward in attack. No one talked to his woman like that. No one. He closed the gap, using his height to intimidate and get all up in Dr. D-bag's business.

But before he could do his usual "fists first, questions never" thing, Kinsey slipped between them, her hands on Luke's chest. Protecting her ex—and Luke from his own brutish impulses.

"Luke, don't." Her eyes implored him not to undo all her good work making over his reputation. "He's not worth it."

Just as she had calmed him at the firehouse post-Lisa and this morning, when she covered his angry fist with her small hand as they sat at his kitchen table, her tender touch absorbed all his negative energy. With one last "fuck you" glare at the doc, Luke rolled his shoulders and backed off.

Which is when Kinsey turned and landed a right hook to the Douche's jaw.

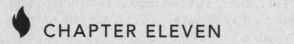

CHAPTER ELEVEN

That steaming pile of cheating excrement.

Of course, Kinsey had suspected it all along. When she arrived in Chicago in February and David told her six weeks later that he had met someone else, the odds of him *not* going for a test drive with his pretty nurse had struck her as slim to none. Now her ability to do simple addition taunted her, making it very clear how David had spent those cold, oh-so-lonely early days in the Windy City.

Fucking—and impregnating—the nurse.

A child. He was having a child, though by the looks of it, Blondie was carrying quadruplet hippos. David had claimed he didn't want children, some logically reasoned argument about how fatherhood wouldn't suit him or their lifestyle, and she had let him lead there, too. But it was Kinsey who hadn't suited him.

He just didn't want children with *her*.

Stunned senseless, she plowed aimlessly over the hot sand, its burn on her feet a match to the scorch marks over her heart. She flexed the hand she had used to strike her gutless ex. It hurt—all of it. Her head, her chest, her knuckles, which looked as raw as she felt. Her throat was thick with unshed tears, which she desperately staved off by making each step more deliberately forceful than the last. Walk it off, Taylor.

Walk. It. Off.

"Hey, watch it," an aggrieved voice called out. She might have trod on the voice's towel. Or his sand castle. Or his stupid face.

Fury fueled her off-kilter pivot. She refused to let one more man walk all over her today. "Watch what, asshole?"

Any forthcoming answer was lost on the lake breeze as a strong arm circled her waist and gathered her to a solid chest.

Luke.

The comfort she took in his body was more shocking than the events that had led to this moment. For too long, she had been starved of a man's affectionate touch. For too long, she had relied on her own resources. It felt so good to rely on someone else for a little while.

Stiffness in every part of her gradually gave way to Luke's strength, a muscularity that was as much mental as it was physical. It must have taken sincere mental strength not to want to comment on the scene he had just witnessed. Make her feel better with murmured platitudes. Fill the gnawing silence. Instead, he was just there for her, his hold tight and sure and a touch rougher than she was used to.

It was perfect.

Peeking up from where her head was burrowed into his left pec, she found those lake-blue eyes holding her prisoner. While the competitor in her was tempted to see how long this stare down could last, the woman in her needed something else. Something only this man could give.

"I've got you," he whispered.

With strong hands on her butt, he raised her body, her lips to his, and the resulting union streaked through her like fire. Their mouths might be made for sniping, but mostly they were made for this. Better they should be used for this. A perfect melding of lips and tongues, the tangle so sweet, the chemistry so right.

I've got you. For the first time in what seemed like forever, someone had her.

Afraid he'd pull away before she was done taking her fill, she climbed closer, tighter. The kiss turned more assured, the intimate taste of him more intoxicating. Faced with the knowledge that she couldn't satisfy one man, she needed to know she was desired. That despite all those character traits that men found so off-putting—her bossiness, her selfishness, her drive—she still had something to offer the man who could match her word for word, kiss for kiss.

Blood saturated with him, she reluctantly drew back and blew out a shaky breath against his lips. "Thanks," she said simply.

"Anytime, sweetheart. Put these on." He fell to one knee and slid her foot into her flip-flop, then the other, with a reverence that stung the backs of her eyelids.

He stood again. "You might recall my theory about how violence satisfies men's sense of justice, makes us feel good, and always improves our odds with women."

Baffled, she stared at him. "I do."

"Goes both ways," he said, his grin twinkly and dangerous. "That little outburst considerably improved your odds of getting lucky with me. How's the hand?"

Laughing, though she still hurt everywhere, she stretched her hand and relished the oncoming stiffness. "Worth the bruise I'll have later."

"Good girl."

Dwarfing her uninjured hand in his, he led her to a path at the back of the beach, the one that headed to the beach house shaped like an ocean liner. He never let go, just threaded his way through college kids with lithe bodies and older hipsters who surveyed the youth with a mix of wry amusement and jealousy. Finally, they reached the rooftop bar and found a table near the balcony overlooking the volleyball courts.

Luke raised an eyebrow in query. "Watered-down beer or watered-down cocktails?"

"Beer would be fine."

Scanning the crowd, he connected with a server who had clearly already spotted him. Six four of rock-solid brawn with the face-body combination of a god was hard to miss.

"Hey, you're the hot firefighter!" the waitress squealed.

"Yeah, just trying to enjoy a quiet moment with my girl here. Any chance we can keep that on the down low? There's a good tip in it for you."

"Undercover firefighter-slash-model? Your secret's safe with me as long as you give me your autograph later." She shimmied, displaying her autograph book.

Luke kept his face carefully blank.

"Lucky girl," she murmured to Kinsey, before bouncing off with Luke's order for a pitcher of cold stuff and a bowl of ice.

He met Kinsey's testy gaze. "Hey. You started this. Don't get all crabby because you don't like the monster you created."

She *hmphed*, irked that her disapproval of Miss Sign-My-Jugs was so obvious.

"So Dave the Douche likes 'em sweet and adorable," Luke said, shooting right to the heart of the matter.

Kinsey snorted. "Something I could never be accused of."

"No, you're not sweet. But you're pretty damn adorable when you're drunk off your ass."

"Is that what I need? Copious ingestions of alcohol to make me palatable to the opposite sex?"

He stared, all badass and sexy. "I wouldn't change a thing about you, Kinsey."

Her heart jerked to a stop. She willed it to beat again. "That's easy to say in the early phase of a relationship." Brilliant. Just bandy the R word around, why don't you? "What I mean is—"

"That your particular brand of 'in your face, I am woman, hear me roar' does the trick for attracting men, but gets old in a hurry and doesn't work in the long term."

How embarrassingly astute of him. "Yep. Men claim strong women are sexy, but by the time the wooing is over and you're no longer shaving above the knee, by the time the sex has wound down from every night to once a month—if you're lucky—and especially when the man you admired because he saw you as an equal starts to see you as a rival, then we can safely say most men prefer the soft, ultrafeminine replacement. The Stepford Wife."

"Don't tar us all with the sins of your ex, sweetheart. It could be you two were just incompatible."

That's what David had said when he dumped her. She'd assumed it was one of those breakup buzzwords men throw out to justify their boredom with a longterm relationship and their embrace of the new and shiny. Ten years with someone who she may never have been compatible with. How did it come to this?

Luke strummed the table. "What was all that shit about winning?"

"David thought I was too competitive. I always had to run faster than him, beat him in the bedroom, win at poker—"

"Back up there a sec. The bedroom?"

With marvelous timing, their perky server returned with a pitcher of beer, a bowl of ice, and a flirty smile for Luke. He poured a glass and passed it over, then tipped water into the ice bowl and dipped Kinsey's stiffening hand in the frigid solution. His no-nonsense attitude in caring for her reached inside to some private, untouched place.

"You were saying?"

"No, *you* were saying."

"How did you beat him in the bedroom?"

She sighed and took a draft of beer. The cool swallow refreshed, but couldn't quite temper the hot burn of failure knotted behind her breastbone.

"I didn't see it as beating him, but he did. He wanted to be in total control, and while I like that every now and then . . ." Heat scalded her cheeks, but she was already in too deep to turn back. "I also enjoy a more proactive role."

A muscle twitched in his jaw. "In what way?"

"Telling him what I liked. What I needed." *Shut up, Kinsey.* "How hard I wanted it."

The muscle went ripe bananas.

"Most guys would be happy to have a woman so vocal about her desires," he said in a voice several degrees huskier than before. "Half the time, we have no clue if a woman is enjoying herself."

"Really?"

"Not me. Just trying to represent for my maligned gender. So what made this guy so bad at keeping a woman like you satisfied?"

"Sometimes I needed more, and if I took care of it myself, he saw it as an indictment of his skills, a threat to his manhood." God, she couldn't believe the words spewing from her mouth. Never had she been this open about her sex life, not even with her girlfriends. Luke assessed her with no judgment, just a whole lot of heat.

How had she devoted so many years of her life to a man like David?

Tears threatened, and Kinsey took a long swig of her beer to steady her fading calm. She saw now how ridiculous it looked, how she had been holding on to this relationship that had been half past dead for so long. The fear of being alone had trumped her better judgment. Or maybe she had no clue what was best for her.

She knew now, or thought she did. Putting herself first—career, ice cream, orgasms, in that order—that's what she needed.

"Maybe I'm too hard to please," she said, immediately backtracking on her attitude of, *You go, girl*.

Luke gusted out a sigh. "Don't go all pity party on me, Kinsey. This dickhead screwed up, plain and simple. He should have done everything in his power to satisfy you. To make sure you knew how special you were." Leaning in, he cupped her jaw and swiped at her bottom lip with the pad of his thumb. "If you were mine, baby, I'd never let you forget that."

If you were mine . . . It wasn't fair of him to speak to her like that, not while she was feeling ditch low. Desperately, she dug for her indignation at being called "baby," but it was nowhere to be found. On his lips, that word made the broken woman in her feel treasured. Cherished.

What would it be like to be caught in the emotional crosshairs of a man like Luke Almeida? To belong to him, body and soul? The prospect warmed her some. Scared her more. With Luke, she suspected there would be no half measures.

Not like David, who took eight and a half years to pop the question. More fool her, she had let him set the pace of their relationship because she wasn't sure she deserved the attention of a man in such an exalted position. In her current hot mess, she wasn't sure she deserved the attention of any man, including the one sitting across from her.

The sickening flash of recrimination at David had her drawing back from Luke's touch. "You shouldn't say those things . . . it's too much."

He stared with unerring intensity, his gaze a million times steadier than her heartbeat. "Is it?"

"I—*we* have a job to do and we should be keeping it professional." *Preach it, sistah.* What had happened down on that beach with David only served to confirm what she'd known for some time: she was a loser in love and her career was all she had left. Jeopardizing it by having a fling with an assignment was suicidal.

His voice was a low rumble of sex. "You're a smart woman. I'm sure you've figured out by now that professional ain't my middle name." Abruptly, he stood and towered hugely over her, looking three times her size, and pissed to all hell at her. From his pocket, he extracted two twenties and threw them onto the table.

"C'mon."

"But I haven't finished my beer!" And he hadn't even touched his.

"Get that sweet ass of yours in gear, Kinsey, or I'm going to carry you out of here." He inclined his body, close enough for them to share a breath. "You don't want me to make a scene, not after all the good, *oh-so-professional* work you've done turning me into a heartthrob."

Growling because she knew he was right, and because she felt like growling, she stood and pounded toward the exit to the stairway. The man was a complete ass, with his *baby this* and *sweetheart that* and surliness that gave her whiplash. Well, she'd show *him* surly.

When she reached the bottom step, his fingers curled around her arm, and before she could jerk away, he had muscled her through the restroom door. She spun around to face him, grasping for outrage that immediately fizzled on seeing his face. His eyes blazed hard and true.

Instinctively, she stepped back, and her butt met the cool porcelain of the sink. It was one of those single restrooms with its own lock. Which he turned. The click set her heart thrashing like a wild animal struggling to escape her throat.

"Luke, people need to get in," she said in her most reasonable tone. Yes, let's be reasonable here. People needed to empty their bladders, and Luke Almeida was planning . . . well, she was unsure what exactly he was planning. But those feral eyes of his—oh, they told her it would be something wicked.

The air was drenched with masculine spice, aggression, and danger. In a split second, he was on her, swarming her senses, his hands stroking and inciting before settling at her hips. They fit just right. Everything about him fit. His Semper Fidelis tattoo gleamed on his chest and her jaw dropped to the undoubtedly filthy tile as if she was seeing that chest for the first time.

Kinsey, get a grip. It's just a chest!

"I think it's time you realized how goddamn sexy you are, Miss Taylor."

"But we—we can't. Did you not hear a word I said about keeping it prof—" She lost her train of thought because Luke's sandpaper-rough hands had started swirling tight, erotic circles on her back . . . her hips . . . her ass.

"I've—I've given up on men."

"Wait until tomorrow, baby." He nuzzled along the line of her jaw, his lips igniting volcanic heat across her skin. "Today, let this man take care of you the way you need." His hands kneaded her rear in a way that made her mindless with desire.

"I can take care of myself," she moaned, then added, "and my orgasms," in case her implication was unclear.

She felt the curve of his lips in a smile against her neck. "I don't doubt it, but why should you have to?"

"Luke, stop. You're already in enough trouble—"

But trouble was what found her when Luke's lips brutally claimed hers. His hand shaped her neck, his thumbs held her jaw in place for his assault. She surrendered, no fight left in her, no longer wanting to be the difficult woman. She let him work her mouth, slide his tongue inside, map the roof of her mouth. She let him use her.

He broke the kiss, his eyes hazy with a strange brew of lust and compassion. "That's okay, baby. Next time, I expect your full participation, but right now I'm drivin' this train."

Yes. She was so tired of trying to do it all, wear the pants and the skirt. Giving herself permission to submit was as arousing as anything Luke Almeida brought to the table.

He turned her so she faced the cracked mirror, its luster diminished but still bright enough to show her body's potent reaction to this astonishingly sexy man. Nipples a lot perkier than she felt, hair the wrong side of sexy tousled.

"You need to see how beautiful you are, Kinsey. How powerful."

Trailing a blunt hand along the border of her bikini bottoms, he tested the boundaries. She shuffled her feet apart. His grin turned disgracefully wicked.

"Do you want to direct?"

"No, just do it right, Luke. Make it good."

He bit down on her earlobe, a tender puncture to that sensitive flesh, then yanked her bikini bottoms halfway down her thighs so roughly she gasped at the contrast. Moisture flooded her sex at the thought of what would come next.

One strong forearm banded beneath her breasts while his other hand tunneled through her tawny curls, parting her swelling folds to where she was already shockingly hot and slick. Reaching up, she cupped the back of his head and set anchor. He kissed her wrist over her rocketing pulse.

"That's my girl," he whispered. "Hold on tight."

He slid a finger inside her.

Then, giving her the intimate stretch she needed, a mind-melting two.

"Fuck, you're so wet and tight. You really need this, don't you? You need me deep inside you, baby."

"Yes. God, yes." Every fluid thrust massaged her clit perfectly on the return, and increased the spirals of want low in her belly. The raging evidence of his own need jutted into her spine.

"There, right there." She grasped his hand and pressed it closer to where she needed it.

He chuckled. "Seems you can't resist taking charge."

Mind in a blur, she froze. That's what David had hated. Her assumption of the role of aggressor, her pleading for him to deliver more than he had to give.

The rules were so hard to follow.

"Don't stop, Kinsey. If you need to tell me what makes you feel good, do it. I'm yours to command."

Thoughts vaporized. Muscles dissolved. Desire flew loose in her core as those words smashed her senseless.

"I need . . ."

"What, baby? Tell me what you need."

This. You. Everything you have.

"Your fingers . . . your fingers spreading me. A little rougher than—" Oh! He followed her instructions, the callused sides of his rough-cast fingers abrading her sensitive folds as he plunged inside her.

"Like that?"

"And my breasts. Squeeze my nipples."

His meaty paw yanked away, then replaced, the triangle of fabric over her aching breast. He covered her easily, molding her soft flesh to his rough ministrations.

"Please, Luke," she begged. "More."

Another bite on her earlobe, a further pinch of her nipple, and he adapted quickly to her raw, desperate needs. An invisible thread of pleasure shot straight to her sex and produced another gush of pleasure on his hand.

The blatant look of male satisfaction on his face said he approved.

Faster, he rubbed against that taut bundle of nerves, drawing the blistering sensation to a peak. All she could do was writhe. And watch. And feel. His dark, cocoa skin against her gilded flesh heightened their contrasts, yet also showed how well they complemented each other. She stood cradled in his arms, half dressed, a sleazy mess, which made it filthier and sexier and so, so good.

"Need your mouth, Kinsey."

Angling her head, she offered herself up to his ruthless kiss. The thrusts of his tongue mimicked the possessive invasion below and spun her higher toward that place she was desperate to reach. Where no man could touch her. Hurt her. She was close, her moans rising in volume.

"That's it, baby," he growled. "Let go."

Pound. A loud noise pulled her out of her sex-crazed fog.

"Hey, people are waiting out here!"

"Luke," she gasped.

"Finish." With eyes so heated she wondered how the mirror was still solid, he held her gaze. Bold, resolute, compelling her to release. But it was gone. People would know what they were doing and her moans . . . she couldn't suppress them if she tried.

Another thump on the door shot a bolt of panic through her.

". . . come on, open up . . ."

"Finish, baby."

"I can't," she said, tears of frustration leaking from the corners of her eyes. On noodle legs, she collapsed her weight against him. "I'm sorry."

He moved his hand still soaked with her pleasure away from her swollen sex and held it to her mouth.

"Lick."

Oh. My. "God."

"Lick," he demanded.

This was outrageous. *He* was outrageous.

Yet.

She felt her lips parting, her mouth watering, something deliciously obscene switching on. Obeying him, she alternated long lewd licks with gentle kitten ones. Combined with her musky taste, Luke's bossy self-possession renewed the slippery warmth between her thighs and recharged her libido to dizzying heights.

"Now bite down and finish."

In a pleasure-stung haze, she bit down on the two fingers he placed lengthwise in her mouth. His other hand found her glistening sex, while against her ear, he whispered wicked words of encouragement. All the depraved things he wanted to do to her. Filthy promises she reveled in. Within seconds, she was bucking against him, riding long, shivering pulses of pleasure, her cries of release muffled against Luke's hand. Finally, she went spineless, safe in the knowledge he was sheltering her through the squall. They stayed that way for a few precious, breath-grabbing moments.

When she opened her eyes again, he had turned her to face him while he rearranged her clothing. So kindhearted, so unexpected. He laid his forehead against hers, his eyes dark with liquid heat.

"You are somethin' else, Kinsey," he whispered. "I could spend the rest of my life watching you come."

She closed her eyes against the perilous fondness she felt for him, until an angry thump against the door wrenched her eyelids apart and ushered in the reality she had suppressed during that brief moment of oblivion. The customers who needed to pee away the watered-down beer.

"Ready to face your public?" Luke's grin was pure evil. He was loving this. "I wonder how the woman who spends her life cleaning up after the bad behavior of others is going to get out of this pickle."

She slid a glance to the door. The barbarians were at the gate and she had just been serviced by Chicago's sexiest, *and most recognizable,* firefighter.

In the words of her boss, a PR-fucking-disaster.

"Do I look"—she chewed her lip—"like I just—"

"Had your world rocked? Oh yeah."

Her hands flew to her hair as if that could minimize the lover's flush on her cheeks or the desire-drunk lethargy of her limbs. The flutter in her chest turned into a full-scale flapping.

His eyes gleamed, smug with it. "You've done such a good job handling my reputation. Let's see how I do handling yours. On three . . . two . . ."

"Luke, I don't think . . ."

"One . . ." He threw open the door and cannoned through the waiting crowd, most of whom were too focused on the hard glory of Luke Almeida's chest to pay a passing glance to his disheveled, wholly satisfied companion. Assuredly, he pulled Kinsey with him toward the bar's exit until they broke into the safety of the sun.

"Made it!" he whooped, like he had just performed the most daring rescue.

He caught her incredulous stare and shrugged, the movement as good as a smile. So much for keeping it professional.

In comfortable silence, they walked back to the volleyball courts. Back to his family and her new friends and postorgasm reality, all while one phrase beat a tattoo in her head.

Luke Almeida, my hero.

CHAPTER TWELVE

Kinsey was quiet on the way back to their spot on the beach, and Luke wondered if she had regrets about what had happened. All that need and messiness she had bottled up during her years with Dave the Douche had exploded like a firecracker in that restroom.

Under Luke's command.

Kinsey coming all over his hand had been a sight to behold, an experience he wouldn't forget anytime soon. As for the Douche, he might be a piece of work, but he had one thing going for him. If he'd been less of a D-bag, then Luke would not be in this situation. One he was liking more and more each second.

Back at the courts, they found only Wy left, sitting and staring out at the lake. Too often, Luke had tried to get inside his brother's head but to no avail. However, today, Wy's know-it-all lip twitch coupled with an eyebrow lift made his thoughts as clear as the sky over their heads.

Luke responded with his own patented look of, *Fuck the hell off.*

"Larry's been on," Wy said. "You need to call him

back." He squinted at Kinsey. "Your phone's been ringin', too. *1812 Overture*."

Kinsey fished out her phone from her beach bag. "It's the mayor."

While she wandered a few feet away to get some privacy, Luke called his godfather back. Two minutes later, he had hung up and so had Kinsey. A few electrifying moments ticked over as their gazes locked.

"The commissioner said I'm back on the job, because apparently, the mayor is pleased with my level of cooperation. You know anything about that?"

She opened her mouth. Closed it again.

"Kinsey . . ."

"You're overestimating my influence—"

"Don't believe I am." The few feet between them vanished, and then she was in his arms while he kissed her fiercely. "I'm thankful, baby. Truly, I am."

She blushed, sliding a glance at Wy, who was still in full-on smirk. "It's where you belong. I just made sure they knew that. We still have the community party, but the part of the assignment involving you specifically is finished."

They stared at each other like idiots. Like horny idiots. Because now there was nothing to stop what came next.

"Probably should still keep it professional, though," he teased, lobbing her mantra back at her.

She grinned. "Agreed. I expect to be serviced very professionally indeed, Mr. Almeida."

Chuckling, he lifted her off the ground to the tune of her gasp and held her tight. He was a little bit crazy about this woman.

Wy sniffed as he stood. "Anyone need a ride? No? Okay. Later."

Luke parked the truck outside her place on Erie and flipped on the hazards. Kinsey turned, a wicked smile hooking the corner of her mouth. "There's a parking garage around the corner."

"Can't. I have to report in. Larry said I'm needed on shift tonight."

Kinsey's naughty smile quickly faded into a skeptical frown.

"The holiday weekend is different from the usual," he explained. "They need all hands on deck. Have to be in by six and I'll be off at eight tomorrow morning."

The implications of that hung in the air, so he went for the kill shot.

"I can be inside you by eight sixteen."

She gulped, the slender column of her throat bulging. "That sounds very . . . precise."

"It'll take me fifteen minutes to drive and park—"

"And then wham bam, it's the Fourth of July down here?" She gestured to her lap and he couldn't help but laugh. Nice to see her sense of humor was intact, especially as she'd had such a shitty time of it earlier during that run-in with her ex. He liked to think that orgasm helped. However, she also made an excellent point.

"When you put it like that, it might be better if I come over later in the day."

She shook her head. "No. What you did for me back there, Luke—I want to make you feel that good and I refuse to wait." Along his thigh, she slid a hand over the fabric of his shorts. Any higher and he was going to take her here, traffic be damned.

But joking aside, he didn't want to do her quickly. He wanted her slow and sweet, between cool, crisp sheets while he teased those sexy moans from her. Maybe a few screams.

"The thing about fires, Kinsey, is that it does something to me. To all of us. Around the Fourth is one of our busiest times. Lots of calls with barbecue and firework accidents, and when I finish my shift I'll be all hopped up on adrenaline. Horny as hell, too, and I usually need to take the edge off quickly."

"Are you warning me about your premature ejaculation problem?"

He slanted her his most condemning look. She took it like a champ.

"It's not quite that bad, but I'm so hot for you that it's gonna be close. I could always take a shower, take care of business before I saw you. That way I can do you right. Otherwise, I'll want to fuck you really fast and then I'll probably fall asleep right on top of you."

"Wow, you're really selling it, Almeida."

Shit, he sounded like an idiot who had no control over his dick. But he knew that one look at her, all sleep-softened and beautiful tomorrow morning— like when she woke up hungover in his bed—and he'd want to nail her to the wall. They wouldn't even make it to the bedroom, and he wanted to show her every way it could be good when he was balls-deep in her honeyed heat.

She leaned in, skated a tongue over her lower lip. No help, whatsoever.

"So you'd take a shower at the station, jerk off

on city property, and then come on over, ready to shamrock my world?"

"You make it sound so romantic."

Her soft breath warmed his lips. "When the clock strikes eight tomorrow morning, you will come straight to me. Do not shower. Do not pass go. The only thing you will be doing is *me*, Luke. I want to be the one who takes the edge off. And you'd better be able to handle it."

His shorts were not loose enough for this. "You're killin' me here, baby. Not sure I can last."

"Oh, you'll last. Because while you might rock a good impression of a guy who can't control his passions, I think you're the opposite. I think you like to be in control of the situation with your family, your job, your sex life. And even though you can't stand to lose, this is the one race where coming second will make you happy. You're going take care of me and then I'm going to take care of you."

She had him pegged. He loved how she cut through his crap with those sharp eyes and even sharper observations.

"I'm pretty sure I already took care of you, Ms. Greedy."

"I am greedy, I want it all." She patted his erection with that hand she used to punch her ex, a sexy sliver of a smile on her lips when he expanded under her touch.

"I want *you*, Luke. And now there's nothing stopping me from having you."

She brushed her lips across his in a tantalizing sweep, that wicked mouth of hers an instrument of torture. Unable to resist, he cupped her face and ravished her for a few brain-destroying seconds. Then he pushed her back.

"Go. Now, Kinsey. Or I won't be responsible for what happens next."

"Luke . . ."

"I will fuck you right here, right now if you don't get out of the truck."

"Be still, my heart." After grabbing her bag, she opened the car door, checked for oncoming traffic, and skipped to the sidewalk.

Look back, baby. Gimme one sweet look.

Over her shoulder, she threw him a smile and a wave, and he flat-out nearly came in his shorts. This was going to be the longest short shift ever.

"Engine 6 and truck 53 are on the scene of an occupied two-story ordinary, single-family, approximately twenty-four by forty. We've got a working fire."

Luke radioed in the report as the truck halted halfway down the block on Leavitt, about a mile away from the station. Flames curled like greedy fingers from one window on the second floor, the smoke billowing from the first still gray. The crowd viewing the spectacle made no moves to get to safety, but then he supposed this counted as entertainment.

Fourth of July weekend. Amateur hour, filled with the ranks of the trashed and the stupid. It might have started with a splash of lighter fluid on the grill or an illegal cherry bomb in the backyard. Whatever, it was now his problem.

"Honda Civic blocking the hydrant, Lieutenant," Derek called over from the other side of the street.

Phelan had started in on that lieutenant shit the minute Luke showed up at six, already feeling a hundred feet tall after those precious moments with Kinsey. Oh yeah, and the fact that he was a freakin' firefighter again. Gruffly pleased that Luke was back in the rotation and that the "YouTube probation shit" was over, Venti had assigned him to fill in for the B platoon officer who was on vacation. As far as the crew was concerned, Luke was God tonight. At least until the battalion chief made it on scene.

Luke side-eyed Wyatt. There were ways of doing this without damaging a good citizen's property, but . . .

"On it." His brother headed over with the Halligan and made that Honda owner regret parking his piece-of-shit car within fifteen feet of a water source. Thirty seconds later, the hose was punched through the now nonexistent side windows and screwed into the hydrant.

Don't fuck with the CFD.

Luke began barking out orders. "Phelan! You're on the pipe. Take two hundred feet off the side and meet me at the front door." Rapid fire growth in an occupied dwelling called for urgent tactics: quick water from the engine's five-hundred-gallon tank into the attack hose line. It would be empty in two minutes, hence the hydrant hookup, but putting wet stuff on the red stuff ASAP was the priority.

Luke's crew got to work. Murphy pushed the bug-eyed bystanders back. While Phelan readied to hand off the charged hose line, Luke strapped on his mask, ensuring the seal was airtight and the air regulator on his bottle was turned on. As acting officer, Luke's job was to go in to investigate what they were up against, knowing that simultaneously his crew was moving the truck's aerial ladder into position to gear up for roof ventilation.

One minute later, Luke was back outside with a grab-and-go, a badly burned civilian who had tried climbing to the second floor where her son was sleeping.

"He's still in there!" the woman screamed, her voice splintering in panic. "My Robbie!"

"I know, ma'am." He passed her off to Gordie, the EMT, and spoke up to counter the sound-muting effects of the mask. "We're going to get him out."

Wyatt and Phelan looked to him for the assessment. "First floor's clear. It's really rollin' on the second and stairs are already impassable. Seven-year-old kid in the front bedroom. Where are we with ventilation?"

A shriek fractured the air. Glass shattered like hail to the ground. All eyes fired upward to where a wild-haired kid stood with a telescope taller than he was. He dropped it to the floor, its job as window breaker done.

That took care of the ventilation and made CFD's job ten times more dangerous. The fire would burn hotter and faster now that it had a new source of fuel: oxygen-rich air. Giver of life, but in this case, bringer of death.

"It's too hot!" Robbie placed his hands on the shard-laden windowsill before drawing back, visibly shocked at his cut-up palms.

"Stay still, kid," Luke called out. "We're comin' for you." Heavy black smoke poured out of the top half of the double-hung window. A hundred more degrees and the whole room would be totally engulfed in flames.

"He's got a minute, maybe two at best," Wyatt said.

At that instant, Battalion Chief Lonny Morgan swung onto the scene, ready to run the fire as Incident Command. The guy had a mouth as sharp as his chin, but he knew his job. About a hundred feet down the street, a local news van was perched, drooling for disaster. Wonderful.

"Report," Morgan barked as he hopped out of the buggy.

"Wy, you and Derek get in there with the hose and slow that bastard down. Buy me some time," Luke ordered, expecting that Morgan would pick up the specifics quickly.

In thirty seconds Luke was up that aerial ladder faster than a chimp on steroids. Eighty percent of runs these days were EMT calls: motor vehicle accidents, pin-ins, cardiac arrest at a nursing home, dehydration at a summer festival. Of the fire calls, it was mostly suppression and no rescue. People usually escaped on their own or the fire was too far gone by the time CFD made it on scene. Seven years on the job, and Luke had made only six rescues, including the woman he had pulled out three minutes ago. Beck had five, Gage had three, Wyatt had them all beat with eight, the house record. Alex had zilch. Firefighters can go decades without a rescue to call their own.

On the way up the ladder, the already dicey situation took a turn to shit: the kid disappeared from the window, likely overcome by the thick black smoke now pushing out of the opening.

"Robbie! Fire Department, call out!"

Nothing but the distant crackle of burning paint. Of death approaching.

Luke hauled himself into the room through the broken window, testing his footing in case he encountered the kid. But all he hit against was a large solid object—the telescope. Visibility was zero, the air so hot Luke started to feel the burn on his ears through his Nomex hood, a sure sign that he was in too deep.

"Robbie!"

Dropping to the floor where the heat was less intense, Luke started a catlike crawl, feeling his way to the door. In a smoke-filled room with senses diminished and adrenaline competing with reason, the space always felt vast, though it might be no more than eight feet square.

With thick gloves, distinguishing a table leg from a kid's can be tough. He grabbed what felt like a drafting desk. That sizzle in his ears only intensified with every hard-fought foot of floor covered.

He found an edge and Brailled his way upward for a couple of feet. The door. The damn open door. He swung it shut.

Instantly the temperature dropped and his visibility improved, the air more charcoal than squid ink. *Jesus, kid, where the fuck are you?* If he'd left the room, he was a goner, because no one was making it off that landing alive.

First check was behind the door he'd just closed. Ignoring it was a rookie mistake. No kid.

"Robbie!"

Kids usually gravitated to the bed, thinking the fire and smoke won't find them there, but not this one. Nothing over, nothing under. That left . . .

Score! A sneakered foot poked out of a half-open closet. Pulling the door out with one hand, Luke grabbed the limp kid from inside.

"Robbie, can you hear me?"

The kid moaned, and Luke's heart, already pumping overtime, kicked his ribs with joy and gratitude. His seventh grab, and no save had ever felt sweeter. Damn, this day just rocked.

"Come on, kid. Let's get outta here."

CHAPTER THIRTEEN

Despite a restless night, her dreams steamy and studded with Luke, Kinsey was showered, shaved, and caffeinated by 7:30 a.m. She had already ignored a "too early for God, but not too early for the mayor" call on the grounds it was Independence Day, and that went double for the chains that bound them. Unless city hall was burning with him in it, she didn't want to know. On hearing Eli's voice mail asking if she'd like to stop by the barbecue he was hosting for a few friends (assumption: you must be lonely), she was glad she'd let the call go. It would be hard to say no to him personally and, with Luke on his way, she'd rather play the day by ear.

Not unlike this entire thing that was happening between them.

Casual relationships were not her thing. She had started dating David in college, but they had parted when he did his residency in New York, the long-distance thing too much pressure. If they were meant to be, they would get together again. Postresidency, he ended up as an attending at UCSF (his third choice, by the way) and they picked right up where they left off. But for the three years they were on a break, she had dated a couple of nice guys in San Francisco.

A lawyer who did pro bono work. A guy who ran a software start-up in Silicon Valley. The operative word being *dated*. Three dinners before they got to second base, two more before they saw her special-occasion lingerie. Sleeping with a man based on little more than animal attraction was not her usual.

No one could mistake what Kinsey and Luke were doing for dating. This was a down-and-dirty affair.

Kinsey tried to assess the flutter in her stomach. Was she apprehensive because this was not standard Kinsey behavior and she felt a little slutty, or because she wished there was more to it? Luke Almeida was a man of many faces: the hothead, the family stalwart, the guy who gave back, the hero. But ultimately, he was a man who knew his way around a woman's body without needing GPS. As attractive as those other facets were, she needed to remember what this was about. Sex. Pure and simple.

And yet, something did not agree with her sensible, reasoned conclusion. Something nagged at her brain, insisting to be heard.

It was those godforsaken flip-flops.

After she had pulled a Luke Almeida on David at North Avenue Beach, her fantasy-made-flesh had wrapped her in his arms, then kneeled before her in the sand to take care of her feet. The solicitude didn't end there. She flexed her hand, enjoying the memory—and not just because she had gone batshit on her ex. What followed had lodged its way into her bruised heart. In his practical manner, Luke had taken care of her stinging knuckles with ice, and later, her other desperate needs with fire.

In all her time with David, not once had she felt

cherished like that. Ten years together off and on, planning a life on the corner of picture and perfect. Throughout their relationship, she couldn't recall a single moment that rivaled the tenderness Luke Almeida had shown her yesterday.

Yeah, dating was so overrated. Brain-scrambling orgasms with the inked thug fireman were the way to go. Glad they got *that* cleared up.

An incoming FaceTime call on her laptop saved her from further navel gazing: 5:45 a.m. in San Rafael, and the Colonel was on the line. Always an early riser, her father still lived life like he was on the base at the Presidio back in the good ol' days. Better known as the Cold War.

"Hi, Dad."

"Happy Fourth, punkin."

She smiled at his weathered face upon hearing the endearment. As much as she liked to present to the world as the take-charge career woman, hearing her father's soft words made her squishy. "You, too, Dad. Everyone coming over for the cookout-slash-animal sacrifice?"

Retired army physician and colonel Jackson M. Taylor IV spent his days coming up with new ways to flavor chunks of dead cow. Kinsey's vegetarianism was a source of playful conflict between them.

Her father chuckled. "Cole and Tina are stopping by with the girls. Jax is bringing some flibbertigibbet he met at a bar."

"He's not with Alison anymore?"

"No, that's who he's bringing. Alison."

She rolled her eyes. "They've been dating for a year, Dad."

"Until he puts a ring on her finger, she's only temporary." Thirty-five years ago, then Lieutenant Jackson Taylor IV, on leave from Okinawa, had wooed Kinsey's teacher mother by showing up at her first-grade classroom to sweep her off her feet. The Colonel's views on love and romance were clear: find woman, claim woman, marry woman.

Needless to say, David had never measured up.

Her father seemed to realize that his comment might be considered insensitive to his recently dumped daughter. "Sorry, Kinsey. I wasn't thinking. How're you holding up?"

In other words, had she collapsed into a self-loathing mess? Not quite. After the farce with David yesterday, she really should be feeling pretty ropy, but she was surprisingly okay. Revenge orgasms for the win.

"Not bad. I've met some—" *Steady there, girl.* "People. Making friends, you know."

"That's great, Kinsey, but . . ." He trailed off, his hesitancy surprising her. The Colonel did not usually mince words.

"What's up, Dad?"

"Now might be a good time to reconsider things. You got great scores on the LSAT and you know I'd help you out. Berkeley's law program is one of the best."

"I love what I do."

He shook his head disapprovingly. "Working with crooked politicians? How can you get any job satisfaction out of that, punkin?"

This tired old argument had been making the rounds for seven years. In a family of overachievers like the Taylors, her ambitions were far too small for highly motivated military men, physicians, and lawyers. At times like this, she wished her mother, with her softening influence, was still around. She had died when Kinsey was eight, leaving Kinsey in a cauldron of overbearing men. Character building, but exhausting.

"If I was working with a crooked politician back in California, would that make you feel better? I've got some feelers out to see if Max Fordham needs someone for his campaign." She had interned with Max while getting her degree, when he was still a small-time San Francisco councilman. Word was out that he was considering a run for state senate—and she wanted to be in on that.

She could feel her father's attitude adjustment all the way from the Bay. He'd tolerate her cozying up to corrupt politicos if it meant seeing her more regularly.

"Kinsey, I'd love to have you here every Sunday lunch, eating the big steak I grill for you."

She laughed. "How can a salad lover resist?"

Her intercom buzzed and she checked the time on her laptop. Only 8:06, but her heart thudded insanely fast. It had to be him. Luke.

"Hey, Dad, I've got to go—um, delivery."

"On the Fourth?"

"Give my love to everyone. And eat two steaks for me." With her father's chuckle echoing in her ears, she headed to the door to let in the man who was about to set her body on fire. She'd be having her own cookout right here in her apartment.

"Do you smell smoke?"

The woman in the elevator up to Kinsey's apartment wrinkled her nose and stared pointedly at Luke.

He cleared his throat, flashed his pearly whites, and proceeded to lie his ass off. "No, ma'am, I don't."

Momentarily thrown by his politeness, she squinted, then clutched her tiny yapper of a dog to her low-hanging bosom. Mercifully, she elected to stay on her side of the car, because if she were to get any closer, she'd smell smoke all right. On his clothes, in his hair, whispering from every pore.

It had been one helluva night. When oh when would people realize that splashing kerosene on charcoal was not the way to get a nice, healthy blaze going on the grill? But then nobody ever called the fire department for doing something smart. He supposed he should be grateful for the job security.

Saving that kid, though—there was something both elating and humbling about it. After the shit storm of the last couple of weeks, he felt renewed again.

Might also have something to do with Kinsey. With her, he just *felt* again.

At the twelfth floor, the woman left with her dog, but not before they both treated him to a suspicious glare. Only four more floors to go and the excitement was heightening in his chest. *Th-thunk. Th-thunk.*

The elevator stopped and the doors parted. Two steps out. Look left, look right.

Hot damn.

Kinsey stood at the entrance to her apartment, three doors down. There was highfalutin art on the hallway walls and plush carpeting underfoot, but the details were fuzzy because all he could see was her.

"Mr. Almeida."

The way she said that, rolled it over her tongue,

pumped an extra shot of blood to his groin. As did her outfit, a Berkeley tee, and that was about it. It hit her thighs at butt-skimming level and all he could think was, *Turn around, baby. Show me that heart-shaped ass of yours.*

"Hey, sweetheart."

"Tough night?"

"No more than usual." He locked his arms around her perfect ass and hoisted her up around him. Kissed her slow and deep. He had missed her taste. "I really should take a shower."

She tunneled her fingers through his hair, coming away with ash and grime.

"Shower later. Right now, I want to smell what you do on my body. I want to smell what means so much to you on my skin."

Those words rendered him mute—and unbearably aroused.

He carried her inside and closed the door with his foot. The possibilities tripped through his lust-mushed brain . . . against the door, on the floor, on the . . . yes, the counter. He sat her down beside her laptop. Knowing Kinsey, he bet she'd been working before he arrived.

Peeling off her shirt with a languor that surprised him considering the speed of his depraved thoughts, he took a moment to appreciate her body as every delicious inch was revealed. He had washed his hands but missed a couple of black streaks on his knuckles. He grazed the pink buds of her breasts, gratified when they dirtied up under his touch. His mark.

She tugged at his tee and he pulled it off with one hand.

"How did you get this?" Her cool hand stroked the scar tissue on his shoulder.

"Dumb move during my rookie days. Kind of mistake I wouldn't make now."

She laid feather-soft kisses over the sign of his stupidity. "Tell me."

"Two months out of the Quinn—that's the Firefighter Academy—and I—"

"Hello . . . Kinsey?" A strange male voice boomed God-like into the room.

"Oh shit!" She slammed the lid shut on the laptop. Yeah, the laptop.

A shiver of dread curled through Luke's overheated blood. The Fourth, a time for connecting with friends and family. Please, Christ Jesus, don't let that be—

"Sweetheart, tell me that was an old college pal. Or your personal shoe shopper. Or the assistant to your personal shoe shopper."

Both hands covered her flushing face. "That was my father. I was talking to him before you arrived and I must have forgotten to end the call."

Unable to help himself, Luke burst out laughing. Fucking priceless. "You are determined to destroy your reputation, PR princess."

She looked like she was going to slap him. Then she did. Well, more of a punch to his shoulder.

"Not funny!" In a mad scramble, she pulled on the shirt she had been wearing pre-strip, forcing him to agree with her assessment wholeheartedly. A not-naked Kinsey was not funny at all.

She bumped him aside with her hip, then took a deliberate moment to compose herself and arrange the laptop so Luke was out of the frame. With a couple of shallow breaths, she flipped it open and redialed.

"Hi, Dad. Ah . . . again."

"Hey, punkin, sorry about that. I was getting ready to call your brother in Park City. Realized sort of late that the previous connection was still up."

An awkward pause joined forces with a downright uncomfortable one.

"So," her father finally said. "Package delivered okay?"

The old man sounded amused, thank God, so Luke felt safe in raising an eyebrow in Kinsey's direction. Too soon, apparently. She blasted him with a look of outright censure.

"Yes, Dad. Safe and sound." Seeming to come to a decision, with an exasperated wave, she adjusted the laptop to face Luke. A white-haired man with bushy eyebrows and a strong jaw stared out from the screen. "Luke, this is my father, Retired Colonel Jackson Taylor IV. Dad, this is Luke Almeida. He's—"

"—a Devil Dog," her father finished.

That's right. Luke was shirtless with his Semper Fidelis chest tattoo on display.

In the apartment of the daughter of a retired colonel.

At 0800 hours on the Fourth of July.

Kinsey's crafty smile told him she was back on top. *Luke, meet my father, the tough-as-nickel-steak, all-American hero who could happily arrange to have a Tomahawk cruise missile shot up your ass before breakfast.*

"Former Devil Dog, sir. Discharged in '07. First

lieutenant, 2/24, Chicago's Own," Luke said, referring to his Marine Corps service as part of the Second Battalion, Twenty-fourth Marines, also known as the Mad Ghosts.

"You boys held it together in the Triangle of Death back in '04. What are you doing now you're stateside?"

"Fire Department. After Iraq, it's a picnic."

Retired Colonel Taylor laughed knowingly. "I can believe that. Good to meet you, Luke."

"Sir." Man-to-man nod.

"Bye, Dad. For real this time." She shut the laptop definitively and went back to the desperate face holding. "That did not just happen. What a disaster."

"Nah, he liked me."

"Of course he did. You guys have a million things in common." A frown puckered her brow. It bothered her that he and her father might be alike in any way.

Why, this just got better and better.

He led her by the hand to the sofa, a bland piece in an apartment that was sterile and impersonal in the way of these short-term accommodations. No photos, no plants on life support, no attempts to make it homey. That she hadn't settled in or rented a more permanent solution frosted him a bit, but he warmed right up again when he remembered where they had been headed a few moments ago.

She sat down, her eyes wide, her mouth delectably mobile.

He sat beside her. "Now, where were we before we were so hilariously interrupted?"

"We were giving my father an eyeful of his only daughter about to be debauched."

"By the big bad wolf . . ." With downright debauchery in mind, he pulled up the hem of her shirt all the way over her head, leaving her hair beautifully tousled.

"With my smoke-smudged hands . . ."

Which he now used to peel off her panties. Cute pink ones, like sexy shorts.

"On our nation's birthday."

He now put his filthy, un-American hands to the task of laying her flat against the cushions and opening her up to him.

"To life, liberty . . ."

". . . and the pursuit of orgasms," she picked up, flashing that naughty smile he adored.

Ah, finally she was getting into the holiday spirit. He kissed her breast, licking over the smoky smear he had imprinted there. He suckled, taking long, slow sips of her nipples, enjoying her gasps of pleasure, hoarding them for later fantasy time. Then he recalled that she liked a little roughness, and he nipped her.

"Luke," she moaned, his name on her lips a prayer. Her hands found his hair and she held him fast, encouraging him to suck deeper. The quiver in his balls picked up.

Raising his head, he met her lusty gaze. "I thought about you all night, Kinsey. Couldn't wait to see you like this. At my mercy, wild for me." He applied an open-mouth kiss to her belly. "I rushed out this morning, floored it in my truck." More kisses on her silky soft skin, the connection between them ratcheting up with every motion south on her body. "In my hurry to get here, I didn't even eat. And I never leave the firehouse without fueling up."

Her fretful glance slipped to the kitchenette. "You want me to make you something?" Asked in a tone of, *You've got to be shittin' me*.

"Yeah, I do." He parted her legs and draped them over his shoulders. The view was spectacular, all pretty pink and juicy succulent. The scent of her arousal hiked his pleasure higher and his mouth watered with the need to take his fill. To bury his face in her heaven.

"I want you to make some of that honey so I can feed off your sweetness."

She squirmed against the sofa, seeking relief. "This is all for you, Luke. I need your mouth on me. Now."

Bending to his enviable task, he licked her already soaking seam. God, her taste. He could happily live and die here. Against his tongue, the pulse of her beat like a heart, and she made those sexy sounds he had enjoyed so much yesterday. He fed on the hot silk of her sex, every throb like an infusion of fire into his blood.

Around his ears, her thighs clenched, and he redoubled his efforts, licking her long, thrusting his tongue deep, nibbling when he realized she was close. Holding off would make it better for her, so he told his balls to behave. Little fuckers could wait their turn. His woman needed his A game.

He gave her his all. Loved her with his hungry mouth, tested her limits, tested his own. Because a woman as amazing as Kinsey would expect no less. Deserved no less.

And maybe he wanted to hear her beg.

Twenty seconds later, she screamed his name, followed by *pleasepleaseplease* and some very vulgar language. Achievement unlocked.

Finally, after taking her to the edge and pulling back too many times to count, he brought her home. The woman was so loud he wouldn't be surprised if that yapper dog on the twelfth floor was climbing the walls.

"Okay, sweetheart?"

Not a peep.

"Kinsey?"

"Can't move," she finally gasped out. "Orgasm paralysis."

He chuckled. Bonus points.

"Bedroom?" He scooped up her limp body and held her close. She buried her face in his neck, and the sweet vulnerability of that almost undid him.

"Behind you," she mumbled. "Second door."

As he carried her to the bedroom, a swell of protectiveness surged through him, like how he had felt yesterday when she was under attack from her ex. Taking care of her physical needs was one thing, and he supposed it was nice to know she needed him when she was at her lowest. It was a firefighter's lot and something he went through every day. He ran in when the rats and roaches were running out. People needed him when the shit hit the fan, when they'd screwed up and it was all about to come tumbling down.

For a strong woman like Kinsey to need him when she was down was something. But wouldn't it be something if she needed him when she was up? Not just the bad times, but the good times, too.

Where the hell was this coming from? Clearly, his brain was on the last train to Sleepville.

He lay her down on the bed and watched her honey

blondeness spill over pristine, white sheets he was about to dirty with his smoke-marked body and grimy hair. But he no longer cared about keeping this pure and sterile. Kinsey wanted this. She wanted the sweat, the calluses, the guy who could give it to her as hard as she needed. Maybe it wasn't the same as wanting *him*, the man behind the billboard, but he'd take it because he was desperate for her. He shucked his jeans, and of its own volition, his hand went to his cock because damn, it needed attention. Was weeping for it.

From his pocket, he pulled a condom, tore the wrapper, and positioned it over the tip of his dick. It was so sensitive to the touch that he closed his eyes a moment.

"You planning to keep this a solo operation, Luke?"

His eyes snapped open. "Just doing a before check. I've a feeling you're going to work me so hard my dick won't be recognizable after you've gotten through with me."

A flash of mischief tugged at her mouth. She removed the condom from his hand and placed it on the nightstand.

"Kinsey, I won't—"

"Me, neither. But I'd like to touch you skin to skin, first." Her slender hand captured him and squeezed. "Is that okay?"

If it wasn't, what would that say? That he couldn't take a little stroking and fisting and—Jesus H. Macy, she licked the underside of his shaft and his balls went into nuclear meltdown.

"'S fine," he managed to choke out.

She continued with teasing licks and rougher

strokes, perfectly timed to bring him close and then haul him back from the brink. Finally, he'd had enough and he drew back. There was no way he was getting off outside rather than in.

"Time to do this my way, sweetheart."

He sheathed himself, and covering his body with hers, settled between her beautiful thighs. One thrust, maybe two would be all it would take to send them both over—and yeah, she would be coming and screaming his name again—but he liked the leisurely way they were going about this. He also liked the vulnerable look that came over her as he notched his cock at her slick opening.

"Kinsey, you are all woman."

A soft sound left her throat, a whimper of appreciation for *his* appreciation of her and her many parts. Strong, soft, ballsy, tender. The complete package, and any guy would be lucky to be in this position.

He rolled on his back, and in one fluid movement, pulled her down on his aching shaft.

Or in this position.

She had no witty comeback, and he was done with the back-and-forth that had characterized their relationship so far. In this bed, it was just a man and a woman who wanted each other beyond all reason. As he watched her looming over him like a golden angel, all thoughts of the past and future fled, leaving this soul-melting instant of honesty. Of now. Her hazel eyes held his as she moved up and down, feeling out her pleasure, her body softening with each smooth motion.

And right then, he knew he could hold it forever, because this was a forever kind of moment.

But it seemed Kinsey had other ideas. "It's okay, Luke. You can . . . you can let go now."

"Did you just give me permission to come?"

In answer, she squeezed those velvet muscles around his cock. "You don't have to take care of me. You already did."

Gripping her hips, he stayed her sensual rock. "Baby, don't deny it. That greedy little pussy of yours needs more of what I've got."

Her mouth fell slack with desire and a low moan escaped her throat. This lusty woman of his liked a little dirty talk.

"Luke, I know you're close."

"And I know I can hold this for as long as I need to. I was a Marine, for Christ's sake." Were they really arguing about this? And was he really enjoying it?

She laughed, low and raspy. "If you were a Navy SEAL, maybe, my expectations might be higher—hey!" she squealed as he gently pinched her world-class ass to punish her insolence.

"This isn't quid pro quo, Kinsey. You need more, I've got it to give." Damn, he would give her anything. He leaned up and cupped her jaw to let her know he meant business. "My body is yours. My cock is yours. Use it to take what you need."

Those words seemed to affect her like none he had uttered so far. Her eyes flew wide with emotion. Her lower lip trembled. Never taking her scorching gaze from him, she clutched the headboard with one hand. He gentled her toward him, and together they sought the angle that would hit her spot just right. The friction she needed at the juncture of their slick, naked bodies. She didn't have to do it alone. He would take care of her.

It felt like he'd been put on Earth for this very purpose.

"Luke . . . that feels so good. So . . . oh, God."

Inclining forward, he took her inviting breast in his mouth, and the full-throated sound she made almost sent him over the edge. Hell, he hadn't even begun to explore the mysteries of her body, all those sensitive places waiting for the right touch. What only he could give her.

"Yes, Luke. More."

He glanced a thumb over her clit, a light pressure that sent her bucking like a rodeo queen. Giving her the more she needed. That they both needed, because what was good for her was fucking transcendent for him. The intensity ratcheted up, coiling the pressure in his balls, and damn, if she didn't come soon—

She broke on a scream, her snug, hot channel milking him to near release.

He flipped her over and entwined his fingers with hers. Her hands were small, strong. Those tiger-striped eyes, lust-blown with all that unleashed passion, stared back at him. Begging him to let go and love her as only he could.

He drove in once. Twice. The equivalent of a flashover ignited every cell and he came with such force that starbursts exploded behind his eyelids.

Sweet Christ, that was amazing.

Several perfect moments passed and he knew that if he didn't leave her now, he would fall asleep right there in the cradle of her body. So tempting to let that hook of hers impale itself deeper. Mustering a half ounce of energy, he rolled off and panted his way back to an even draw.

Don't close your eyes. Do not close your eyes.

"Should go," he murmured into the darkness. Yep, he had closed his eyes. He needed to get up, get dressed, and get gone, because it was close to nine in the morning and Kinsey probably had stuff to do that did not involve him.

His cock twitched as gentle hands rolled off the condom and a cool sheet landed on his hot, damp skin.

"Kinsey, I . . ." But the words faded, replaced with the heavenly sensation of soft, naked woman curling up into his side.

"Sleep, Luke," she whispered.

With barely enough consciousness left for one last thought, he said, "Your father likes me."

Nothing from Kinsey on that, so he guessed she was out. His eyelids fell, dragged shut by the twin weights of comfort and repletion, but then he heard a growl followed by "Oh, shut up."

If it wasn't perfect before, it sure as hell was now.

On a featherbed of satisfaction, and with a smile cracking his face in half, Luke slipped away into a dreamless slumber.

Resting her shoulder against the door to her bedroom, Kinsey drank in the sight of the long, lean, muscled male lying facedown across her bed. The sheet she had placed so lovingly over Luke's tired, sexed-out body over four hours ago had fallen to reveal the spectacular curvature of his ass.

So, maybe she had pulled it down a few inches

about thirty minutes before. She was only human, and the man was the most delicious specimen of masculine perfection she had ever seen.

Touched.

Smelled.

Kinsey slipped a strand of her hair under her nose. The scent of smoke made her mouth water, conjuring up memories of Luke's hard body moving inside her. The next time she burned toast she was going to have a freaking orgasm.

As if sensing her dirty thoughts, Luke turned over, twisting his body in the sheet. Oh my. The circus had come to town, the big-top tent at full mast.

She really should wake him up. No doubt he had things to do on the holiday. Family stuff. Important errands. She really should not be standing here, reveling in the pornographic view.

His hand slipped under the sheet and—*holy wow*—stroked his afternoon wood.

"Damn," she purred.

His eyes flicked open and sleepy confusion gave way to sharp-eyed awareness. Didn't move his hand, though. Just kept it there, at the ready.

"What time is it?" he asked, sleep-hoarse.

"About one. I was coming in to wake you." After she'd ogled him for another hour or five.

"You should have woken me sooner so I could get out of your hair."

"I figured you could sleep here just as comfortably as you would at home." In the bedroom he used to share with his wife. Annoyed that her mind had even gone there, she added, "And the sleep after sex tends to be the best."

"Especially when the sex is that incredible."

Assurance she hadn't thought she needed calmed her racing pulse. It *had* been incredible. Not just that, but fun and bawdy and filled with unexpected generosity. Luke Almeida was a giver, in so many ways.

Undeniable intimacy stretched between them while they both considered the incredible sex. And just in case there were any doubts about how fantastic it had been, his hand began to move under the sheet. A slow, rhythmic stroke that put a hitch in her breathing.

"If you want to take a shower and . . ." Eat, talk, keep pumping that gorgeous piece of equipment she needed inside her now.

"Come here," he said, his voice sexy-serious.

She moved toward him, noting with satisfaction that certain previously underused muscles ached pleasantly. Soreness had never felt so sensuous. She sat at the edge of the bed.

"Closer," he said, his eyes dark and hooded. He sat up to meet her halfway.

The sheet dropped. Her jaw dropped with it. The man was simply magnificent—and magnificently erect. She squeezed her thighs together.

He noticed. Smirked. "This is all for you if you're good, baby."

"And if I'm bad?"

"Bad girls get it harder. Now, don't make me come over there."

"Maybe I want to be bad."

With those quick-as-lightning reflexes that kept him safe on the job, he pulled her into the cage of his strong arms. "How's the hand, killer?"

She made a fist in mock threat. "Stay on my good side, Almeida."

"Sure plan to." He brushed his lips over the still-reddened knuckles and her dumb old heart whispered, *flip-flops*. "I've got today off. Want to hang?"

"Is that some weird bondage thing?" she joked, foolishly relieved he'd brought it up but still too wary to read anything more significant into it.

He smiled. One of those "it's okay, baby, I can tell you're nervous" smiles. "I've been invited to a cookout at the house of some friends later. You'd like them. We could watch the fireworks, make some of our own. What do you say?"

The last question was framed in a cut-the-crap sort of way. No more quips, let's just be honest that we might like to spend time together.

She thought about what she needed. What was right for her. "Luke, I want to . . . I just . . . I want to be clear. I'm not looking for anything more than a little company. After what happened with David, I'm working on myself for a while." That came out more serious than she'd intended, so she dug for the humor. "You can use those fake blue eyes on me all you like, but I refuse to fall in love with you."

He took a long, unsettling look at her. Had she thrown him for a loop with her candid speech or her accusations of eye color fakery or, perhaps, that troublesome mention of the L-word? After walking on eggshells for years with David, muting her strong personality in deference to her ex-fiancé's ego, she was no longer interested in playing games.

Luke's granite features broke into a smile. "So you only want my body."

"You can talk. Just keep the chat at gutter level."

The smile stretched wider. "I'm fine with that. I'm especially fine with the part that involves working on you. On your breasts, on your ass, on the sweetness between your thighs." One big, callused hand slipped to the hem of her T-shirt and cupped her butt. "Think of me as your sex coach until you get back on your feet."

In two seconds, he had flipped her on her back under his hard—extremely hard—body.

"Which means, to do the job well, I plan to keep you off your feet for as long as possible, Miss Taylor."

CHAPTER FOURTEEN

"This'll do," Luke muttered.

Kinsey narrowed her magnificent hazel eyes at him and cocked a jaunty hip. Damn, she was looking sexy fine today in an orange-and-white-striped minidress that showcased her legs to perfection. Her beautiful, braless breasts strained at the thin fabric, the top part remaining in place by virtue of a tie around her neck. The only thing between his tongue and Kinsey's rose-pink nipples was a simple bow knot.

File that under *I* for infuriating.

She held up the list in her hand. "You're not even taking this seriously."

"I said I'd just do it online."

"Luke." She placed a hand on his chest, step one in working what he now knew was the Kinsey Taylor soft soap. "While human society has managed to make practically everything possible in the online environment, this is one area where the virtual cannot replace reality. Now, get on that bed, stud, and tell me how it feels."

She gave him a not-so-gentle shove and he fell easily on the first mattress that had filled his visual field as soon as they walked into the store. He'd planned to buy a new bed this weekend. A little clickity-click on the Web. Done deal. But then he'd made the mistake of mentioning it to Kinsey.

She advised research.

They're all the same, sweetheart.

She produced research.

I'll just pick the top-rated one on Mattresses 'R' Us.

Now, thanks to his big mouth, they were in a brick-and-mortar store with a list of dos and don'ts on how to buy a mattress, when he'd much rather be back at her place putting *her* perfectly good mattress to use.

She took a seat at the end, frustratingly out of reach. "How do you feel?"

He was shopping when he should be pounding beers, carbonizing steak, and making up for his year-long sex drought. How did she think he felt?

He remained silent.

"The research advises lying for ten minutes in your regular sleeping position."

Throwing out his arms and legs in a sprawl, he took up as much room as possible.

"That's your regular position?"

"When I'm alone. When I have company, I'm more generous."

"What a lucky girl."

The grin he shot her covered his true reaction to that throwaway comment. He got it. This was temporary, and that stuck in his craw more than he'd like to admit. "Just get over here and play stand-in for the next woman I grace with my gifts."

Her sigh was more amused than annoyed as she

kicked off her flip-flops and swung her legs up onto the mattress to lie down beside him. After a few seconds squirming her way into a comfortable position—which he was positive she did to piss him off—she laced her hands behind her neck.

"What do you think?" she asked.

Not too firm, not too soft. Goldilocks would definitely approve. With the woman lying beside him, it felt close to perfect.

"Feels good. Like . . ."

"A mattress?" She turned on her side and inched closer. "Why are we here, Luke?"

"Because you insisted I do this in person. On July Fourth, when there are a million other things I'd rather be doing." Like her, for example. He couldn't believe they'd found a mattress store open on the holiday, but then he supposed that was why the founding daddy-os had gone all revolutionary on those British asses. For the right to sell mattresses on any damn day of the year they pleased.

"No, why are you buying a new mattress? I've slept on the other one and it seems fine."

His gaze shifted to the rest of the store, empty except for the lone salesman who eyed them surreptitiously, waiting for the slightest encouragement to unload his spiel. Luke thought about how to put it delicately, then figured a straight shooter like Kinsey could handle it.

"My current bed is where my ex-wife fucked my ex-friend for several months."

Eyes alight with understanding, she leaned up on her elbow. "Is this something you know or, uh, *know*?"

Oh, he knew all right. "There's not enough bleach in all of Costco to cleanse my eyes of that image."

As if it wasn't bad enough that his wife and her man-slut were screwing like rabbits, they had to do it in his home. In the bed he and Lisa had bought together when they'd married. His life had teemed with possibility then: he would fill Lisa with babies in that bed, she would breastfeed their kids in that bed, they would build a good life in that bed.

"So it's been more than a year," Kinsey said, puncturing his misery bubble.

"Right."

"And you've been sleeping in that bed this whole time?"

"No, I sleep on the sofa." At her mouth twitch, he clarified. "Don't worry, I change the sheets every couple of weeks. You weren't sleeping in the original crime scene." He wasn't that fucked up that he'd maintain the bed linens as some sort of shrine to his ex-wife's cheatin' heart. But otherwise, he had let the room fossilize. The furniture she chose, the robin's-egg-blue paint on the walls, the raw silk drapes he wasn't allowed to touch with his smoke-smudged fingers.

And then there were the other things that had been off-limits.

Wash up first, Luke. You know I can't get in the mood when you're dirty like that.

A stray lock of honey-blond hair had escaped Kinsey's hair tie and he pushed it behind her ear. Out of her power suits and kneel-before-me heels, she looked years younger and not unlike this ideal he had crafted in his mind for the future. This pliant, easygoing woman who would bow to his will. Of course, his libido knew better. Reluctant to leave, he let his thumb rest on her cheek.

"Lisa was always looking for more, expecting that I had all these extra layers that she'd unveil as we got to know each other better. But . . . I'd shown her all I had. There were no hidden depths. No inner child struggling to break free. I'm just a simple guy. I love beer, sex, and hockey. I hate liars, Sting, and art that doesn't have people in it."

She laughed, which was his intention. He saw no reason why a conversation about his ex and all the ways he had failed her should ruin the mood.

He looked up to the ceiling. One of the tiles was loose. "I thought keeping her safe and loving the hell out of her would be enough, but it wasn't. She didn't think I had sufficient emotional intelligence, whatever the hell that is. What it boiled down to is that I wasn't ambitious enough for her."

"In your career?"

"Yeah. She's a lawyer, and the blue-collar thing floated her boat for a while, but she wanted me to strive for more. Lieutenant, arson investigator, out of the FD altogether. She said my family held me back."

Serious again, her gaze turned sharp. "Do they?"

"I told you already how important it is that I protect them. For now, that's all the ambition I need."

She nodded her acceptance, not a nod of, *I get it*, but one that said, *We'll come back to this*. He wanted to resent it, but found he liked her approach.

"I wasn't a great husband, Kinsey. I should have talked to her more. Listened to her needs." *In that bed.* Now he sounded like a new spin on the Chinese fortune cookie game, except instead of the "between the sheets" postscript, it was this latest catchphrase.

You will get your life fucked over. In that bed.

The sympathy in Kinsey's eyes killed him a little. "Sometimes we like to assess past decisions through the filter of shoulda, coulda, woulda, Luke. Maybe you should have given her more attention and listened to her problems. Or maybe she shouldn't have been a skanky-assed, open-her-legs-for-any-dick whore."

The crack of laughter he let fly loosened something rigid in his chest. It also drew the attention of the salesman, who made a move, only to have Kinsey hold up her hand to stop him. The imperious gesture had Luke's entire body going hard. This woman was some kind of special.

"Tell me how you really feel."

"Just sayin'. I've been there, remember?" She lowered her head back to the mattress. "So what are you looking for in a bed?"

"Too easy, Taylor."

That netted him a gorgeous grin. "Soft, firm, adjustable . . ." She leaned over the side to grab the list from where she'd dumped it on the floor, and the view of her golden thighs as her dress rode up put his groin on alert. Back up top, she gave him a good-natured look of, *I know your game*. "There's pillow-top, sateen cover, no-flip mattress . . . The options are endless."

"I want one . . ." He considered for a moment, giving it much more thought than it probably deserved. Who knew buying a mattress could be so complicated? "Where I can get great sleep."

"Of course."

"Amazing sex."

"A given."

Turning, he drank in her fresh California beauty. "And have conversations that matter."

Her smile wobbled a little around the edges, and that his words had an impact on her contracted the space around his heart. Suddenly they were kissing, touching. Connecting. Putting the cherry on top of what had started out as the shopping excursion from hell, but had now taken on this frighteningly new significance.

Somebody coughed.

The kiss continued because Luke really did not care.

The very annoying somebody coughed again.

Kinsey broke away, blinking those big hazel eyes above cheekbones tagged with a watercolor pink bloom. She shot up to a sitting position.

"Um, sorry about that," she said to the salesman, who hovered menacingly at the end of the mattress.

"That's okay," Sales Guy said. "I've seen much worse. Lying on a bed, even when that bed is in public, can be a very intimate experience."

Evidently doing her utmost to avoid Luke's gaze, Kinsey rubbed her kiss-swollen lips. Yes, sweetheart, it had felt very intimate indeed.

The salesman patted the end of the bed. "This is one of our most popular models. Serta SmartSurface, FireBlocker Fiber, Body Loft Anti Microbial Fiber, and PillowSoft Foam. It also has Cool Twist Gel Memory Foam, one-inch Support Foam, one-inch PillowSoft Foam, and the Insulator Pad. And all purchases over $599 get free delivery in the Chicagoland area."

"Sorry, dude, but I understood about every fifth word there. What's the bottom line?"

Sales Guy checked the tag at the end of the bed as if he didn't have this shit memorized. He spent all day with these mattresses—he knew what they cost.

"This model is $799. A great price for a great night's sleep."

Luke bolted upright like the bed was covered in fire ants. "Eight hundred fucking dollars! For a mattress?"

Kinsey placed a calming hand on his arm and flashed a conciliatory grin at the salesman. "Could you give us a moment, please?"

Curding the air with his oiliest smile, Sales Guy sidled off.

"Luke, you cannot put a price on great sleep, sex, or conversation."

"Yes, I can. Apparently it's eight hundred dollars plus tax."

Gracefully, she jumped up, pulling her dress down as she did, which only served to draw attention to her shapely legs. And the gorgeous swell of her breasts. And how he wanted nothing more than to take her home and bang her boneless.

Stupid mattress shopping.

As she shrugged her feet back into flip-flops, she gave a cursory wave around the store. "Look at all the beds we've yet to try."

He groaned. "We have to look at more?"

"Sometimes the first one doesn't work out."

Never a truer word. Sometimes it took practice and a truckload of experience. Mattress buying as a life metaphor. He was learning so much.

Unfolding to a stand, he circled her in his arms, resigned to this not being easy. None of it. A woman like this would never let him off the hook about anything. Foreign satisfaction warmed his chest at that.

"I probably should practice my talking-in-bed skills, and where better to do that?"

She kissed his chin with those soft, supple lips. "By the time you whip out your credit card, we should know each other very, very well."

"Do you mind if I ask a personal question?"

Luke grunted, then drew his knuckles along the crest of Kinsey's breasts. The man was trying to sidetrack her again, which he had been doing all day with the ultimate in fun distractions: glorious, amazing sex. Now she looked forward to christening the rooftop deck of her building, where surprisingly they had the outdoor lounge area to themselves.

Earlier, they had attended a holiday barbecue at the home of some of Luke's friends, and met up with the rest of the Dempseys. The company was great, the food delicious, the cicadas and easy laughter the perfect summer soundtrack. After an hour of Luke's smoldering stares burning erotic holes in her sundress, they made their excuses. By the time they'd turned into the garage around the corner, she'd lost her panties, most of her brain cells, and was three-quarters of the way to an orgasm.

It didn't get much more patriotic than sex in a Chevy on the Fourth of July. God bless America.

"We did waste an entire afternoon talking about me," she said, making her case for being allowed a few personal questions. The shopping trip had been a revelation—for Luke. On each mattress, he polished his talking-in-bed skills by laying the groundwork.

Find a comfortable position.

Hog every inch of available space.

Trap her left leg beneath his strapping thigh.

Only when the circumstances were to his liking would he begin the interrogation.

Lying on the Serta Sedgwick Euro Top, she had started with Jax, her ortho surgeon brother who would happily break Luke's arm if he hurt his baby sister, then fix it up for him (Hippocratic oath, she had reasoned with a smile). As they repositioned themselves on the next bed, Cole, the only one of her brothers to follow Dad into the military as a JAG, got the treatment before she rounded off with Tate. He was her favorite brother, though she would die a painful death before she ever told him as much. A champion skier, he acquired weird levels of fame every four years during the Winter Olympics before fading into obscurity in between.

What would her brothers think of Luke? They'd always been wary of David, who was too precious for them, reluctant even to play touch football over Thanksgiving because of his fragile cardiac surgeon's hands. All the Taylors were men's men and couldn't abide any behavior that whiffed of wimpery.

She suspected Luke would pass muster with flying colors.

Not that they would ever meet each other. It would never come to that, because this whole thing was just good, dirty, casual fun. But even as she reprimanded her treacherous mind for jumping ten steps ahead, she couldn't shake one indisputable fact: her father liked Luke. It disturbed her how much that disturbed her.

Two hours after they'd first entered the mattress store, Kinsey had spilled what felt like her entire life story. On the Tempur Cloud Prima, she'd shared that her mom died when she was eight. The Northfield Vista Firm bore witness to her dream to work with more interesting community causes, and maybe one day, a big political campaign.

Through it all, Luke listened, pinning her to their plush surroundings with that serious blue gaze. Hanging on every word like it was the most important thing he'd ever heard. By the time he made his mattress choice—the Riverside Plus—he knew enough to make her uneasy about the knowledge imbalance.

Now, enjoying the sunset twenty floors above Chicago's River North neighborhood, Kinsey let herself get lost in the feel of Luke's solid chest to her back and the comforting weight of his claiming forearm over her breast. Now it was her turn.

"You can ask me anything," he murmured against the shell of her ear.

"Why did you spend only four years in the Marines?" She'd seen his file at city hall and, while he'd been honorably discharged, she had to wonder at his truncated service time. Getting out before the full eight was virtually impossible without an injury or kicking your CO's head in.

"Worried my hot temper got me booted?" he asked, reading her mind.

"It did occur to me."

He was silent for a few moments, then said, "Sean

and Logan died. Wyatt and I were both serving in different units; he was in Afghanistan, I was in Iraq. We had to make a decision about who would leave. It's allowed under hardship rules."

"For Gage and Alex?"

He nodded against her temple, the scratch of his rough stubble sending a thrill of sensation through her body. "They were still minors. Beck had just turned nineteen, and in the eyes of the social services that wasn't good enough. My godfather, Larry, would have stepped in, but he was going through chemo at the time. There had to be someone else around to look after them."

Realization struck her hard. She turned in his arms, needing to see him face-to-face. "Or they would have ended up back in the system."

"Alex had been adopted by Sean and Mary and she was seventeen, so her status was secure. But Gage . . ." He paused. "He was sixteen. Too old to be fostered by anyone else and too young to be without an official guardian. He would have ended up in a group home."

She heard the pain in his voice. It wasn't just that he'd be in the home . . .

"You were worried he'd be bullied."

He nodded. "Gage has always known he was gay. You should have seen him when he arrived at the house, Kinsey. This scrawny, crazy-eyed ten-year-old waltzed into the kitchen with Sean's hand on his shoulder, and announced, "Hey, everyone. I'm Gage and I'm a homosexual." I mean, who does that? I've known countless Marines, firefighters, all manner of tough guys, and none of them can hold a candle to that kid's bravery. But, in that situation, without us backing him up, I'm not sure he'd have been okay."

Her heart liquefied, and she felt like she knew him a little bit better than a moment before. It was intoxicating. "Why you and not Wyatt?"

"Wyatt was closest to Logan. Biological brothers."

"They don't have the same last name."

"Same mother, different fathers. When Logan died, Wy needed to stay away from us for a while. Marines was the best place for him. Focus on the job." He kissed her forehead, then held her gaze firmly as if he needed her to understand what he was saying. "It wasn't some great, heroic sacrifice, Kinsey. I love them and I'd do anything for them. Besides, we're Dempseys. It's what we do."

Said with Swarovski clarity, conviction in every word. Wow, she sure enjoyed those tingles that thrilled across her skin every time Luke got his family man vibe on. This guy would make some woman very lucky one day.

Not her, though. She didn't need a man to look after her, and she had a feeling a throwback like Luke wouldn't enjoy the kind of relationship dynamic where a woman was equal in all things. He likely wanted a wife who was happy to remain in the background, content to pump out mini Almeidas who would look so frickin' cute in their CFD onesies.

"Can I ask something else?"

He cocked a brow. "Would there be any point in denying you?"

"How come Alex is the only one of you who was adopted?"

"Well, if you were to ask her, she'd say it was because Mom and Dad loved her best." He grinned. "With kids in foster care the preference is to return them to their birth parents, so that's what happened for most of us through our teens. In care or with the Dempseys when our parents couldn't cope, back with them when they were doing better. Sean and Mary tried to adopt us all, but it's harder than you think to sever parental ties. If one parent refuses to give their kid up for whatever reason and there's a chance they could still do the job, you're looking at legal battles that could be drawn out forever."

"So your parents—?"

"Still wanted me?" His barked laugh was bitter. "No. Mommie Dearest was already toast—literally— because of a crack house fire, and my father was a guy who skirted the edges of the law. I lived with my grandmother for a while, but when she couldn't take care of me, I stayed with the Dempseys. Bio Dad was a stubborn prick who had clear ideas about ownership. And even though he had no chance of a relationship with me because he was rarely around, he wouldn't sign on the dotted line. He died about five years ago."

How awful for him. She stroked his shoulders, absorbing his agitation into her body.

"It was variations of the same for the others except Alex, who was a toddler when she landed at Camp Dempsey. None of us needed it signed and sealed. Sean is my father. Mary is my mother." His lips brushed hers softly, then deeper, more possessively. "Of course, being a Dempsey isn't hearts and shamrocks 24/7. Getting away from them for a day or two can be pretty fucking awesome."

"Anytime you need a haven from your crazy family, come on over."

He met her gaze with a warm, inviting one of his own. "Feels a little like that up here. Under the stars, a sanctuary on the roof, this pocket of peace in the city."

With fairy-tale timing, fireworks lit up the sky over their heads.

She squeezed his shoulders. "You knew that was going to happen!"

"Not exactly, but I know the city throws a big show for the holiday. And I seem to recall promising you an explosion down here." He brushed his thumbs under the hem of her dress, higher, higher, then over her satin panties, sending her sex into a quiver. "Never thought I'd be thankful to our illustrious mayor for anything, but it looks like the city of Chicago is cooperating to make this really special."

It sure felt special. Perhaps it was this vulnerable place she'd been in since moving here, but she liked to think she was not hostage to her emotions—or the emotions between her legs. This connection she felt with Luke might be a right man/right now kind of thing, but it felt like more. It felt like right forever.

Danger, Kinsey Taylor! She needed to take a baseball bat to that dangerous line of thought. Just enjoy the here and now.

Thankfully, he seemed to be on the same wavelength. Slipping his fingers to the nape of her neck, he undid the halter of her sundress and leisurely tugged it south. Feral heat darkened his eyes at the sight of her perky nipples.

Going braless had been an excellent sartorial choice.

She unbuttoned his jeans, and after some maneuvering, she took out his thick, potent erection, its skin smooth and silky hot under her touch. As he rolled the condom on and she lowered her body onto him, fireworks burst overhead while the magic of bodily connection created its own shower of sparks below.

Inching slowly, surely, she found her claim. So good, so right.

Too right.

Damn. Blinking away the sudden rush of emotion that equaled more than she wanted to deal with, she focused on a starburst in the sky. Anything to avoid that eye-to-eye connection that might send her over too quickly, or drop her into the abyss.

"Kinsey." Clear strain underlay his words. "Look at me, sweetheart."

Tempted to be petulant and ignore him, or even to say a resounding no—Luke Almeida was not the boss of her—instead she closed her eyes against the onslaught of him.

"Kinsey, I want you so bad," he whispered. "I've never wanted anyone the way I want you."

"Luke, please—"

"I've got you, sweetheart," he groaned. "Trust that I will always have you."

Liar. Yet she could no more deny him than she could deny this pleasure detonating every cell into oblivion. Her eyelids fluttered open of their own accord and she sealed her gaze with his heavy-lidded one.

Unavoidable.

Necessary.

His large, hero-roughened hands kneaded her butt and guided her up and down, up and down. Slowly, intimately, tearing down every defense. Sleek and thick, he filled her body, while those terrible blue eyes filled her heart with a need for connection beyond the physical.

"That's it, baby. Keep it there, right there. Stay with me. I've got you."

And she wanted to be got. With every fluid stroke, he tapped into raw nerves of emotion. Riding him in time to that age-old rhythm, she swore they were sharing a pulse. A heart. The give and take of their rise and fall nudged her close to the edge and when he told her to come for him, she gladly obeyed and toppled over that cliff into the sweet, hot flood.

CHAPTER FIFTEEN

Feeling as light as air on a gorgeous Friday afternoon, Kinsey walked from city hall to the "L" on Washington to take the Red Line up to Wrigley Field. She was meeting Luke for game two of the doubleheader between the Cubs and her home team. Smiling, she adjusted her Giants cap. The competition never ended.

The city was in fine form today, its gleaming buildings reaching for the sky, its friendly natives burbling in excitement for the weekend. Up ahead, she could see the Gehry-designed band shell in Millennium Park with its billowing stainless steel ribbons, peeling back to reveal the stage. She hadn't even begun to skim the surface of what Chicago had to offer.

Dragging herself from the bed of one sexy firefighter would be a good start.

As she passed the Hotel Burnham on the corner of Washington and State, her phone rang with a San Francisco number she didn't recognize. A twinge of panic had her questioning if something had happened to her father or brothers.

"Hello, this is Kinsey."

"And hello, this is Max."

It took her a moment to recognize the voice of

Max Fordham, now a member of San Francisco's powerful board of supervisors.

"Max! How are you?"

"Fine. Just fine." After a few minutes playing catch-up, he got to the point. "I heard you were looking for a way back into city government here in San Francisco."

"Wow, your hearing is excellent from all the way on the West Coast," she teased.

He chuckled. "I'm a lot easier to work for than that megalomaniac in Chicago. Though I hear you're handling him with your customary flair."

"He's just a man, Max. Easily manipulated like all of your gender." He laughed, and she was glad he didn't take offense at her gentle man-bash. "So, you're about to declare on the Calderon seat?"

"State senate? No, Kinsey. I'm going straight to the top—national race in the midterms."

Whoa, not expecting that. It was sixteen months away, but still sort of late to throw his hat in the ring of a U.S. senatorial campaign. She had assumed she'd have to wait a few years to get a bite of an apple that tasty, but to have it dropped in her lap right now was too perfect.

"Who else are you talking to?"

"The usual suspects." He named a few people she knew in PR out in California. "But we worked well together before. I loved what you did on the breast cancer campaign here and I've been watching you closely for a while now. That's the kind of social issues thinking I need on my team."

She smiled at his somewhat hyperbolic description of their past connection. As a lowly intern during her practicum at Berkeley, there hadn't been much working together at all, but it had been a formative experience. He had sparked her interest in city government and in devoting her career to community-focused messaging. Communicating his platform would be so much more gratifying than what she was doing now.

But.

Things were ticking over nicely in Chicago. Spending time with Luke, making friends, gaining the mayor's trust, goodwill she was sure would soon translate into better assignments . . .

Double but.

She had also vowed not to let her emotions trump her judgment again—which is why the next words out of her mouth were so shocking.

"Can I think about it?"

"Where's Mickey?"

Luke's query was met with a chorus of "I dunnos" and those loose-boned shrugs bored teens seemed to have a patent on. Next, he dialed up the flinty gaze. The crowd, two boys and two girls in the thirteen-to-fifteen range from St. Carmen's, gamely withstood the onslaught.

"I see him." Wy zoomed over to where Mickey stood in a huddle with a stranger near the east entrance to Wrigley Field. Strong-armed, the kid was walked back to the group.

"Tryin' to sell his ticket," Wy muttered.

Jesus. "Okay, here are the rules. No sneaking off." Luke double-glared at Mickey, who remained unfazed. "No fighting. No cursing—there are a lot of kids here and their parents would rather teach them how to swear themselves. Got it?"

Grumble, grumble.

"You can each have one hot dog and a pop, which we're going to buy before we take our seats."

"What about a baseball cap?" Kevin asked, snapping his gum.

"Maybe a baseball cap."

"A Cubs T-shirt?" Anton, pushing his luck.

"We'll see," Luke said because he was a soft touch. "Anything else?" He looked at Wy, whose eyebrow tweaked indiscernibly.

"Oh right. Bathroom breaks are only with me or Wyatt."

Abby squared her shoulders. "I ain't goin' into no bathroom with you."

"We'll let you pee alone, Abs, but you'll have an escort to the entrance."

"Ooh, an escort," Sharon, her pal-in-crime, said.

"I can take the girls," Kinsey offered.

Dressed in jeans that rolled midway up her smooth, golden calves and made her ass look picture perfect, Kinsey adjusted the peak of her Giants cap. Quite deliberately, Luke was sure. The woman was clearly enjoying the prospect of the Cubbies getting whipped by her home team.

She smiled at him. Then added a cheeky wink.

Oh yeah, she was loving this.

He had invited her along because he wanted her to witness something that meant so much to him. Let her see another side of Luke Almeida, hothead fireman. Also, because he wanted to spend every minute of his spare time with her.

That's right. Luke had officially turned sap, and the craziest part was he couldn't have been happier about it.

"You don't have to do that, but thanks, sweetheart."

"Thanks, sweetheart," one of the boys mimicked, sending the rest of them into laughter that quickly devolved into elbow-shoving. Because that was the next logical step.

"All right, let's do this."

Wyatt rode point through the turnstile while Luke hung back, one eye on his charges, the other focused on protecting his girl all the way to her seat. "Thanks for hanging with us today," he whispered in her ear.

Kinsey gave him a kiss, no less heated for being so quick. "It's going to be fun."

Ahead of them, Anton gave Mickey a push. Amid muttered curses and accusations that made no sense to anyone but a bunch of teenagers, Luke heaved a weary sigh.

"I'll see if you still think that in an hour."

An hour later, Luke was 99.99 percent positive that Kinsey should have been ready to bail, but every sneaky glance in her direction found her watching the Olympic-level whining and nonstop antics with obvious amusement.

The Giants hit a double and the crowd booed, but in a resigned way. The lot of being a Cubs fan. Bottom of the fourth, and they were already down six-zip.

"This is so *boooring*," Abby moaned for the fiftieth time in the last hour. "Can't I check my messages?"

"No phones," Luke said, a rule he'd instituted two minutes after they all sat down and started playing

Candy Crush. "This is a tech-free zone except for emergencies."

Abby waved toward the field. "I'm gonna die if somethin' don't happen soon. That's a *fo*-real emergency, Luke."

"Yeah." Sharon nodded her agreement. "Like, *fo-real*."

"Anthony Rizzo is kinda cute," Kinsey said, her eyes trained on the game.

Sharon, the slightly less mouthy half of the Shaz-Abs tag team, turned to her. "Who?"

"Yeah, Kinsey," Luke growled. "Who?"

"Anthony Rizzo. He's up at bat right now and he fills out those tight pants real nice. Great glutes."

Abby and Sharon exchanged guarded glances, but couldn't help checking out the situation on the diamond.

"Can hardly see him," Sharon said. "He's like an ant out there."

"One more reason not to get the Jumbotron," Luke muttered. The long-suffering renovation proposal that would bring Wrigley into the twenty-first century was on hold while the local residents sharpened their pitchforks. Luke had always been on the side of the neighborhood, no more so than now. Keep those great glutes at a great distance.

Kinsey rifled through one of those gigantic purses that seemed to hold everything a woman needed whenever she needed it and produced . . . binoculars. Itty-bitty, fun-sized ones.

Luke made a noise of disbelief. "Are you fuckin' kiddin' me?"

"Hey, you said no cussin'!" A chorus of grumbles

ensued from the kids mixed with a healthy glare of disapproval from Wy.

"You go bird-watching in your spare time?" Luke asked Kinsey once the complaining had subsided.

"Just butt watching." She sun-blasted him a gorgeous smile. "I was a Girl Scout. Always be prepared." She peered through the lenses, adjusted the rims, then passed them over to Sharon, who was sporting a clown grin.

"Wow!" Sharon squinted through the bins. "That guy's totally ripped. Even better than Luke on that billboard."

"Lemme see!" Abby grabbed them and looked for a few reverent moments. "He's got a good body. Muscular."

"He's too old for them and too young for you," Luke said to Kinsey, but only the sultry air was listening. She and the girls were already deep in a discussion about Derek Jeter's enchanted butt muscles (*vintage*, according to Kinsey, since the Yankee had retired). Soon, phones were being powered up so the relative merits of Major League Baseball asses could be argued.

"I said those phones were only for emergencies," he said.

"Derriere discussion in progress, babe," Kinsey said as she dialed up a pic of Barry Zito. "Nothing more important."

With a sassy smile, she turned back to the girls. "Ladies, check out this BuzzFeed tribute to Baseball's Finest Butts."

Luke sat back, resigned to being on the losing end of this argument but not minding one iota. He liked watching Kinsey with the kids, that ease she exhibited with people. She had upended every expectation he had for how a career-focused, suit-wearing professional woman might act. All this time, he had been subconsciously—okay, maybe consciously—comparing her to Lisa. Now he couldn't help but compare his ex to a good-looking date. At the end of the night you can't remember a thing she said, but at least she was pretty.

Kinsey wasn't just pretty. She was whip smart and compassionate. A keeper.

Except she didn't want to be kept. Or, more accurately, she didn't want to be kept by him.

When he shared with Kinsey about the demise of his marriage, he had kept some details back. Not only had he failed to measure up to Lisa's lofty standards of twenty-first-century evolved male, but he'd been too demanding, too intense in more ways than one. His ex-wife had laughingly called him "her bedroom brute," but like all jokes, there was an unmistakable grain of truth in there. And it was no different for Kinsey.

Luke was her toe-dipping rebound. Her dirty fling. The guy who hit all her sweet spots and made her scream until she saw God—but hell no, you don't bring him home to Daddy. Witness her horror that he might have anything in common with the Colonel. Her last relationship might have been a dud, but she clearly had a type in mind for the next time she got serious.

Someone not like Luke.

Kinsey couldn't believe how devoted Luke was to these kids—and not just the close to a hundred dollars he had spent on each one, from the ticket to the exorbitantly priced hot dog and soda, never mind the hat and T-shirt (thirty bucks for a tee!). She knew that money had to come out of his pocket, because no care home had the extra funds to drop on a kid who was a ward of the state. But also, his devotion shone in how he talked to them. On their level, with no phony adult-to-child condescension.

Overcome with curiosity, Kinsey leaned in to Luke. "How much time and money do you spend on this program?"

"Not that much." He gave a negligent shrug, but she could tell from how his mouth tightened that the casualness was forced. "Most of these kids are too old to be taken in by a family, so whatever we can do to keep it as normal as possible is worth a few dollars and hours of my time. Besides, what else am I going to spend my money on? My best girl only eats vegetables. Cheapest date ever."

Heart squish. "The calendar profits will help."

"It will for St. Carmen's, but there are over seven thousand kids in foster care in Cook County, a couple thousand of them in group homes who will probably stay there and age out of the system. They're forgotten by everyone."

"What needs to happen?"

He stared at her, blatant surprise creasing his brow. Surely he knew by now that she was a woman of action. "People need to know how they can help. Money for books, games, days out. Then we need more people to take these kids into their homes. Give them that foundation you can only get from being part of something solid."

Kinsey considered that for a moment. "The kids need better PR."

"They do."

"What would you say if I talked to Eli about shining a spotlight on the foster care system?"

"I'd say your boss doesn't give a flying fu—" Frowning, he curved his gaze around her shoulder to the kids, then back again. "It's not a very sexy issue for our fearless leader." He smiled. "But I think if anyone could make it happen, it'd be you."

His confidence in her thrilled her to the marrow. With David, his job had always taken priority, and he had never once let her forget it. More worrisome, she had allowed him to diminish her ambitions. Kinsey was starting to think that nurse and her buffalo sextuplets might be the best thing to ever happen to her.

A sly peek found Luke grinning, that knock-her-dead smile the bright relief in his five o'clock shadow.

"What's so funny?" she whispered into the languorous air.

"I like watching you plan."

"You do?"

"Yeah, you get this adorable crimp between your eyebrows, and your world domination look takes over. Nothing sexier than a woman who's got the bit between her teeth."

Nothing sexier than a man who appreciated it.

He interlocked his hand with hers, so easy and natural, like they had known each other for years. The man certainly knew his way around a palm, another area where Luke was the opposite of David, who was never tactile. Too worried he'd use up his precious surgeon hand mojo on his fiancée.

To think she and Luke had once been enemies. She couldn't imagine going back to that, but neither could they go any further. Or could they? Why else would she have hesitated when she spoke to Max Fordham? The man had offered her the chance of a lifetime, a foot on the bottom rung of a U.S. Senate campaign. A job with Max would be a better use of her talents, yet here she was all starry-eyed because a gorgeous guy was making up for the attention she'd lacked from her loser fiancé.

Snap out of it, Kinsey.

Luke's assassin blues imprisoned her in their swirly depths, and she held her breath, waiting for . . . she wasn't sure what.

"Keep your eye on the MLB butt, sweetheart, and then later I'll show you why CFD is better."

Phew. At least one of them was thinking straight and keeping it at the hormonal level of sizzling sexual chemistry. That catch to her heart was relief, not disappointment.

She was sure of it.

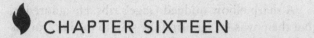

CHAPTER SIXTEEN

Brady hadn't called.

Which should not have been surprising, because Brady had never called. Gage was the one doing all the running in this—whatever it was. Not a fucking relationship, that's for sure. That surly bastard probably didn't even have Gage's number, because Gage had only ever called him at the restaurant. But he knew where Gage worked, at Engine 6 and at the bar. He could call or stop by anytime he wanted.

But he hadn't. And that pissed off Gage in the extreme.

Looking forward to blowing off some steam on his shift, Gage tightened the strap on his helmet and refocused on the current run: a single-car collision on Western and Division at one in the morning. Probably some drunk on his way home from the Division Street bars or an idiot with an overpacked, rowdy car.

As the truck swung around a corner onto Western about a mile off from the site of the accident, Gage looked up to find Jacob Scott watching him from his spot opposite in back, his eyes as mean as a snake's. The homophobic prick was always staring at him like he was scared he would catch gayness just from breathing the same air.

"Whatcha lookin' at, buddy? Careful, someone might call you a homo."

Jacob colored and looked away.

A sharp elbow nudged Gage's ribs. He ignored it, but there was no ignoring the slap to the back of his helmet, the one that made his teeth rattle.

"What the hell was that for?" he barked at his sister.

Alex narrowed her eyes. "Want to tell me why you're acting like Aunt Flo has come to visit?"

"Just in a bad mood. I'm allowed sometimes." Being the life and soul of the party 24/7 took its toll on occasion. There was no good reason why he should be mad about this Brady situation, or the distinct lack thereof, but he was furious. And not a little sorry. *Sorrious*. It felt like he had lost some great opportunity, when opportunities for easy ass abounded in every bar on the Great Pink Way, aka Halsted Avenue. Well, no more missing out for some silent dude with an ink addiction and zero comm skills. As soon as his shift was over, Gage would grab some Zs and then head out to get well and truly laid. This nonsense ended here.

They pulled over to the scene and jumped out. A blue Lamborghini had somehow managed to jump the median, not crash into oncoming traffic, and was now resting on the opposite side of the street with the driver's side wedged against another car. Besides whatever damage was done to a parked Camry, a broken headlamp seemed to be the worst of it for the luxury vehicle. The driver was still inside, on his phone, air bag not deployed.

Gordie Sanchez, the EMT who had arrived before

the truck, approached Big Mac with a lazy gait, no urgency whatsoever.

"Driver's okay."

"Why's he still in the car?"

"He's not injured but the door is stuck," Gordie said, still in no hurry. "Think he's trashed."

The driver pounded on the window so hard that all eyes turned back to the car. The guy had somehow managed to crash his car without injuring himself or anyone else, and he had the balls to get snotty about not getting out quickly.

"Ah, hell no," Gage heard Alex mutter. "Do you know who that is?"

Gage squinted and took a harder look at the driver. Oh snap. They had media mogul royalty on their hands.

Sam Cochrane.

Gage locked eyes with Sanchez, who shrugged. So that's why they weren't busting their asses to get the guy out. He wasn't in any immediate danger, and the code of firehouse brotherhood was at play here. In taking aim at Engine 6 through the mouthpiece of his newspaper, Cochrane had made one monolithic enemy out of the entire Chicago Fire Department. Pissing off the people who might someday hold your life in their hands seemed less than smart but, hey, the world was filled with the stupid.

Gage was not about to join those ranks.

He walked over to the car. "Mr. Cochrane, don't worry, we're going to get you out of there as soon as possible."

Those words spoken by a member of the CFD were usually enough to calm children, dogs, and pregnant women, but Sam Cochrane was not buying it. Red-faced fury mottled his face as he snarled through the partly open window. "Well. If it isn't Pretty Boy Dempsey."

Had Gage heard that right? This guy seemed to have forgotten that he was trapped in a steel cage, and more to the point, that his exit from said cage was dependent on the public servants surrounding his vehicle.

Deep breaths. Keep it professional.

"Get me the Halligan," he called over his shoulder.

"You'd better not put a dent in this car, Simpson, or I'll have your fag ass in stirrups at city hall."

Alrighty, then. No worries, Gage had heard much worse including from his own mother, who on her many psychotic breaks from reality liked to remind him that the only thing separating him from damnation was a bathful of Clorox. An aversion therapy she had been unafraid to use. Nothing this fucker said or did could hurt him.

"That's okay, Mr. C. I'll do my best not to slobber my fag saliva all over you while I pull you to safety. You can kiss my homosexual ass later."

Alex handed him the Halligan, the all-purpose tool that was Gage's first choice where possible. *The right tool for the right job*, Sean used to say whenever Gage visited his father at the firehouse. The heft felt good in his hand, the perfect extension of his profound dissatisfaction with everything in his life right now.

No, not everything. Just Brady.

"Okay?" Alex asked.

"Yeah, no problem. He's a bit belligerent. Think he might have had a few."

Cochrane's face lit up like the Fourth of July when he spotted Alex. "And here comes the other one who thinks she deserves her place ahead of better-qualified men. Just a dyke using the system."

Alex blanched. "Whoa, what's his problem?"

"Just drunk. Ignore him until he pulls a Mel Gibson and starts calling you Sugar Tits."

Accident sites were usually fairly tense, but the vibrations rolling off Alex were hiking the anger up to red-zone levels. The sooner they got Cochrane out and on his way, the better. Angling the blade of the Halligan into the gap between the door and the frame, Gage pulled, but the door refused to budge.

"Jesus Christ, find me a firefighter who's not a filthy fag. Even that wetback brother of yours could do a better job," Cochrane slurred, a nod to Gage's brother Beck, who was seriously involved with the Big C's daughter, Darcy.

Beck would no doubt get a kick out of that backhanded compliment about his extraction skills. Provided Gage made it out of this situation with his head still screwed on straight enough to tell him once Beck had returned from his vacation, because all of a sudden everything started to go kind of fuzzy.

Shit, not now . . .

Gage found the muscles in his arm locking up tighter than corded wood. His body felt both too heavy and like he could float away at any moment. Sound fell away in dimming echoes, replaced by Cochrane shouting, bellowing . . . just like the kids in the group home. Bullies he tried to shut out with relentless cheer and an attitude of, *Don't give a fuck.*

It had been more than ten years since he'd had a panic attack, but he could feel the wave hitting the shore in his chest, each suck of the surf claiming an inch more of his calm. This must be what it was like to get up close and personal with a Dementor.

Someone gently taking the Halligan from Gage's hand brought him back from the ledge.

"Go over there," Alex said. Or he assumed it was Alex. Her voice sounded distant, like a flickering lightbulb deep in a cave. "I'll take care of it."

Gage moved back—and then way back—needing a couple of lengths of fire truck between him and Cochrane before he did something stupid. Like grab the Halligan back from Alex and smash it through the window. He used deep, wracking breaths to fill his lungs and control the rising panic. Called on good memories, as well. They always worked best. Sean's soothing words, spoken in that gruff Chicago accent, echoed in his hammering heart.

It's okay, son. You're safe with us now. No one can hurt you anymore.

Days like this, Gage missed his father so much.

"Simpson." The lieutenant strolled over to the back of the pumper where Gage stood with arms braced, struggling to get a grip. McElroy had hung back to flirt with Maria, Gordie's partner on the EMS truck, but was now realizing he should be on hand to do his job of leading the run. "What gives?"

"Nothing. I'm just . . ." Fucking losing his mind in chunks because of a boy. Brady Smith had him all twisted up. "He's Darcy's father." When Big Mac looked blank, Gage clarified. "You know, Beck's girl."

"Ah. Doesn't like his connection to you lot?"

Something like that. But the vitriol spewing from Cochrane was positively biblical. Beck said the guy hated the Dempseys because of some beef with Sean back in the day, but this seemed on the wrong side of unreasonable.

Gage didn't have time to think on that. A pumping whoosh followed by the screech of splintering metal turned his head, and the visual before him put lead in his feet. The passenger door to Cochrane's car lay at a broken angle off the hinges. A huge gash half-way through the roof had opened it up to the warm summer air.

Holy fuck.

Somewhere along the way, Alex had swapped out the Halligan for the Hurst tool, also known as the Jaws of Life, though in this case it might be more appropriately called the Jaws of Death. As in your career is over. Standing back to assess her handiwork, which looked oddly like a modern art installation in the middle of Western Avenue, she peeled off her helmet. With a shake of her fire-streaked hair, she flashed those green eyes Gage loved.

"We live to serve, Mr. Cochrane."

CHAPTER SEVENTEEN

"I've left messages for Beck and Darcy," Gage said, his eyes troubled. "Probably too busy partying in Phuket."

Luke paced the kitchen of the house he grew up in, his muscles knotted in white-hot rage. "Are you expecting Darcy to be able to put a sweet word in? Because last I heard, she and Daddy Cochrane were not on the best of terms."

Gage grimaced. "I just thought—"

"Thought?" Luke yelled. "Thinking is clearly not what anyone at that scene was doing. Did McElroy have two thumbs or just the one up his ass while Alex was pulling out the Hurst tool and shredding the roof of Cochrane's car—?"

"Hey, don't get all pissy with them," Alex interrupted. "This is down to me, and me alone."

Luke glared at his sister. He loved her more than life itself, but right now his palms itched with the need to throttle her slowly. "I haven't even started with you, Alex. Goddamn it, we're already a target for Cochrane and his paper."

"And whose fault is that?" Gage could always be counted on to stick his neck out for Alex, and vice versa. As kids the two of them were an inseparable force of nature, defense of each other beating out defense of anything else, even the rest of the family. "You brought this down on us all with your You-Tube Luke-Smash, and now it's open season on the Dempseys."

Luke looked to the adults in the room for support. Wyatt sat at the kitchen table, watching the tennis ball exchanges, biding his time before he pronounced judgment. At four in the morning, Luke had been enjoying a postorgasmic sleep with Kinsey pancaked across his body, every curve clinging to him like a cliff face. But then he was wrenched to the cold shock of reality by a phone call from Wyatt. Wyatt, who never called because he despised talking on the phone. Wyatt, who would rather gouge wells under his nails and pour battery acid in them before he would punch out the numbers and go verbal.

But right this second, Luke wanted to hear from Kinsey, who had insisted on accompanying him back home. He was this close to boiling over to ballistic, and her presence was the only thing keeping him at a simmer.

"What did Cochrane say?" Wyatt asked Alex, all reasonable and shit.

Luke's head felt really hot. Maybe he was having an aneurism. "Who cares what he said? Nothing he said could justify this reaction."

Kinsey opened her mouth and clamped it shut again. Whatever she had, she may as well get it out now at the family meeting.

"Spill it, Kinsey," Luke said.

She cleared her throat. "Well, what Cochrane said is important. If it's considered in any way inflammatory to certain segments of the city's voter base such as gays and women, then it could be used to present a case of incitement. Maybe even hate speech."

Alex's face lit up. "He called Gage a fag, me a dyke bitch, and his future son-in-law Beck a wetback." She finished with her mouth set in a mulish line and glared at Luke as if this was all his fault.

"Hit all the major food groups there," Wyatt muttered. "Sounds pretty inflammatory to me."

Kinsey held up her hand. "Don't get me wrong. The city's not going to support an employee who destroyed a citizen's property over name calling, but we might be able to exert pressure on his team when he calls for Alex to be prosecuted for criminal damage. Which he will. He might be content with her termination."

Distress cut up Alex's features and her shoulders slumped in defeat. Despite his fury, Luke's heart clenched. "So I'm definitely going to lose my job," she said in a quiet voice.

Kinsey shrugged helplessly. "I can talk to Eli, but he's relying on Cochrane for the endorsement and campaign donations. With the election not so far off, it's too risky for him to go to bat for you."

"And why would he?" Alex said bitterly, her anger reigniting. "He'll probably be thrilled to see another unqualified female firefighter get pushed out. He's no different than Cochrane." Alex's phone pinged at that moment with an incoming text, and a blush bloomed on her face. She blinked up at Luke. "The mayor wants to see me at his house now. How did he get my number?"

How about, *He's the fucking mayor, sis.* "Probably

from Larry." Luke had already spent a bust-your-ass ten minutes on the phone with his godfather, trying to shield Alex from the worst of it. Cooper's urgency did not bode well.

"Can he just fire me on the spot?" Alex asked, her unsettled gaze flitting around the room.

"Nope," Wyatt said. "Union won't allow it."

Kinsey's phone buzzed. "I've been summoned, as well." She shot a glance at Luke, and he saw the worry etched there.

Over the last few weeks they had been finding common ground with every new intimacy. Her touch was a magical balm. The chemicals in her kiss were a drug he couldn't get enough of. He was exercising patience because she claimed she didn't want anything serious, but the timing of this was, well, shit, to be honest.

"Gotta do what you gotta do," he said, and then winced at how wounded she looked. They were back on opposite sides, it seemed, no matter how sexy and personal the truce had been. In unspoken agreement, everyone stood and made moves for the door.

"You can't all come with me," Alex said. "As much as I'd like to have you there, I have to face this alone."

"I called Petie Doyle, the union rep, but he's out of town on vacation," Gage said. "You have to go in with a second, Alex."

"I'll go with her," Luke said.

"No fuckin' way—"

"You've got to be kidding—"

Luke gasped a lungful of air while his siblings made the vociferous case for his sitting this one out. *Christ, family, tell me how you really feel.*

Alex rubbed his arm. "Thanks, Luke, but you won't be able to keep your temper on a leash, and right now, I need cool heads around me. Especially if I have to talk to him."

Meaning the mayor? Since when did his sister have a beef with Cooper? Luke was about to ask a follow-up when Wyatt cut his query dead with a stony stare. "I'll take care of her."

Luke nodded. "Just don't let her be bullied, Wy."

Gage hugged his sister. "We're going to fix this."

Alex remained silent, just let Gage hold her tight to his chest. Then she nodded once and walked to the front door, looking like she was heading for the firing squad at dawn.

"Need a ride, Kinsey?" she asked over her shoulder.

"I probably should arrive separately."

Didn't that just say it all? Hard to reckon which aspect of this pissed off Luke more: the fact that his sister was up shit creek, paddle in smithereens, or that whatever he and Kinsey had started seemed to be slipping like sand from his grasp.

Alex headed out with Wyatt, leaving Kinsey and Luke standing in the hallway.

"Guess we're back to opposing corners," Luke said, knowing he shouldn't blame her but needing to say it aloud.

Kinsey looked hurt. "We're on the same team here. We all work for the city of Chicago and now it's under threat from an outside force."

That was one way of looking at it, he supposed. "But when push comes to shove, Alex will end up trampled."

"Luke, she fucked up. Big time. I'll do what I can, but the city cannot afford to fight a lawsuit against the likes of Sam Cochrane. Someone has to pay here, and it's not going to be the mayor."

"She's got a temper. She's loyal beyond reason. This family means everything to her." He pounded the wall. "Usually I'm on that shift, but schedules have been changed up with vacations. If I'd been there, none of this would have happened."

"Or maybe we'd be erecting the tombstone on your career instead." She opened the door.

"Kinsey . . ." The words stalled in his throat. Their time together so far had been amazing, every minute a precious gift. Now it was like there was a rip in the fabric between them. "Just . . . later."

With lips pressed together and a curt nod, she walked out.

Early morning traffic was light, making Kinsey's cab ride to the mayor's house in the upscale Lincoln Park neighborhood short. Too short. Though she had stopped off for coffee first to give them a head start, she still arrived at the same time as Wyatt and Alex. Not good. Her professional allegiance was with the city of Chicago, but her heart was with the Dempseys.

One Dempsey, in particular. She had not enjoyed how Luke had assessed her in his kitchen, as though sizing up the enemy, and now she had to put on her game face for the mayor. Straddling these two worlds was getting harder and harder.

Before Wyatt and Alex emerged from their car, Kinsey bounded up the steps to Eli's ivy-covered brownstone and rang the doorbell. The door opened and Eli stood there, looking weary, sullen, and more casual than she had ever seen him, in a hunter green tee, board shorts, and running shoes.

"Kinsey." His expression turned as dark as a pocket at the sight of the Dempseys.

"Is this all there is?" he asked Alex. "I thought the situation would be considered serious enough to warrant a visit from your entire family, Miss Dempsey."

"We didn't want to overwhelm you," Alex said, stepping inside without waiting for an invitation. "Wyatt's here to make sure there's no funny business."

Out of nowhere, a huge ebony-coated dog jumped on Alex, standing on hind legs that made him almost as tall as her. Laughing, she rubbed his ears and settled him down to the ground. "Who are you, big boy?"

"That's Shadow," Eli said in a voice brimming with pride. "He makes a terrible guard dog because he likes everybody." The mayor offered his hand to Wyatt. "Mr. Fox. I understand you're late of the 3/5. Darkhorse."

Coming from a military family, Kinsey knew that was a reference to Wyatt's Marine battalion and its nickname. The two men shared an understanding glance over their handshake before Eli turned and strode ahead, the assumption being that they should all follow.

Kinsey had never been to the mayor's house before, but she knew it had been his childhood home and the site of his parents' murders. Their path into the kitchen was flanked by photos, mostly of Eli as a kid, proudly displaying trophies and game fish, his parents on either side. Happy memories all sliced to ribbons by a senseless act of violence when Eli's father, then Cook County state's attorney, was targeted by a mob boss he was prosecuting at the time.

How he could still live here blew Kinsey's mind. An exchanged glance with a goggle-eyed Alex confirmed she wasn't alone in that opinion.

"Sit down," Eli ordered, with a flick of his hand to a large farmer's table in the pleasantly appointed kitchen. Sunlight streamed through the window blinds, bathing the room in buttery stripes.

Everyone sat, including the dog, who stretched out companionably at Eli's feet. The mayor went back to what he had been doing before they arrived—making coffee. Only when he had measured, apportioned, and pressed the start button on the maker did he return his attention to the merry little band.

"So you've switched sides, Kinsey," he said in a dangerously low voice.

This is what she had been afraid of. "There are no sides, Mr. Mayor. Only a need to minimize the damage caused by this situation and make sure the city has zero liability."

"Spoken like a true spin doctor." He sharpened his fierce gaze on Alex. "What the fuck were you thinking, Alexandra?"

In Kinsey's limited experience, she had surmised that Wyatt Fox had two looks, Cool Indifference or Mighty Pissed Off, and the expressions for both were pretty much the same. But with Eli's very familiar address of Alex, Kinsey encountered a new expression from the eldest Dempsey: surprise. Gray-blue eyes flew wide as his gaze ping-ponged between Eli and his sister.

"Is this an official interview?" Wyatt asked the mayor.

"Do you think I usually ask people who screw with my city over to my house at 0600 if I want to discuss official business? I invited you here because I'd rather get her side of it before the shit hits the fan later today. I've spent the last two hours talking to Commissioner Freeman, Media Affairs at CFD, and Sam Cochrane. That car cost four hundred thousand dollars!"

"Take it out of my wages," Alex said petulantly, biting down on her lip.

"You mean the wages you'll no longer be earning?" Eli inhaled deeply, palming the counter like he could draw on an inner calm from some deep-seated place. "Okay. Tell me what happened."

Alex's cheeks flamed. Eli's conciliatory tone had not gone unnoticed. "He was rude. He called Gage a fag, Beck a wetback, and me a dyke."

Eli threw up his hands. "The world is rude, Alexandra. It's filled with incredibly rude and shockingly bigoted people."

"Oh, I know," Alex said pointedly.

He arched an expressive eyebrow, the jibe not lost on him. "But we're public servants, and those rude people pay our salaries."

"And fund your campaign." Alex stood, the effect of her height nothing short of staggering. "That asshole chose to insult the people who were sent to extract him from a single-car collision which he caused. He was drunk and could have killed himself or others."

"There was no evidence of DUI."

Alex's mouth fell open. "He smelled like a brewery! He was about to be Breathalyzed by CPD as we were leaving the scene."

Eli folded his arms. "The result came in under the legal limit."

That revelation seemed to take the wind out of Alex's sails, but in typical Dempsey fashion, the deflation didn't last long. She turned to Wyatt and swore in colorful language more suitable to an army mess hall. "That pigfucker hates our family because Beck's in love with his daughter. Ever since Luke's fight with Dickwad McGinnis, Cochrane's sided with the CPD in his paper, and now he has them in his pocket."

Kinsey watched Eli's reaction carefully. He covered it well, but she could tell the truth of Alex's assertion resonated. Nonetheless, he remained unshakably political.

"Unfounded accusations of corruption aren't going to help you here, Alexandra. There's still the little matter of damage to a very expensive car. Drunk or not, he will now likely sue the city."

"Oh, I'm sure you can figure something out, Eli. You entitled big shots always flock together."

"Firefighter Dempsey." Kinsey shot a sharp glance at Wyatt, who had settled back in his chair with arms crossed and an avid curiosity in the exchange before him. This situation was hurtling out of control, and big brother was supposed to be making sure Alex's best interests were considered, not looking like he wished he had a box of Milk Duds in one hand, an extralarge Coke in the other. Wyatt met Kinsey's gaze for a moment and, evidently unaffected by the desperation he saw there, turned back to the action.

For the love of her ovaries, did Kinsey have to do everything?

She sent a pleading look Eli's way. "Mr. Mayor, she's upset and—"

"No, wait a second," Eli said, holding up his hand to curtail Kinsey's defense. His gaze bored into Alex. "Do you even know the meaning of 'entitled'? Because if you looked it up, there'd be a holiday photo of the clan Dempsey, Alexandra. You think because you've got dead firefighters on your family's résumé and your godfather is the commish, you're a special snowflake? That's not how it works. You're very small in the grand scheme of things, and fucking with Cochrane does not make you look bigger. It makes you look stupid. I'd put it down to some tigress-defending-her-cubs dynamic, but I'd risk accusations of being a patriarchal woman-hating asshole."

"I was raised to be proud of my family and to not take shit from people who screw with them," Alex shot back.

Eli's eyes flashed with admiration—there were Oscar-worthy levels of eye flashing going on—but they quickly dimmed to indifferent. "Oh, be proud, Alexandra. Be proud all the way out of a job."

"Fine! I'll resign."

"Alex," Wyatt warned. "Not another word." *Finally.* He stood and looked the mayor right in the eye. "Firefighter Dempsey will cooperate with any and all hearings."

Eli glowered right back. "CFD HQ will be in touch later on today about the next steps." His tone was dismissive, and everyone took it in that spirit, except Alex, who hunkered down to rub Shadow's ears, making the dog thump his tail in joy. Kinsey suspected she was trying to compose herself and using the dog to get her emotions under tether.

Wyatt moved toward the front door. Kinsey rose to join him.

"Stay a second," Eli said.

Kinsey froze, her chest filling with dread because she knew she was going to hear it.

"Not you, Kinsey. Be in my office as soon as you get to city hall today. Alexandra, I want a word in private."

Wyatt bristled. "Anything you have to say—"

"It's okay, Wy." Averting her attention from the dog, Alex stood and touched her brother's arm. "If I'm not out in five minutes, you can send in the search squad to retrieve my body. And make sure they play Green Day at my funeral."

Wyatt still looked torn, but one hairy-eyeballed glance at Eli was apparently enough to convince him Alex was not going to be compromised by the big bad mayor. That military brothers-in-arms code, perhaps.

However, Kinsey wasn't completely out of the woods yet, as the mayor turned to her for a parting volley. "You're walking a fine line here, Kinsey. Be careful about aligning yourself with a volatile bunch like the Dempseys."

Alex made a strangled sound of disbelief.

"I'm not going to do anything that runs counter to the city's interests, Mr. Mayor," Kinsey said firmly. Or her own, she insisted to her Luke-muddled brain.

"Good to know you have my back," he said with a knife-edge smile she didn't believe for a second.

Kinsey followed Wyatt out to the house's entryway, where they stood for a few awkward moments looking at the walls, the grandfather clock, and anywhere but at each other.

Finally he huffed out a disgusted sigh. "Since when are my sister and the mayor on a first-name basis?"

Kinsey pounced on the subject, grateful for any crumbs of conversation. "As far as I know, they've met only once. The mayor and I were having dinner at Smith & Jones and we ran into Gage and Alex."

Wyatt digested this information. Or at least, Kinsey thought that's what he was doing. Unlike Luke, who wore his heart on his sleeve, Wyatt was impossible to read.

"I thought you were here to make sure she didn't get bullied," she said into the lengthening silence.

"Is that what we're calling what happened in there?"

Point taken. What they had witnessed was more like a mating ritual between two hopped-up, hoof-pounding moose. In that moment, Kinsey realized that Wyatt had done exactly the right thing in hanging back and leaving his sister to duke it out with Eli. If anything could save Alex, it was Eli's attraction to her.

Not too shabby, Mr. Fox.

A minute passed in silence.

Then two.

"Tell Alex I'll be in the car." Wyatt stepped outside, and Kinsey released the breath she'd been holding. The guy still freaked the shit out of her.

Just as the five-minute mark loomed, Alex emerged, her cheeks fire red.

"What happened?"

"Let's just go," Alex muttered, throwing open the heavy oak door.

Kinsey caught up with her on the stoop. "What

did he say?" Silence. Alarm soaked her chest. "Did he . . . did he make a pass at you?"

Horrified, Alex shook her head like a dog coming out of water. "Of course not! He just—" Her cheeks still burned and she raised her hand to her face to cool them. "Where's Wy?"

"He couldn't stand to spend one more second in my scintillating presence, so he went to the car. Are you going to tell me what happened or do I have to go back in there and extract it from Eli?"

Alex muttered something unintelligible.

"What's that?"

"We talked about the dog. He's a Lab retriever–Border collie mix."

"The dog?"

She gave an embarrassed shrug. "He wanted to know how I was holding up."

Ah, that was more like it.

Alex waved Kinsey's smirk away. "Oh, don't worry. The sympathy thing lasted all of five seconds before he defaulted to his usual cocky, I'm-the-man self. He told me I made him so mad that he would like nothing better than to put me across his knee."

"He can't say that to you! It's sexual harassment."

"*Hello,* have you seen where I work? He wouldn't go there if he didn't think I could handle it."

Perhaps, but it was still outrageous behavior from a sitting mayor. Kinsey huffed her indignation. These politicians and their power trips. "I hope you gave him a piece of your mind."

"I said, 'Do that, Mr. Mayor, and prepare to live testicle-free for the rest of your miserable days.'" She broke into a nervy giggle that morphed into slightly hysterical. Oh, God. The woman had Eli ensorcelled in her glimmer and she was positively giddy on the power.

"Damn," Kinsey said, "I'd better stock up on flashlights and bottled water."

"Huh?"

"There's going to be some sort of 'end of days' deal when you two get together. Earthquakes, riots, swaths of prime real estate on Chicago's Gold Coast falling into Lake Michigan."

Alex tripped down the walk to the street, a rather inappropriate spring in her step considering her precarious situation.

"Don't worry, the world is safe. Mr. Metrosexual and the girl who snacks on the leftover Chinese food she finds in her hoodie? Uh. No."

"I'm not saying you have to birth his babies, but you could scratch an itch. I know you've thought about it." Every conscious female in the Western hemisphere had thought about it.

As if powered by the loud snort she issued, Alex moved more quickly along the tree-lined streets of Lincoln Park. Kinsey pounded her feet double time to keep up.

"Not enough mirrors in my bedroom to satisfy his need to check his hair while he's doing it."

"Bet there are in his, though," Kinsey said with a grin.

"Look, I might have the worst dating record of any woman in Chicagoland, but believe me when I say I'm not desperate enough to go *there*." She headed toward where Wyatt was waiting, a dark curtain descending over her face again. "Right now, I need to be focusing on how to get out of this mess, K. What am I going to do?"

CHAPTER EIGHTEEN

Gage dipped the puke-sodden mop in the bucket and wrung it out. He had thought this week could not get any worse, but hey, here he was.

Alex on suspension while she waited for her hearing. Luke snapping Gage's head off whenever he so much as parted his lips to apologize. And now some drunk dickhead had thrown up in the can at the bar, leaving a Jolly Rancher–colored stream of—was that curry?—all over the tile.

He had eliminated the Brady situation from his litany of Life Sucks. That shit no longer made the list.

Of course, that didn't stop him from checking his phone every five minutes on the off chance there might be a call from Mr. Surly. Three weeks since the farmers' market kiss-and-bolt, and Gage could still feel Brady's stubble-peppered jaw against his. Every day since, Gage had jacked off to the visual of the habanero-hot chef pushing him hard against the SUV, all that need leeching from his mouth and pores. The feel of his cock rubbing—

Don't torture yourself, man. The guy is just not into you.

But deep down, Gage knew different. Disinterested

men did not lose a few seconds of sanity and tongue the guy who carried their veggies around for them.

What was holding Brady back? Normally Gage would be pumping his sources for information by now, but his only connection was the mayor, and that wasn't happening, not when the Dempseys were *familia* non grata.

With the last of the mess mopped up, Gage stowed the equipment, washed up, and made tracks to the bar. In the corridor, he spotted—*shit*—Jacob Scott coming his way. Despite being coworkers on the truck, he and Jacob had never really gelled, something Gage put down to the guy's DEFCON 1 level of disgust anytime he came within touching distance of Gage. So his typical play was to walk on by with a quick, not unfriendly nod.

However, tonight Jacob stopped him with a hand on Gage's arm. "How's Alex?" he asked.

"Hanging in there. Her hearing will be in a few days." Jacob nodded. Then nodded a few more times.

"Okay, dude?" Gage asked, because the guy seemed all tweaker agitated.

Jacob stared at him for a moment, his eyes darting back and forth. When their gazes clashed again, Jacob leaned in and . . .

Kissed him.

Jesus.

Gage pushed him away, shock vibrating through his body. "The fuck!"

"S-sorry." Jacob was panting hard, his breathing serrated like he was having an anxiety attack. "Sh-shit, man, I'm sorry."

"You want to tell me what that was about?"

"Just too much to drink," Jacob muttered.

Uh-uh. No way could that be laid at the feet of an extra pint of the black stuff. Gage took Jacob's arm and steered him toward the back office. "This isn't college, Jacob. You can't experiment with your coworkers, and you certainly can't lay one on them without warning."

Jacob ran his hand through his blond buzz cut while an ugly red flush crept up his thick neck. "I know, Simpson. I guess . . ." He swallowed and stared at Gage directly. "I guess I just like you."

Shit on a shingle. That was about the last thing he would have expected out of this guy's mouth.

"Well, that's not really how it works. Just because I'm gay and you're—" He paused. "You are gay, right?"

Jacob nodded sadly, a slump in his massive shoulders.

"Just because we're both gay does not mean we're supposed to hook up. It's not a proximity thing." Sometimes it was, but this minute? Nah-ah.

Blowing out a heavy breath, Gage leaned against the office desk laden with paperwork. He'd had a couple of nice encounters on this desk, but there would be no repeat performance tonight. Jacob Scott—who the hell would have thought it?

"Look, I know someone like you would never be interested in someone like me," Jacob said. "I mean, you're gorgeous and cocky and . . . you know who you are."

Hell if that didn't make Gage feel pretty shitty about all the times he'd been less than nice to Jacob. He couldn't remember a moment when his sexual orientation hadn't been woven into the very fabric of his being. Owning it early was his way of coping with his mom's cruelty and narcissism, of sticking it to the mean kids, of surviving. He had reveled in his difference, so it was hard to fathom denial when he saw it. Denial of self. Denial of happiness.

"I'm sorry, man, but . . ." He trailed off, because the guy was doing the "sad-eyed, you killed my puppy" thing and Gage didn't much relish his role of dream destroyer.

He supposed Jacob wasn't half-bad looking with his smooth, boyish features, doofus grin, and bull-like physique. And to top it all off, he was part of the anointed: Chicago Fucking Fire. That last checked box alone meant Jacob would be fighting them off with a freakin' Halligan in any bar in Boystown.

Jacob continued to stare at him intently, like he was working up to say something, and Gage braced himself. But it was not what he expected at all.

"What if I could help your sister?"

"And how exactly would you do that?"

"I have a video of Cochrane's meltdown, Alex with the Hurst, the whole thing."

Gage's ears perked up to the ceiling but he kept his voice bland. "Which doesn't exonerate her."

"But we all know that the perfect sound bite can beat out a dry newspaper report anytime. Get a video to the press with Cochrane running his mouth off and people immediately start to sympathize with her. With the whole lot of you. Then it looks like you're being persecuted."

The man made an excellent point. "And what would I need to do to get this favor from you?"

Jacob tilted his head and placed his hand on

Gage's chest. It had been awhile since Gage had been touched with any intimate intent, not since Brady, who couldn't slough off whatever demons lived in his head. Sure, it was Jacob Scott, recent addition to the Pink Posse, who Gage wouldn't have looked at twice even if he were dressed in a sparkly thong on a Gay Pride float in June. But he had something Gage wanted, and the heady brew of being able to extract Alex from this mess *and* that someone actually wanted him was downright intoxicating.

Didn't mean Gage would make it easy for the blackmailing little fuck, though.

Unmoving—and strangely unmoved—he watched as Jacob ran a hand over Gage's shoulder, testing, gulping down a lump of nervousness as he did it.

"You been with a guy before?"

"Just anonymous hand-job stuff at the gym."

Gage could see that. It wasn't his thing, but he knew every kind of hookup was imaginable in the steam rooms at Equinox. Evidently taking Gage's silence as an invitation to proceed, Jacob's thick fingers curled around his neck, and Gage closed his eyes, imagining it was Brady. Imagining the gruff chef's lips roving his jaw, his neck, his chest.

But reality was far too vivid. The weight of Jacob's hand was all wrong, the skin too soft to maintain the lie. Or perhaps the burning knot behind Gage's breastbone was telling him how whack this felt.

He opened his eyes and placed a hand over Jacob's, readying to push him away. He probably had the video on his phone. Gage could get it from him without blowing the last guy on earth he would ever think of in that way.

But of course, the moment couldn't just go to shit—it had to go to nuclear crap levels, because Gage was having that kind of day. A noise at the door arrested his attention, and Gage raised his gaze to find sharp black eyes boring into him. The red, mottled skin on the new arrival's face looked more raw than usual, matching the grim line of his mouth.

Gage knocked Jacob aside. "Brady."

He was already gone.

God*damn* it.

"Don't move," he barked out to Jacob as he rounded him to follow Brady. Chasing this guy down was getting to be an ugly habit.

Considering that Brady was a bit of a hulk, Gage was surprised to find he was already out the door by the time Gage made it to the bar. Drilling though the crowd, with Alex calling out that she had sent Brady back a moment ago—*thanks for the heads-up, sis!*— his mind pinwheeled in panic. He was going to lose this before it had even started.

"Brady!" He caught up with him about a half block down the street as he was throwing a long leg over . . . a Harley. The guy drove a frickin' Harley and this was the first Gage knew about it?

Focus, Simpson.

"That wasn't—"

Brady's eyes snapped up, slitted and accusing.

"Okay, maybe it was."

"None of my business," Brady bit out. But he remained still on the bike, a column of moored energy, and the fact that he had not yet punched the gas flooded Gage's chest with hope.

Brady had come *here*, to Dempsey's bar, obviously

with the intention of . . . God knew what. Now Gage had to work with the knowledge that this man, who had the communication skills of a parking meter, had something on his mind.

Well, sometimes the best way to find out what someone wants is to tell them what *you* want.

"You're right, it's none of your business, but I want it to be," Gage said. "I need more from you. I need proof that you even think of me that way."

Brady's frown deepened. "Then I'm sure you can find any random dick on Halsted to give it to you. Don't even have to go that far. Door's behind you."

"I don't want a random dick. I want you."

"Why?" Brady shook his ravaged, fucked-up head. "I don't get it. You're the most beautiful man I've ever seen. At that market, every single guy was staring at you. You're on billboards, for Christ's sake! I'm just a guy who can't even——" He clamped his mouth down on the words.

Gage edged forward. "Can't even what?"

Brady lifted his gaze, and what Gage saw there— the pain, the out-and-out sorrow—smashed him to the ground. Terrified the bejesus out of him, to be honest. Maybe he didn't want to know what Brady's problems were. Maybe he couldn't handle the demons fighting at the gates of his soul.

"Can't even what?" he repeated, moving closer into Brady's space, a sneaky shift into the lion's den. Not especially brave, but baby steps.

Brady held his breath, and Gage could see him fighting to let that breath go, to push it out, so he could haul a deeper one, but his chest muscles were in a rigid lockdown. The moment teetered on the edge of intimacy, and despite his best intentions, Gage's cock roused. Getting close to Brady, getting close to his truth, turned Gage on.

"I'm just some challenge to you," Brady grated. "Is that it?"

Gage choked out a laugh. This idiot. This beautiful, broken idiot.

"Yes, you are. But not the way you think. I'm not in the business of bringing reluctant gays over to the dark side. I'm not here to be your spirit guide into Queerlandia. When I met you, I was scared shitless, because I'd never experienced that with anyone before. You knocked me on my ass, you—you asshole! I want to cook with you and wake up with you and give you the best blow job you've ever had. And then I want to start the day all over again. With you!"

All color drained from Brady's face, except for the hamburger meat zigzags on his right cheek and temple.

Whoops, that might have been a bit over the top. Gage searched for words to temper it. Tell him that Brady made him so mad it inspired Gage to spew mouth shits. Tell him that he didn't really want to reach inside this man's chest to pry open his locked-up soul. They could take it slow. Just have fun.

Brady and fun? *Puh-lease.* Send in the frickin' unicorns.

"And what if I can't give you what you're looking for?" Brady's brow crumpled in rather endearing bafflement that made Gage want to smile.

"And what if you can?"

Brady's answer was to blow out a breath, giving Gage a blessed moment to catch his own. "I came over to see how you were. Saw the stuff on the news about your sister."

"I'm handling it." Or he had been, before Brady showed up and unloaded a big ole jealousy bomb on him, because that could be the only reason he was vexed about this.

"That's what you do? You handle it?"

"I'm not one for games, Brady. I see something, I take it. There's a problem, I fix it."

"Think you can fix me?"

"Think you need to be fixed?"

Brady stared with those dark, sinful eyes, and again Gage felt that sorrow rolling off him. Whatever had happened to him was keeping him just out of Gage's usually long reach.

"It'll take more than a blow job, Gage. I'm unfixable."

"Sucking your dick sounds like a great start. We can work up to the hard stuff later."

It was the wrong thing to say. Brady's face shuttered, his shoulder muscles went taut.

"You've got a willing fuck ready for you back there." Gripping the hog's handlebars, he stamped the gas pedal with a vengeance. "I can't give you what you need."

In a haze of ear pollution, Gage watched Brady drive out of his life. Whatever, the man was right. He couldn't give Gage what he needed because Gage didn't need anything. He had his family, his job, and a keen awareness of who he was. And back in that bar, he had a guy desperate for whatever Gage had to offer.

Brady Smith could go screw himself, because Gage

sure as hell wouldn't be begging for the opportunity. Come willingly or not at all.

He headed back into Dempsey's. From behind the bar, Alex mouthed at him "You okay?" and he nodded, then issued an order to Jacob Scott, who had not stayed put as requested.

"With me. Now."

In the bar's office, he waited on the balls of his feet, with fists scrunched and fire in his veins. Ten seconds later, Jacob trudged in, a sheepish look on his face.

"Was that your boyfriend?"

Gage white-knuckled the edge of the desk. "No."

Jacob's expression turned smug, like he thought he had the power to make a difference here. Like he could hold this over Gage and screw with his head and his family.

"C'mere," Gage said.

Jacob shuffled forward a few steps, his eyes alive with anticipation.

Gage ran a finger down the front of Jacob's shirt, feeling each button of his Oxford all the way to the slight paunch on his stomach. Jacob's eyes lit bright, and for a moment, Gage considered giving in. It would be so easy to push him to his knees and shove the hard-on with Brady's name on it into that slack, inexperienced mouth. Lord only knew, when it came to sex, Gage's default was easy.

Shaking those thoughts free, he focused.

"Here's how it's going to work. You will give me that video. I will not beat you to a pulp. And maybe, just maybe, I'll introduce you to somebody more your speed."

"But—"

"No buts, Jacob. Because if you don't hand it over, I'm going to have to tell everyone what you tried to pull here and I won't be able to stop the hellfire that rains down on you after that. Do we understand each other?"

"You think I'm afraid of your brothers?"

Gage coughed out a mirthless laugh. "Oh, you *wish* I was talking about them. Hope you enjoy eating through a straw. Should I call her in now?"

Jacob blanched with the realization that he risked incurring the wrath of a certain green-eyed brunette. As had been recently demonstrated, a Dempsey female was not to be trifled with.

His mouth twisted peevishly. "You'll take me out with you one night? Cruising on Halsted?"

Gage smirked. "You're gonna have so much cock aiming for your throat you'll need plastic surgery to make your mouth bigger. Now, give me the fucking video."

CHAPTER NINETEEN

In the mayor's office up on the fifth floor of city hall, Kinsey employed several strategies to avoid staring at Eli as he viewed the latest video tainting the reputation of the Chicago Fire Department.

She picked at some imaginary lint on her pencil skirt.

She uncrossed and recrossed her legs.

She focused on the history that dripped from every crack in the wood-grain wall paneling. Photographs of previous mayors shaking hands with the notable and the not-so-notable peppered the walls, including one of Mayor Daley and a young assistant state's attorney, Weston Cooper, father of the man who sat across from her behind the antique mahogany desk. If these walls could speak . . .

Gage had brought the video directly to Kinsey. When she asked him why he didn't just blast it online and let the chips fall where they may, he countered with the argument that they needed to protect Darcy, Sam Cochrane's daughter, who was like another sister to Gage. Darcy might not get along with her father now, but Gage knew she didn't want that to be the final chapter in the story, and neither did he want to be responsible for causing any irreparable damage. It would be better all around if Kinsey could use it as leverage against the badly behaved billionaire.

Which was why she now sat in an uncomfortable chair in the mayor's office, lashes and head lowered in humility.

As Sam Cochrane's homophobic, racist, and chauvinistic rant gave way to the earsplitting sound of shredding metal, she risked a peek and found Eli's mouth stretched in an ear-to-ear grin. That made her duck her head to hide a smile of her own. She was relying on two things: the mayor's innate sense of justice, and his even more innate attraction to Alexandra Dempsey.

He put the phone down, propped his elbows on the desk, and steepled his fingers, all traces of amusement now replaced with gravity.

"So?"

"It's not a very flattering portrait of Mr. Cochrane, sir."

Eli arched a "don't even bother" eyebrow at her use of *sir*.

"What I see here merely confirms the sequence of events. This can't damage him. It only makes it worse for us."

"So far, we've only heard reports of what Cochrane said."

"Leaked by someone at CFD HQ who was privy to Firefighter Dempsey's statement."

Kinsey might have had something to do with that.

"The words in print don't mean much, but spoken aloud, heard and viewed by millions, they acquire power." Kinsey stood, needing the stretch to make her point. She was back at Berkeley, persuading her classmates in Public Speaking 101 that smoking wasn't so bad for you, that transfats had benefits, that Stalin was a goddamn saint.

"We want to get out in front of this. We have to show the public that Cochrane is a foul-mouthed, drunken bully who verbally assaulted the brave men and women sent to save him from his own worst excesses."

Shaking his head in disbelief, the mayor swiveled his lantern jaw toward the other person in the room. Madison Maitland stood with her back to them both, her regal gaze drinking in the city streets like Boudicca surveying the Roman enemy before heading into battle.

Without turning, she spoke. "There was no evidence of drunkenness and he apologized for his behavior in that press conference. He's contrite and slick."

Kinsey suppressed a growl. Cochrane had handled this better so far for sure, first with his finagling of that Breathalyzer test in his favor—she was still uncertain if it was CPD corruption or just old-fashioned ineptitude—and then blaming his potty-mouthed tirade on his claustrophobic panic at being left too long in a "steel coffin" (his words). Kinsey had listened to his statement so many times in the last twenty-four hours she could have recited it word for word.

. . . And while my behavior is in no way excusable, the situation does make me question the suitability of this firefighter who could be so easily baited. But then, Alexandra Dempsey comes from one of those entitled firefighting families who believe the rules and

regulations do not apply to them. Less than a month ago, her foster brother instigated a brawl against the brave officers of the police department and was allowed to buy his way back on the job by flaunting his naked body on billboards. Now we have yet another example of this family's blatant flouting of the rules. There's a physical exam requirement, lowered some years ago to accommodate female applicants, but perhaps we need a psychological aptitude test for the fire service. Or perhaps Firefighter Dempsey's judgment was impaired for other reasons.

When questioned about that cryptic statement by reporters, Cochrane made an offhand comment about how Alex herself should have been Breathalyzed at the scene (oh, the irony), a baseless implication that took the heat off him and transferred it to her in one fateful stroke. He offered a halfhearted apology, but the damage was done and had wormed its way into the city's hearts and minds. The jury of Alex's peers was already questioning her judgment.

They needed to fight fire with a nuclear bomb.

But Kinsey could understand how this placed Eli in a delicate situation. Cochrane had both media and financial clout, both of which Eli needed in the next few months as they drew closer to the election. The only thing Eli had going for him is that Cochrane would be loath to switch to Eli's opponent so late in the race after he had invested so much in the mayor as incumbent.

"He was drunk," Kinsey insisted, "no matter what CPD says. You saw him stumble out of that car."

"Unsteady after being rescued from a car crash," Madison countered.

"And his slurred speech was due to claustrophobia and post-traumatic shock?"

Madison locked eyes with Eli. Some intimate knowledge passed between them.

"Cochrane's not a politician," Madison said after a few taut seconds. "The public won't care about the meltdown of some guy they barely recognize. Do you think people are going to boycott his paper, stop going to Cubs games?" All endeavors in which Cochrane had a substantial financial interest.

"I think we can get people on Firefighter Dempsey's side. On our side," Kinsey shot back. "We need to use her. She's photogenic, a woman working her ass off in a male-dominated profession, a sister defending her gay brother and the rights of twenty-first-century women everywhere to break the mold. It's David versus Goliath. We couldn't have come up with a better poster child."

Eli strummed the table, then pivoted in his chair to look out the window. "It was so much easier in the desert."

Agh! Channeling the patience of a saint, Kinsey managed to keep from screaming her head off. Frankly, she didn't have time for Eli's "war is hell, ain't it great?" reminiscences. Alex's job was on the line, and they had a smoking gun that smelled so sweet.

"Print is dead, Eli. You might not need Cochrane as much as you think. Your coffers for the election are healthy, and it's not as if he can donate above the campaign finance limits." Ethics rules prohibited any one individual from giving more than five thousand dollars to a Chicago mayoral campaign. Of course,

Cochrane had so much influence he was able to use his friends and employees to contribute above the threshold.

"Who else has seen the video?" Madison asked.

"Gage Simpson brought it to me. The only other person is the firefighter who took it, but Gage said he could be controlled."

Eli's eyes shot up. "She hasn't seen it?"

"We—I thought it best."

The remaining Dempseys were in the dark because Gage insisted Luke would go ballistic if he actually saw what had gone down. Knowing the man, Kinsey was inclined to agree. She and Luke hadn't spoken in two days, not since they had all crowded around the kitchen table in the Dempsey kitchen the morning after the Cochrane incident. The times they had spent together—mattress shopping, up on the roof, the baseball game, the sex (God, the sex)—had been touched with some sort of magic that vanished like an illusionist's trick as soon as that call came in from Wyatt. She knew Luke was working, but that wasn't the only reason behind this sudden distance. They had retreated to their respective corners, and while she had tried to explain that they were on the same side, she understood his reluctance to see her point of view. Minimizing the damage to the city would likely lead to maximizing the damage to his family.

Yet again she found herself on the wrong side of the divide. Luke's protective streak was a mile wide, and she wanted to find shelter inside the wagon circle. To be his first and last thought, not the woman who was collateral damage in the battle to save his family.

"I can persuade Cochrane not to sue, Kinsey," Eli

said. "It's worth more to him to have the city on his side while he has several real estate development projects in the works. But someone has to pay."

There was something else, something he wasn't telling her.

"Maybe it's time to cut Cochrane loose."

A muscle in Eli's jaw contracted and she could see how much effort he made not to look in Madison's direction. "Decisions made above your pay grade, Taylor."

Understanding dawned. Cochrane had dirt on Eli. It was the only explanation for why he'd stick with such a liability.

Kinsey's eyes bored into the mayor's. "And Firefighter Dempsey?"

She thought she saw regret in Eli's stark blue gaze, but it could have been a trick of the light. "She was never going to come out of this with her job, but at least she won't be in debt for the rest of her life."

Kinsey's heart sank to her soles. She'd really thought she could pull out a win here. And she hated to lose, especially like this.

There was one last hand to play.

"You like her," she said to Eli. It came out of her mouth, sounding like an accusation. Sounding desperate.

"Like?" Eli leaned back in his chair, faintly amused. "God, no. It's just . . . she's so damn young, filled with all that loyalty and fire. Even a jaded soul like me can appreciate it, but there's only so much I can do." He shook his head, strangely subdued. Where was *his* loyalty? Where was *his* fire?

"And even if I did like her, Kinsey, it wouldn't

affect how I do my job. You're letting your fucking hormones rule your judgment. I don't care that
you're sleeping with Almeida and I don't care that the
Dempseys are your new besties, as long as *you* don't
forget who pays your salary."

Rage made her muscles seethe. It was pointless
to deny her relationship with Luke, not that it could
be characterized as that, especially of late when they
were barely on speaking terms. Neither did it matter
how the mayor knew that she and Luke had crossed
that line—the most powerful man in Chicago probably had spies everywhere—but no way would she
stand for accusations of "decision making by vagina."

"That is not why I'm advising you to play this
differently."

He shot her the dangerously pointed glare he used
on the city council when they wouldn't cooperate
with one of his proposals. "Kill the video, Kinsey,
and one more thing . . ."

She was barely listening to him now, her mind
racking up frequent-flier miles as she worked all the
angles. Anything to counter the slow, sick spin of failure in her stomach.

"Kinsey."

Looking up, she found him glowering. "I want this
whole Dempsey-McGinnis cluster stitched up and gift
wrapped ASAP. What we discussed the other day—"

He halted on seeing the frown she knew was cemented on her face. What they had discussed was a
move that was only going to pull the pin out of the
grenade-shaped head of a certain Cuban Irish fireman.

"I've given you far too much latitude with this
situation. Bring Almeida to heel. Now."

She switched on her "yes, Mayor" expression. "The community party at Engine 6 is all set for a week from Saturday." Bouncy house. Check. Face painting. Check. Gathering representatives from fire and police together for a cozy how-do-ya-do, axes and Halligans within spitting distance. Goddamn priceless.

"And the rest?"

"It'll go exactly as planned, Mr. Mayor."

CHAPTER TWENTY

Riding the elevator up to the fourth floor at city hall, Luke mentally shit-kicked his brain for his poor timing. It might only be an hour past the official end of his shift, but it was close to zero hour for the working stiffs on the nine-to-five, and he was sardine-canning it with everyone on their way into the office.

It had taken him forever to leave the firehouse, between ensuring that the handoff to the next shift went smoothly and completing the briefing reports he had to fill out because he'd taken over for Big Mac, who was on vacation. Usually a relief lieutenant stood in, but Luke had pulled rank—what little he had—and persuaded the cap that he could handle it in McElroy's absence. This wasn't the time for strangers to take up residence. With the shit soup Engine 6 was wading in, the company needed to see the next few weeks through as a cohesive unit.

It was Luke's job to make sure that happened, especially as his meltdown had put them dangling on the precipice.

The Dempsey dynamic was the perfect microcosm of Engine 6 at the moment—a crap load of tension, everyone sniping, and no one getting along. Alex knew she'd screwed up, but they all looked to Luke, either to blame because he'd set this whole downward spiral in motion with his fist in McGinnis's face, or to fix because that's what he did. He was Mr. Fix-it for Team Dempsey.

The elevator clunked to a grinding halt at the second floor to let off the lardasses who couldn't walk up one floor. While the bodily real estate was rearranged, a woman beside him sniffed and gave him the twice-over. Yep, that's the scent of a hard night's work saving lives, honey.

You're welcome.

Weird, but since he had promised Kinsey that one time to hold off on the firehouse hygiene routine, he'd been heading out every time smelling like brimstone. As if the mere repetition could conjure up the memory of riding that elevator to her apartment and all but running to her at the end of that hallway. What he wouldn't give for a chance to wrap his filthy body around her, breathe her fresh, clean scent, lay her on cool, white sheets . . .

Three days had passed since the family powwow in the Dempsey kitchen, and communication between them was bordering on nada. She had left a couple of messages, and like the broody bastard he was, he had ignored them, which was oh-so-high-school of him. He was here to man up.

The third floor came and went—Lisa's floor. It was a testament to where his scrambled brain was at that he'd not spared his ex-wife a thought when he hopped onto the elevator in the very building where she worked. Huh, go figure. Finally the elevator hit four, and the doors split apart. In the suite opposite,

Kinsey's cute assistant was chatting on the phone and as he stepped inside, she hung up.

"Hi, Luke." Eyelash fluttering ensued.

"Hey, Josie. How are the cats?"

Her eyes brightened. "I adopted another one—a gorgeous calico." She tap-tapped on her phone and pulled up a photo of a kitten who looked like he'd rolled around on a wet Jackson Pollock canvas.

"Isn't that—?"

"Yes! Your costar on the photo shoot, Millicent. I call her Millie. Most calicos are female, you know, which of course is why she was such a peach in your arms." She sighed wistfully. "She got a taste of fame that day, so I figured it was a shame to put her back in the shelter."

He nodded at Kinsey's closed door. "Her Majesty in yet?"

Josie's look was filled with *naughty, naughty*. "She's in a meeting right now, but her nine o'clock is up on the fifth floor, so she'll be done any minute. Have a seat."

She gestured to the edge of the desk where he had happily parked his ass on his last visit. He'd come straight here that day from CFD HQ, determined to tear strips out of Miss Taylor. Instead they'd engaged in a fiery battle of wills that ended with him staring avidly as she bent over that desk. Like the secrets of the universe were made manifest with the wiggle of her gorgeous ass.

"I'll sit over here." He settled himself on a sofa off to the side of Kinsey's office and checked Facebook. Darcy and Beck had posted more pics of their island hopping around Thailand. They looked tan, happy, in love. He smiled, let his mind wander. Maybe one day he'd get a chance to indulge that California beach fantasy of his with his own California beach girl.

Not a couple of minutes had passed when the sound of muted laughter and a shuffle of movement told him Kinsey's meeting was done. The door opened and out stepped . . .

Daniel McGinnis.

Daniel "Suit Wearing, Smooth Talking, Wife Stealing" McGinnis. He was gripping Kinsey's hand, pulling her toward him ever so subtly. Enticing her into his body.

Cold fury grabbed Luke by the throat, his body oozing rage. He stood. Kinsey had her back to him, but her relaxed stance and upturned face told him everything he needed to know.

"Glad we could finally meet, Kinsey," Dan was crooning. "Though I feel like I already know you so well with all those calls you left. Sorry I've been so busy."

"That's okay, Detective. I'd much rather you were out catching the bad guys. Just glad you could take a few moments to talk."

"If there's anything I can do to make it go more smoothly, you let me know." He released her hand with a slow slide, savoring the skin of Luke's woman. "Good luck with Almeida. It's going to be a tough sell."

"What is?" Luke snapped, unable to keep quiet any longer.

He had to give it to Kinsey: as she spun around to face him, she didn't look like she'd been caught with her hand in the cookie jar of dicks. Not like

Lisa's shocked, openmouthed gasp when he found her with his so-called friend in their marriage bed. Kinsey was too cool a customer, and Luke supposed it wasn't the same.

It just felt like déjà fucking vu.

"Luke," McGinnis said, lifting his chin in acknowledgment, eyes the color of regret. "See you soon." He left, his designer loafers silent as he glided across the carpet.

Luke stared at Kinsey, his molars crunching hard enough to expel bone dust from his ears. "What's gonna be a tough sell?"

"Would you like to come in?" she asked.

No, he would not. He had half a mind to chase down McGinnis, jury-rig the elevator so the doors slammed on his skull. Again and again and again. Then throw him down the stairs. All three flights.

Kinsey remained silent while soul-sickening understanding rolled off her. Frozen in a furious block, he could do nothing but stare. When he still made no move—when he couldn't—she turned to Josie. "Could you call upstairs and tell them I'll be late to the meeting?"

"How late?" Josie asked, hand already on the phone.

"As long as it takes." Without looking at him, Kinsey pivoted and walked into her office, and Luke followed her in like the blind fool he was.

Inside, he found her leaning against her desk, the smooth lines of her skirt hugging her stellar thighs. He had missed her body. He had missed her. But he was so rigid with rage that he wondered how he could do this.

He had never been good at compartmentalizing his problems. Stuff tended to bleed across the boundaries, his anger so amorphous it spilled over into his work and his relationships. Now hurt and resentment tangled up inside him so much he could barely think straight. In this moment, he had a choice. Approach the situation rationally and calmly, or let his anger do the heavy lifting.

"What the fuck was he doing here?"

So, seemed he was going down the road rage route, then.

"We've set the date for the community party at Engine 6 for a week from Saturday," Kinsey said, her tone clipped. "That's why I was meeting with Detective McGinnis."

Luke knew McGinnis would be attending so they could put a cast on that fracture between the CFD and CPD. Maybe everyone could sign it like a yearbook. What he failed to see was why Kinsey had to have one-on-one time with the man who had destroyed Luke's marriage and prompted a fistfight that almost deep-sixed his career.

"I know he has to be there for appearances' sake, so if you're worried I've got a problem with that, then don't be. Does he have a problem with it?"

"He's fine with coming to the event, and the mayor would like to see him and his colleagues from the Third District there—"

"But?" Because he could hear it coming as clear as day.

"The mayor would like you to ask him."

"What?"

"He'd like you to formally invite McGinnis onto

your turf. That's why I was meeting with him first—to make sure he didn't get all high and mighty when you talked to him. I know it's ridiculous, but it would go some way to smoothing this over."

"You mean I'm supposed to apologize."

"In a manner of speaking. Luke, I know he's an asshole, but as far as the mayor's concerned, you're in the wrong here. You threw the first punch, and while you might have the moral right on your side, you don't have the mayor. He doesn't know . . . the full story." Her eyes softened. "And you need him. Especially now."

Because of this situation with Alex. "My sister is going to lose her job anyway. How exactly are you doing on that, Kinsey?"

Annoyance furrowed her brow like a corduroy swatch. "I'm working on it. The priority is to limit the city's liability—"

"Yeah, because it's not to save my sister. That's right, PR princess, you keep spouting the party line. Your job is to make sure Cochrane doesn't sue, even when CPD is covering up the fact he was driving drunk."

Kinsey threw up her hands. "Luke, come on, you can't prove that and I can't fight it. At the moment, I'm doing my best to make sure Alex won't be financially ruined, which is what will happen if she's made a party to a lawsuit against the city." Her sigh was impatient, exasperated. "But yes, her job is likely toast unless the union can pull a rabbit out of its hat. And I've been told to wrap up the Rehab Engine 6 campaign so I can move on to other projects."

His body's radar went haywire. He'd known it

was coming, that this forced time together while she kissed his boo-boo better would come to an end. He wasn't ready for it to come to an end. He wasn't ready for them to be over.

But his vision field was filled not with her beauty and smarts, not with mental snapshots of the amazing times they had spent together, but with that image of McGinnis cupping her arm possessively. His ears still heard the tinkle of laughter as she wrapped up her schmooze. Every muscle in his chest went rigid at the idea of Kinsey and McGinnis talking about Luke and his propensity to fly off the handle at the smallest thing.

Unaccountably, his cock stirred, remembering how it felt to work his way inside her, to feel those silky muscles tighten around him in need. But Kinsey didn't need Luke, not really. She just needed him for how he could serve her. Give her an orgasm. Make her look good to her boss by kissing McGinnis's ass.

Well, Luke wasn't going to be doing that anytime this century, so Kinsey would have to find another way to impress the mayor.

"McGinnis and his pals can join the party, but you can tell Cooper that there won't be any gold-plated invitation or apology from me. And seeing how cozy you and the detective were a few moments ago, I'm sure you can use your particular methods of persuasion to get him on board."

She tilted her head, folded her arms, and cocked a hip—the trifecta of pissed-off woman. "I hope you're not suggesting there was anything more to that meeting with McGinnis than a request for his cooperation."

"Me? No, no, Miss Taylor. I'm just a blue-collar stiff, too emotionally stunted to see what's in front of his face. I'm not so good at reading between the lines."

"Luke—"

"Gotta go. You know where to find me."

A moment's regret that he was being such an ass nagged at him. But then it was swallowed up by the knowledge that Kinsey had met with McGinnis so they could craft a strategy on how to bridle Luke. Make sure he acted like a good little soldier. How had he ever thought she would be on his side in this?

Stiffening his resolve, he left her office, letting a good head of righteous indignation fuel his exit. The misguided notion that he had gotten off easily with a slap on the wrist and a few embarrassing photos of his chest on billboards slammed through him. Sometimes there are worse punishments, like the blow to a man's pride. Playing host to that bastard, welcoming him into his firehouse with an invitation to make himself at home—not gonna happen.

He'd take ten suspensions, the loss of pay, and a year's worth of shrink sessions before he said sorry to Daniel McGinnis.

Kinsey stared at the door through which Luke Almeida had just stormed out in a full-throttle hissy fit.

That pigheaded, obstinate idiot.

Perhaps she could have handled that better, but Luke had caught her off guard by showing up unannounced. He hadn't even given her a chance to ask why he was here at nine in the morning after ignoring her texts and calls for days. Clearly straight from his shift, too, smelling like he'd put in a hard day's night and he needed some TLC. Then seeing her with his sworn enemy first thing . . .

She could understand his being annoyed. Pissed off, even. But to accuse her of using her body as a tool of persuasion? To imply that she was some kind of shrew willing to open her legs to get ahead in her job? As if she would ever do something like that—and with the sleaze bucket who destroyed his friend's marriage? Just. No. She knew firsthand how much betrayal hurt.

Ugh. Her skin still crawled with having to play nice with McGinnis on orders from the mayor. The good detective—yet another guy who acted like his dick should have its own zip code.

But no matter how mad Luke Almeida made her, what he had said about Alex struck a chord in her heart. His sister had screwed up, but Kinsey did not like how the influence of one powerful man was determining Alex's future. Or how Eli Cooper was refusing to sac up and take a stand against Cochrane.

Josie popped her head around the door. "Kins—"

"What?"

The poor girl blinked at Kinsey's grouchy tone.

She sighed. "I'm sorry, Josie. It's just been one of those days." And not even nine thirty yet.

Kinsey, down here. That was the bottle of Grey Goose in the bottom drawer of her desk, letting her know she had a friend.

Her assistant smiled her sympathy. "The fifth floor called down wondering if you were going to the meeting. You're running eight minutes late."

"Tell them I'll be there in five. No, ten." Those fifth-floor jackasses could wait. A wide-eyed Josie backed out slowly.

The scent of smoke lingered in the air, and Kinsey felt that familiar flutter down south. Damn her hormones. Damn Luke Almeida.

On her phone, she hovered over Luke in her contacts list, but then scrolled back up and hit another four-lettered name. As she waited for the recipient to answer, her heart careened around her rib cage like a pinball. This was the right thing to do, she insisted. The only thing to do. Once connected, she hauled air into her lungs and started talking before she could lose her nerve.

"Hey. I need a favor."

CHAPTER TWENTY-ONE

Kinsey knocked on the door of Gage and Alex's house and waited, bone-shaking fear hurtling through her veins. She had made a decision and put a plan into action, and now she had to live with the consequences for her career, her future, and, well, maybe her love life. But that was not why she had done this.

Keep talking the talk, Taylor.

Gage opened up and yanked her inside. "Did you get ahold of her?"

Kinsey nodded. Earlier, she had called Gage looking for Darcy Cochrane's number. The time difference between Chicago and Thailand meant she had caught the woman as she was heading to bed—a very active bed judging by the husky Spanish murmurs in the background. Beck Rivera, another Dempsey who apparently knew how to rock a woman's world. Those damn Dempsey men. They had a way of sneaking into your blood and heating it so much your heart boiled over.

"Now we wait," Gage said.

"Not for long."

Alex stood up from her spot on the sofa as Kinsey walked into the living room. "Gage told me what you did."

Kinsey held up a warning finger. "Not me. The moment it was taken, there was always a risk that it would escape into the wild. But if it gets into the right hands and gains maximum coverage, then as a concerned citizen, I am grateful."

Eli would skewer her head on a pike if he found out she had been the source. When he found out. But it wasn't as if the video was a lie. She didn't agree with him that putting a lid on it was the right strategy. Bullies like Cochrane deserved to be exposed, which is why she had called Darcy and explained what was on the line. Gage's instincts not to shame his future sister-in-law's father were noble, but when faced with the prospect of setting back reconciliation with her father versus Alex's career, Darcy had not hesitated in her support of the Dempseys. She had chosen her side.

Like Kinsey.

"Turn on the TV," she said to Gage.

The video led the local news on NBC, just as Kinsey had been promised when she met anchorwoman Marisa Clark for a late liquid lunch that afternoon (extra-dry martini, Ketel One, two olives). There was no sugarcoating Cochrane's language, the bleeps making it sound even more profane. More perfect. With every piercing cover-up of a not-suitable-for-network-TV word, Kinsey could feel the meter of public opinion tipping to Alexandra's side.

But the best was yet to come.

Marisa laid it out: *"The firefighter in question, Alexandra Dempsey, is currently on suspension and her administrative hearing is scheduled for Tuesday. Sources inside CFD say it's unlikely that Firefighter*

Dempsey will escape with her job intact. However, a petition demanding that she be allowed to keep her position on the grounds that she acted overzealously under extremely difficult circumstances is now available online."

A Web address pulsed on the screen.

Marisa's male coanchor snuck a glance at his counterpart. *"A woman scorned. That's one way to handle it,"* he said with a suggestive wink.

A class act all the way, the Emmy Award–winning newswoman rewarded him with the brittlest of smiles before bringing the spot home. *"Think I'd want to have a firefighter like that on my side. How about you, Chicago? Before you check out the petition, vote in our online poll. Should Firefighter Dempsey lose her job over this?"*

Kinsey stood and cheered. Score one for the home team!

"Is your hot tub harboring a silent killer? Find out after the break."

Gage muted the TV, his expression stunned. "There's a petition?"

"Releasing the video was just part one," Kinsey explained as she paced with fists clenched on hips. "All campaigns need a call to action. There's no guarantee it'll work or that Alex will keep her job, but—"

Alex launched her Amazonian body at Kinsey and pinned her to the sofa. "I can't believe you did this for me. I can never, ever, ever thank you enough, K. Never."

"I don't like to see jerks like Sam Cochrane getting their way." Kinsey squirmed, looking for a more comfortable position. Alex Dempsey was not exactly a delicate flower. "But we're not out of the woods yet. The petition is far from binding."

"It's already got . . . five hundred and fourteen signatures," Gage said, holding up his phone. He tapped it a few more times. "And the video has six—no, seven thousand views already. Might overtake Luke's fifteen minutes of fame before the night is out."

"Because that's just what we need. Another video of a Dempsey behaving badly." Everyone turned to the source of the voice.

Luke. He stood at the door, hands shoved deep in pockets, body language taut and menacing. Completely badass.

"We had to do something, bro," Gage said. "We tried to use it as leverage without releasing it but it didn't work. It was time for plan B."

"And you didn't think to discuss it first? As a family?"

Alex sat up and shared a guilty look with Gage. "We wanted to take care of it. You're always getting us out of hot water. This time, we wanted to solve it ourselves."

"I see." Luke's face was a stone wall as he stared at Kinsey accusingly, making every cell in her body tingle.

It was good to be reminded of why she wanted to punch him in the penis with a fire extinguisher.

She stood, annoyed to discover her legs swaying like reeds. "I'd better go. I have a feeling I'll be getting a call from my boss very, very soon."

"Kinsey, thank you so much," Alex said, her eyes glossy with gratitude. "I owe you big time."

Boom! Kinsey's phone exploded with the *1812*

Overture, her bombastic ring tone for Eli. "I'll take this outside."

She brushed by Luke, who refused to stand aside as she passed. Ruggedly handsome jerk. Out in the Dempseys' backyard, she stared at Eli's name flashing like a red alert on her phone screen. Music swelled. Cannons exploded. She half expected SWAT teams to descend and haul her off to screw-with-the-mayor jail.

There was an excellent chance she had lost her job here.

Coward that she was, she let the call go to voice mail. Only to have it promptly start up again a moment later, because this was the mayor and the guy was annoyingly persistent like that. Time to pull on her big-girl panties.

"Mr. Mayor," she said, her tone aiming for casual but falling somewhere north of high, squeaky, and guilty.

"Kinsey," came the clipped reply.

Lying was not her intention. She had known it would be obvious that she was the source and it would be disingenuous to pretend otherwise. "Eli, I'm sorry—"

"I told you to kill it, Kinsey, but we all know that it's like locking the stable door. I can't blame Simpson for doing everything in his power to save his sister."

True, but . . . that was unexpected. What she wouldn't give to be in the same room as him, checking his expression for clues. He couldn't possibly think she had nothing to do with this, could he?

The urge to come clean warred with her instincts for self-preservation. Honesty won out. "Well, he wasn't working alone—"

"I don't doubt it. The Dempseys are well connected, so I'm sure they had plenty of people telling them how to play this. We just have to figure out how *we're* going to play it."

That mention of *we* flushed up another well of guilt. If she continued to play dumb, how the hell would she look him in the eye? She actually liked Eli, liked working for him, and she owed him the truth.

"Eli, I have a confession to make."

He snorted. "Are you finally going to fess up about your relationship with Almeida? Because I already told you I know and I don't care. Listen, Kinsey, this isn't an automatic 'get out of jail free' card for Dempsey. There's still the hearing, but this puts a different color on it. Should we expect marches in her defense on city hall?"

Only if the petition didn't work. Plan C.

Kinsey cleared her throat. "I doubt it'll go that far. I think people appreciate her exuberance in trying to extract one of the city's favored citizens under such trying circumstances. As long as the voters feel they're being listened to by their representatives."

She could almost see Eli rolling his eyes at that, but she knew that deep down he cared what the voters thought, especially his key demographics of women and gays. In the background, the choppy noise of a TV indicated he was channel surfing.

"They're already calling her America's Favorite Firefighter over on CNN. Where *do* they come up with this stuff?"

From the brain of Kinsey Taylor, that's where. She'd worked with Gage to ensure the moniker was planted on several firefighters' Web boards and social media, knowing the brotherhood would spread it quickly. The twenty-four-hour news cycle was always desperate for new content, and the combination of a woman doing a man's job and a prominent media kingpin behaving like a jackass was a match made in news coverage heaven.

And the fact that she had engineered this whole damn thing needed to be told!

"Eli, this is all my—"

"Prepare a statement and have it on my desk by seven a.m. tomorrow." She heard a soft click. "That's Cochrane on the other line. I'd like to let him stew but it'll just get ugly if I do. Night, Kinsey." He ended the call.

She stared at her phone, feeling like she had been bludgeoned over the head by Steamrolling Eli. Perhaps that was his sneaky intention. The situation had plausible deniability written all over it, so maybe that was the angle Eli was taking? A classic politico's gambit.

Tomorrow she would talk to him and set the story straight. If he didn't fire her on the spot, he might be curious to know why she risked everything she had worked for, and she would trot out her defense about Truth, Justice, and the American Way. Maybe throw in something on the inalienable rights of women and gays with a few nods to the Constitution. Because the real reason she had taken this leap off a cliff was something she was not yet prepared to examine.

But as is so often the case, sometimes we have no choice but to face head-on what we try so hard to ignore. Her core had started to hum, her body already hyperaware of a raw, physical presence.

She turned . . . right into an intractable wall of muscle named Luke Almeida.

He was so *there*. That rock of strength, the heart of his family, who now clearly felt threatened by her lady kick-assery yet again. She was beginning to think there would be no satisfying him—or any man for that matter.

"Kinsey, we need to talk," he said gravely.

Kinsey's eyes almost popped out of her head. He was going to scold her yet again? She had worked her butt off to clean up his world: first the fist-shaped mess of his own making, and now his sister's bid for self-destruction. She had walked a fine line between peacekeeper and bulldog. She had risked losing her job, and indignation at his assumptions about her since this fiasco with Alex rose to score her chest—and mutate into the beginnings of a thumping migraine.

Basically, she'd had quite enough.

"Listen up, caveman," she said, pointing a finger in his chest. "If you think for a single second I'm going to stand here and take whatever you're-on-my-turf bullshit you feel like spouting today, then you need your Neanderthal skull examined. Gage brought that video to me because he knew your first instinct would be to go berserk and throw it online. We wanted to try a more subtle tack, and when that didn't work, we wanted to control the release. And it looks like it might have paid off, so get off your high horse, get your head out of your ass, and get on board with the solution."

"You finished?"

She fisted her hands on her hips, took a fighter's stance with a rock back on one heel, and squared her shoulders. "I haven't even started."

"Good. As long as you finish with me."

That self-congratulating, macho asshat. He thought he could just—

Wait. *What?*

In one swift motion, Luke curled his hand around her waist and jerked her into his body. His mouth greedily took control and stole her bubbling outrage with a kiss so dizzying it left her breathless.

Yeah, this.

Drawing back after a few moments, he searched her face, his eyes flaring with naked desire, his mouth swollen and wet. "Are you still employed?"

"For the moment."

"But you could have lost your job."

"There was always that chance." In fact, she wouldn't write off the possibility just yet. "I tried to come clean, but Eli kept cutting me off and—"

He kissed her hard, fierce, pushing her back against the gable of the house as he worked over her mouth. "You did this for me."

Oh, the arrogance! Of course he had found a way to bring it back to him. So what if she had, he needn't be so damned sure about it.

"I didn't do it for you." She kissed him again with her dirty lying mouth, loving how the hard ridge of his erection slotted into her body perfectly and made every part of her go soft. "I just don't like bullies."

"You did this for my family."

"No," she insisted, her resolve melting into the warm night. "I did it for gay rights and gender equality and for everyone who's ever felt small in the face of unlimited power."

His talented thumb found her nipple and rolled

over it. Delicious pleasure thrummed through her. "I don't know what the fuck you're talking about, but it's really hot that you did this for me."

"I didn't, you idiot."

"Uh-huh."

Then he kissed her until she forgot why she had ever done anything else her entire life except kiss him back.

Kinsey.

Take-no-prisoners, sexy-as-all-get-out Kinsey.

The risk she had taken to help Alex—to help his family—knocked Luke's world off its axis. She went out on a limb. For the Dempseys. Not just crawled out there inch by inch, checking to see if the bough could support her weight. She went full tilt and hung from the branch's weakest twigs.

Luke knew about taking risks. It was part of his thrill-seeking makeup, a requirement of his job. But it wasn't a requirement of Kinsey's. So she claimed she wasn't looking for a relationship, but surely her decision to come down on the side of the Dempseys in this counted for something. Knowing that it might mean more—that *he* might mean more—nurtured a seed of dangerous hope in Luke's heart.

They needed privacy, so he steered her to his house, never taking his hands off her. Once in his kitchen, he pressed his body against hers, chest to chest, hip to hip. Mouth to mouth.

"Now, where were we?"

"You seemed to be under the impression that my decisions are all about you." A shaft of moonlight caught Kinsey's eyes like stones shining in a stream. He could never get tired of looking into those eyes. He could never get tired of her.

Ah shit.

"I don't care about your reasoning, Kinsey," he lied, not ready to push her—or himself. "What you did for Alex goes a long way with me. With all of us."

He felt like his skin had been flayed and every nerve was exposed. It had snuck up on him, this depth of feeling. One kiss at a time, one scorching touch. One woman who made his knees buckle along with his brain.

The moment sat like heavy objects between them.

"Take me to bed, Luke." A wisp of air left her lungs and mingled with his breath. Despite his brain urging against it, his heart tried to interpret it. Disappointment that he hadn't stepped up to admit that this meant more? Or relief that her plea took the edge off the moment?

Except it hadn't. Not in the slightest.

He led her up the stairs by the hand, and at the bedroom door, he switched on a light that cast a muted glow over the room.

Her golden eyes sparked in recognition. "New bed?"

"New everything. Gage helped me pick out different furniture." On his brother's recommendation, Luke had gone with a blond-wood bedroom set, and he had to admit that the lift it gave the room lifted a weight off his chest. Maybe it was silly to put such stock in the "out with the old" ploy, but apparently the Psych 101 stuff works wonders for moving on.

She sat down on the edge of his brand-new mattress and jumped her fine ass up and down a few times. "Excellent choice, sir."

He grinned. "Best eight hundred bucks plus tax I ever spent." Moving closer, he felt a thrill course through him when she parted her thighs to bracket him. He cupped her chin and directed her up to face him. "Wanna christen it?"

She clutched a hand to her chest in pretended surprise. "You mean . . . you haven't yet?"

"I might have thought about you last night when I was all by myself, but getting off solo is no replacement for the original. You're the only woman I want in my bed, Kinsey. And I mean to show you how grateful I am for what you did."

That earned him an "oh, really" tilt of her head.

He winced. "That didn't come out right."

"Gratitude sex. The kissing cousin of pity sex." She placed her palm flat on his denim-clad erection. "Perhaps I should earn more of this gratitude you're so eager to dispense." The zipper scraped down slowly, and from beneath her lashes, she watched as his breathing picked up.

The moment—and Luke's erection—grew larger as she inched down his boxer briefs, making a small noise of appreciation on finding him hard, huge, and ready for her.

"Thank you," he whispered, no longer caring if she took it the wrong way. His lungs were filled with it. With her.

Peeking up with those eyes that killed him a little every time he fell into them, she grasped him in her firm grip. She might be the death of him, but what a way to go.

"No, Luke. Thank you," she said, before she put her mouth to better uses.

Sweet, wet suction coated his cock, every stroke of her tongue a promise of the pleasure to come. There was something so very, very sexy about a strong woman with her do-me lips wrapped around him. But as much as he enjoyed the alternating soft and hard suction she was expertly applying, tonight he planned to show her just how much he appreciated her.

He drew her head away from him. "I want to take care of you, sweetheart."

Her expression was petulant. "I'm in the middle of something here. If you absolutely must participate, then take off your shirt and jeans."

No slouch, he did as he was told.

"Lie down, Luke." She raised a hand to cut off the argument he had no intention of making. "Tonight, we do this my way."

He stretched out, knowing if he dawdled she would have pushed him anyway, and waited to see how she would play it. With a look of obvious female appreciation, she surveyed his body and bit down on her lip. "I'm going to enjoy this."

Surprised it was even possible, Luke became harder at those words.

With infuriating slowness, she stripped to her underwear, something pink and lacy and feminine that pushed up her breasts and molded her ass cheeks perfectly, and then mental hypoxia set in when she straddled him. She ground her exquisite softness against his hardness.

"Let's try this again, shall we? And this time, no interruptions." Starting at his throat, she let her luscious lips do the talking. She got chatty with his nipples. Loose-lipped with his abs. Downright gabby with his . . . *groan*. She took him into the sweet, wet nirvana of her mouth, and he bucked off the bed.

"Kinsey," he moaned. "Baby . . . that's so . . ."

Slick.

Hot.

Perfect.

He burrowed his fingers in her hair, holding her where he needed her, drawing her off for a couple of inches as he rolled his hips. That's when she slipped a nail across one of his balls, causing him to jolt and thrust between her lips. That smart-tart mouth of hers, the one that could alternately cut him with a sharp remark and make him melt with a quirk of her lips, continued its erotic assault.

Taking him fully, her cheeks hollowed out, and her wet up-down sucks created a sensual rhythm that quickened his rampant pulse. His hips danced to her beat, begging for more. At the base of his spine, a sizzle built and spread to his balls. They felt as big as melons.

"Kinsey . . ." He should warn her. Some women needed the time, but this woman—*his* woman—knew what was coming, and best of all, she wanted it. She wanted him.

Just at the moment that his thrusts heralded his orgasm and his vision blurred, she peeked up at him with those gorgeous hazel eyes. The spark, the intelligence, everything he loved, was there. Encouraging him to let it all out because she would take care of him through the crash.

Him, Luke Almeida, the guy who took care of everyone because it was all he'd ever known and what he'd always wanted—his needs came first with this woman. That knowledge didn't just send him over the edge, letting out a piercing groan as he gave himself over to convulsing sensation. It damn well blew his mind.

CHAPTER TWENTY-TWO

Hours later, Kinsey lay sated in Luke's strong arms. The sex had felt different tonight, alternately urgent and dreamy, every kiss from Luke treasured, every plunge of his hips a gift.

She was tired, and so was he, but there was something in the air that made her think he had something to say. Waiting him out, she caressed his hard bicep and listened to his thunderous heart against her cheek. Its *th-thump* found a fast-paced rhythm with her own.

After a few minutes, he faced her, then curled a strand of hair behind her ear. "Tomorrow would have been my sister's twenty-fifth birthday."

Would have been. "You had another sister?"

"Mom was a meth head and she died when I was eleven. My father was in and out of our lives and my grandmother couldn't cope with us all the time. Jenny and I—" He stopped and she rubbed his shoulder in encouragement. "We were split up because there wasn't room for both of us. She was five years old and ended up with a family in Winnetka."

At her querying look, he added, "Fancy North Shore suburb. Mansions, country clubs, that kind of thing. She was hit by a car while she was out playing on the street. I thought she was safe. After all the shit she survived with Mom being so high she barely got fed to child care by drug dealers, you'd think the white-bread suburbs would be safe for a little girl."

"Oh, Luke." Her heart wrenched at his pain and the sobering awareness that no one is safe. Life was short and precious and could be stolen away at any moment. No wonder he defended his family like a wolf defends the pack.

"They didn't tell me for a month. I was emotionally fragile to start with, and they were worried I'd go nuts at the funeral." He lifted hard, blue eyes to hers. "I would have, and not much has changed. If anything happens to them . . ." He shook his head, unable to finish, but they both knew. Lord help anyone who came between Luke and his family.

That knowledge simply turned her on from head to toe.

"Anything happens to them and you'll be there. Like you've always been."

"But that can't be all I am. As important as they are to me, I have to think about where I'm going, as well."

Finding that balance between work and life, the needs of family and self, was so hard. And not just for a woman, she now realized. Luke had taken on the role of parent and nurturer a long time ago and let it define him. But he needed more. We all do.

"You want to be a lieutenant," she whispered, incredibly proud of him.

He nodded. "They sorted this problem out by themselves. Well, they did it with you, which means they're a lot more resourceful than I gave them credit for. I've been trying to be parent, brother, friend, all things to them, and the stuff I wanted became buried under all that."

She stroked his stubble-rough jaw, the intimacy of talking to him in the bed they had chosen together striking her as strange. A good strange.

"You can still be all that to them. I know that working together at the same house you feel as though you're fulfilling a pledge to your father and Logan, but you can still be their rock. If you become a lieutenant and get transferred somewhere else, they'll internalize everything you taught them and—"

"Still fuck up?"

"And still fuck up," she deadpanned, then seriously, "They'll make mistakes but maybe the next time one of them wants to trash a four-hundred-thousand-dollar car belonging to one of the city's VIPs, they'll think 'What would Luke do?'"

He groaned. "Oh, baby, now I know they're screwed."

She laughed and he joined in, alternating husky chuckles with scorching kisses. She loved this side of him—the vulnerable man who sought her counsel, not because he was weak but because he was strong enough to handle her opinion.

This mattress had been chosen for its ability to facilitate good conversations after all.

"I'm sorry about what happened at city hall, Kinsey. I saw McGinnis there, touching you, laughing with you, and I lost it. You belong with me."

It terrified her to agree, to even think it, but it was true.

"I'll call him tomorrow, invite him to Engine 6 for

the big shindig." His breath whispered against her lips. "Put it behind me. Behind us."

"Good. It's the right thing to do."

He looked thoughtful, and again she felt that sense of something important thrumming in the space between them. "And once the party's over, once your job of reining me in and cleaning up my house is done," he said, sounding like he was choosing his words carefully, "you'll be moving on to another assignment."

"That's usually how it works."

"You said once you were on the lookout for other opportunities." He paused. "Away from Chicago."

Yes, she had said that. When she was on the business end of her breakup, her heart a pulpy mess. Before this.

Before Luke.

"I did."

"Ever think that maybe this big, bold city might suit a woman of your talents, Kinsey?"

She thought it suited her very well, but it was more fun to disagree with him. "You mean the backwater that has only two seasons—winter and construction? The daylight robbery sales tax?"

"Makes it easy to calculate tips in restaurants. Just double the tax."

She pooh-poohed that. "The coldest winter I've ever had the misfortune to live through?"

"Better than damp, foggy summers in Frisco."

"Only tourists call it Frisco, Almeida."

"I know. Just messin' with you, Cali girl." He kissed her, a soft whisper of warmth that turned fierce within the span of a heartbeat.

She smiled, liking where this was going. "I dunno. Chicago could never beat San Fran."

"Oh yeah?" He coasted a lethal hand down her body, lighting her sensitized skin to flame with every inch claimed. "Do I need to convince you?"

"Persuasion is more my area of expertise, Almeida. And you'll never convince this California native that suffering through a frigid, Chiberian winter is worth it."

"Oh, I've got moves you've never seen, Taylor, and a ton of reasons why Chicago is the place to be," he murmured. "How about the beach is never more than fifteen minutes away?"

"The eight-month winters sort of ruin it."

His coarse palm kneaded her breast, plucking pleasure from every nerve. "Or the friendly people without that bicoastal-sized chip on their shoulder."

"Those chips are well earned," she said with a lusty giggle. "We've got a real ocean with salt water and everything."

The attack on her hormonal and mental well-being continued with Luke's lips grazing her jaw. Talented fingers parted her thighs and found her wet and welcome. Ready for him.

"Am I getting through to you, Kinsey?" He skimmed her plush folds with exasperating tenderness.

Needing the pressure, she ground against his hand, begging with her body what she refused to admit aloud. "Not in the slightest. You might need to . . . to take your argument up a notch."

Never one to back down from a challenge, Luke raised his game to that next sizzling level. His fingers pierced her, abrading her responsive flesh. She rocked against him, seeking, imploring.

The lure of his voice caught, hooked, and held her. "Then there's that one day in March when the clouds crack open and the sun punches through like it's escaped a cage and you can lose the heavy coat."

"Only to have to put it back on the next day," she countered on a moan.

"Yeah, but on this one day, everyone's in the best mood because the worst of it is behind us." His thumb moved in tight, sensual circles over her clit. Teasing out her pleasure. "There'll be a few more cold days, but now we know there's hope."

Hope. She hadn't dared to think it was possible, but in Luke's arms, it seemed fantasies, wishes, dreams could be rewritten.

"Luke . . ."

"It's like you have to experience all the bad days to appreciate this one day all the more, you know?"

She did. Oh, God, she did.

There was a time there when she didn't think it would get warmer. Literally, on her move here in February, and then figuratively, while she bore the pain of David's betrayal. And then that day happened. The clouds parted, she shed the wool and lifted her face to Mr. Sun.

She knew which day, maybe not at the time, but she knew it now. On a lakeside beach, Luke Almeida wrapped her in his big, hard body and held her like she mattered.

In truth, it had been more than one day, an avalanche of moments. Spending July Fourth, her new Independence Day, getting to know each other while trying out every bed in the mattress store. Making love under a firework-bright sky. Watching the passion he held for his family and those foster kids who should have been strangers to him. Every moment tore her apart and put her back together with how right it felt.

How right *this* felt.

She moaned her displeasure when he removed his hand, but he put her at ease as he spread her thighs and slipped inside her. Filling her completely. He plundered and dominated, and still, he talked. Seducing her body and soul, tying her to him inexorably.

"Screw the winter, baby. 'Cause I'll always be here, keepin' you warm."

He continued his thrusts, deep, consuming strokes that held her in place as he let her fall. The force of her orgasm caught her by surprise, but he was right there with her, capturing her pleasure-cries with his mouth—and seizing complete ownership of her heart.

CHAPTER TWENTY-THREE

Under the shelter of a picture-book-blue sky, the community party to heal the rift between fire and police, and put the finishing touch on CFD's rehabilitation, got under way. Everything was going according to plan, and why the hell not? Kinsey had organized this event to within an inch of its life. Both fire and police were out in force, split between flipping burgers under Chef Brady Smith's direction and eyeing their brothers in blue suspiciously. She had pulled in media, the community, and enough dignitaries to be worried about how the city was running in their absence.

It was the perfect punctuation to what had been one hell of a week at city hall.

Courtesy of the online petition, which had hit 350,000 signatures, Alex Dempsey was still employed by the Chicago Fire Department. Eli had commented dryly that when a petition includes the signatures of both Superman *and* Mickey Mouse, who was he to deny the wishes of the people? Between that and the countless calls from women's groups, concerned citizens, and even a celebrity ambulance chaser offering to represent Alex in the lawsuit to end all lawsuits, Eli risked his bid for reelection if he fired her. So she hung on to her job by the skin of her teeth, just like Eli did with Sam Cochrane's much-vaunted clout.

In some undoubtedly shady backroom deal, the mayor had managed to prevent Cochrane from bringing suit and dropping his endorsement. Kinsey was inclined to think that losing Cochrane's support might not have been such a bad thing, but she recognized that there was more to this situation than met the eye. Those monster egos needed each other. Cochrane wanted Alex gone, but his lawyers advised that the video evidence of his jerkwad—and according to public opinion, patently drunken—behavior was too damning. He should cut his losses and move on.

The people had spoken.

Kinsey had won.

Feeling rather pleased with herself, she surveyed the crowd on the firehouse forecourt until her gaze found the metal to her magnet.

Luke.

He was in rare form today. Checking in on the face-painting station. Ensuring that the visitors got their tax dollars' worth on the firehouse tour. Flirting (harmlessly) with some of the yummier mummies. Amid the happy chaos, the man even found time to pull her into the bunker gear room for a little one-on-one.

"I need to talk to you, Miss Taylor."

She rubbed his hard, bulging bicep—she would never get tired of touching this man's sinfully sexy body—and tried not to get distracted by his raging handsomeness. She had a job to do. "Luke, I'm working."

"Sure are, sweetheart." He kissed her slow, wet, and deep. "Workin' it good."

Fighting her impulse to jump his bones, instead she splayed a hand on his chest. "So you know what you have to do?"

He grunted. He knew, but he didn't like it, and she didn't blame him one bit.

"You're just going to shake hands with Detective McGinnis, smile for the camera, and then go about your business of making sure everyone knows this is your house."

Luke sucked in a breath. "So shake hands, get him in a sleeper hold, and shove a two-and-a-half-inch-diameter hose where the sun don't shine."

"That doesn't sound very sporting, Firefighter Almeida. At least let him be conscious when you insert the hose."

Laughing, he shook his head in disbelief. "You must be so sick of baby-sitting me and my family, Kinsey."

"Oh, the pros far outweigh the cons."

"You calm me down, you know that?"

"Not completely, I hope," she whispered against his lips before she brushed them, knowing he'd do his thing and take over. To her surprise, he kept it soft and sweet, nibbling gently, languorously, like they had all the time in the world and didn't have to walk out into the firehouse forecourt and put on a show.

"Hey, kids, we ready to get this horse-and-pony gig on the road?" she heard behind her.

Gage.

Luke rolled his eyes as Kinsey scooted away from him. "Are you actually cock-blockin' me in my own firehouse, bro? Got something against me gettin' it on?"

"Gettin' it on?" Kinsey asked, amused.

"Marvin Gaye is my second language. And that one"—he pointed at his brother—"needs a fucking bell."

Gage held up his hands. "Consider it a favor, Mr. July. You don't want to get into even more trouble by using city property for conduct unbecoming."

"Excuse me, sweetheart, while I kick some fraternal ass," Luke said to Kinsey as he made a move toward Gage, who promptly hightailed it out of the gear room.

Laughing, Kinsey trailed the brothers outside, back into the fray. Out front, she held back near the firehouse entrance and watched Luke scoop a kid off the truck ladder and pop a plastic helmet on his head. Her ovaries jumped in revolt. David had claimed not to want kids, though clearly the rat bastard had changed his mind on that score—or his wandering prick had changed it for him. She had fallen into the trap of thinking a career-oriented woman shouldn't need children to feel complete. But she realized that she did. She always had. A friend in San Francisco had insisted the man's only contribution should be the baby batter. Two kids later, she was living her dream—tired, happy, and alone.

That was not for Kinsey. She wanted a partner in all things, a man who supported her professional goals and worked with her to ensure that she—*they*—could handle it all. Marriage, career, a family of fearless blue-eyed moppets she would teach to ski off the side of a mountain.

Blue-eyed? She was in so much trouble.

Beside her, she felt a shadowy presence accompanied by a hint of Chanel No. 5. Turning her head, she met the deliberate gaze of Madison Maitland.

"You've done a great job, Kinsey. The mayor's approval rating is up and it's got a lot to do with how you've handled this whole CFD-CPD business. If I cared about community-focused PR, I'd offer you a job."

Kinsey felt a warm glow in her chest at Madison's appreciation. "I'm hoping to get the mayor working on a campaign for foster kids." While she had the ear of the most powerful man in Chicago, she needed to use her connection.

Mayor Cooper moved to a podium that had been set up near the grills, ready to charm the crowd.

"*Aaaand* show time," Madison murmured.

"I'm not going to patronize you with some speech imploring us all to just get along," Eli said. Patronizingly. Kinsey knew he was over it and just wanted to put the whole sorry mess in his rearview mirror.

"As the city's first responders, it's imperative that fire and police work together for the safety and well-being of our citizens. Cooperation saves lives, is fiscally responsible, and means I can keep the gray out of my hair for a little longer."

This was met with dutiful chuckles, though Kinsey could have sworn she heard a mutter of "There's always Clairol Nice 'N Easy" in what sounded suspiciously like Alex's voice. Whoever it was got a bigger laugh from both fire and police. Nice. Finding a common enemy in management was always a guaranteed way of uniting the troops.

The mayor's raised eyebrow acknowledged the jab, but with a flash of that voter-baiting smile, he plowed on. "Thanks to everyone who came out today—CFD, CPD, esteemed members of the press, and most important, the community we serve."

His beam arced over the crowd, shining especially bright for the female citizenry, who clapped loud and long. The mayor was having a rather awesome hair day.

"Oh, he *is* good," Madison said under her breath. "At times like this, I wonder why I gave him up."

Startled, Kinsey turned to Madison. "You and . . . Eli?"

"The first Mr. Maitland," she said with a wry smile, "for all of thirty seconds about twelve years ago."

No effen way. Kinsey's gaze landed on the mayor once more as her conversation with Madison over cocktails in the Signature Room trailed back to her in pieces. Madison's first husband who had been too young and unformed to get it . . . but he was fully formed now. Perfectly so.

Buckle up, Alex Dempsey. It's going to be a bumpy ride.

The mayor was finishing up the hands-across-America speech and now paused for the reason they were all here. "Firefighter Almeida, Detective McGinnis?"

Eli looked left and right at Luke and McGinnis, who eyed each other warily like old prizefighters deciding if they should push each other around the ring for appearances' sake or go straight for the knockout punch.

Kinsey held her breath. *Come on, babe, you can do this . . .*

Luke stepped in. McGinnis followed suit.

After a taut moment, Luke threw out his hand

toward the man who had bedded his wife and almost destroyed his career. McGinnis nodded and shook the proffered peace gesture with a firm grip. The official photographer snapped a candid for posterity and both men separated as quickly as they had come together.

"Excellent," Eli said. "Now, there's still plenty more fun to be had. And I believe the desserts will be coming out soon."

As the mayor spent a few moments glad-handing with the (female) voters, Kinsey locked eyes with Luke, who shot her a wink and a cheeky smile. Pride in how he had handled this mingled with respect, affection, and a whopping case of *wow*. Caught in the tractor beam of his gaze, she couldn't imagine being anywhere else, with anyone else.

Nothing else mattered, only Luke.

Only this moment.

At the face-painting station, Gage was getting made up like his favorite superhero, Spider-Man, ostensibly because it was fun for the kids, but really because he was a nine-year-old trapped in a twenty-four-year-old's body.

"Hey, Spidey. How's it goin'?"

Gage hadn't heard that voice in an age. Squinting up, he found his brother Beck, a scruffy-jawed grin on his face and his lady love on his arm. The beautifully inked, amazingly badass, former heiress Darcy Cochrane. They had been traipsing all over Asia for a month, and Gage had never been happier to see anyone.

He jumped up, almost knocking the face paint artist over, and clasped Beck in a bear hug.

"Hey, watch it," Beck said. "Don't get your paint on my fine, fine threads."

Gage pushed his brother back and assessed him. Tailored linen pants and a silk shirt were not Beck Rivera's usual. *Ooh la la.*

"Your doing, *princesa*?" he asked as he embraced Darcy, who didn't seem to mind a little paint.

She raised her hands in defense. "This was all him. We brought home an extra suitcase dedicated to his Bangkok tailor shopping spree."

"You like dressing me up, *querida*," Beck murmured. "Admit it."

Darcy's smile stretched wider. "I prefer stripping you down, handsome." Grin fading, she turned back to Gage, trouble clouding her eyes. "Sounds like we missed all the crazy."

Gage nodded. "Yeah, it's been wild." Though he knew Darcy was referring to the CFD drama, Gage felt his gaze inevitably drawn to the big grill they had set up at the north end of the forecourt, and the big hunk of crazy hunched over it. Brady Smith, assigned to community party cookout duty by his buddy the mayor. Gage had already been blessed with the "didn't I know you once?" nod from the guy when he walked by thirty minutes before. Now the bustle of neighborhood kids and parents, as well as single women looking to hook up with Luke, were milling about, creating not nearly enough of a distraction.

". . . I'd like to believe my father wouldn't say or do any of those things but . . ." Darcy waved a hand before his eyes. "Earth to Gage."

Gage jerked his gaze away from the jerk who was still taking up far too much of his mental real estate.

Beck followed Gage's treacherous eyeballs. His face lit up. "Hey, Darcy, look who it is. Brady!"

"You know him?"

"I do his ink." Darcy's green eyes gleamed. "Beck met him a few months ago around Christmas."

Small world. If Brady knew Beck and Darcy, why the hell hadn't he said so? Oh yeah. Because that would be far too personal for a guy as closed off as Brady "Can't Do You" Smith.

"More to the point, how do you know him?" Darcy asked, mischief in her tone.

Gage shrugged. He didn't know him, not really— he only wanted to.

Beck put a hand on his shoulder. "What's going on?"

Ignoring his brother, Gage directed 100 percent of his attention to Darcy, the brains of the operation. "Tell me everything."

"Well, he's a Marine Corps vet, several tours of Afghanistan. Served with Eli Cooper—that's how we met, actually. Eli's an old friend of the family, and he and I were having dinner in Paris about three years ago. Brady was apprenticed at this amazing restaurant there, L'Astrance and . . ." At Gage's impatient look of, *Get to the good stuff*, she rolled her eyes. "He's been a good friend to me, especially when I came back to Chicago last year. He doesn't like to be touched and I think it's because something happened to him overseas. He makes himself suffer for the ink."

He makes himself suffer for the ink, but he couldn't go that far for Gage.

"How do you know him, Gage?" Darcy asked again, this time more softly.

"Your pal Cooper." The mayor stood shoulder-to-shoulder with Brady, talking up a storm with no visible response. How the hell were those two friends?

"Good old Eli," Darcy mused. "Not sure I would have thought of the two of you together, but hey, if it works." At whatever she saw on Gage's face, her lips thinned in concern. "So which one of you is being the dumbass here?"

"No one. I dunno, maybe me." Gage had pushed too hard, come off as too desperate. No surprises there. "I thought he was interested but I had it wrong. He's wound so tight I don't want to be around when he blows."

"Coward," Beck muttered.

Irritation ignited in Gage's chest. "I am *so* glad you're back from your travels, Becky. We've been missing all that Puerto Rican charm."

Beck scoffed. "You're so used to getting all the dick you want that at the first sign of resistance, you turn tail."

Gage lasered his best glare at his brother, who he'd probably admit to being his favorite Dempsey. After Alex, anyway. Right now? Even Wy was beating out this jagoff with a smart mouth.

"I don't have time to chase the reluctant."

"Why? You on a deadline to tap as much ass as possible before you're twenty-five?" Beck's gaze turned measuring. "I wouldn't have pegged you two for a couple, either. But if you saw something there, then it had to be for a reason."

Beck had a point. There had been something there, and Gage intended to find out exactly what it was.

CHAPTER TWENTY-FOUR

During the mayor's speech, Brady had disappeared, and Gage guessed he had finally decided to leave his station to take a leak. Inside, he found the man himself in the house kitchen, offloading bottles of barbecue sauce onto the counter.

"Hey, great food," Gage said.

Brady raised his head, every move of his bull's neck like it was doing him an injury. "Thanks," he responded after a lengthy silence. "Figured your crew might like the leftover sauce. Should keep for a while."

Gage grabbed two containers, and together they loaded that and a few tubs of slaw into the cool confines of the communal fridge.

"Nice paint job," Brady muttered on closing the fridge door.

Having stopped itching awhile back, Gage had forgotten he was wearing the mask of Peter Parker's alter ego. "Spidey was always my favorite."

"Mine, too."

Well, howdy-fucking-do. This felt strangely like progress, the air suddenly alive with promise. How far could Gage push it?

"We appreciate you giving your time today,

though I guess when the mayor issues an order, you hop to it." Gage leaned against the counter and folded his arms, his bones buckling with the effort to stay casual. "Was he your CO in Afghanistan?"

Brady dipped his head, but not before Gage caught the barest hint of a smile. The way it transformed that ground-up face sent Gage's heart into a pitter-patter.

"I was his. The team was mine."

Brady bossing Cooper around? Gage would've paid good money to see that. Hell, he'd pay good money to have Brady bossing *him* around.

"You ever wish you were back in the Marines?"

"Never. The structure is good, but it starts to wear on you after a while. I prefer where I am now." Again, that look of visceral pain marred his face, like the night he'd told Gage he was unfixable.

"Do you?"

"Do I what?"

"Prefer where you are now?" 'Cause as far as Gage could tell, this man was living a half life.

The impact of Gage's question seemed to hit Brady like a two-by-four, but just then they were interrupted by a couple of the C shift making a noisy entrance into the kitchen. Shit.

"Can we go somewhere to talk?" Brady grunted.

"Come with me." No way was Gage passing up a chance to have Brady open up to him. He walked them back to the locker room, opened the door to the bunk room, and held it ajar, like he was trying to woo a puppy for a walk. Brady cast a suspicious glance around the room and stepped inside. Gage turned the lock on the door.

"This is the most private area of the firehouse."

The oversized chef was already scoping out the bunks with one hand, testing for comfort or lack thereof. "You sleep here?"

"Sometimes. Getting shut-eye is hard because we're one of the busiest houses, but I can usually sleep anywhere. I'm pretty adaptable."

Brady's shoulders lifted on a labored inhale and a few moments passed before he spoke. "Listen, I'm sorry about how I insulted you the last time we talked. I was accusing you of stuff and . . . I don't know you well enough to talk to you like that. I don't know you well enough to assume your fuck patterns and how often you need it."

Gage was so stunned by Brady's apology that for a moment he was rendered speechless. First time for everything.

"You didn't insult me. I just want to know why you're blowing hot and cold."

Brady smiled again and *yowza*, Gage almost jack-knifed to his knees right there and then. "Guess I like you some."

Gage took a step closer. "No take-backs, Brady."

"I'm not gonna take it back, but it doesn't mean anything. This . . . this can't work."

"Aw, shit, you didn't lose it in A-stan, did you?"

"Lose what?"

"Your sex drive? Your dick? Your southern-fried mind?"

Brady glowered. Bring on the sex-ay. "No, I didn't lose it, you little shit. I—I'm just not comfortable with anyone touching me. Not yet."

So Darcy had that much right, but that's not what struck Gage hard. It was those two little words. They stayed suspended on wings, kept aloft by the raw need thickening the air.

Not yet.

Gage sat on the nearest bunk and had to psychologically restrain himself from patting the space beside him. "So how are we going to work this out? Because this no-touching thing is sort of harshing the vibe."

"I know a guy like you won't want to wait."

"There you go making assumptions about me again."

The blush staining Brady's cheeks drew Gage's smile. So fucking cute. "Gage, I want to touch you, but—"

"You'd be okay with touching me?"

The big man nodded.

"But I couldn't touch you back."

Another nod.

"You're describing the fantasy of every guy, gay or straight. Getting off without giving back. But while the old me would be fine with letting someone blow me without having to return the favor, that's not who I am anymore."

Since when, Simpson? Since about a month ago when he strutted into this guy's kitchen and just about doubled over with lust and want and other scary shit his dumb gray cells refused to examine this minute. Stellar timing on the sex-life-changing epiphany.

Why couldn't he have picked someone easy? Guys with layers were not his thing, but man, he wanted this guy and all his messed-up layers. "Some of the stuff I've done, Brady, I could do with dialing it back, know what I mean?"

Brady shook his head, adorably confused.

"I'm young and I'm hot. Maybe it's time I took it a bit slower in my old age."

"You're twenty-four years old, asshole!"

Brady getting agitated was about the sexiest thing Gage had ever seen. Oh man, this was going to be fun.

"I'll let you in on a little secret." Gage gave a faux shifty look, left-right, and leaned forward. "I'm a bit of a ho. Just sayin' I'd be cool with taking it easy, seeing how it pans out." He cocked his head. "How old are you?"

"Thirty-five."

Older than he thought, and even more of a turn-on. But then, Brady turned Gage on by merely breathing. "So. Even though you don't want me to run my hot hands all over your hard body just yet, you still have fantasies about me, right? You touch yourself and think of me and my billboards?"

Brady mumbled something.

"What's that, Chef Smith?"

The barest of smiles snuck up on his lips. "You know it, Golden."

Feeling smug, Gage leaned back on his elbows, which had the deliberate, and very fortunate, effect of lifting his tee enough to show a sliver of tanned skin at his abs. Brady's eyes darkened to almost black.

"I need you to touch me, Brady. Now."

Brady swallowed, his Adam's apple so pronounced it made his thick neck bulge. But then he backed up a few steps, hurtling Gage's heart into a free fall. What the hell?

He checked the lock on the door. "I've already scared half the kids out there. Don't want to scare the other half by getting caught at this."

Gage's heart clenched at that, but the discomfort fled the moment Brady walked over—stalked, really—with surprising animal grace for one so mountainous. Kneeling down, he moved a big bear paw to Gage's thigh, and that simple touch set Gage to shaking. Up, up, up he slid his hand to the zipper of Gage's jeans. His dick bucked liked a bronco in anticipation of being let out of the gate.

"Remember what I said, Gage. Hands to yourself."

The guy had barely touched him and he was ready to blow his wad. As Gage fisted the bunk bed coverlet, he could hardly push the words out. "That's going to be . . . really . . . really . . . difficult."

Brady chuckled and rubbed over the denim at the crease of Gage's thigh and groin, hard but not hard enough.

"I'm about to go down on Spider-Man. This is mighty fucked up."

That was the least of it. Gage had no idea which was weirder: that he was about to be blown by an ex-Marine, five-star chef with hard-core intimacy issues or that for the first time in his life, he was not in charge of a sexual encounter.

Brady pulled down Gage's zipper and glanced his knuckles over the rampant bulge straining against his boxer briefs. Just a tease, to let Gage know he was in control.

But then the bastard had been running the show since day one.

Out in the Engine 6 forecourt, the party was kicking into high gear. Finally finished with his voter schmoozing, the mayor strode over to Kinsey and Madison.

"Nice speech, Mr. Mayor," Madison said.

Without acknowledging her compliment, the mayor said, "Mind if I have a word with Kinsey in private, Mads?"

"Sure," she said, a wrinkle in her usually smooth brow as she split a look between Eli and Kinsey. "I think there's a slice of cake with my name on it."

Eli watched his ex-wife walk away—Kinsey was still reeling from that shocker—but even when Madison was out of earshot, he remained silent. Quiet built like a fortress between them, almost bruising, and her stomach turned queasy. Every time Kinsey had stopped by Eli's office over the last week to confess her sins, he'd been out on official business or in meetings. Now it was time to welcome those dang chickens home to roost.

"I was hoping to talk to you about some of the campaigns I think we could tackle next, but first, I have a confession—"

"You can have a week to clear out your office, Kinsey, but I imagine you'd prefer to wrap things up sooner."

Oh. Her dumb heart plummeted to the tarmac, where it flopped around like a landed fish. *Fired.* One of the most powerful and influential men in the country had just fired her.

"How long have you known?"

His expression said she was an idiot, naive, or both. So that's how it was. The bastard had been playing dirty pool all along.

"You're not the only one with an insider at NBC,

Kinsey. I suspected immediately, then had it confirmed about ten seconds after it aired." He shook his head. "You could have let the Dempseys go it alone, but the petition, the management of it all . . . well, I can see why you would want to craft that yourself. Even when you're disobeying a direct order, you do it in the most professional way possible."

Hadn't she suspected he knew the moment she hung up the phone with him after the release? For the video to be sourced directly to the mayor would have been an open declaration of war on Cochrane. Much better if Eli could plead ignorance when it went viral. This way, he kept Cochrane's backing, the city safe from a debilitating lawsuit, and Alex Dempsey's job intact. Kinsey's position? Collateral damage.

Indignation rose up, swift and certain.

"The minute I brought in that video, you knew it was the way to save Alex, but you didn't want its release traced back to you. I was relying on your sense of justice, but you were banking on mine. I played your game, did your dirty work, and I'm still out of a job?"

Inclining his head, he spoke in a voice underlined with steel. "I told you to kill that video, and instead you ran a shadow campaign that resulted in me almost losing a top donor and an important endorsement. Don't pretend you didn't understand the risks here. There was no guarantee it would have such a positive end, but the means . . ." A spark of something softened those piercing blue eyes. "We would have made a great team, you and I. But I can't abide disloyalty, even when it works out for the best."

True, she had gambled, and she'd known her job

might be the casualty. But Eli had strung her along, let her think she was safe. Let her fall deeper into this new life she was crafting. This new love she was embracing.

What a penis.

Her head spun as she tried to wrap it around the labyrinth of this man's mind. "Why didn't you fire me the minute you found out I had ordered the release?"

He moved his gaze over the crowd in the forecourt. "Given your special relationship with Almeida, I didn't want to put this event in jeopardy. Christ knows how far off the rails he'll fly when he finds out I've canned you."

Nice to know she had her uses, even if it was merely as lion tamer for a roaring beast. Shame on her. She had underestimated Eli, a common mistake when dealing with people possessed of stunning good looks.

"That's not what this was about," she said, back to his jibe about Luke even as she acknowledged the truth of Eli's statement. Desperation to hold on to her core values of dedication and professionalism compelled her to defend yet another decision made with a man as the engine.

"Ah yes. You were making a stand for the sisterhood and defending the rights of our pink citizenry."

He was right. She had moved cross-country for one man, and now she had sacrificed her job for another.

She was a fool—and she had no one but herself to blame.

CHAPTER TWENTY-FIVE

Dempsey's on Damen was in full swing tonight since the Engine 6 community party, declared a "rousing success" by the CFD brass and the sharp-clawed media, had gone some way to sealing the fissure between the city's first responders. The bar was traditionally blue, so Luke was glad to see the police again rubbing shoulders with their brothers in the fire service. It was good for morale—and profits.

He also had another reason for his cheerful mood.

This afternoon he had taken the lieutenant's exam, and now he had a couple of weeks to wait until the results. But he was sure he'd aced it because he was already a CFD lieutenant in everything but name. The only crimp in his happy was that Kinsey wasn't here. She had returned to San Francisco to visit her family, and three days without her was making him scratchy.

Off in the corner, he spotted Josie, Kinsey's assistant, playing darts with a gaggle of Trixies-in-training. She bounced over and leaned across the bar, her eyes big and expressive.

"Luke, are you okay?"

"Never better. You?"

Sadness tweaked her pretty face. Shit, maybe something had happened to her cat.

"I'm fine. I mean . . ." She squeezed his arm. "It's awful about Kinsey getting fired, isn't it?"

"*What?*"

Her mouth formed into a perfect O. "You didn't know?"

Pulse hammering, he blinked rapidly, as if that could somehow change what he had just heard. Kinsey had been fired? And she hadn't said a word?

Josie seemed to take his silence for encouragement to continue. "I don't think it's public yet or anything, but it was inevitable the mayor would find out about her part in the whole Cochrane video thing, and of course, he's not going to stand for that kind of disloyalty . . ."

His heart was still pounding. Josie was still talking.

". . . Not when he told her to keep it on the down low . . ."

Luke gulped down a boulder of guilt. Shit, she'd lost her job—because of the Dempseys?

Because of you, shithead.

". . . And it's all anyone can talk about at city hall because she was one of his favorites. He'd bypass his top press guy to get her opinion, though Porn Stache John was probably the worst person to represent the city. I mean, would you trust a guy with that kind of facial hair . . ."

Luke tuned Josie out. He needed to talk to Kinsey. Now. His aggravation at being kept in the dark was overpowered by concern for her. She must be crushed, at home in San Francisco licking her wounds, not wanting to worry him. He took a few blind steps away only to freeze as the last thing out of Josie's mouth penetrated his skull like a hollow-point bullet.

"Say that again."

"I guess it's a good thing she has that job lined up back in San Francisco."

"What job?"

Josie looked both annoyed at his ignorance and taken aback by his snappishness. "With that politician, Max something. I heard her talking about it on the phone when she came in Monday morning to pack up her office. I wasn't eavesdropping, but she usually leaves her door ajar because she always has, or had, this open-door policy and . . ."

The thump of his blood boomed in his ears. His swallow sounded unnaturally loud.

She already had her next job lined up.

In San Francisco.

He pulled out his phone and, in a daze, studied the last text she had sent him earlier that day. He'd wanted to share news of the exam with her, but then thought it would be better to surprise her when he officially passed. When she was in his arms again. Instead he had asked about her day.

Dad's trying to force bacon on me!

His response: *Suck it up, baby. When you're back, I'll make you all the damn salad you want.*

She had replied with a smiley face. A fucking smiley face.

She wasn't coming back. Not permanently. She hadn't even confided in him about losing her job. Why the hell would she keep him in the loop about her life plans?

Maybe Josie had the wrong end of the stick. God knows what sort of game of broken telephone went on down at city hall with everyone *not* eavesdropping and the bathroom stalls buzzing with half-truths and gossip.

He needed to calm. The. Fuck. Down.

"Back in a sec," he said to Gage, who nodded absently, too busy flirting his ass off with all comers at the bar.

He stepped into the hallway near the restrooms, drew a deep breath, and hit call. She picked up on the end of the first ring. "Hi."

"Hey, how's it going?"

"Good . . ." Her voice faded out and then he heard her hiss, "Jax, quit it!" She came back on the line. "Sorry, that was my brother Jax. He's making up for months of not being able to torture me in person. So, how are you?"

Not so hot. "I heard the strangest thing. Apparently you were fired, but I thought that couldn't possibly have happened because you would have told me about it." He knew the words came out pissy, but there was no honey-coating his fury. She had lied to him, and while she might not owe him a future, she owed him the truth.

The pause was full, weighted. "I didn't want to worry you. I knew as soon as you heard you'd feel bad about it because—"

"You did what you did for my family." For him.

"Right, and I needed to figure out my next move." *Alone*, she left off the end of that sentence. This was to be a Kinsey-only decision.

He took a deep breath. "And does your next move involve an actual move back to California?"

There was another pause, and it sounded as though she was walking somewhere. He heard a low squeak, like the opening of a screen door.

"I'm not sure," Kinsey said finally. "There's an

offer working with someone I admire here in San Francisco. It's a U.S. Senate race and I'd be a fool to pass it up."

Then be a fool. Come back to me and plug the void that could only be filled with your smile, your smarts, your compassion. Be a fool for me.

But she had been here before when she moved for her ex, compromising her career and her principles for a man who did not deserve her. Luke knew he didn't deserve her either, and prostrating his body before her would only make a proud man feel low.

Or lower.

Kinsey had never promised him a thing. She was supposed to be his rebound, the first woman since Lisa. And clearly that was the function he fulfilled for her.

But for him it was more. So much more. She'd saved both his and Alex's jobs, kept his family together at Engine 6, and pried open a heart that had been closed for an eon. He had somehow managed to convince himself that playing Dempsey Dad was enough, but it wasn't. Kinsey had shown him that it was okay to want good things. To strive, to use his skills as a leader, to speak up when he saw something that needed to be rectified. He would make an excellent lieutenant.

He wanted to share that with her.

He wanted to share everything with her.

But of course she wouldn't care. She was like Mary Poppins, swooping in with a spoonful of sugar to help the medicine go down. Making his crapfest of a life palatable with her quick wit and gorgeous smile, and now she was on to her next challenge. Boxes checked, mission accomplished. Luke Almeida had been domesticated and returned to normal society.

"Luke, are you still there?"

Barely. He felt insubstantial, transparent. Surely this was happening to someone else. "Listen, I gotta go, we're gettin' busy in here."

"Oh . . . okay." She sounded like she had more to say, and he waited, praying there was something else worth saying. But when she spoke again, it was to bid him good night.

It sounded a lot like good-bye.

Well, that went down like the *Titanic*.

Sagging in her own skin, Kinsey gripped the marble countertop in her dad's kitchen and shot for a logical analysis of her feelings.

Coward.

No matter how she sliced and diced it, that was the one word that taunted her. She was a coward for not telling Luke she'd been fired. She was doubly a coward for not telling him about the job offer from Max. And ding-dong, three times was the cowardice charm for not telling him how she felt. She missed him. Terribly.

But she had missed David, too, when he put them on a break to complete his residency in New York. She had missed him when he left for Chicago to take the next step in his high-powered career. Missing someone who's filled a gap in your life, no matter how briefly, was not a sound basis for life-altering choices. She was the poster child for piss-poor decisions fueled by hormones, from her cross-country move to her management of the Cochrane video, and damned if she would let her hoo-ha get the jump on her common sense again. Sure, she could find a job in Chicago and see where this journey with Luke led, but what about the opportunities here and now?

This morning, she had met with Max Fordham at city hall, fully prepared to fess up about why Eli had fired her. But he already knew.

Eli had called Max, not to scuttle her chances, but to sing her praises. He had canned her—then come through with a glowing reference. After Kinsey explained what happened, Max had looked at her differently. Oh, she knew he had respected her before, but now she was the moral heavyweight who stood up to the powerful mayor of Chicago.

Max had loved that.

Short of something embarrassing popping up on her background check, she was a shoo-in for the job. She was under no illusion that Max was any less jaded than Eli or any other politician she'd worked for, but she wanted to be in at the beginning. Crafting his message from scratch was the new challenge she needed. The guy might be a senator, maybe even president one day.

All this should have made her feel better.

Dispirited, Kinsey returned to the backyard of her father's house in San Rafael, where Dad, Jax, and Ali—Jax's girlfriend—sat at the picnic table. The sun was hitched on the horizon, its peachy glow promising a beautiful day tomorrow. But despite the warm air, the chill of regret she'd brought with her from Chicago remained in her bones.

"We okay?" her brother asked, that familiar worry

crinkle bisecting his brow. He topped up her glass of Pinot.

"Fine." She took a sip, then put the glass down.

"Easy there, tiger, we've only got three bottles left," Jax said, and when Kinsey looked she was shocked to see the glass was half empty.

Her father was watching with eyes narrowed to curious slits. "Was that Luke?"

Ali perked up. "Who's Luke?"

"Her firefighter fling in Chicago. Used to be a Marine." Jax's expression was filled with brotherly disgust. "Sounds like a tool with a hero complex."

Since the David debacle, her brothers had become more protective of her. But because they were men and had the emotional subtlety of grizzlies, this protection took the form of insulting any man in her immediate orbit. Case in point: Eli Cooper was, in Jax's words, "a lily-livered, hair-obsessed tyrant."

"A firefighter who's ex-service?" Undeterred by Jax's assessment, Ali leaned in conspiratorially. "Tell me more."

Kinsey squirmed in her seat. Where the hell had all the oxygen gone? "There's nothing to tell."

Her brother cocked a "you shittin' me" eyebrow. "According to his Facebook fan page—yeah, this tool's got a fan page—he's an Irish Cuban split, likes to punch people who piss him off, and gets off on showcasing his abs on billboards. In fact, he's such an exhibitionist, he and K are not averse to broadcasting their sexcapades to the whole family. FaceTiming it to whoever's online."

"Dad! I can't believe you told him that." More to the point, she couldn't believe Jax would have such top-notch weaponry in his arsenal, but was only firing off a round now.

"What's this?" Ali proceeded to collapse in giggle fits as Jax regaled her with his version of the caught-on-cam story (which wasn't even *his* story). By the time he'd finished, it had become ten times more naked and twenty times more pornographic.

Her father gave an unembarrassed shrug. Military men. Unshockable. "After I got over the surprise of interrupting my daughter as she was about to . . . you know, I found it to be quite funny. I like your beau, punkin."

"He's not my beau, Dad. He's—"

"Just a fling?" Ali smiled, the epitome of coy.

He was the man who restored her faith, one kiss, one touch, one heartbeat at a time. "Just a nice guy who made the Windy City a little more bearable."

On a grunt, Jax raised his glass. "Like I said. A tool."

They were talking about him in reverent, worried whispers. Or, Gage and Alex were. Luke imagined Wyatt listening with a barely raised eyebrow as they discussed "How do you solve a problem like Almeida?"

He strode into the kitchen, tempted to whistle to see if it would throw them. In the week since he'd found out about Kinsey losing her job, Luke had gone about *his* job, which made them all suspicious.

Each Dempsey had different MOs when it came to the crapshoot of relationships. When Gage broke up with someone, he cooked. A lot. Until they had chicken marsala coming out of their ears. Alex "scared guys dickless," so there was no protocol there. As for Wyatt, he lived like a monk, except for the mysterious overnighters he refused to talk about. And Beck was all loved up with Darcy.

After Lisa, Luke had punched things and shouted at people and punched more things, then spent months becoming one with his couch and making a very fine acquaintance with the bottom of a bottle. That he wasn't curled up in a fetal ball of Jack-soaked misery worried them.

Ignoring them, he poured coffee, then pulled out his ringing phone. He frowned on seeing it was Alex—as in the same Alex who was sitting behind him at the kitchen table.

"What?"

"Just checking that your phone is working," his sister said. "Kinsey said you haven't answered any of her calls."

Luke's neck prickled at the mention of her name. He rearranged his expression to neutral as he did the turn-and-sip.

"What are you going to do about it?" Gage asked. Today's T-shirt announced: I'm a firefighter. To Save Time, Let's Just Assume I'm Never Wrong.

"About what?"

Gage's look was cutting. "I really like her."

"You have enough friends."

"*You* really like her," Alex said.

"It was just a fling, sis. Nothing more." The lie felt blasphemous on his lips—at least ten Our Fathers at confession, Mary would have said. He took a gulp of coffee to keep from screaming.

"Bullshit."

Luke's eyes zeroed in on Wyatt. "Bullshit?"

"Woman's perfect for you. Puttin' up with your hoverin' crap. Givin' us all a break."

"My hovering crap?" He moved his gaze around the kitchen and was met by eyebrow shrugs. "You mean the fact I care about you a-holes enough to actually want to know where you are and when you might be home? You mean that hovering crap?"

"But that's the problem, isn't it?" Alex chewed on her lip, Dempsey determination taking over. "You're always thinking of us. Worrying about us. You can't be there for every run, for every mistake."

"Someone has to be!" He turned and slammed the coffee cup down, not caring that its contents splashed the counter. Who would look after them if he weren't here? Wyatt? Wyatt was useless as a caregiver. Great to have by your side in a fire or a foxhole, but he was so hands-off with the juniors, they may as well be unrelated.

"There's a box of nails under the sink," Wyatt said. "Should be strong enough to keep you up on that cross."

"Oh, shut it, Wy," Alex snapped. "Give him a break."

Gage sighed, ever the peacemaker. "We're adults, Luke. We're trained professionals—"

Wyatt huffed at that.

"—and sometimes we mess up, but it's not your job to fix it."

"I'm just looking out for you all. That's not going to change. It's ingrained in my DNA." He couldn't fight for Jenny. He was powerless then, but not anymore.

"I need to speak to Luke alone," Wyatt said.

Luke turned back in time to catch the surprise on Alex's and Gage's faces. Wyatt never made a request like this. All family matters—not that this was a family matter, but it was the nature of the Dempseys to stick their noses into everything—were discussed as a group. Wyatt and he might talk about the kids when alone, but they never asked anyone to leave the circle.

Acutely aware of the significance, Gage and Alex exchanged worried glances, but obeyed and left the kitchen.

In the pause so heavy it could have crushed a fire truck, Wyatt stared at Luke.

"I wasn't here," he said finally in a low voice. "When Sean and Logan died, there was no discussion about who would stay."

"I was happy to do it." He did it as much for Wyatt as for the juniors. Given the choice, he would do it all over again, no hesitation.

"You've every right to be bitter about that," Wyatt continued as if Luke hadn't spoken, "and not just because you loved the Marines. I was no use to you or the kids." His chest lifted on an inhale. Luke might have called it the most demonstrative display of emotion from Wyatt he'd ever witnessed, except that was bordering on melodrama.

"It was tougher for you, Wy. Logan was blood." Luke knew what it was like to lose your blood. Wyatt's pain had cut so deep that the regimented life of the Marines was the only thing keeping him somewhat steady during the storm. Mourning Dempsey-style was too messy for his personality.

Wyatt didn't argue the point, just nodded his acceptance of Luke's conclusion, and in that moment, Luke had never loved him more. They had always understood each other.

"No one expects you to give up your life anymore, Luke. You've got to think about what you need. This woman of yours . . . what she did for Alex . . ." He frowned. "If she'd had it in her power, Lisa wouldn't have lifted a bony finger to help and you know that. Kinsey gets you. She gets *us*."

Yeah, she did. She put her job on the line and it came back to bite her beautiful ass. But that did not change the cold, hard facts. "She doesn't want me. Jesus, she didn't even tell me she got fired, Wy. She's already planning her life thousands of miles away."

"You tell her already how you feel?"

Luke delivered the look of, *Hell no*. It was not as if he was emotionally well adjusted like Gage or anything.

His brother shook his head, the wisp of a smile almost strange on his lips. "She needs the grand fuckin' gesture. Like all chicks."

An inappropriate laugh burbled up from somewhere deep and painful. Wyatt dispensing relationship advice was about the funniest thing he'd heard in a long time.

"And I should be taking tips from the guy who never dates because . . . ?"

"Forget it. Just tryin' to help."

Evasion would no longer get a pass here, not when Wyatt had opened the touchy-feely door. "I need to ask you something. When you're gone overnight, is it for a woman?"

"Nope."

"Is it illegal?"

Wyatt looked affronted. Damn, screw the risk of offense—Luke had to be sure. Visions of Wy drag racing the Camaro down Western Avenue darted through his brain. Luke needed to know that he could trust his brother to be here if he wasn't.

If he wasn't.

Holy shit. He was really considering this.

Wyatt took a slug of his coffee. "Years ago, I let a girl go. I knew she was mine, but I wasn't brave enough to claim her, and she moved on. If I could do it over, I'd make sure she knew she was my woman. In no uncertain terms."

If Wyatt had said he was joining the circus, Luke wouldn't have been more surprised. His oldest brother was the most private person Luke knew, and it had to be hard for him to, one, spill anything personal, and two, cop to being deficient in the bravery department. The latter admission, especially, was something no Dempsey ever made. Fearlessness was treasured more than Hawks tickets, and just because they were talking about all this emotional crap did not change the rules.

Luke had been living in a state of comfortably numb for the last year. Longer. Lidocained by the security blanket of his family, he had a role, a reason, and the self-deluding assurance that it was enough. But it wasn't.

He would happily crash through the flame-hot door of an apartment building to rescue someone, yet he didn't have the sac to take Kinsey Taylor into his arms and tell her he wanted her forever. His useless heart was in shreds without her. He needed her like he needed oxygen. If there was a chance he could make this right, what in hell was he doing sipping coffee in his kitchen?

Wy slid a glance toward the door and Luke felt the

beginnings of a smile mixed in with a little sadness. "You can come in now," he said.

The door pushed open, bringing Gage and Alex tumbling into the kitchen, ready to pick through the rubble of the truth grenade that just exploded.

"About time," his sister griped. She wrapped her arms around him and lay her head on his shoulder. "I'm sorry, Luke. About Cochrane, about Kinsey losing her job. It's my fault she's gone. Well, it's that cretin Eli Cooper's fault, but I know I have some share in it. I've never been anything but a pain in your ass."

He smiled against her hair. "True that, but we're not going to armchair-quarterback this anymore. It's done and now we have to move on."

She held him tighter. "You've always been my favorite brother."

"Jesus wept," Gage muttered, and everyone laughed, breaking the tension after what seemed like weeks of disharmony and stress in Camp Dempsey.

The kitchen door opened and in strode Beck and Darcy. They halted at the scene before them.

"What's goin' on here, then?" Beck asked, his blue eyes narrowed in suspicion.

"Luke just extracted his head out of his ass," Wy said.

With a sigh, Darcy made a move on the cinnamon rolls. "There we go missing all the excitement as usual. Can you do it again? In superslow motion."

Luke divided a look among his annoying-as-all-fuck family members. "Any more opinions or comments before we wrap this up?"

Gage eyed him shrewdly over his coffee cup. "Yeah. I suggest you take off your dress and go get her."

CHAPTER TWENTY-SIX

The pop-pop synth of Röyksopp and Robyn's "Do It Again" kept Kinsey's feet on track as she punished the streets of San Rafael, but it did squat to keep her thoughts from straying to Luke. His sharp blue eyes haunted her. Watching, wanting, ready to spark into laughter or desire at any moment.

She turned up the volume.

Her querulous mind churned up images of Luke's hard body joining with hers. Much better. Objectify that beefcake. Think of him only as the guy you had a hot fling with during a sultry Chicago summer. The last few months had been like a vacation from real life. An internship of sorts with the mayor's office. Campaigns realized, crises averted, worth proven, and even though it ended on a less-than-stellar note with that awkward firing business, she had still come out ahead experiencewise. And she'd managed to get some hot firefighter lovin' while she was at it.

Not bad. Not bad at all.

Except . . .

There was no except—and to prove it she picked up the pace. There was only the past, filled with unworthy men standing in the way of her goals. If she couldn't stay strong on this, then what kind of sister was she?

Was she doomed to repeat her mistakes and the mistakes of women before her? This wasn't why women marched and burned bras and fought for respect. Not that her job was to represent the entirety of womanhood, but she had to do what worked for her, for once, and right now taking the job with Max Fordham was it.

But Luke Almeida also worked for her. In the bedroom. In his Chevy. In her heart. He worked for her so damn well he had taken up permanent residence in her brain. Ten years with David and now she barely spared him a thought. Ten days without Luke and she could think of nothing else.

But he clearly was not thinking of her. She had called him several times in the week following that heart-sickening phone conversation, with no response. It was one thing for her to insist he was a fling; it was quite another to have it so unmistakably affirmed by his silence. Anyway, what would she have said to him if he'd answered one of her calls?

Great knowin' ya, babe—thanks for all the orgasms?

Yanking out her earbuds, she rounded the drive up to Dad's ranch house and slipped through the passage at the gable. Masculine voices carried on the warm breeze. Jax must be here for brunch already. She ambled into the backyard to say a quick hello before hitting the shower.

Only it wasn't Jax.

Heart slamming madly, she took a long, lingering look to soothe her parched brain. Once again, she was sharing the same time zone as Luke Almeida.

"Hey," he said coolly, as if the idea of him popping in for brunch at her father's house two thousand miles from Chicago was perfectly normal.

Words refused to form. Man on fire in the garden, lady IQ plummeting.

Her memory had done him no justice. He wore jeans, those soft ones that molded to his powerful legs like old friends. God love the man, she would never tire of how he looked in denim. His tee was gray, its simplicity only serving to accentuate the man's incredibly powerful chest. It had never been *only* a chest. She was glad to see he hadn't dressed up to meet her father. He was just as he should be—the sexy, take-me-as-I-am warrior she loved like crazy.

She loved this man.

"Luke's been filling me in on his service in the Marines," her father said, hauling her out of the Luke fug she'd become lost in. In her dad's voice, she heard approval. Acceptance. They were cut from the same cloth, these two. Good, family-oriented, value-driven men.

Find woman, claim woman . . . oh dear. She'd fallen in love with a guy like her dad. Her brothers would never let her hear the end of it.

"I'll grab the orange juice," her father said, never mind that there were two pitchers already perspiring on the picnic table. He raised a raggedy eyebrow as he passed her.

Message received, Colonel.

Luke's gaze, that piercing, unnatural azure, traveled across her face as if it were the first time he'd laid eyes on her. "Surprise," he said softly.

"I'm all sweaty," she blurted, because she knew what was coming next and oh, God, if he touched her now she was going to lose it.

"That's how I like you, Taylor. Sweaty, pliant, and at my mercy." And the next thing she knew, she was in his arms and his mouth was fire-hot, man-hot, and it was as if everything distilled to this pure moment of heat-infused peace.

The kiss was perfect, the man even more so. Damn him.

He laid his forehead against her damp brow. "I would say we need to talk, but I much prefer what we're doing now."

"Solving the problem with sex?"

He grinned. "Even with my mad skills, I couldn't pull that off before your father gets back with a third pitcher of OJ. Looks like dehydration won't be an issue."

She let loose a laugh that staved off the threatening tears and smothered about 50 percent of her nerves. Maybe 55.

Luke drew back, his air now grave. "Have you started your new job yet?"

"My final interview is tomorrow."

"You should have told me. About everything."

"I know. It's just . . . losing my job like that, I thought I was prepared for it after the decision I made with the video, but it wrecked me. I couldn't think straight." Around him, she meant. In Luke's orbit, her brain came unglued and her heart started calling the shots.

"Baby." A murmur, not judging, just understanding.

She rubbed his biceps. She had missed these arms, and the familiar motion distracted from her guilt at running like a quitter. "When did you get in?"

"Yesterday."

At her obvious disapproval of the fact that he

had been here overnight and had not contacted her sooner, he pulled her flush again. "Kinsey—"

"Why, hello, there," she heard from her brother Jax, who had rounded the corner into the yard.

Luke eased up on his grip but didn't release her, just switched his arm to circle her waist possessively.

"Hey," she said to her brother. "Jax, this is Luke. Luke, my brother Jax."

Luke thrust out a hand and shook Jax's firmly. Avidly, she watched for signs of her brother's feelings in this.

Oh hell, what did any of it matter? Luke was here to do the caveman club-and-drag back to Chicago, and surrendering to his demands was an impossibility. She would not be a fool for love. Not again. Still, her heart stirred that he would fly across the country to claim her. She'd have to be made of stone not to be floored by the pure romance of the gesture.

Her father came out, sans OJ. Luke shot her a sidelong glance, his lips curved in amusement.

Now for the true test. "I should take a shower." She braved a peek at Luke to see if the idea of being left alone with the male Taylors bothered him, but those impossibly blue eyes betrayed nothing.

"You do that, sweetheart."

As she stepped away, his fingertips brushed hers, a touch as intimate and arousing as the smoldering kiss he'd laid on her before.

Better make that shower a cold one.

Forty minutes later, she headed downstairs and found Luke, Jax, and her father in the kitchen. Luke was cooking French toast—suck-up—and her father was plating so much bacon she wondered how many pigs had been sacrificed to supply it. Their laughter stopped abruptly on her entrance.

Jax shot her a look of, *Well, isn't this special?*

Yes, she got it. The man had come a long way, and of course her father was going to appreciate that. Dad was a soppy old romantic at heart, and he recognized a kindred soul when he saw one.

But Kinsey wasn't a romantic. She couldn't be swayed, no matter how many grand gestures Luke pulled out of his hat. The risk was too much to bear.

"There's our girl," her father said, handing off a piece of bacon and kissing her on the forehead. Luke winked at her, in on the joke.

Brunch wasn't quite as rambunctious as a Dempsey family meal, but after a few minutes, they found an easy rhythm once Luke and Jax fell into trash-talking hockey and baseball teams. Still, around the ebb and flow, every thread of conversation wound back to Luke's unfaltering gaze seeking her out. She found herself heating under his inspection, and when she looked away, it was worse. Worse not to stare at him, and worse to have to meet the wiseacre grin of her brother and the knowing scrutiny of her father.

Both of whom made no secret of their approval. Twenty-three minutes in, her father invited Luke fishing. At the thirty-seven-minute mark, Jax had clearly revised his opinion of her summer fling as "a tool with a hero complex" and was assuring Luke he'd take to skiing like a duck to water. You know, for that trip to Vail that Luke was welcome to join over Thanksgiving. By the end of brunch, Kinsey suspected the cozy male knitting circle would have decided the color scheme of the invitations, along with the wedding china pattern.

"So, Luke. Have you been to San Francisco before?" her father asked.

"No, but what I've seen impresses me."

"One day," Kinsey said, "and you're that impressed."

"It's where my woman is. That's all I need to know."

Something lurched in her chest. What the hell did that mean?

The Colonel interpreted that as a sign to make himself scarce. "Luke, it was great to meet you. In person." With a squinty-eyed grin, he stood and extended his hand.

Luke rose and gripped firmly. "Likewise, sir."

"We'll get you on the slopes and then we'll see what you're made of, Almeida." Following her father back to the house, Jax sent Kinsey a significant glance of, *Do not fuck this up*. So fickle, that brother of hers.

Luke sat down again, pulled his chair closer, and took both of her hands in his. "I missed you."

Her heart clattered wildly, panic sharpening some fuzzy knowledge that existed on the outer corner of her mind. "You said you arrived yesterday. Why didn't you come visit sooner?"

"I had dinner last night with John Carson. He's a fire chief over at SFFD in the Mission District."

"Old friend of yours?"

"Never met him before in my life."

Every thought in her brain spun out like bowling

pins, and still she refused to go there. This could not be happening. "Picking up tips for the CFD?"

His smile was droll. "Feeling him out for a job."

"You mean—"

"Yes."

She swallowed against the sand-dry lump in her throat. He had cooked up a batch of French toast, sat through brunch, joked with her father, endured her brother, and now he was dropping this on her?

"I—I thought you were here to bring me back," she said, astonishment pitching her voice too high. "I thought that's why you came."

"You made up your mind, Kinsey. Following a man, staying put for one, is off the menu. I would never expect you to compromise. It's why I'm so damn crazy about you." He raised her hands to his lips and brushed fire across her knuckles. "There's no reason why I can't move here."

"There are a million reasons and they're all called Dempsey," she said, shocked. "Luke, your family. You can't leave them." For her? He would do that for her?

He nodded thoughtfully. "It'll be hard at first. I'll miss them, but I have to start thinking about what I want. What I need. It's right here before me. I thought I wanted someone easy who'd let me run roughshod all over her. Instead I get you, Kinsey. Bossy, strong, sexy as hell, a pain in my ass. A gorgeous pain in my ass. My heart hurts when I'm not with you and"— he squeezed her hands tighter—"shit, baby, it hurts when I'm with you, too, but it's that good hurt, you know? You've got your hook in me. You're the barb I can't get loose."

She couldn't breathe. "Luke, your job—"

"Carter at SFFD said with my experience, I can probably take the lieutenant's exam in a year. It'll be a slight step down at first, but it's doable."

Doable? How about insane? Her summer fling couldn't have become so serious that he would give up everything and everyone he had ever known, the people and city he had vowed to protect, to be with her. She adored her family, but for Luke it was different. It was a biological imperative that he watch over them. Could she live with knowing she was the reason he was here, separated from the people he loved?

"Luke, this is"—*crazy, stupid, the most romantic thing anyone had ever done for her*—"not going to work. We hardly know each other."

"I love you. It'll work."

She lowered her eyelids. He loved her, and those words had never sounded sweeter or more sincere. But the realist beat the romantic into submission as she sought out fissures in his argument. "This job I'm up for, if it works out, it's headed to Congress in sixteen months. D.C. What happens then? Are you going to turn your own life upside down every time I move to a new job?"

He slanted her a look. "I haven't thought that far ahead. Instead of thinking about all the reasons we can't be together, think of all the reasons why we should. Right now, all I know is that when I'm not with you, I'm unhappy. With you, I am. The rest will sort itself out as long as we observe that simple truth."

Truth was never simple, but this one toppled her.

Luke Almeida toppled her. He was her ideal mate, a man she could trust to hold and protect her, the one she wanted to father the children she had pretended were not a factor in her lonely future. He understood her like no one else. Respected her like no one else. She could build a miraculous life with this man.

But she could not take him away from his family.

"I appreciate that you came all this way . . ." At the flash of hurt on his face, she considered backpedaling, but there were no safe spaces that would leave either of them happy. "That you thought for even one moment of moving here to be with me, but there's not enough between us to justify a decision so drastic."

He bolted upright to a stand. "I know you hate to lose, Kinsey, but I never thought I'd see the day that you hate to win. Have I somehow lost points with you because I've compromised here? Because I'm not stubbornly holding on to your idealized version of manhood?"

"No, Luke, that's not it. That you would think of doing this for me is terribly flattering." She cringed at how false those words rang out. Nothing sounded right.

"Terribly flattering," he said, his voice robotic. "I didn't intend it as a compliment, sweetheart. I intended it as me laying out my truth so we could start our life together. I love you and I know that you feel the . . ." As he trailed off, realization crept over his face by degrees. It horrified her to watch where his mind veered.

"Say it," he growled.

"Luke . . ."

"*Say. It.*"

She didn't pretend to misunderstand, and she stood because he deserved directness. "I care about you, Luke. I want only good things for you but"— may God not strike her down—"I don't love you."

He blinked a few times, and with each shutter of his eyelids, the light in those gorgeous blue eyes dimmed, darkened. Died. There was a moment of terrifying unknowability between them, as if a door was being cemented shut.

"Damn, you'd think after years on the job I'd have developed better instincts than this." Slowly, he scrubbed his mouth. "Have I really got it that wrong?"

In that moment, she hated herself. The list of why was endless, but up top was that she had made him doubt those instincts he usually trusted implicitly to keep his body and family safe. She wanted to scream that he wasn't wrong. This wonderful man standing before her was so right that she could barely move for needing him. She wanted to tell him that she loved how he took this problem between them and solved it with his head instead of his fists. But she worried for his heart—that huge, pumping engine in his chest. It needed care and love.

Dempsey care. Dempsey love.

Stealing him away from them would shrivel his heart to a raisin. She couldn't possibly be enough for him. She hadn't been for David. While she had no doubt Luke would fit her life like a glove, and that everyone she knew would come to love him as much as she did, there would always be that nagging thread of tension bordering on resentment between them.

I gave them up for you. Now prove to me I didn't make the mistake of my life.

She just couldn't live with that pressure.

"I'm sorry, Luke," she said as her heart shattered into a million screaming pieces. "I . . . I hope we can be friends."

He took a step toward her. Not a friendly step.

Then another.

Fighting every instinct to shrink, fall, run like the coward she was, she stood her ground and let him curl one strong, rough hand around her neck.

For the last time.

The reveal of emotion turned his handsome features harsh. She thought she knew all the ways those blue eyes of his could speak. She'd seen anger, lust, laughter, but not this. Not heartbreak.

He searched her face, staring into her soul, looking for evidence of her lie. But she pokered up, all while inside a part of her caved in and died. His thumb carved a line along her jaw, and she started to shake because she needed his touch like a drowning woman needed air. Because any second now, it would be over.

Abruptly, he lowered his mouth to hers and kissed her.

No, that was too tame a word for what he did. He ravaged and destroyed, pouring into it every ounce of his passion. His mouth owned hers, held her suspended on the edge of something indescribable, and the sweet, heartbreaking taste of him imprinted on her senses. Tattooed on her heart.

Then he tore his lips from hers for the last time.

"That's why we can't be friends, sweetheart," he breathed, the words like blows.

He turned and left the garden, a tower of virility, her proud man to the last. And she thanked her stars that he didn't look back. Better that he never saw her break, wiping away the first tears she had cried since her mom died.

CHAPTER TWENTY-SEVEN

Luke studied the departures board at San Francisco International Airport. His flight was delayed by two hours. Of course.

For a split second, he considered heading for the rental desk. He'd heard the Pacific Coast Highway drive was scenically epic, and the idea of jumping in a car and driving to LA (or into the ocean/off a cliff) sounded ultra appealing right now.

So much for the perfect plan. Luke was not a hearts-and-flowers kind of guy, but even he had to admit that what he had just done—or tried to do— was special. He had offered her everything. His heart, his world, it all belonged to her, and here he was, backing it up with decisive action.

Well, *whoop-de-doo*. Apparently he knew dick about women, and to top it all off, she had played the friends card.

How in the hell had he thought a woman as driven and sophisticated as Kinsey would want him for more than a few bouts of vigorous, mind-blowing sex? Had he learned nothing from the crash-and-burn of his marriage? He clearly didn't have anything to offer beyond his callused hands, his billboard body, his brutish skills between the sheets. Fling material, not good enough for the real thing.

But . . .

For a moment while he held her that last time, felt her tremble beneath his touch, he had thought the gods might cut him a break and affirm his gut on this. But, no, the gods were too busy laughing their asses off.

His phone buzzed and he pulled it out, hoping, wishing. But it was only Wyatt, which made it twice in a month. Some kind of record.

"Hey."

Typically Wy, he got straight to the point. "Kinsey called Gage. She was worried about you."

Nice to know *those* two were still friends.

"That's the last time I take advice from you, Fox. So women love the big gesture? You've been watching too many chick flicks."

Wyatt gave an unapologetic sniff. "Come home, Luke. The kids want to take care of you."

"They there with you?"

"Hangin' on every fuckin' word."

Luke smiled though it hurt like a rotted tooth. He could see them clearly, jockeying for position, working so hard to keep their lips sealed while Wyatt played spokesman for their collective love. The ache in his chest eased slightly, but right now, the Dempseys were the last people he wanted to see.

Without quite knowing how it happened, he found his feet had moved him outside the terminal to the car rental shuttle stop. Whichever one arrived first would be the recipient of his business.

He couldn't remember the last time he'd taken

a vacation, other than one enforced by his bad behavior, and it had been even longer since he actually relaxed. Apart from a firefighter safety conference in Dallas, his tour of Iraq, and now this effed-up pleasure ride to California, he had never left Chicago.

"I need a couple of days, Wy. I'll call Venti and let him know—"

"Consider it done," his brother said. "As long as you want."

The Avis shuttle rounded the corner of the terminal and came to a halt in front of him. *Ding, ding, ding,* we have a winner.

In the pause before he hung up, he heard Gage call out, "Love you, Luke."

Hell and damn, that kid killed him sometimes.

A few days away might help to screw his head on straight, but he'd need longer to plug the gaping hole in his chest.

Five days later, Luke was back in Chicago and his chest still felt like it'd been scooped out to make a canoe. And then there was his scalp, which was still on fire from driving in a convertible on the PCH without a hat.

Totally worth it, though. The sheer majesty of the twisting, cliff-hugging route down the coast had knocked his socks off. Might have been nice to share it with a California native—one California native in particular—but he needed to terminate that line of thinking stat. One day he might be able to acknowledge that it was good to take a chance and put himself out there. He couldn't imagine what that day would look like, but he wasn't as resentful and bitter as he had been a year ago in the aftermath of Lisa.

It was 6:45 a.m. as Luke strode through his firehouse, past the gym, past the trophies for the softball league and Beck's four straight wins at the Battle of the Badges, past the photo collage with the smiling faces of Engine 6, a mix of current crew and friends long gone.

This was his house and these people were his family, both Dempsey and the brotherhood of the CFD. The best company in Chicago, this city born of fire. Not such a bad place to be.

In the locker room, Luke found Gage changing for his shift. Since hooking up with his chef, he looked a little older, wiser, and a whole lot more happy. Chatterbox Gage and the mute Marine. Pretty crazy.

"Mail's in."

The kid held up an envelope. Luke didn't need to squint to know what it was.

"Give it here, bro."

"Not before I've gathered an audience of your peers." Gage released a high-pitched whistle.

"They're not dogs, idiot," Luke muttered, his stomach roiling with nerves even as he tried to play it cool. He had thought he'd aced the exam two weeks ago, but given his rusty instincts of late, who the hell knew?

"What are you doing here?" he asked Alex and Beck as they tromped in with the rest. Neither of them were due on shift.

"Gage told me to stop by," Alex said. "Heard there was a big announcement."

Beck merely shrugged. "I was hungry. Best food's here."

Wyatt strolled in, sparing a cursory glance for the crowd. He removed the envelope from Gage's hand and handed it over to Luke.

"Just open it and put them out of their misery."

"Come on," Alex urged. "You're cutting into my beach time, Luke."

After tearing open the envelope, he unfolded the sheet of paper, praying he had made the grade, because if he had to endure any more of the sad eyes from his family, he'd be back on a plane heading anywhere quicker than you could say "Fly the friendly skies."

He sighed and watched the faces of his siblings drop. "Only . . . a ninety-six."

"What?" Panicked, Alex looked at her brothers. "Don't worry, Luke, next time—hey, wait. That's a pass, isn't it?"

"With flying colors," Beck said. "Good job, Luke. No one deserves it more."

The rest of them crowded around, and soon the entire A shift had trod through with back claps, congratulations, and not a small amount of speculation about where he might be assigned.

"Engine 69 needs an officer," Derek said. "My cousin works over there."

This was met with a chorus of profanity and lewd suggestions as to what exactly happens at 69. Amid the raucous noise, Luke reflected on how it felt like the end of an era. His entire career in CFD—his entire life—was dedicated to protecting his family. It would be strange not to work with them anymore.

He caught Wyatt's eye. His brother nodded imperceptibly, an assurance that he'd do whatever it took to keep their pledge. Whether he stayed at 6 or was transferred out, Luke knew one thing.

It was time to move on with his life.

Kinsey poured herself a cup of joe, needing the boost before she hit the shower after a twilight jog. Her muscles ached and she was glad of it. She had it coming.

Her phone rang and her heart hitched, then dropped on seeing who it was.

"*What?*"

"Sounds like you need to get laid," Jax said. "But of course you had your chance and you blew it." Her brother was still pissed at her for turning down a solid guy like Luke. Apparently, they had "really bonded."

"Your bro-crush is showing. If I can get over it, so can you."

He ignored that. "You finally meet a guy who I wouldn't be ashamed to have a beer with and you go soft. Stop feeling sorry for him because you're so amazing that he wants to move across the country to be with you. He's probably thrilled at the chance to get away from his blood-sucking family—"

"Yeah, my time away from you lot was the best six months of my life."

"See? That's the kind of ruthlessness I know and love from my baby sister." He chuckled. "Time to bring it, Kinsey. Time to step up."

"Thanks, Coach. Is this why you called?"

"No, but my wisdom, even when unsolicited, has a price. I want your help picking out an engagement ring for Ali. Meet me for lunch tomorrow."

She growled. "Congratulations. My commiserations to your clueless bride."

On his laugh, she hung up on him. That he and Ali were getting engaged didn't surprise her, but it would be awhile before she could appreciate it.

"Hey, punkin. Good run?" Her father had strolled in from the backyard to top off his glass of wine.

She nodded as she let the coffee bring her back to life, at least for a little while. It couldn't do right by her heart, though.

"You know you can stay here as long as you need to. No hurry to find your own place."

"Living in the city makes more sense, Dad." For now, she'd commute, but she had begun a halfhearted search for an apartment closer to the new job she would start tomorrow.

"Kinsey—"

"Are you going to tell me I should be enrolling in law school, Dad? That these politicians are bad news?"

His mouth tightened with concern. "No, I was going to ask if you'd heard from Luke. It's been a week since his visit. "

Guilt that she had snapped at him flooded her sore chest. Her father's gaze was overflowing with love she didn't deserve right now. She was undateable, unlovable. Just *un*.

"No, I haven't heard from him and I don't expect to. I really hurt him, Dad."

Her father chuckled when she could have done with some sympathy. "You're so like your mom, Kinsey."

"I'm hoping you mean that in a good way. I really need to hear something nice right now."

He rounded the kitchen island and put his strong arm around her.

"I mean it in the best way. Do you know how long it took to get her to marry me?"

Oh, God. First Jax, now this. She was so not in the mood for a recounting of the romance to end all romance. "All of sixty seconds. You showed up in that classroom and swept her off her feet and the rest is history."

"No, Kinsey. That was just the beginning of the long, hard road to capture that woman's heart. She didn't want to make the kids cry by turning me down, so instead she kissed me and led me to the corridor, then told me that I was going to have to do better than that."

Kinsey blinked. This was *not* the version of the fairy tale that had entered the Taylor annals. Everyone knew Dad was on leave from Okinawa and then— *hey presto!*—he and Mom were together. Those were the facts. The end.

"But how could you do better than that? What you did was perfect." She should know. The same thing had happened to her exactly one week ago.

Her father shook his head, smiling in memory. "Not for your mother, it wasn't. She was a practical woman. She didn't want to live on a military base in Japan, and she didn't want her first months or years as an army wife to be spent alone, so she said as soon as I was stationed stateside, she'd reconsider. So I worked on that, and a year later, when I was reassigned to the West Coast, she agreed to marry me. 'Cause she was stubborn."

Setting aside the fact that everything Kinsey

thought she knew about her parents' courtship was a barefaced lie, she readied herself for the usual defense. "Dad, this isn't a case of female orneriness or a woman being difficult. You know what happened with David."

"Luke's not David, Kinsey. Would David have come for you like that? The minute you turned that corner into the backyard, Luke's face lit up like the Golden Gate. He was so excited to see the girl he loves."

Then she ruined his day. His week. Maybe his life. Maybe her own.

"Love's not the problem," Kinsey countered. "I can't allow him to give up everything he knows, and if I go back to Chicago, I'll feel like I'm giving in. Like before."

He pushed a strand of hair behind her ear. The gesture curled up and pressed on the space under her heart. "Oh, honey. Sometimes I wonder if I shouldn't have married again. Given you a positive female role model."

"So I could understand my place better?" she joked, not really feeling it.

"So you could understand the art of compromise. Why is this a competition? Why can't you both win? Even as a kid, you always had to beat your brothers. Had to be the best at everything. No such thing as a draw in your world."

Her chest ached like it was on fire. "Dad—"

"No, listen. You were with David for a long time, but it never seemed like you were truly with him. It was as if his life was on one path and yours was on another. Side by side for a while, sometimes veering off, but never crossing. Never coming together as one.

How long did it take him to finally pop the question? To make a true commitment to you? And you didn't push him to do right by you, either. Neither of you wanted to change for the other, not really. It was never meant to be and you know it."

She did. She guessed she always had.

"You can be the best at something and still rely on someone—if it's the right someone," her father continued. "A guy who deserves you, who understands priorities. Who gets how strong and stubborn and amazing you are. Luke came for you, punkin. He was prepared to give up his people to make it so *you're* his people. The one person he can't do without. And I don't think you can be without him, either."

The truth of those words shivered through her vitals. Kinsey might be standing in her physical home, but this man was the home of her heart. Her internal compass was pointing true Luke.

"I can't take him away from his family, Dad. I couldn't possibly be enough." She thought she had no more tears to shed, but it seemed the supply was endless. "You should see him with them. They are everything to him."

Strong paternal hands cupped her face and swiped at her leaking emotion. "And so are you. You're his one person and he is yours. That's the bottom line. And when I said you were like your mom, I didn't mean that you were stubborn like her, though you are, or that you're competitive like her, though you're that, too. I meant that you're practical."

Her father gave her that look he used on his company back in the day. "You're a smart girl, Kinsey, the smartest of my children, though I wish you'd spend

your talents on something more worthy than help-
ing those crooks lie to the public. This problem with
Luke? Use your big Taylor brain and work it out."

Wisdom dispensed with typical no-nonsense flair,
Retired Colonel Jackson Taylor IV headed out to the
patio so he could read his Patton biography and sip
his Syrah and plan which meat would get the spice
treatment on tomorrow's grill.

Kinsey plunked down at the kitchen table, her
thoughts racing to keep up with her hammering
heart. She reached for logic, her tried-and-true friend,
but the bitch was on sabbatical. Maybe that was for
the best. What the hell had logic ever done for her?

She had always believed that it's not about how
much you want your dreams, but how much suffering
you'll endure to achieve them. Something *always* had
to give. Relationships invariably came last, or that
was the perceived wisdom, wasn't it? There was no
such thing as a silver-plattered life filled with rain-
bows and puppies—or firemen and kittens.

Her father was right. She and David hadn't worked
hard at their relationship. There had been something
missing, some deficit that they didn't even question
because they were so focused on the outside instead
of the in. Their lives together had been comfortable.
Safe. But they were lives, not a life. Living in the same
house, moving on different paths.

Kinsey had put food on her table. She had been
responsible for her own orgasms because no way in
hell could she rely on a man for completion. But
there was more to consider outside that list. There
was passion. There was living. There was getting
someone.

There was that spark of recognition when you realized someone got you.

Was she ready to resign herself to a life of if-only? Suffering through late, lonely dinners in tower-high restaurants, eyes misting over about the one who got away? Relying on a handsome waiter to serve up joyless orgasms along with the Glenfiddich eighteen-year-old? If she was willing to put in time for the job, then why wasn't she willing to put herself out there for the personal?

This man of hers—nothing had come easy for him, and still, he had been prepared to make it harder on himself. Take on a new challenge.

Kinsey.

Uproot his life and move to a place where he knew no one but the woman he loved.

Kinsey.

Six months ago, she had done that for David, for the wrong man, and now she was back where she started, running scared, unable to comprehend the magnitude of the right man's love for her. Because it was beyond anything she could have ever imagined.

All this time, she had known it was huge that Luke was prepared to move to San Francisco for her, like a googolplex was huge or a sequoia was huge, but the true enormity of his gift had escaped her. Not the part where he left his family behind, but the part where he thought she was worthy of that choice.

Luke thought she was worth *everything*. He came here with respect for her choices, generosity in his heart. He loved his family, his foster kids, his job, his city, his country. And he still had room in that big heart for her.

The question was not whether this man was worthy of her. That point had been proven, over and over. The question was whether she was worthy of that heart-stopping sacrifice and soul-deep love—and did she have the balls to take what he offered so lovingly?

CHAPTER TWENTY-EIGHT

Luke stepped out of the shower and wrapped a towel around his hips. Last night had been a doozy, with five runs between ten and four. Pretty unusual for a Sunday, but after years on the job, Luke had learned there was nothing typical about a CFD shift.

Out in the locker room, he could hear the standard insult-o-rama winding down. He smiled. On a call earlier this week, Wyatt had accompanied a blue-haired old lady from her nursing home to the emergency room. But en route she seemed to perk up real quick, judging by her constant ass grabbing. Now his brother was griping about the bruises (*this one's shaped like fuckin' Florida*).

Luke walked out to the locker room. "Christ on a crutch, Wy, put your ass away and—" His voice cut out because shit had gotten real quiet.

As he took stock, his gaze locked with the golden-umber one of the woman who was still embedded in his skin, a hook so deep he relished the sweet pain of it.

"Hi, Luke."

Unlike that first time she had strutted into his firehouse, this version of Kinsey was not quite so put together. She wore fraying-hemmed sweatpants, a hoodie with the faded letters of UCAL across her chest, and flip-flops—one pink, one orange. Her matted hair would make a nice home for a family of robins. She carried with her a wild-eyed excitement, the kind you got from too much coffee or not enough sleep.

She looked beautiful.

Gage walked into the locker room with a cheery, "Hey, Kinsey." His reward was an elbow jab from Alex, who treated Kinsey to a skin-flaying glare. Hell hath no fury like the sister of a Dempsey scorned.

"Hi, guys," Kinsey said, unfazed by Alex's frosty reception. "Any chance I could have a word with Luke?"

His family made no move to leave, loyalty shining off them like love. Even the rest of his crew, who didn't know the full story but recognized trouble when they saw it, stayed put. This woman was trouble all right. Had been the moment she waltzed in here and made him feel again for the first time in years.

"It's okay," Luke finally said to the attack dogs. "If she gets difficult, I'll whistle for help."

Everyone trudged out reluctantly, casting baleful looks over their shoulders as they went.

Kinsey looked around. "I think we've been here before."

"Are you saying nothing has changed?"

She bit down on that fleshy lower lip he wanted to suck on. His little ball buster was nervous. "Actually, I'd say a lot has changed since I walked in here close to two months ago." She paused. "But not much has changed since you came to see me in San Francisco."

What in the Sam Hill did that mean?

"Did you forget something?" He waved a hand over her. "Your power suit? Your heels?" The molten brand she used to stamp her ownership of his ass?

"Yeah, I forgot something." She stepped in and his heart constricted painfully. How someone so slight could possess so much of his space he would never understand. "I forgot how lucky I am to be loved by you."

Stark vulnerability was etched on her face, and he so wanted to say, *Thank you, Jesus,* for sending her back to him. But twice now, she had twisted a knife into his chest, and it would take more than Kinsey Taylor's glossy eyes to bring him home.

"Two weeks ago, you left without a word that you were fired. One week ago, you insisted you didn't love me. Excuse me if I'm a little reluctant to take this at face value, sweetheart."

That vulnerability was displaced by open-eyed shock. It killed him to hurt her, but there would be no half measures for him. If they were doing this, he needed to know it was real.

"Luke, I love you."

His heart went berserk. Dumbass heart. Punching it down, he plastered on his most bored expression. "Uh-huh."

Kinsey's lush, supple mouth worked in that cute way she got when she was about to go absofuckinglutely nuts. "Luke . . . I . . . what are you saying here?"

"Oh, I think you know, PR princess. This is what you do, right? You sell ideas, opinions, people, or at the very least you put a good spin on them." He leaned against his locker and folded his arms, projecting a hundred times more casual than he felt. "You need to convince me this is the real deal."

He wouldn't have thought it possible for those beautiful eyes to get bigger, but they did. And then they ignited with fury.

Did he mention that outrage looked so damn fine on her? Good thing, too, because he was about to spike her mad even further.

"Use your words, Kinsey."

For a moment, he thought he'd gone too far. That the line he had crossed was in his rearview mirror and fading into the distance. She was breathing heavily, her perfect, cuppable breasts rising and falling with her distress.

"Do you see what I look like, Luke? Is this making any impression on you? When I realized my mistake, I didn't even bother to change out of this outfit because I had to get to the airport to make the red-eye. I didn't even bring socks!" With a shaky hand, she pointed at her mismatched flip-flops. The varnish on the nail of one big toe was chipped, a lovely detail that cheered him immensely.

"I had to take these off and walk through security in my bare feet. God knows how many diseases I picked up! I look like I've been yanked through a hedge backward. I look like a bedraggled, nationless refugee, and you're asking me to make a case for loving you?"

"And you'd better make it good."

She looked like she wanted to make it good all right. Maybe a slap upside his head or a fist to his groin with a terminating twist of his nuts.

She looked like she wanted to walk right out the door.

Until this moment, Kinsey hadn't realized just how deeply she had cut Luke. Somehow, she had expected that the mere fact of her presence, the message it sent, would be enough for him to understand why she was here. How she couldn't draw a full breath without him. But apparently, working with egocentric politicians for so long had given her some arrogance of her own, and Luke was refusing to play his part in the big finale.

He was right to be wary. He had been betrayed by one woman, rejected by another. Entering a burning building only to risk having his heart incinerated again was a tall order.

In the past six weeks, she had turned Luke Almeida into Chicago's Sexiest Fireman, his sister into America's Favorite Firefighter, and had recovered from a cheating ex who was about to have octuplet walruses with a nurse. Meet the queen of tall orders.

Deep breath. Squared shoulders. Fists on hips.

Let's fucking do this.

"You didn't give me a chance to finish, Mr. Almeida. A few moments ago, before you rudely interrupted me"—she shot him her best stink eye—"I was saying how lucky I was to have you love me. Well, it's not just me. Every person who knows you is blessed to have a man like you giving us everything you have. Because that's who you are. You leave every piece of your heart and soul out on the field of battle."

Moving in close, she tipped back her head to take a long, hard look at this man she loved.

"Fire." She coasted a hand over his shoulder and that raw strip of scar tissue. She had yet to hear the story behind it, but she intended to find out.

"Country." She traced the edge of his sculpted chest muscles over his Semper Fidelis tattoo.

"Family." She stroked her fingertips over the inked

cuffs of his biceps, *Sean* on one side, *Logan* on the other.

Finally, on tiptoes in her flip-flops, she brushed his lips. A gentle press she knew that, despite his stubbornness, he was itching to return.

Only sheer willpower prevented her from throwing her arms around him instead of placing her hands on his chest for emphasis. "Now, I wouldn't want to be accused of using my feminine wiles as a weapon here, Luke. You need cold, hard facts. You need an intellectual argument, because an emotional or sexual appeal won't be enough."

Those had-to-be-fake blue eyes heated to midnight. She suspected he was starting to enjoy the emotional (and sexual) appeal, but she wanted to give him more. She wanted to give him everything.

"I've never been as brave as you. I chose one man because I thought he fit into this glossy-magazine-cover life I'd envisioned. He hurt me, so I shut down, determined not to let anyone get that close again. And then I met another man. We butted heads, we danced around each other, we challenged, and we fought. It was messy and infuriating. I mean, you really pissed me off sometimes."

A gentle lift at one corner of his mouth registered his pleasure with that conclusion. God, he was so annoying.

"But I'd never felt more alive. Through it all, during these moments with the most exasperating man I've ever met, I realized that I'd only been living in black and white. Burying myself in my work. Using it to avoid passion and fire and love."

"Know what that's like," he murmured.

"Stop." She held up a hand. "You don't need to make it easy on me, Almeida. Yes, you're some sort of emotional savant who figured out what you needed to fill this gap in your life, but I'm not as smart as you. I thought I would lose everything I'd gained by accepting all this love you had for me. That it was some sort of capitulation—"

"Sweetheart."

"I know." And she did. At last. "It took me awhile to realize that love doesn't make me weak. That together we are so much stronger than we are apart. That I don't want to end up alone in fine restaurants, sipping top-shelf whiskey and relying on the waiter for orgasms."

He frowned. "Wouldn't wish that on anyone."

Losing the plot here, Taylor. She hadn't slept a wink on the flight, too keyed up about seeing him. "Sorry, I'm explaining this badly. I have a question for you. Just one." She curved her hands around his towel-wrapped hips. A trickle of moisture vied for her attention as it traveled an eager trek down his chest, but she stayed the course.

"Would you still move to be with me?"

"To the ends of the earth."

Still. Still, this man would do anything for her. She was his first and last thought. He was the hero she needed.

"You make me strong, Luke. I feel invincible with you, like I can do anything. And I think I do that for you, too."

He leaned his forehead against hers as if he could draw from their collective strength. Her heated blood rushed to where they connected.

"Yes," he said above a whisper. "Yes, you do."

Her teary smile was filled with relief. "But you also need something else to be strong. Your family. They mean everything to you and leaving them would kill you."

"Aw, baby, is that why you shut me down in California?"

"That, and fear that I wouldn't be enough for you. You have so much, Luke. What can I offer you? What do you give the man who has everything?"

One thick finger traced the pulse at the base of her throat and blazed an erotic trail over her collarbone. "You give him the one thing he can't do without. This ball of fire inside you. Your heart, Kinsey."

That ball of fire combusted, shooting sparks of joy through every nerve ending.

"It's yours, Luke. I know I can trust you with it. I know you're the one man who can hold it safe. I also know that the best place to do that is here. In Chicago."

Bafflement rumpled his brow. "What about your job?"

"I don't have one now, but I'm really, really good at what I do. There are tons of opportunities for a woman with my particular skill set."

Sexy lip twitch.

"My *professional* skill set, perv."

For the first time since she was sixteen, she was unemployed and not entirely sure what her next step was careerwise. But she knew this much. "Going forward, I'd like to work on causes and campaigns I actually care about."

"So rehabilitating the rep of a hit-first meathead is not your cause of choice?"

"As much as I enjoyed making you sweat for that calendar, my days of wrangling kittens and recalcitrant firemen are over."

Swallowing her fear, she let him see every ounce of the vulnerability she had spent her life hiding. From her brothers, from her bosses, from any man who had knocked at the door of her heart only to find it padlocked. Because Luke Almeida was waiting for her with the key.

"As long as I know you have my back, as long as you know I have yours, then we can do anything." And wasn't that the truth of it?

Finally, finally he took her face between his big, caring, made-to-love her hands. "You fuckin' slay me, Kinsey." Then he kissed her to the depths of her soul, a kiss so transcendent her brain spun at the possibilities. In far-off galaxies, worlds were created with this kiss. In this one, her new life began.

Against his perfect mouth, she whispered through trembling lips, "I thought I'd screwed up."

"Well, you did. But you came to your senses in the nick of time." Those eyes, like fierce blue suns, dragged her in deep. "You sure about this, baby? About us?"

"Maybe I'm not as good at this PR business as I thought. Haven't I convinced you, Luke?"

"You have. But it sounds like I'm getting the better end of this deal. I get to stay put in my hometown, I get to continue my campaign of chronic interference in the lives of my family, and I get the girl." He broke out into a huge grin. "I even get to be a lieutenant."

She gasped. "You took the exam?"

"Results came in yesterday."

"Luke, that's amazing! I'm so proud of you." She kissed him, then broke away before her brain turned to mush. "You're right to question who's getting the better deal here, Mr. Almeida. I'm seeing a bit of an imbalance in our relationship already, and you know how much I hate that. What are you going to do for me?"

He considered this, and she felt that thrill of anticipation at what he'd come up with.

"Here's my promise to you, Kinsey. There'll be talking and laughing and loving. There'll be fighting, as well, because we're both damn stubborn and we won't agree on everything, but that's okay, 'cause we'll figure it out like adults. I will never blindside or disrespect you. I'll listen as long as you're not yammering on about other women's hair or clothes or what shade of paint should go on the walls of our bedroom."

"But I value your opinion. Especially when it comes to paint."

"Don't interrupt. Declarations of love are in progress." He gifted her that sexy, so-help-her-Luke grin. "There'll still be surprises. Every now and then I'll do something so romantic it'll make you cry."

She sniffed. Blinked rapidly. Must be something in her eye.

"Yeah, you, Kinsey Taylor. I'll make you cry with my rare romantic gestures. And then there's the sex."

"That's more like it."

"I said no interruptions. Now, where was I?"

"The sex."

"What about it?"

She squeezed his biceps. "You were making promises, Luke. Wonderful, wonderful promises."

"Okay, I'll offer up a few surprises there to keep it fresh. After my shift, I'll race home smelling of smoke and need and so beat I can barely stand. But that won't stop me from taking what's mine. And when I'm buried so deep inside you that you won't know where I begin and you end, I'll make sure you understand why you're here with me in the city I love and with the family I love. Why you are the woman I love and how I'll never forget that you came back to me."

His smile was killer, those astonishing blues filled with all she could ever need or want. Filled with his love for her. Her heart hurt with the joy of it all. It was a good hurt, though. The best hurt.

He molded her tight to his hard, sinful body, and cupped the ass that belonged to him. Completely.

"Welcome home, sweetheart."

She looked into the eyes of the man she refused to live without and let him see how much she adored him.

"Best city in the world, right?"

He nodded. "It is now."

EPILOGUE

The siren blared as the truck burned rubber through a largely residential neighborhood on Chicago's north side. Single-family homes, modest flashes of green, a good place to raise kids. By the time they made it to their destination, Luke was about ready to leap out of his skin with anticipation.

With a smooth drop to the ground, he surged forward, ignoring the shouts of his crew. For some runs, a man had to go it alone.

He approached his quarry, but no obstacle was tall enough to defy him, no barrier wide enough. The front door fell open. The stairs disappeared under his long stride. At the top, he paused and listened.

All quiet.

But not for long.

He threw open the door to the bedroom and assessed the scene.

"Did someone call the fire department?"

"You're late, Lieutenant," said the vision lying beneath a crisp, white sheet that barely covered her golden skin and delectable assets.

"It's only eight twelve, sweetheart."

She gave a languorous stretch on the bed they had bought together and raised a sultry eyebrow.

"You promised me eight sixteen." Lifting the sheet, she pointed a slender finger to the treasures that lay below. "In here. And because you take so long getting your gear off, I very much doubt you're going to make that deadline, Mr. Almeida."

"Why, that sounds like a challenge, Miss Taylor."

He curled his thumbs under the suspenders of his bunker gear and let them fall to his sides. Normally, he would never leave the firehouse wearing them, but this morning he had plans. Wicked plans.

"You like the slow reveal, Kinsey." He ran a hand over his erection, which hungered to break free and find her warm, wet haven.

She sighed, resigned to the accuracy of that statement. "I do."

In the month since she'd come back to him, they had moved into a two-flat rental a few blocks away from Engine 6. It was fitting that they start their life in a place not filled with the toxic remains of his marriage. They had the rest of their lives together to figure out a more permanent solution.

"Tough night?" she asked, as she always did.

"No more than usual," he replied, as he always did, knowing there would be time later to share his recap of the shift's events. Two house fires, a multi-car pileup, and a guy who handcuffed himself to his ex-girlfriend's radiator. Everyone lived, though the ex-girlfriend looked like she might have murder on her mind. It was a good night for his first stint as lieutenant on the A shift, taking the place of McElroy, who had transferred to Engine 69.

Returning to his striptease, he unsnapped his bunker gear.

Pop.

She squirmed. He enjoyed that immensely.

Pop.

She arched her back and slipped her hand below the sheet.

Pop.

"Luke," she rasped, her voice so needful he could barely stand it.

He ripped off his tee, shucked the rest. Five seconds later, he was settled in the embrace of her body. Where he belonged.

But that didn't mean it would be easy. Nothing with his woman ever was.

On his way to twining his fingers in all that honey blondeness, he encountered a hard edge under her pillow. He pulled to reveal . . . Jesus, Joseph, and Mary, the damn *Men on Fire* calendar.

"Came in yesterday," she said with a husky giggle. "Josie sent a box of them over to M Squared. Madison and I spent all afternoon checking each and every photo over martinis. Quality control, you know."

Unsurprisingly, Kinsey had managed to talk her way into a job with Madison Maitland at the top PR firm in Chicago. She would be running their new non-profit division, pairing up worthy causes with corporate sponsors. The Cook County foster care system was the first project on her slate.

He was so damn proud of her.

But there was this matter of the calendar.

"It's not even open to July," he said, uncertain if the gravel in his voice was because of the sexy game they were playing or his annoyance that she was getting juiced up with Mr. March, one of those rescue squad show-offs from Engine 57.

"Oh, that's just the appetizer, babe." She flashed him a naughty grin, then her hand found him and gripped hard, just how he liked it.

That calendar went flying over his shoulder.

"Now I'm ready for the main course."

Needing no further invitation, he slipped inside her in one long, possessive, perfect stroke.

Eight sixteen on the dot. He'd always had exquisite timing.

With each pump of his hips, both new and familiar pleasure rolled through his veins. Along with fire and smoke, this woman was in his blood, and every day he thanked the gods for bringing her back to him. She was the center of his universe—and that was where she would stay.

Those stunning hazel eyes, drunk on desire, imprisoned him in their depths. "Love you, Luke."

"Love you more, baby."

Because they were never not competing.

As she crested toward her orgasm, and the pleasure wound tight and built toward his, his overriding thought was how to top this happiness. Only one thing might. These days, he was a man of unstoppable ambition. Making this woman Mrs. Luke Almeida would be his next lofty goal.

Oh, who was he kidding? If his woman had her way, it would be Mrs. Taylor-Almeida. And she'd get no complaints from him.

ACKNOWLEDGMENTS

To my amazing editors, Elana Cohen and Lauren McKenna, for your energy and dedication in making this book awesome. Thanks for taking a chance on me.

To the great team at Gallery and Pocket Books, thanks for my hot-as-the-hinges-of-hell cover and all the work you do making me look good. And to copy editor Faren Bachelis, your insightful notes and catches of my errors made me sound less stupid, and your smiley faces at my jokes were just what I needed in the homestretch.

To Captain Jerry Hughes of Truck 33 and his crew, thanks for making me feel welcome at your firehouse and for your patience with all my questions. And extra thanks for the amazing food. CFD chefs are the best!

To Nicole Resciniti, my agent, cheerleader, and friend, thanks for your faith in me. I hope to make you money one day!

To Monique Headley and Lauren Layne, who are the best beta readers a writer could ask for. I really should send you flowers.

Finally, to my family, both Irish and American. I feel blessed to know you all and have your support.

Keep reading for a sneak peek of

PLAYING WITH FIRE

Book two in the sizzling
Hot in Chicago series

by KATE MEADER

Available Fall 2015 from Pocket Books!

Alex Dempsey considered herself a highly skilled woman.

Prop a fifty-foot ladder against a burning building and watch her blitz that baby in sixty seconds. Hauling a thirty-pound hose bundle up multiple flights of stairs and down again? Child's play. She could even drag a body to safety without breaking a sweat (she also knew a few prime locations for hiding one).

But for the life of her, she could not master the art of wearing a thong.

Unfortunately, this painted-on dress that left nothing to the imagination required that particular skill. Because going on her thirty-fourth date in ten months required that she wore this particular dress. Once a week, the results always the same. No callbacks. What she had been doing before clearly wasn't working, so time to bring out the big guns—aka the girls.

As for other weapons in her arsenal . . . Tonight, she was test-driving smoky eyes that were more emo panda than sex kitten along with a pair of inadvisable heels—inadvisable because she was already too tall at five ten. On the plus side, courtesy of a bout with a hair iron, her usual rumpus of chocolate curls now knew who was boss.

Looking across the table in the farmer-chic restaurant Smith & Jones, three days before the New Year, Alex prayed she might finally be reaping the benefits of her itchy underwear, low-cut dress, and overlong primping. Her embarrassingly long dating résumé included prospects from all walks of life: stockbrokers, artists, auto mechanics, to name a few. A miscellaneous lot, they enjoyed the novelty of dating a female firefighter, but once the honeymoon was over—usually by dessert of the first date—doubts scudded like petulant storm clouds across their faces, the forecast always the same.

How can I be the man if you're being the man?

God, she was so over it.

She didn't crave excitement—she got that in her work. She just wanted someone who wasn't a complete dick and could stand up to her occasionally abrasive personality. Tonight's ~~victim~~ opportunity bashed a hockey puck around a rink with her brother Gage and was a Chicago police detective who she hoped had enough self-confidence to handle hers.

Detective Michael Martinez, are you the one?

"So, America's favorite firefighter, huh?"

Don't judge him yet, she cautioned. It was inevitable it would come up.

"I have good people on my PR payroll," she said with a deferential smile.

"Remind me not to get on your bad side. Plenty of nights on the sofa in my future, huh?"

No nights if he didn't quit being such a jackass. But then it seemed she was a magnet for jackasses. Five months ago, she had made headlines all over the country when she took the equivalent of a chain saw to the Lamborghini of one of Chicago's wealthiest and most influential men. Mega mogul Sam Cochrane had drunkenly crashed his car and miraculously not injured himself or others. When he wasn't extracted quickly enough from the pin-in, he leveled a chauvinistic, racist, and homophobic rant against Alex and her family. The upshot? She extracted Cochrane out of that car all right.

Through the large opening left by the sawn-off door. There was also the two-foot gash she'd carved (unnecessarily) into the roof.

Pretty.

Also pretty stupid. She knew that. So, not her finest moment, but anyone who messed with her family risked her wrath. Growing up Dempsey meant all other considerations fell by the wayside.

"Good thing someone filmed it," Michael continued, sounding like it wasn't such a good thing at all. "Got the women and the gays on your side. Put the mayor in a difficult spot."

Real good thing. Alex had escaped with her job and damp toes from her dip in the fifteen-minutes-of-fame pool. Her semi-celeb status as "America's Favorite Firefighter" (thanks, Wolf Blitzer) had faded quickly as real news stories took precedence. Now she saw no reason why that unfortunate incident should have any impact on her professional—or her love—life.

Except that everyone kept bringing it up.

"You know how the news blows stuff out of proportion," she said with a minimizing shrug. She'd noticed that on her most recent dates she had started channeling a softer version of herself. More datable.

More lovable. Less likely to use the Jaws of Life on the personal property of anyone who pissed her off.

She leaned in, a tip she had read today on HuffPo's Lifestyles section. Boobs out, smile wide, voice low. Being sexy was exhausting.

His gaze fell to her cleavage. Spectacular stuff, she knew, but rarely did the girls get this much air.

"Do you like the squash blossoms?" Alex asked, her voice dropping to bedroom-husky as she tried to get the date back on track.

"The what?"

She gestured to the dish of tempura-fried goodness between them. Chef Brady Smith, who was currently groping Gage on a semi-regular basis, had sent it over with his compliments.

"Oh, yeah, they're good." He shrugged, looking a little embarrassed. "These flashy places don't really do it for me. Overpriced food, undersized portions. Gimme a burger any day."

She laughed, feeling at ease for the first time that night. "I know. Gage is a big foodie, so he's always dragging me to restaurants with stuff like veal cheeks and charred orange and—"

"Seaweed and shit."

"Yes!"

He chuckled and she joined in. Everyone around them was the epitome of hipster, looking like they drove Priuses and had Lolla ticket stubs in the pockets of their ironic bowling shirts. The restaurant did feel cheerfully festive, though, with beautiful holiday wreaths hung over the large antique mirrors. But it also had a bread program, which, while delicious, was unforgivably pretentious.

"I sort of know the chef," she whispered to keep her traitor-talk out of the hearing range of Brady's server spies, "so I thought it might be a good place but . . ."

"Next time, we'll get a burger."

Next time. *Score!* But she needed to rein in her runaway thoughts. It wasn't over until the ginger-bread pudding had made an appearance.

His phone pinged—again—and her heart sank as his expression morphed to cop-serious. "Got to take this, sweets. Back in a sec."

"Sure."

He headed off toward the restrooms, leaving her to wonder if he had designated a buddy to dial in for rescue at a certain point into the date. Like "call a friend" but in reverse.

Time to do her own check-in. She took out her phone and conference-texted her posse: Gage, who was on shift at Engine Company 6, where they both worked, and her friends/future sisters-in-law, Darcy and Kinsey. Otherwise known as Team Get Alex Laid.

He's left the table 2x in 10 mins. Either his gun's digging into his tiny bladder or he's on a coke break in the can.

Five seconds later from her brother: *Stop looking for faults!*

Gage said she was impossible to please. As his standards up until meeting Brady six months ago involved being pleased fifty ways from Sunday by any guy who raised an eyebrow of come-hither in his direction, she'd say she might have the moral high ground here.

The need to complain wouldn't let go. *He keeps staring at my tits.*

Darcy chimed in with, *That's what they're fucking for!*

Touché.

Next up on deck was Kinsey, who could usually be relied upon for a healthy jolt of common sense. *Try channeling your inner sexpot. Suck on a straw.*

Real subtle, Alex texted back.

Subtle does not lead to man-made orgasms! Gage again.

Alex found it rather priceless how people started to channel the love child of Yoda and Oprah the second they bagged a regular sex partner. But she wanted what they had with a heady desperation that sometimes left her breathless. She wanted to be smugly in love.

Her phone buzzed again, and a smile tugged her lips at the prospect of yet more oh-so-sage advice from her loved-up peeps. But the new message wasn't from her crew.

Her pulse rate skyrocketed as it always did when she heard his name or saw him on TV or spent a single moment in his presence. Of course, he had no idea how much he affected her. She planned to keep it that way.

Try the quail, the text read. *It's excellent.*

He was there. In the restaurant. Either that or he had surveillance trained on her, which, given her past behavior tainting the good name of the CFD, might not be so far-fetched. While she pondered how to play it, another message came in. *Check your six.*

If she ignored him, it would look like she actually cared, and yet the idea of turning her head because he issued an order was equally galling.

Deciding that following his "suggestion" sat with her better than letting him think his presence bothered her, she twisted her shoulders and met the raw blue gaze of Mayor Eli Cooper. He was seated alone in a booth near the back, paperwork and an iPad laid out before him, long fingers curled around a tumbler of scotch.

He didn't smile. She wouldn't have believed it if he had. There was something predatory about him, like a lazy python lying in the sun ready to uncoil and strike at any moment. Before he straightened to his full six two, she knew he would come to her table.

She wanted to look away as he approached, but it was only twenty feet and again, *So don't care.* Watching him walk over, she mused that Eli Cooper was the sort of man who knew how to use his physicality. Beneath his handmade shirts and tailored suits, a street fighter hummed through every loose-limbed motion. But that impression did not extend to his face, which was structurally perfect. High cheekbones. Superhero jaw. A mouth that should have a government warning. There were no signs of past trouble with a jealous husband or an abandoned girlfriend. No one had ever broken his nose. No one had busted his lip.

Strange, because her first instinct on seeing him was to roundhouse-kick him into the next millennium.

"Alexandra," he drawled.

"Mr. Mayor."

He sat without invitation. "How's your date going?"

"Just dandy. Probably won't appreciate a threesome, though."

The words were hardly out of her mouth, and she longed to bite them back. That well-worn smirk, like a stray comma at the corner of his full-lipped mouth, activated.

"No one would like to share you, I imagine, Alexandra. However, you're so difficult you'd probably need several CPD officers to handle you."

Passing over the fact that he knew her date was Chicago blue, she blew out a bored sigh.

"Slow night on the campaign trail? I would think you'd want to get out there if your latest poll numbers are anything to go by." She tsked. "Less than two months to the election and you're hovering under forty percent."

"All that matters are the numbers on the night."

"Still, I'm sure you have babies to kiss, MILFs to ogle." Donor dicks to suck. "Don't let me stop you."

"Given your recent popularity, I should have you stump for me, but there's no telling what might come out of your mouth from one second to the next."

She raised her fruity Cab to her unpredictable mouth and took a ladylike sip instead of her usual gulp. Now would be a fabulous time for her date to reappear.

"I'm not for sale, Mr. Mayor."

"Call me Eli. You did before."

One mistake, a lifetime of regret. "You bring out the worst in me."

"Oh, it doesn't take much to get you riled, Alexandra. All that passion just looking for an outlet." It was never Alex with him, which everybody and their aunt called her, but her full name. Just another dig that ensured her XX chromosomes would not be forgotten.

But this time, it didn't feel like a dig. It felt like . . .

a caress. She lowered the glass of wine to the distressed mahogany table and stared at it accusingly because that was just, well, loco.

Done blaming the alcohol for that ludicrous flight of fancy, she lifted her chin and thought she saw his gaze snap up as if he'd been looking at her chest. Not likely, except to disapprove. Eli Cooper disapproved of her from his perfectly pedicured feet to his overly produced hair.

Hell and damn, so the man happened to be an exceptionally good-looking son of a bitch. The gods had been generous, giving him a strong brow beneath that wavy, black hair. Ice-blue eyes that hinted at secrets and numerous ways of uncovering hers. A dimple, too. Not that she'd ever seen it up close because he had never smiled at her, not a real smile, anyway. But she'd seen it on TV, a sunshine pop in the hard plane of his cheek. Practically every woman in Chicago had a lady boner for him, even the ones who hated his politics. Put her in the latter camp—not the lady boner part, just the politics-hating.

"Feel free to call me Firefighter Dempsey or plain Dempsey. That seems more appropriate for a boss-employee relationship."

His brows rose. "You consider me your boss?"

"I consider you an asshole."

He laughed, deep and rich, and the sound corkscrewed down her spine with a pleasurable thrill she resented. Fascinating how a basically nice person like herself could turn nasty, but then she always felt slightly unhinged around him.

"Ah, but you put it so much more colorfully before when you called me a *patriarchal woman-*

hating asshole. In this very restaurant. Over there."
He pointed to the booth where he'd been sitting. His
regular table, she supposed.

Twice in the last six months she had crossed
swords with Mayor Eli "Hot Stuff" Cooper, the most
arrogant, chauvinistic jerk of her acquaintance—and
she should know, because he had stiff competition
from the throwbacks she worked with at CFD. (Except for her firefighter brothers, who were generally
cool with the presence of a woman on the job. They
had to be or she'd kick their asses.)

The first time she ran into Cooper, he had made
it clear that he thought firefighting and breasts were
incompatible.

The second time he was pissed to all hell at her,
and she was woman enough to admit he might have
had good reason. That foul-mouthed big shot with
the Lamborghini? Only Mayor Cooper's preeminent
donor, another guy who thought his dick had its
own zip code. After her luxury car slice-and-dice, the
mayor had summoned her to his town house in Lincoln Park—by text, which was why he had her number—and proceeded to bawl her out. For a long time.
The guy did not like Alex or her family or the CFD.

Goes both ways, Mr. Mayor. Alex did not like a
man who had no respect for what she devoted her life
to, day in, day out.

"My opinion of you hasn't changed," she gritted
out. "Putting aside your caveman pronouncements
about what women can and cannot do, during your
reign of terror, you've managed to cut funding to
libraries, bring city pensions to the brink of bank-
ruptcy, and reduce social services to a fraction of

what they were before. All so we can beautify the tourist traps of our fair city and fete George Lucas for the Star Wars museum."

Because he was undoubtedly used to the blows from the opposition, her words had no discernible effect on his ice-compacted heart. "Hard decisions are made by people in charge every day. Someone in your profession should know that."

She imagined she heard a compliment in there, but her passion rolled right over it. "And don't think I've forgotten how you fired your press secretary for taking my side and almost ruined everything between her and my brother." Thank God Kinsey had come to her senses and returned to Chicago, though Luke had been ready to up sticks and move to California to be with her. Eli Cooper's megalomania had almost lost Alex a friend *and* her brother.

"The course of true love never did run smooth," the mayor said quietly. "Firing Kinsey was the best thing I could have done. Made them face what's important. And I *still* haven't received that thank you card."

"Is there anything you won't claim credit for?"

Eyeing her speculatively, he took a sip of his scotch, undoubtedly something expensive and triple-distilled from the tears of Scottish virgins. Everything about him screamed privilege, from his monogrammed cuff links to his Wall Street suspenders.

"I even paired off Gage with Brady. Perhaps I should add that to my campaign ads." He swiped a hand across an imaginary billboard. "Vote for Cooper, the Matchmaking Mayor."

She snorted. "Well, you can forget about the Dempsey vote."

His steely stare penetrated to the blood boiling beneath her skin. "Oh, I know," he murmured. "In fact, you and your family seem to take great pleasure in doing what you can to make me look bad."

"Believe me, when I was cutting up Cochrane's car, you were the last thing on my mind."

"Exactly. You don't think."

She tamped down on the growl fighting to escape her throat. *Do not engage.*

He flicked a glance over his shoulder. "I must say your date is taking an awfully long time. Perhaps he's a little intimidated by all this passion of yours, and he'd rather risk a twisted ankle by escaping through the restroom window. Getting on your wrong side could be costly for any man."

Unavoidably, her gaze traveled toward the restrooms just as Detective Martinez appeared, ankles none the worse for wear. Praise Jesus.

"Looks like this one is brave enough to stick around and take me on, Eli."

Shit. She said his name. The dimple did a jig.

"Beware of men who claim to be able to handle you, Alexandra. While I've always found our exchanges extremely provocative, I doubt others will be as entertained by you as I am."

"I'm not here for your entertainment." Covering a yawn with one hand, she picked up her phone with the other. "I'm going to delete you from my contacts list. If you text me again because you're bored, I won't know who you are. As I was raised to never speak to strangers, it's unlikely we'll be chatting again."

The dimple quickstepped into a samba. "I'm in your contacts list?"

"Yep." Discombobulated by that dumb dimple, she turned the phone to him, grasping for the upper hand in this unnerving conversation. "BFT."

As he leaned in, the smokiness of the whiskey and something indefinably male struck her nostrils. Her stomach gave a treacherous flutter.

"Best Friend *Totes*?"

"Big. Fucking. Tool." She plastered on a saccharine grin. "But I don't need a contacts list entry to remember that." She went ahead and deleted it, each tap more indignant than the last.

"Want to know what I've called you in mine?"

Her heart rate spiked. "*Dying* over here."

He tipped the screen toward her to reveal "Splinter" in the contact name field.

Splinter?

"Short for Splinter in My Side. I was going to call you Thorn, but you're not worthy of a thorn, Alexandra. You're a minor annoyance."

"Glad to hear I don't rate too much on your radar. Would hate to think you're wasting valuable mental real estate thinking about me and my family and all we do to make you look bad."

The detective arrived at the table, his expression curious. Eli—*no, Mr. Mayor*—uncoiled to a stand. Just running her eyes over all that slickness drew her shiver, but neither could she help comparing his physique to that of her date. Eli Cooper had a couple more inches in height on Michael and maybe, just maybe, slightly more girth on those biceps. She would think with all his fancy tailoring he could find a shirt that fit him properly instead of one that outlined his bull-like shoulder muscles so obscenely.

"Enjoy your meal, Alexandra. As I said, the quail is excellent." He nodded curtly at her date. "Detective Martinez."

As he walked away from the table, three things stuck with her:

One, the jerk's personality did *not* improve on acquaintance.

Two, in less than five minutes, he'd managed to sour the most promising date she'd had in months.

Three—and how she hated herself for even going there—those gray pin-striped pants shaped his ass really, really well.